THE SEVENTH CROSS

THE SEVENTH CROSS

ANNA SEGHERS

Translated from the German by
MARGOT BETTAUER DEMBO

virago

VIRAGO

This edition first published in Great Britain in 2018 by Virago Press
Originally published in German in 1942 as *Das Siebte Kreuz: Ein roman aus Hitler-Deutschland* by El Libro Libre, Mexico D. F.

1 3 5 7 9 10 8 6 4 2

Copyright © 1946, 2000 by Aufbau Verlag GmbH & Co., Berlin
Translation copyright © 2018 by Margot Bettauer Dembo

A CIP catalogue record for this book
is available from the British Library.

HARDBACK ISBN 978-0-349-01066-3
C-FORMAT ISBN 978-0-349-01067-0

Printed and bound in Great Britain by
Clays Ltd, St Ives plc

Papers used by Virago are from well-managed forests
and other responsible sources.

Virago Press
An imprint of
Little, Brown Book Group
Carmelite House
50 Victoria Embankment
London EC4Y 0DZ

An Hachette UK Company
www.hachette.co.uk

www.virago.co.uk

This book is dedicated to Germany's antifascists, living and dead. Its publication in Mexico came about through the friendship and joint efforts of German and Mexican authors, artists and printers.

—ANNA SEGHERS

CONTENTS

CHARACTERS

GEORGE HEISLER	A prisoner who has escaped from Westhofen concentration camp
WALLAU, BEUTLER, PELZER, BELLONI, FUELLGRABE, ALDINGER	Prisoners who escaped from Westhofen at the same time
FAHRENBERG	Commandant of Westhofen concentration camp
BUNSEN	Lieutenant at Westhofen
ZILLICH	SA squad leader at Westhofen
FISCHER, OVERKAMP	Police commissars (Gestapo)
ERNST	A shepherd
FRANZ MARNET	George's former friend; works at the Hoechst Dye Works
MR AND MRS MARNET	
AUGUSTA	Their daughter
LENI	George's former girlfriend
ELLI	George's wife
ALFONS METTENHEIMER	Her father, a paperhanger
HERMANN	Franz's friend; works at the Griesheim Railway Workshops
ELSA	His wife
FRITZ HELWIG	Gardener's apprentice
DR LOEWENSTEIN	A Jewish doctor
MRS MARELLI	A seamstress for artistes' costumes

PAUL ROEDER, LIESEL ROEDER	Friends from George's youth
CATHERINE GRABBER	Paul Roeder's aunt, owner of a haulage business
FIEDLER	A fellow worker of Roeder's
GRETA	IIis wife
DR KRESS	
GERDA	His wife
REINHARDT	Fiedler's friend
A WAITRESS	
A DUTCH SEA CAPTAIN WHO TAKES ALL KINDS OF RISKS	

I

PROBABLY no trees ever cut down in our country were as unique, as strange as the seven plane trees growing at the gable end of Barracks III. Their crowns, for a reason to be revealed at a later time, had previously been cut off and a board had been nailed across each of the tree trunks at shoulder height. From afar, the seven plane trees looked like seven crosses.

When the new camp commandant arrived – his name was Sommerfeld – he immediately had them all cut up into kindling. He was quite different from his predecessor, Fahrenberg, the old warrior, 'conqueror of Seeligenstadt', where his father still has a plumbing business on the market square today. The new camp commandant had served in Africa as a colonial officer before the war, and after the war he had marched on red Hamburg with his old major, Lettow-Vorbeck. We found out about all this only much later. While the first commandant had been a fool responsible for terrible, unpredictable acts of cruelty, this new one was a sober, calculating man whose actions were predictable.

Fahrenberg would have been quite capable of having us all beaten. Sommerfeld, on the other hand, was just as likely to line us up and then have every fourth one pulled out and beaten to death. Back then we didn't know this. And even if we had known, what difference would it have made in the face of the emotions that overwhelmed us when we saw the six trees being cut down and then the seventh one as well! A small triumph certainly, measured against our general helplessness, our prison clothing. And yet it was nevertheless a triumph to suddenly feel our own power after who knew how long; a power that even we had for a long time considered just one of many ordinary powers on this earth, a power to be discounted as merely moderate when actually it was the only force that could suddenly grow immeasurably, incalculably.

That evening, for the first time, our barracks were heated. The weather had just changed. Today I'm not so sure any more whether the few pieces of wood that they fed into our little cast-iron stove were really from that same pile of kindling. Back then we were sure they were.

We crowded around the little stove to dry our clothes, profoundly moved by the unaccustomed sight of an open fire. The SA guard had considerately turned his back on us and was looking out of the barred window. A soft grey drizzle, at first not much more than mist, had suddenly turned into a hard rain, blown from time to time against the barracks by powerful gusts of wind. Even a hard-boiled SA man hears and sees the arrival of autumn only once each year.

The wood crackled. Two little blue tongues of flame indicated that the coals were glowing too. Five shovelfuls of coal had been allowed us, only enough to warm our draughty barracks for a few minutes, not enough even to dry our clothes completely. But we weren't thinking about that yet. We were thinking only of the wood burning before our eyes.

Hans said softly, with a sidelong glance at the guard and without moving his lips, 'It's crackling.'

Erwin said, 'The seventh one.' On all the faces there was now a faint, peculiar sort of smile – a mixture of unmixable things, of hope and scorn, of helplessness and boldness. We held our breath. The rain pounded against the wooden planks and on the metal roof. Eric, the youngest of our group, said with a glance out of the corner of his eye, a brief glance that nonetheless revealed his and our innermost concern, 'Where might he be by now?'

I

In early October a man named Franz Marnet left his relatives' farmstead in the community of Schmiedtheim in the Taunus foothills on his bicycle a few minutes earlier than usual. Franz was of average height, a sturdy, stocky man, about thirty years old with a calm, almost sleepy expression when he was among people. But at this moment, riding along his favourite stretch, the steep descent between the fields down to the main road, his face expressed a simple, powerful joy in life.

Perhaps later on no one will understand how Franz could have been happy in his situation. But at that moment he was happy; he even let go with a joyful shout as his bicycle bounced over two earthen ridges in the road.

Tomorrow the flock of sheep, which had been fertilising the Mangolds' adjacent field, was to be driven to his relatives' large apple orchard. That was why they wanted to finish harvesting the apples today. Thirty-five trees, each with a powerful, bristly tangle of branches reaching up into the bluish air, and heavily hung with Golden Pearmain apples. They were shiny ripe and gleaming in the early-morning light like countless little round suns.

Franz had no regrets about missing the apple harvest. He'd helped farmers dig the soil long enough for mere pocket money. Still, after all the years without a job, he ought to have been glad of the work, and the farm of his uncle – a calm, decent man – had been a hundred times better than a work camp. But now at last he had landed a job at the factory and had been bicycling there every day since the first of September. He was pleased about this for many reasons, and his relatives were glad too, because he'd now be staying with them through the winter as a paying guest.

As Franz was pedalling past the neighbouring Mangold farm, they were in the process of setting up ladders, poles and baskets under their mighty Mollebusch pear tree. Sophie, the oldest daughter – a strong girl, a bit stout but not fat, with delicate wrists and ankles – was the first to jump up on a ladder, at the same time calling out something to Franz. Although he couldn't make out what she'd said, he turned around briefly and laughed. He was overcome by a feeling of belonging. People who feel and act feebly will have trouble understanding him. For them, belonging means having a particular family, a specific community, or a love affair. For Franz it meant simply belonging to this bit of soil, to its people, and being a member of the morning shift cycling to the Hoechst plant, but above all it meant belonging to the living.

Once he had gone beyond the Marnets' farmstead, he could see across the gently downward sloping open land and look down at the fog. Somewhat farther on, below the country road, the shepherd was just opening the sheep pen. The sheep pushed their way out and were immediately clinging to the hillside, as still and dense as a little cloud that quickly separates into smaller little clouds, then draws together and fluffs up again. The shepherd, a man from Schmiedtheim, also called out something to Franz. Franz smiled. It was Ernst the shepherd with his bright red kerchief; he was a cheeky fellow, quite unshepherd-like. Farmers' daughters, feeling sorry for him in the frosty autumn nights, would come from the villages to his little wheeled hut.

The land dipped in wide, gentle waves behind the shepherd. Even though you couldn't see the Rhine from there since it was still an hour's train ride away, everything here already indicated that the river wasn't far off: the wide, sloping hillsides with their farm fields and fruit trees and grapevines farther down, the factory smoke you could smell all the way up here, the turning of the train tracks and streets to the southwest, the glittering, shimmering spots in the fog, as well as the shepherd with his bright red neckerchief standing with one arm on his hip, one leg thrust forward as if he weren't watching his sheep but an army.

They say about this land that the projectiles of the last war unearthed the projectiles of the one before. These hills aren't a mountain range. On Sundays any child can go to visit his or her relatives in the next village for coffee and streusel cake and be back home in time for vespers. But this ridge of hills had long been the edge of the world – on the far side began the wilderness, the unknown country. The Romans had drawn their borderlines along these hills. So many battles had been fought, so many tribes had bled to death here in this place since the days when they had burned the Celtic altars to the sun on these hills, that they believed they had at last fenced in the world they could hold and cultivate. But the city down there had kept neither the eagle nor the cross in its coat of arms, but rather the Celtic sun wheel, the same sun that ripened the Marnets' apples. This was where the legions had camped and with them all the gods of the world, city gods and peasant gods, the Jewish God and the Christian God, Astarte and Isis, Mithras and Orpheus. The wilderness once reigned here; here where Ernst from Schmiedtheim now stood with his sheep, one leg forward, an arm on his hip, and a corner of his kerchief sticking straight out as if a constant wind were blowing. In the valley at his back, peoples had been cooked into a stew by the gently misted-over sun. North and south, east and west had simmered into one another, but the land remained untouched by all that, even as it kept some traces of it all. Empires rose like bubbles from the land at Ernst the shepherd's back and burst again almost instantly. They left behind no borders and no triumphal arches and no army highways, nothing but a few broken golden bands from the ankles of their women. But they were as tough and indestructible as dreams. And the shepherd stands there as proud and as imperturbable as if he knew all this and were standing there for that very reason. And maybe, even if he knew nothing about any of it, he really was standing there because of it. There, where the country road joined the highway, was where the Franconian army gathered when they were trying to find a way to ford the Main River. Here between the Mangolds' and the Marnets' farms, this was where the monk rode up into a total wilderness that no one had entered before, a gentle man on a little donkey, his chest protected by the armour of his belief, girded with the sword of salvation – bringing with him the Gospels and the art of grafting apples.

Ernst the shepherd turned towards the bicyclist. The kerchief around his neck already felt too warm, and he pulled it off and tossed it like a battlefield banner on to the stubbly field. One might have thought the gesture was one being performed before a thousand viewers. But only his little dog Nelly was watching. He resumed his inimitable, arrogant, mocking stance, but this time with his back to the road, facing the plain and the place where the Main flows into the Rhine. At their confluence lies Mainz. It provided the Holy Roman Empire with its archchancellors. And back then all the flat land between Mainz and Worms – the entire shore – was covered by the tent camps of the imperial elections. Every year something new happened in this land, but also, every year, the same things were repeated: the apples and the grapes ripened in the gentle, misted-over sun and with the exertions and worries of the people. For wine was needed for everything and by everyone: by the bishops and the landowners for the election of their emperor; by the monks and knights to found their orders; by the crusaders to burn Jews – four hundred of them at a time on the square in Mainz that today is still called The Brand, the fire; by the spiritual and secular princes once the Holy Empire disintegrated and the celebrations of the Great Ones continued, more merrily than ever before; by the Jacobins dancing around their liberty trees.

Twenty years later an old soldier was standing guard on the Mainz pontoon bridge. As the last members of the great army, bedraggled and sombre, straggled past, he remembered how he had stood guard here when they had first marched in with their tricolor banners and human rights, and he wept openly. The old soldier standing guard was withdrawn too. It became quieter, even in this region. And the years '33 and '48 came to this land too, lean and bitter years, two little threads of coagulated blood. Then once again there was an empire, which today they call the Second Empire. Bismarck had its inner borders drawn – not around the land, but straight through it so that the Prussians got a piece of it. For the inhabitants weren't exactly rebellious; they were resigned like people who have experienced all sorts of things and will experience more.

Were those really the sounds of the Battle of Verdun that the schoolboys heard when they lay down on the ground on the other side of Zahlback? Or was it only the constant trembling of the ground under rumbling railway cars and marching armies? Some of these boys were later tried in court. Some for fraternising with the soldiers of the occupation army, others for placing explosives under the rails of their trains. The flags of the Allied Commission were flying on the courthouse.

It hadn't even been ten years yet since they hauled down those flags and exchanged them for the black, red and gold ones that the empire still had at that time. Even the children remembered this recently when the 144th Infantry Regiment marched over the bridge once again with its band playing and drums drumming. Oh, the fireworks they had that evening! Ernst could see them from up here. The burning, hooting city on the other side of the river! Thousands of little swastikas coiling and twisting in the water! How the little flames flitted over them! Yet the next morning the calm bluish grey of the river where it left the city beyond the railway bridge was quite pure. How many battlefield banners has it carried off, how many flags. Ernst whistled to his little dog and she brought him the kerchief in her teeth.

Now we are here. What happens from now on is happening to us.

II

Where the dirt road joined the Wiesbaden Road, there was a little house where they sold soda. It irked Franz Marnet's relatives every single summer evening that they hadn't rented the little house when they had the chance, for the heavy traffic had turned it into a veritable gold mine.

Franz had left home early that morning because he liked cycling alone and wanted to avoid getting caught up in the pack of cyclists coming from the Taunus villages every morning all headed for the Hoechst Dye Works. And so he was a bit miffed to find one of his acquaintances, Anton Greiner from Butzbach, waiting for him at the little soda shack.

The strong, simple, joyful look on his face vanished instantly. His expression turned tight and wooden. The same Franz who might have been ready to give up his life without any ifs and buts was annoyed that Anton Greiner could never cycle past the little house without stopping to buy something. The guy had a nice, faithful girl in Hoechst to whom he'd later give the little bar of chocolate or bag of fruit drops he'd bought. Greiner was standing at an angle so that he could watch the dirt road. What's the matter with him today? Franz wondered, for over the years he'd developed a fine feel for facial expressions. He could tell that Greiner was waiting impatiently for him for a definite reason. Greiner jumped up on his bike and joined Franz. They hurried so as to avoid the swarm of riders who were becoming ever more numerous the steeper the downhill incline.

Greiner said, 'Hey, Marnet, something happened early this morning.'

'Where? What?' Franz said, his face assuming the expression of sleepy indifference it always had whenever you expected him to be surprised.

'Marnet,' Greiner said. 'Something must have happened this morning.'

'Well, what was it?'

'I don't know,' Greiner said, 'but something definitely happened.'

Franz said, 'Oh, you're imagining things. What could possibly have happened so early in the day?'

'I don't know what it was. But I tell you, something did; you can take my word for it. Something totally crazy must have happened. Something like on June the thirtieth.'

'Oh, you're just imagining things.'

Franz stared straight ahead. How thick the fog still was down below! The plain came towards them quickly with its factories and streets. All round them curses and bicycle bells ringing. At one point the crowd of cyclists was split in two by a couple of SS men on motorcycles, Heinrich and Friedrich Messer from Butzbach, Greiner's cousins, who were also on the way to their shift.

'Why don't they take you along?' Franz asked as if he were no longer curious to hear Anton's news.

'They're not allowed to; they go on duty after work. Well, so, you think I'm imagining things ...'

'But what made you think—'

'Because I'm imagining things. Well, anyway, my mother, she had to go to Frankfurt today to see the lawyer because of the inheritance. And so she went over to Mrs Kobisch with her milk because she couldn't be here for the milk pickup. And young Kobisch, he was in Mainz yesterday where he usually orders the wine for the inn. And so they got to drinking there and it got late and he only got back home very early this morning and they wouldn't let him through at Gustavsburg.'

'Oh that, Anton.'

'What do you mean, "Oh that"...?'

'They've had that closed off for a long time there at Gustavsburg.'

'Listen, Franz, Kobisch is no fool. There was a very rigorous inspection, Kobisch said, and there were guards at the bridgeheads and all the time the thick fog. And so, he thought: Before I run into somebody, and they give me a blood test and find alcohol and take away my licence, I might as well go back to the inn in Waisenau and sit there and have another half pint.'

Marnet laughed.

'Go on and laugh, Franz. You think they allowed him to go back to Waisenau? The bridge was blocked. I'm telling you, Franz, there's something going on; something's in the wind.'

They had finished the downhill stretch. To the right and to the left was the level plain, bare except for the beet fields. What might be in the wind? Nothing but the golden, sun-illuminated dust that rose from the Hoechst houses, greying and turning to ash above them. In spite of that, it seemed to Franz, indeed he was suddenly convinced, that Anton Greiner was right. There was something in the wind.

With bicycle bells ringing, they cycled through the crowded narrow streets. The young girls screeched and rebuked them as they passed. At the crossroads and at the various factory entrances carbide streetlamps had been installed, which they were trying out today for the first time, maybe because of the dense fog. Their hard white light made all the faces look as if they were covered with plaster. Franz brushed up against a girl who grumbled angrily and turned her head to watch him. She'd pulled a bunch of her hair hastily over her left eye. The eye had been disfigured in an accident, and the bunch of hair called attention to it like a little flag, rather than hiding it. The good eye, almost black, focused on Franz's face briefly. Yet he felt as if she'd seen deep into him with that one look, to a place he'd closed off even from himself.

And then came the blaring horns of a fire engine from over on the Main River side, the crazy, garish carbide light, the curses of people being squeezed against a wall by a truck – was he still not used to all that or was it somehow different today? He searched for a word or a look he could interpret. He had dismounted from his bicycle and was pushing it along. He had long before lost both Greiner and the girl in the jostling crowd.

But then Greiner manoeuvred his way to where he was. 'Over in Oppenheim,' Greiner said to him over his shoulder; he had to lean so far sideways that his bicycle was almost pulled out of his grasp. Their respective work entrances were located far apart from each other. Once they had passed the first control station, they wouldn't be able to see each other again for several hours.

Franz kept his eyes and ears open, but neither in the locker room nor in the courtyard nor on the stairs could he detect any excitement other than the usual everyday stir between the second and the third sounding of the siren. It was just that things were a bit less orderly, a bit more boisterous than on other Monday mornings. Franz himself, even as he desperately tried to find the smallest indication of any disquiet concealed in the other men's words or in their eyes, cursed just like the others, asked the same questions about what they'd done on Sunday, made the same jokes, changed into his work clothes as brusquely as always. If someone were observing him now as persistently as he was observing the others, then that person would have been just as disappointed. Franz even felt a stab of hate towards all these men who had no inkling, who hadn't noticed that something was in the wind, or didn't want to notice. Had anything really happened? Greiner's stories were usually pure gossip. Had Messer, his cousin, asked him to spy on Franz? Has he noticed anything about me? Franz wondered. What was it he'd actually said? Just gossip and more gossip. That this fellow Kobisch had got drunk at the wine dealer's.

His thoughts were interrupted by the blast of the last siren signal. Since he'd been working at the plant only a short time, he still felt a lot of tension before the start of work. A tenseness akin to fear. And when the transmission belts started up, his body trembled to the very roots of his hair. Now the belt had reached its ultimate high whir. Franz had completed his first, second, his fiftieth operation. His shirt was soaked with sweat. He took a relieved breath. He began to review things in his mind again, although with only half his attention because he was doing precision stamping. Franz always worked with great exactitude. He could never have done things halfway, even if he'd been working for the devil.

There were twenty-five of them at work up there. Even if Franz were waiting anxiously in the punching department for some sign of excitement, given his nature it would have annoyed him if even one of his plates had turned out less than perfect. Not only because there might be a complaint that could harm him, but simply because the plates had to be precise, even on a day like today. Meanwhile he kept thinking: Anton said Oppenheim – wasn't that the little town between Mainz and Worms? What sort of unusual thing could have happened there, of all places?

Fritz Messer, Anton Greiner's cousin, who was the foreman in this department, came up to him briefly; then went on to the next man. Once Messer had parked his motorcycle and hung his uniform in his locker, he was just one more die puncher among the other punchers. Except maybe there was a change in the tone of his voice that only Franz noticed as he called Weigand over to sweep up. Weigand was an older, quite hairy, little man whose nickname was Woodchip. It was a good thing that his voice blended in with the high and piercing noise of the fan belt. For, as he was vacuuming up the waste dust, he said to Franz without moving his lips, 'Did you hear? At the concentration camp? In Westhofen.' Franz, looking down into little Woodchip's clear, almost innocent eyes, saw those tiny light spots he had been so keenly waiting for: as if deep inside the man a fire was burning and sending its last sparks out through the eyes. At last, thought Franz. By then Woodchip had already passed on to the next man.

Franz carefully set up his piece; placed the punch on the marked line, pushed down the lever, again, and again, and once more. At last, at last, and at last. If only he could simply walk away and join his friend Hermann. Suddenly he paused. Something about this news concerned him directly, personally. Something contained in this information had stirred him up, had sunk its hook into him and was gnawing at him without his knowing just what it was or why. So there's been a camp uprising, he said to himself, maybe even a major escape. Then it occurred to him why it concerned him in particular: George...What nonsense, he thought, to think immediately of George on hearing the news. Perhaps George wasn't even there any more. Or possibly he was already dead. But George's voice, coming from far away, mocking, mixed in now with his own voice: No, Franz, if and when something happens at Westhofen, then it means I'm not dead.

He had actually believed these past few years that he thought of George merely the way he thought of all the other prisoners! As if he were just one of thousands of whom one thinks with anger and sadness. He had really believed that, for a long time already, nothing connected him and George except for the firm tie of a common cause, the youthful years they'd spent under the stars of the same hope. No longer that other painful tie that had cut into their flesh and that both of them had tugged at back then. He was sure that all those old stories were forgotten. After all, George had become a different man, just as he, Franz, had grown into another person...For a second he caught sight of the face of the worker next to him. Had Woodchip told him something too? Was it possible that he would keep on carefully stamping out one piece after another? If something had really happened there, Franz thought, then George is in the middle of it. And then again, he thought, probably nothing at all happened, and Woodchip was just passing along gossip.

He went to the canteen during the lunch break and ordered a light beer; his relatives had packed him a lunch of bread, sausage and schmalz because he was saving up to buy a suit after the long period of being out of work. But how long would he be allowed to wear that suit (and if there was enough money also a zipped jacket)? Just then he heard them saying at the counter: Woodchip's been arrested.

One man said: It's because of yesterday. He was very drunk and told a lot of jokes.

Others said: No, it wouldn't be because of that; it's got to be something else. What else? Franz paid and leaned with his back against the counter. There was a strange, pervasive sibilant sound because suddenly everyone was speaking more softly, whispering: Woodchip, Woodchip...

'He talked too much, put his foot in it,' someone said to Franz; it was the man who worked next to him, Felix, a friend of Messer's. He gave Franz a meaningful look. There was amusement on his regular, almost beautiful face. His strong blue eyes seemed too cold for such a young face.

'Put his foot in what?' Franz asked. Felix shrugged and raised his eyebrows; he looked as if he were suppressing a laugh.

If only I could go and see Hermann now, Franz thought again. But he wouldn't be able to talk to Hermann before evening. Suddenly he saw Anton Greiner, who had forced his way over to the counter. Anton must have wangled himself a permit on some pretence to come here, because otherwise he couldn't get into this building, not even into the canteen. Why is he always looking for me; why is he always wanting to tell me things, me in particular?

Anton touched his arm, but immediately let go again as if there was something conspicuous about the gesture; he went back to stand next to Felix and downed a light beer. Then he came back to Franz. He has good, honest eyes, Franz thought. He may be a bit limited, but he's decent. And he's drawn to me the same way I'm drawn to Hermann... Anton took Franz by the arm and then, even as the midday break was coming to an end, he said, 'Over in Westhofen by the Rhine some prisoners escaped, a kind of convict gang. My cousin heard about it. And they're saying that most of them have already been recaptured. That's all I know.'

III

Even though he had thought about the escape for a long time beforehand, both by himself and together with Wallau, no matter how many minute details he had pondered over, along with the powerful impact a new existence would have, in those first minutes after the escape – with his blood and hair still sticking to the trap – he was just an animal escaping into the wilderness that was his life. Ever since the discovery of their escape, the howling of the sirens could be heard for kilometres all across the land, waking up the surrounding small villages still wrapped in the dense autumn fog. Indeed, the fog dampened everything, even the powerful searchlights that would normally have lit up the darkest night. Now, close to six o'clock in the morning, the lights were smothered by the cottony fog, in turn giving the mist a vague yellowish tinge.

George ducked farther down even as the ground under him gave way. He could sink down and go under in this bog before he'd even be able to get away from here. The dry brush resisted his fingers, which by now were bloodless, slippery, and icy cold. He felt as if he were sinking ever more quickly and deeper; it seemed to him that he should already have been swallowed up. Although he had escaped to avoid certain death – there was no doubt that they would have killed all of them within the next few days – dying in the swamp seemed to him quite simple and not frightening. It would be a death different from the one he was fleeing from. This would be a free death in the wilderness, not one administered by a human hand.

Six feet above him, the guards were running along the willow tree embankment with their dogs, driven crazy by the howling sirens and the thick, wet fog. George's hair stood on end. He heard someone cursing so close by, he was able to recognise the voice: Mannsfeld. Evidently the blow on the head Wallau had given him with the spade didn't hurt any more. George let go of the brush. He slipped even farther down. Now for the first time both his feet came in contact with a firm projection that gave him some support. He'd known about this projection when he still had the strength to figure everything out ahead of time with Wallau.

Then there was something new. But only a moment later, he realised it wasn't something new but something that had stopped: the siren. This was the new thing, a silence in which you could hear the whistles

of the men sharply set off from each other and the commands coming
from the camp and from the outer barracks. Above him, the guards
were running along behind the dogs to the outermost end of the
willow dam. Dogs were running from the outside barracks towards
the willow dam, a thin report and then another, a smacking noise,
and the loud barking of the dogs and right after that another thin
barking sound that had no chance of competing and couldn't have
been a dog, but wasn't a human voice either. For probably the person
they were dragging off now had nothing human left in him. It must
be Beutler, George thought. There's a degree of reality that can make
you believe you're dreaming even though you're as far from dreaming
as you can possibly be. They've got him, George thought, the way you
think in a dream, They've caught him. It really wasn't possible that
there were only six of them left now.

The fog was still thick enough to cut with a knife. Two little lights
came into view, far away on the other side of the highway – just behind
the bulrushes, it seemed. These single sharp points of light penetrated
the fog better than the flat beams of the searchlights. Little by little,
lights went on in the farmhouses; the villages were waking up. Soon
the circle of lights closed. That was impossible, George thought, I
dreamed it up. He wanted very much to sink to his knees now. Why
subject himself to this chase? Simply kneel down, there'd be some
gurgling, and it would all be over . . . Just calm down, Wallau always
used to say. Wallau was probably crouching not too far away behind
some willow bush. Whenever Wallau said that to you – First, just
calm down – you always became calm.

George grabbed some of the undergrowth. Slowly he crept sideways.
By now he was maybe some six yards away from the last tree stump.
Suddenly, he had a glaring, no longer dreamlike, insight and was
gripped by such an attack of fear that he simply remained clinging
to the outer slope, his belly flat on the ground. Then it was over, just
as suddenly as it had come.

He crawled as far as the stump. The siren started up a second time.
He was sure its howl reached far beyond the right bank of the Rhine.
George pressed his face into the ground. Keep calm, Wallau said to

him over his shoulder. George took a deep breath, turned his head. The lights had all gone out. The fog had softened and become transparent, a pure golden tissue. Three motorcycle headlights raced along the road like rockets. The howling of the siren having begun again seemed to swell, even though it constantly diminished and increased in waves of loudness, wildly boring into brains for miles around. George again pressed his face into the ground because the guards were now running back across the dam above him. He peeked out of the corners of his eyes. The searchlights couldn't grab on to anything any more, they'd become weak with the light of dawn. If only the fog wouldn't lift just now. Suddenly three of the guards started climbing down the outer slope. They were less than ten yards away. George again recognised Mannsfeld's voice. He recognised Ibst by the curses, not the voice, which had turned quite thin with rage, almost a woman's voice. The third voice, frighteningly close by – any of the men could have stepped on George's head – was Meissner's, which they always heard at night in the barracks, calling up individual prisoners – the last time, two nights ago, it had called out him, George. Now, too, Meissner struck at the air with something sharp after every word. George felt the little breeze it made. Somewhere around here – Straight ahead – Soon – Keep your eyes open – Come on.

A second attack of fear, like a fist squeezing his heart. All right, stop being a human being now, grow roots, become a willow tree among the other willows, grow bark and branches instead of arms. Meissner climbed down into the rough area and started to bellow like crazy. Suddenly he stopped. He's seen me, George thought. He became instantly calm; not a trace of fear any more; this is the end, farewell.

Meissner climbed farther down to where the others were. They were now wading through the area between the dam and the road. Because they were much closer to him than they knew, George, for the moment, was safe. If he'd suddenly taken off, they would have caught him, then and there. Strangely enough, he actually had, though wild and unthinking, stuck rigidly to his original plan! His own plans that he'd figured out during sleepless nights – what power they have over you in that hour when all plans are foiled; then you feel as if another person had made the plans for you. But this other person, he too was me.

The siren faltered a second time. George crept sideways, one of his feet slipped. A tree swallow starting up noisily scared George half out of his wits, and he let go of the brush. The swallow ducked into the bulrushes, making a loud rustling noise. George listened; he was sure everyone was listening now. Why do you have to be a human being, and if a human being, why me? George asked himself. The bulrushes righted themselves again, no one came; nothing happened; it was after all nothing but a bird bumbling around in the swamp. In spite of that, George got no farther; his knee was sore, his arms worn out. Suddenly he saw Wallau's small pale sharp-nosed face in the bushes... Suddenly the bushes were studded with Wallau faces.

It passed. He felt almost calm. He thought unemotionally, Wallau, Fuellgrabe and I will make it. We three are the best. They've got Beutler. Belloni might make it too. Aldinger is too old. Pelzer is too soft. When he turned over to lie on his back it was already day. The fog had lifted. Golden, cool autumn light bathed the land, one might almost call it peaceful. George now recognised the two large, flat, white-edged rocks some sixty feet away. Before the war the dam had once been the driveway to a remote farmstead that had long ago burned or been torn down. Back then they'd probably drained this land. But now, along with all the shortcuts between the dam and the road, it had turned back into a swamp. Back then they'd probably also dragged these rocks up from the Rhine. Between the rocks there were still some firm, dry spots, but they were overgrown with rushes. A kind of hollow pathway had been created through which you could crawl on your belly.

The few yards to the first white-edged grey rock were the worst; there was hardly any cover. George grabbed hold of the brushwood with his teeth, then he released first one hand, then the other. As the branches snapped back they made a swishing sound; a bird darted up, maybe the same one as before.

Once he was crouching on the second rock in the bulrushes, it seemed to him as if he'd got there awfully quickly, as if on angel wings. If only he didn't feel so cold now.

IV

Long after he had received the report, Fahrenberg, the camp commandant, still felt as if this unbearable reality must have been a dream from which he would soon wake up; in fact, he felt as though the entire thing wasn't even a bad dream but just the memory of a bad dream. It's true Fahrenberg seemed to have quite cold-bloodedly taken all the measures demanded by such a report. But actually it hadn't been Fahrenberg, for even the most dreadful nightmare doesn't require measures to be taken; rather, someone else had worked them out for him, for an event that must never be allowed to happen.

When the siren started howling a second after the order had been given, he stepped carefully over an extension cord – an obstacle in his dream – and to the window. Why was the siren howling? Outside the window there was nothing: the correct view for a nonexisting time.

It did not occur to him that this nothing was still something: a dense, thick fog. Fahrenberg woke up when Bunsen tripped on one of the electrical cords leading from the office to the sleeping quarters. He suddenly began to shout, not at Bunsen of course, but at Zillich, who had just reported to him. But as yet Fahrenberg wasn't shouting at him because he'd understood the report about the escape of seven prisoners all at one time, but rather to get rid of his nightmare. Bunsen, a six-foot-seven, conspicuously handsome man, turned round again and said, 'Excuse me,' and bent down to push the plug back into the electric outlet box. Fahrenberg had a certain preference for electric and telephone installations. In these two rooms there were a lot of wires and interchangeable outlets as well as frequent repairs and new installations. Coincidentally, a prisoner from Fulda by the name of Dietrich who was a professional electrician had been released right after the completion of the new installation, which then turned out to be rather a mess. Bunsen waited – obvious amusement in his eyes but no evidence of it in his face – until Fahrenberg was finished yelling. Then he went out. Fahrenberg and Zillich were left alone.

In the outer doorway, Bunsen lit a cigarette, but took only one drag on it, then threw it away. He'd had the night off; actually he wasn't due back on duty for another half hour, but his future father-in-law had brought him back from Wiesbaden by car.

Between the commandant's barracks, a sturdy brick building, and Barracks III, along the length of which grew a few plane trees, there was a sort of square that they referred to as the Dance Ground among themselves. Here, out in the open, the siren really bored its way into your head. Stupid fog, Bunsen thought.

His men had all reported for duty. 'Braunewell! Nail the map to the tree over there. All right: step up! Now listen!' Bunsen placed the point of the compass on the red dot, 'Camp Westhofen.' He drew three concentric circles. 'It's five minutes past six now. The escape occurred at five forty-five. By six twenty a person going as fast as he can could get to this point. So, presumably he'd be somewhere between this circle and this one. All right – Braunewell! Close off the road between the villages of Botzenbach and Oberreichenbach. Meiling! You close off the road between Unterreichenbach and Kalheim. Let nothing through! Keep in touch with each other and with me. We can't comb the area for them yet. Reinforcements won't get here till fifteen minutes from now. —Willich! The outermost circle touches the right bank of the Rhine at this point. Therefore, seal off the stretch between the ferry and the Liebacher Meadow. Occupy this crossroad. Take over the ferry. Post guards on the Liebacher Meadow!'

The fog was still so dense that the numbers on his wristwatch glowed. He could already hear the horns of the motorised SS squad that had left the camp. Now Reichenbacher Road was blocked. He stepped up to the map. And the guards were already on the Liebacher Meadow. Whatever they could do during these first few minutes had been done. In the meantime, Fahrenberg had sent the report in to headquarters. The old man, the conqueror of Seeligenstadt, must be feeling pretty uncomfortable. On the other hand, he, Bunsen, felt pretty good. And what luck! The whole messy thing had happened while he was off duty. Then coming back a bit too early he was just in time to participate in the manhunt. He wondered if the old man in his barracks was done with his second fit of rage; it was hard to tell with the racket the howling sirens made.

Zillich was alone with his superior. He kept an eye on him while he was fiddling with the telephone to get a direct line to headquarters. This damned Dietrich from Fulda ought to be locked up again tomorrow for his sloppy work. Zillich was fully aware of the time being wasted on this idiotic plugging and unplugging. Precious seconds in which seven dots were moving ever farther and more quickly away, to a point where one would never be able to catch up with them. Finally, headquarters came on the line, and Zillich made his report. Fahrenberg thus heard it for the second time in ten minutes. His face kept the incorruptible hardness that had been imposed on it long ago in spite of a nose and chin that were slightly too short and a drooping lower jaw. God, who only now came to his mind, could not permit this report to be true: seven prisoners from his camp escaping at one time! He stared at Zillich, who returned his gaze with a dark, serious expression, full of regret, sadness, and guilt, for Fahrenberg had been the first person who had trusted him completely. Zillich was not surprised that something always came up to spoil things just when they were going well. Hadn't he got that disgusting gunshot wound in November 1918? Hadn't his farm been auctioned off in a forced sale one month before the new law took effect? Didn't he have to go to jail for half a year for the stabbing because that female back then recognised him? For two years Fahrenberg had trusted him to do what, between themselves, they called 'skimming', that is, putting together punishment gangs composed of selected prisoners and picking the guards to escort them.

Suddenly the alarm clock Fahrenberg had on the chair next to his cot from old habit sounded: it was six fifteen. He ought to be getting up now and Bunsen should be reporting back. Supposedly the start of an ordinary day, Fahrenberg's ordinary day, being in command of Westhofen.

Fahrenberg came to with a start. He closed his drooping jaw. Then in a few brief moves he got dressed. He passed a damp hairbrush through his hair, brushed his teeth. He came over to Zillich, he looked down at the man's thick neck, and said, 'We'll catch them in no time.'

Zillich replied, 'Yessir, Commandant!' Then he said, 'Commandant...' and made a few suggestions, pretty much the same ones that would later be carried out by the Gestapo once no one was thinking of Zillich any more. The suggestions demonstrated a clear and keen understanding of the situation.

Suddenly Zillich broke off; they both listened. Far away they could hear even above the sirens shouted commands, the scraping of boots on the Dance Ground, and a small, thin, at first inexplicable sound. Zillich and Fahrenberg looked at each other. 'Window,' Fahrenberg said. Zillich opened it; the fog came into the room along with the sound. Fahrenberg listened briefly; then he went outside with Zillich. Bunsen was just about to dismiss the SA when there was a disturbance. They were dragging the prisoner named Beutler towards the Dance Ground, the first escapee to be recaptured.

Before the eyes of the SA unit that had not yet marched off, Beutler crawled the last stretch without help. Not on his knees, but rather, perhaps because he'd been kicked, sideways so that his face was turned up. And now as the man crept past him, Bunsen, looking down, noticed what was special about the face. It was laughing. The recaptured prisoner lay there in his bloody smock, with blood in his ears, and his large white teeth showing, and he seemed to be writhing in silent laughter.

Bunsen looked away from the face and turned to Fahrenberg. Fahrenberg was looking down at Beutler. His lips were curled back from his teeth so that for a moment it looked as if they were laughing at each other. Bunsen knew his commandant; he knew what would happen next. What happened now in his own young face was what always happened in such a situation. At this point Bunsen's nostrils flared a little, the corners of his mouth twitched, and an expression of the most terrible devastation spread over the handsome features of a face endowed by nature with the features of a dragon slayer or an armed archangel.

But nothing happened just then.

Police commissars Overkamp and Fischer had just come through the camp entrance and were being escorted to the commandant's barracks. Both stopped when they reached Bunsen, Fahrenberg, and Zillich. They saw what was going on and spoke briefly with each other. Then Overkamp, not addressing himself to anyone in particular, said in a very low voice full of repressed fury, 'Is this what you call recapturing a prisoner? Congratulations. You'd better send out an urgent call for some medical specialists to patch up that man's kidneys, balls, and ears, so that he'll be fit enough for us to question him! Really clever, really clever. Congratulations.'

V

By now the fog had lifted somewhat and was hovering like a low, fluffy sky above the roofs and treetops. And the good old sun hung dully above the bumpy village street of Westhofen like a lamp behind muslin curtains.

If only the fog wouldn't lift just now so that the sun won't burn the crops before the harvest, some people thought. Others thought, If only the fog would lift quickly so that the crops could get the sunshine they need.

In Westhofen itself not many had these worries. Theirs wasn't a grape-growing village; theirs was a cucumber village. The vinegar factory was located only a little distance away, on the road that led from the Liebacher Meadow to the highway. Behind a wide, neatly dug ditch their fields ran right up to the road leading to the factory. 'Wine Vinegar and Mustard, Matthias Frank & Sons'. Wallau had imprinted the sign on his memory. Once George was out of the bulrushes, he had to crawl the next three yards without any cover, and then down into the ditch, and follow its left arm, along the edge of the fields.

When he raised his head above the bulrushes, the fog had risen so high that it revealed the group of trees behind the vinegar factory, and since the sun was at George's back, it seemed as if the group of trees had ignited and were suddenly aflame. How long had he been crawling? His clothes were slippery with mud. He could just continue to lie there; nobody would find him. There'd be no noise or commotion around him except for a little cawing and fluttering. A couple of weeks of being patient, by which time a crust of frozen snow would cover anything that was left of him. See, Wallau, how easy it would be to ruin your meticulous plan? After all, Wallau had no idea how heavy his body was and how hard to drag it along by digging his elbows into any available spot of bare ground. It felt as if he were dragging the whole swamp along with him. The sound of a whistle came from the Liebacher Meadow. There was an answering whistle so frighteningly close that George buried his face in the ground. Crawl! Wallau had advised and, after all, the man had lived through the war and the fighting in the Ruhr and the battles in the centre of Germany; in fact, whatever there was to live through, Wallau had experienced it. Make sure you keep crawling, George. Don't think you've been discovered. Lots of guys were discovered that way, because they were imagining they'd already been discovered and then did something foolish.

George peered out over the edge of the ditch through the wilted shrubbery. A guard was standing where the path that led through the cucumber field joined the highway. He was so dismayingly close that George wasn't even scared but got angry instead. He was so close, standing there on his two legs leaning against the brick wall, that it was sheer torture for George to stay hidden instead of jumping him. Slowly the guard walked down the path past the factory towards the Liebacher Meadow – at his back, in the grey and brown infinity, were George's two glowing eyes. George was sure the guard would have to turn round because of the windmill-like clatter his heart was making, although when faced with death, it beat more quietly than a bird's wing. George slid onwards in the ditch almost parallel to the place on the path where the guard had been standing a moment before. Wallau had explained to him that this was the place where the ditch passed under the road. Wallau himself didn't know whether the ditch went on and where it led after that. He had no predictions beyond that point. Now George felt completely deserted and alone. Remain calm – only those two words stayed with him; he could hear the sound of them, a spoken amulet. This ditch, he told himself, runs on through under the factory, taking any discharge with it. He had to wait until the guard turned. The guard stopped at the bank; he blew his whistle. A whistle came back from the Liebacher Meadow. George now had an idea of the distance between the whistles; on the whole, he knew quite a lot now. Every corner of his brain was busy; every muscle, straining; every second, filled – all of life was incredibly dense, breathless, and close. Then when he was down in the stinking, foul-smelling drainage ditch, he suddenly felt sick. This wasn't a ditch to crawl through; it was a place to suffocate in. And yet, at the same time, he was furious because after all, he wasn't a sewer rat and this was no place for him to give up and die. By then it was no longer quite so pitch dark ahead of him, but there was a stormy torrent of little watery whorls. Luckily the factory grounds weren't very extensive, maybe forty yards across. When he came out on the other side of the wall, the field rose slightly upward towards the highway and a path led diagonally up. In the angle between the wall and the field path there was a pile of rubbish. George could not go on; he had to crouch down and throw up.

Just then an old man came walking through the fields with two pails hanging from a rope over his shoulder. He was on his way to get rabbit food from the factory custodian. In Westhofen they called him Gingersnap. In the course of his short walk the man had been stopped six times. Each time he had identified himself as Gottlieb Heidrich from Westhofen, nickname Gingersnap. Aha, thought Gingersnap as he came walking very slowly across the fields with his rabbit food pails and heard the sirens howling, something's happened again at the concentration camp. Probably a lot like what happened last summer when one of those poor devils tried to leave and they shot him – and the siren kept on howling even after he was already dead. There never used to be shenanigans like that before around here. Why did they have to plop this concentration camp down right here, of all places, right in front of our noses? On the other hand, at least people in the area were earning some money now, whereas before they'd had to skimp and scrape for a living, taking every last little thing to sell at the market. He wondered if it was true that later on they'd lease out the land that those poor devils back there had to dig around in; no wonder they wanted to run away. And the price for one of those leases was supposed to be lower than over in Liebach.

All this was going through Gingersnap's mind, but then he turned round again because he wanted to know why that unbelievably filthy man was crouching by a pile of rubbish over there on the field path. He was satisfied when he saw that the man was just throwing up, because that was a good reason for his being there.

George hadn't seen Gingersnap. And so he kept going. At first he wanted to head towards Erlenbach, far away from the Rhine. But now he was afraid of crossing the main road. So he changed his plan, if you could still call it a plan – this extreme momentary fixation. He plodded on across the field, shoulders hunched, head down, expecting any instant to be hailed, to be shot. His toes pushed into the loose soil. Soon there'll be a shout, he thought, then there'll be a shot – he felt an overpowering urge to simply throw himself down on the ground. Then he thought: they'll shoot me in the legs, drag me off alive. He closed his eyes. Mixed in with the cool, gentle morning breeze was an overwhelming sadness, more than any human being could possibly cope with. He stumbled again, then stopped short. On the path at his feet lay a little green ribbon. He stared at it as if it had just dropped into this field from the sky. He picked it up.

And there, as if she'd emerged from the soil, stood a child in a smock with a parting in her hair. They stared at each other. The child looked from his face to his hand. He tugged at the child's braid and gave her the ribbon.

The child ran off to an old woman, obviously her grandmother, who was suddenly also standing there on the path. 'From now on you'll only be getting string for your braid,' the old woman said, laughing. To George she said, 'You could tie a new ribbon in her braid every day.'

'Why don't you cut the braid off?' George said.

'Oh no,' the old woman said. She looked him up and down. Just then Gingersnap called out from the vinegar factory, which was located close behind them, 'Hey, Jumblegranny!' That was what everybody in Westhofen called the old woman because all her life long she'd always had all sorts of junk around her place, useful stuff and useless stuff, whatever you happened to need, adhesive tape, thread, cough drops. Now she waved with her dry, wrinkled arm towards Gingersnap. Once long ago, she'd danced with him and almost married him. And a horrible kind of flirtatious animation contorted her toothless mouth and wrinkled cheeks – it was as if you were about to hear a bag of bones jingling in a dance.

But when Gingersnap saw the appallingly dirty stranger, who might after all have some connection with the vinegar factory, walk off with the old woman and the child, he calmed down and dismissed a thought that had been nagging at him. George, walking behind the two, felt accepted again among the living, if only for a few minutes. But the field path led not merely to the village as George had thought, it forked into two paths, one leading to the village, the other to the highway. The old woman had stuffed the ribbon into one of her skirt pockets together with all her other junk and was now leading the child, who was trying hard not to cry, by her braid along at her side. The grandmother didn't stop jabbering: 'Did you hear all the commotion before, oh my, oh my! What a lot of noise. Now it's quiet. They've got him. That fellow has nothing to laugh about. Oh my, oh my!' She giggled and wailed. At the fork she stopped. 'The fog's lifted! Look!'

George looked around. And it was true, the fog had lifted; the pale blue autumn sky sparkled pure and clear. 'Oh my, oh my,' the old woman uttered this time because two, no, three gleaming aeroplanes were swooping down out of the blue sky, close to the ground, flying in low tight circles above the roofs of Westhofen, the swamp, and the fields.

George stayed close to the old woman as she led her grandchild towards the road.

They walked for about thirty feet on the main road without meeting anyone. The old woman was silent. She seemed to have forgotten everything – George, the child, the sun, and the planes – and was brooding about things that had happened to her in the past, before George had even been born. George continued to stick very close to her, almost wanting to hold on to her skirt. Of course it wasn't real; it was only in his dream that he was walking with the old woman, holding on to her skirt, and she not noticing anything. He'll wake up soon; Lohgerber would be yelling in the barracks . . .

To the right there now was a long high wall topped with sharp glass shards. They walked along the wall for a few steps close behind each other, George bringing up the rear. Suddenly without any horn blowing, a motorcycle came up behind them. If the old woman were to turn round now, she'd think George had been swallowed up by the earth. The motorcycle zoomed past. 'Oh my, oh my,' the woman grunted, but she trotted on; George had not only vanished from the path, he had vanished from her memory as well.

George was lying on the other side of the wall, his hands bloody from the glass fragments; the left hand had been torn open below the thumb and his clothes were ripped right through to his skin.

Would they get off their motorbikes now to haul him in? Voices came from a low redbrick building with many windows. Many voices, both high and low, and then a chorus of quick boys' voices. What were they trying to impress on him, in the hour of his death, what phrases, what words? From the opposite direction he could hear a motorcycle starting up, but it passed, headed towards the camp at Westhofen. George felt no relief; he now became aware of the pain in his hand – he wanted to bite it off above the wrist.

At the left end of the red building – it was an agricultural school – there was a greenhouse. The main entrance and stairway to the school were at this end of the building across from the greenhouse. There was a shed between the street side of the school and the wall; it blocked his view. He crawled over to the shed. It was dark and quiet inside. It smelled of raffia. Once his eyes became accustomed to the dark, he could make out thick bunches of raffia hanging on the wall, along with all sorts of tools, baskets, and items of clothing. Now that everything no longer depended on his being quick witted, but only what was called luck, he became cool and calm. He tore off a rag and bandaged his left hand, using his teeth and his right hand. He took his time choosing, and finally settled on a heavy, brown corduroy jacket with a zip. He put it on over his bloody, sweaty things. He looked over the shoes. Lots of nice, good-quality things. Only problem was that he couldn't go outside. He looked through a crack in the wooden wall. There were people behind the windows and people in the greenhouse. Now someone was going down the steps and crossing over to the greenhouse. He stopped outside the door, turned towards the shed. Someone called out of a window, and he went back inside the school building. Now it was quiet. The sun glittered on the panes of glass and the metal parts of a machine that lay next to the steps still partly wrapped.

George suddenly sprang to the door and pulled out the key. He laughed to himself. Then he sat down on the floor with his back to the door and gazed at his shoes. This lasted two, three minutes, a final time of collecting yourself, knowing that outside everything was lost and you didn't give a damn. If they came for him now, should he attack them with a hoe or with a rake?

He didn't know what roused him from his daze, certainly nothing external, maybe the pain in his hand, maybe a remnant of Wallau's voice in his ear. He put the key back in the lock. He opened the door a crack and peered out. He couldn't go back to the road and over the wall. The brownish foothills of a mountain vineyard were visible between the top of the wall with its glass shards and the sky; the air was so transparent, you could count the little tips of the vines in the topmost row, silhouetted against the pale brown of the hill. While he was dully looking out at the top row of the vineyard, he was suddenly struck by a bit of advice – he had no idea where it came from. For George could no longer remember whether it was Wallau himself at the Ruhr or a coolie in Shanghai or a member of the defensive alliance in Vienna who had escaped danger by shouldering a remarkable object that distracted attention from himself because carrying such an object gives the journey a purpose and lends the carrier an identity. This adviser now reminded George in his shed with the door a crack open on to a wall topped by glass shards that once before someone like him had escaped into a meadow from a house in Vienna or a farm in the Ruhr or a blocked street in Taipei. Though he didn't know whether the face of this adviser had Wallau's familiar features or was yellow or brown, he understood the advice: unwrap the machine part next to the stairway. After all, you have to get out of here; it might not work, but there's no other way. Your situation is particularly desperate, but mine was, too, back then—

Who knows whether anyone even noticed him and, if they did, thought he was a machine factory employee or the man whose jacket he was wearing. At first he took the path between the greenhouse and the front steps of the school, then out through the courtyard gate to the path running along the side of the school that faced the fields. He had to use his left hand in carrying his load, and the pain was so excruciating that for minutes at a time it even dulled his fear. George walked along the path that paralleled the highway. It led past a few houses that all faced the fields, and whose uppermost windows might even have had a view of the Rhine. The planes were still buzzing around; the haze had burned off and the sky was totally blue; it would soon be noon. George's tongue was dry; he was tormented by a desperate thirst; the blood- and dirt-crusted clothes under the jacket hurt his skin. He had been carrying the machine part, the company tag still dangling from it, lightly on his left shoulder. He was about to put the thing down and take a breather when he was stopped.

It was probably one of the two motorcycle patrols who had caught sight of him through a space between two houses: the outline of a man, tramping through the fields carrying something on his shoulder under the silent noonday sky. The fellow challenged him because they were challenging everyone, even without any particular reason. He waved him on after George identified himself with the company tag. Perhaps George could have gone all the way to Oppenheim and even farther – that was the counsel of the adviser who'd helped him in the barracks. George himself heard the soft, urgent voice calling out:

Keep going, keep going. But the guard's challenge had struck fear into his heart. He dragged the machine part as far as possible away from the road, into the field and in the direction of the Rhine, towards the village of Buchenau. The louder his heart pounded in fear, the softer became the voice advising him against taking the field path, until it was totally drowned out by his wildly beating heart and the midday bells of Buchenau. A high, bitter ringing for all poor sinners. A glassy sky was inverted over the village. Even as he entered the village he already had a feeling, an inkling that it would turn out to be a trap. He walked past two guards who stared at him. He could sense their eyes at his back. He had hardly reached the main village street when he heard a whistle behind him, a thin piercing sound that went right through him.

The village was suddenly in turmoil with whistles shrilling from one end to the other. 'Everyone inside their houses!' came a command. Heavy gates creaked. George put down the machine part he'd been carrying and slipped through the nearest gate and behind a woodpile. The village was encircled. It was shortly after noon.

Franz had just entered the factory lunchroom in Hoechst. And he had just been told that Woodchip was under arrest. Anton had come over to him, grabbed his wrist, and told him what he knew.

At that same moment Ernst the shepherd was knocking on the Mangolds' kitchen window. Sophie opened the door, laughing. She was plump and strong but with delicate wrists and ankles. He asked Sophie to warm up his potato soup because his thermos bottle was broken. Sophie said he ought to come inside and eat with them. Nelly could watch the sheep.

His Nelly, Ernst said, wasn't just a dog, she was a little angel. But he had a conscience and he was paid for doing his job. 'Sophie,' Ernst said, 'couldn't you please heat up the soup and bring it out to me in the field? Sophie, don't look at me like that. When you look at me like that with your adorable little eyes, they go right through me.'

He walked back over the fields to his hut on wheels, found himself a sunny spot, spread out a layer of newspapers, and put his coat on top. Then he sat down and waited. He was happy when he saw Sophie coming towards him. Like little apples, he thought, so round, so ripe, and with delicate, fine little stems.

Along with the soup Sophie brought him some of her potato dumplings with pear slices. They had gone to school together in Schmiedtheim. She sat down next to him. 'Funny,' she said.

'What?'

'Oh, that you happen to be a shepherd.'

'They told me the same thing recently down there,' Ernst said, pointing towards Hoechst. 'You're a strong young man, nature made you for something else.' Ernst's face and the sound of his voice could change incredibly quickly, so that one moment he was Meier at the labour office, at another he was Gerstl at the Labour Front, and at another Mayor Kraus of Schmiedtheim, and at yet another himself, Ernst, but that last one only rarely. —'Why don't you let an older man take your place with the sheep?'

'And I said,' Ernst went on after he'd quickly swallowed a couple of spoonfuls of soup, 'the job of shepherding is inherited in my family since the days of Wiligis.'

'From what sort of Willis?' Sophie asked.

'They asked me that down there too,' Ernst said and mashed a dumpling in with the pear slices. 'Probably because none of you paid attention back in school. Then they asked me why I wasn't married when all the others were already married and had children and earned their daily bread doing much harder work.'

'So what did you say then?' Sophie asked a little hoarsely.

'Oh well,' Ernst said innocently, 'I said, I'd already made a start.'

'In what way?' Sophie asked eagerly.

'Because I'm already engaged,' Ernst said lowering his eyes, although it didn't escape him that Sophie had turned a little pale and limp. 'I'm already engaged to Marie Wielenz from Botzenbach.'

'Oh,' Sophie said, her head down and smoothing her skirt over her legs, 'but she's still just a school girl, little Marie Wielenz from Botzenbach.'

'Doesn't matter,' said Ernst, 'I like to watch my fiancée growing up. It's a long story. Someday I'll tell you.'

Sophie toyed with a blade of grass. She straightened it and then pulled it through her teeth. She murmured sadly but scornfully to herself, 'In love, engaged, married...'

And Ernst, who was having fun teasing her and who hadn't missed a thing, whether the play of her emotions or the fiddling of her hands, put the two plates on top of each other, having licked them clean, and said, 'Thanks, Sophie. If you can do everything else as well as you can cook dumplings, then a man won't go wrong with you. Look at me! Would you please look at me! When you look at me with your two little eyes, I can forget little Marie for ever, if not longer.'

He watched Sophie go off with the clattering plates; then he called, 'Nelly!' The little dog raced towards him and up on his chest, then she put her paws on Ernst's knees and looked up at him, a little black bundle of unconditional loyalty. Ernst nuzzled the dog's nose with his face and rubbed Nelly's head with both hands in a fit of affection. 'Nelly, you know whom I like best? And Nelly, do you know the name of the one I like most of all the females in the whole world and of all the people I know? Her name is Nelly.'

Meanwhile the school caretaker at the Darré Agricultural School had rung the midday bell – fifteen minutes after actual midday. Young Helwig, one of the garden apprentices, went first to the shed to get twenty pfennig out of the purse in the pocket of his corduroy jacket. He owed the money to a student for two Winter Aid lottery tickets. The school taught courses the entire year, mostly to the sons and daughters of farmers from the surrounding villages. But the school also had an experimental farm on which not only students worked but also a couple of gardeners and apprentices with the customary work contracts.

The apprentice Helwig was a tall youth with lively eyes. He searched for his jacket all through the shed, at first surprised, then angry, and then upset. He had bought the jacket the previous week, right after he'd had his first girl. He couldn't have bought it if he hadn't won a small prize in a contest. He called his friends over; they were already sitting down for their lunch. The bright dining room with the clean-scrubbed wooden tables was as always festively decorated with the flowers of the month and with fresh foliage twined around the pictures of Hitler, Darré and the landscapes hanging on the wall. Helwig thought at first that his mates had played a trick on him. They'd all teased him for buying a jacket that was still too big for him and because they envied him his girlfriend. The young boys with their fresh, open faces, in which both boyish and manly features mingled just as in Helwig's, tried to reassure him and started helping him with his search. Then soon there were shouts, 'Look here at these stains! What are they?' and one yelled, 'They tore out my lining!'

'Somebody was in here,' another one said. 'Your jacket's been stolen.'

Helwig tried not to cry. Then the guard came out from the dining room to see what mischief the boys were up to. Helwig told him, pale with anger, that his jacket had been stolen. They called over the teacher in charge and the school caretaker. They opened the shed door wide. Then they saw the stained clothes and the torn lining of an old jacket that was all bloodied.

Oh, if only they'd merely torn the lining out of *his* jacket! There was nothing manly left in Helwig's face. Anger and misery turned it childlike. 'If I find him, I'll kill him!' he announced. And he wasn't comforted when Müller found that his shoes were missing. Müller was the only son of rich farmers and could buy himself new ones. But for him, Helwig, it meant he'd have to start saving all over again.

'Calm down, Helwig,' the school principal, who'd been called away from his family lunch table, said. 'Calm down and describe your jacket in as much detail as you can. This man here is from the criminal police and he'll be able to find it for you but only if you give him an exact description.'

'What was in the pockets?' the stranger, a friendly little man, asked once Helwig had finished with his description, during which he had to swallow hard after the words 'it had zips inside too'. Helwig thought about it. 'A purse,' he said, 'with one mark and twenty pfennig, a handkerchief, a knife...'

They read back everything he'd said and had him sign it.

'Where can I pick up my jacket?'

'We'll let you know, my boy,' the principal said.

This was little consolation for young Helwig, but nevertheless a glorification of the misfortune in that the thief who stole his jacket was no ordinary thief. The school caretaker, as soon as he'd seen the shed, immediately put two and two together. He just had to ask the principal whether he should telephone.

By the time Helwig came downstairs – right after him Müller had to describe his shoes – the entire area between the school and the wall had been closed off. The place where George had climbed over the wall and damaged the espaliered fruit tree had already been marked. Guards were posted in front of the wall and in front of the shed. And teachers and gardeners and pupils were milling in front of the police cordon. The lunch break had to be extended; by now, a skin had formed on top of the pea soup with bacon in the big kettles.

An elderly gardener, apparently unaffected by all the excitement, was working on straightening a path a couple of yards away from where they had cordoned it off. He was from the same village as young Helwig. The youth, his pale face an angry red, had eagerly answered all the questions directed at him. He now stopped next to the elderly gardener, maybe precisely because he thought the man wouldn't ask him any questions. 'They said I'd get my jacket back,' young Helwig said.

'Aha,' the gardener said.

'They asked me to describe it in detail.'

'And did you describe it in detail?' the gardener, whose name was Gueltscher, asked without looking up from his work.

'Of course. I had to,' the boy said.

Then the school caretaker rang the midday bell for the second time that day. They started lunch all over again in the dining room. There was already a rumour that in Liebach and Buchenau the Hitler

Youth had been allowed to join in the search. They asked young Helwig all sorts of additional questions. But he had stopped talking. He seemed to be battling a new, more silent attack of misery. And then it occurred to him that his membership card for the Buchenau Gymnasts had also been in his jacket pocket. Should he report that now as well?

What would the thief do with his card? He might just burn it up with a match. But where would the fugitive get a match? He could just tear it up and throw it into a privy. But can an escaped prisoner simply go into a privy somewhere? Or he'd probably just stamp the torn-up scraps into the soil, the boy thought, and was oddly reassured. He made a detour and walked back to where the old gardener was working. Up to now he hadn't paid much attention to this old man from his own village – most young people don't pay much attention to old people, who are always there and then die at some point. This time, too, he stopped near the old man for no reason. He was now transplanting some bulbs along the straightened path. Young Helwig was in good standing, as a member of the Hitler Youth and at the garden school, and he did well everywhere. He was a strong, honest, handy boy. He was sure the men who were imprisoned in the Westhofen concentration camp belonged in that place just as much as crazy people belonged in an insane asylum.

'Hey, Gueltscher,' he said.

'What?'

'My membership card was in the jacket too.'

'Well, and so what?'

'Should I report that too, even now?'

'You reported everything you had to,' the gardener said. Now for the first time, he looked up at the boy and said, 'Don't worry, you'll get your jacket back again.'

'Oh, you think so?' the boy said.

'Sure. They're bound to catch him, more likely today even than tomorrow. How much did it cost?'

'Eighteen marks.'

'That's quite a bit,' Gueltscher said, as if he wanted to refresh the boy's grief. 'In that case, it'll probably be able to take quite a lot of abuse. You'll be wearing it when you go out with your girl. And he,' – he gestured vaguely into the air over the fields – 'he'll long be dead by then.'

The boy frowned. 'Well, and so what?' he suddenly said roughly and insolently.

'Nothing,' old Gueltscher said, 'nothing at all.'

Why did the old man look at me that way just now, young Helwig wondered.

VI

There were clotheslines stretched crisscross in the yard where George had hidden behind the woodpile. Two women, an old one and a middle-aged one, came out of the house with a laundry basket. The old one looked tough and hard; the younger had a tired face and walked hunched over.

'Oh Wallau, if only we'd stayed together,' George thought as a new, wild noise came from the edge of the village and approached the street, 'you would have looked at me now...'

The two women tested the laundry hanging on the line. The old one said, 'It's too wet, not ready for ironing.'

The younger one said, 'It's just right for ironing.' She began to take it down and put it into the basket.

The old one said, 'It's much too wet.'

The younger one said, 'It's ready for ironing.'

'Too wet,' said the old one.

The younger one said, 'To each his own. You like to iron dry; I like to iron damp.'

The clotheslines were being emptied in a flying, almost desperate haste. Outside the courtyard, the village was in an uproar. The younger woman cried out, 'There, just listen!'

The old woman said, 'Yes, yes.'

The young one screamed in a voice high enough to shatter glass, 'Listen, just listen!'

The old one said, 'I'm not hard of hearing yet. Push the basket over here.'

At that instant an SA officer came out of the house and into the yard. The younger one said, 'And where are you coming from this time, all booted and spurred? Certainly not from the vineyard.'

The man shouted, 'Are you crazy, you two females? Doing laundry now! You ought to be ashamed. Some guy from Westhofen is hiding in the village. We're searching everywhere for him.'

The younger one called out, 'Oh, well, there's always something going on. Yesterday it was the harvest prayer, the day before the Hundred and Forty-Fourth, and today trying to catch an escapee, and tomorrow it'll be the gauleiter [the Nazi district leader] driving through the village. What about the beets? And the grapes, the wine? And the laundry?'

The man said, 'Shut up.' He stamped his foot. 'Why isn't your gate closed?' He tramped through the yard. Only one side of the gate was open; to close the entire gate you had to first open the other side too and then close them both and fit them into each other. The old woman helped him.

'Wallau, oh, Wallau,' George thought . . .

'Anna,' the old woman said, 'bolt the gate,' adding, 'This time last year I was still able to do that.'

The younger one mumbled, 'But that's what I'm here for.' She braced herself.

She had just pushed the bolt through when, from amidst the noise coming from the village, there came another, separate noise: the rapid tapping of boots and then a drumming against the gate that had just been bolted. The younger woman pulled back the bolt. A couple of young Hitler Youths came running, yelling, 'Let us in, we're on the alert, we're searching. A man is hiding in the village. Come on! Let us in!'

'Stop, stop, stop,' the younger woman said. 'This isn't your home, and you, Fritz, go to the kitchen; the soup's ready.'

'Let them in, Mother. You have to. I'll show them around.'

'Where are you going to show them around? Whose place?' the woman called. The old woman grabbed her arm with surprising force. And then the Hitler Youths, Fritz in the lead, stepped over the laundry basket and already you could hear their little whistles from the kitchen, from the stable, and from the bedrooms. Bang! Now there was broken glass too.

'Anna,' the old woman said, 'don't take everything so much to heart. Learn from me. There are things in this world you can change. And there are things in this world you can't change. Those things you have to put up with. Anna, listen to me now! I know you're married to Albrecht, the worst of my sons. His first wife was just as bad. This place always used to be a pigsty. And you've made a real farmstead out of it. And Albrecht, who used to work as a day labourer in the vineyard only when he felt like it and just lazed away the time doing nothing the rest of the year – he's suddenly learned a lot. And the children from his first wife, that hussy, you really changed them; it's almost as if you'd reborn them. Your only problem is that you can't put up with things. But there are certain things you just have to put up with, to endure. Because eventually they'll pass.'

The younger woman answered her a little more calmly now, though her voice was still tinged with sadness about a life that in spite of all her truly tremendous efforts was denied all grace, to say nothing of respect. 'Yes, but then this happened.' She pointed at the house from which came the Hitler Youths' cheeky, shrill whistles, and towards the noise on the other side of the gate. 'This has got in the way, Mother. And the children I straightened out, sweating blood in the process, they're now the same impudent brats they were all along from the start, and Albrecht is again the same old beast of a man. Oh my!'

With her foot she pushed a piece of wood that was jutting out back into the woodpile. She listened. Then she put her hands over both her ears and wailed, 'Of all places, that fellow had to pick Buchenau to hide in. That's all I needed. That thug, coming into a decent village on a Monday morning like a rabid dog. If he's got to escape, why can't he go and hide in the marsh? Does he have to get all of us involved in this? Aren't there enough meadows by the water where he can take cover?'

'Grab the basket,' the old woman said. 'The clothes are still soaking wet. Couldn't it have waited till after the meal?'

'We all do what we learned from our mothers. I do the ironing wet.'

At that moment, from the street on the other side of their gate there came a howling that sounded like nothing an ordinary human voice could have produced. But it wasn't an animal's howl either. Some creatures previously unknown on earth must suddenly have dared to make an appearance – George's eyes began to glow at the sound; he bared his teeth. His throat tightened; it was as if he himself were sheltering something that he had to howl out now, along with this fellow creature. But at the same instant something soft and pure and clear came to the fore from inside him, an inviolable voice that couldn't be drowned out, and he knew that he was ready to die then and there, not as he had always lived but as he had always wanted to, bravely and calmly.

The two women had put the basket down. And black networks of wrinkles, coarse and wide in the younger one, fine and dense in the older one, showed on their pale faces. The boys raced out of the house across the yard and into the street. Then again there was pounding on the gate from outside. The old woman emerged from her paralysis; she took hold of the big bolt with what strength she had and pushed it back, perhaps for the last time in her life. A crowd of Hitler Youths, old women, farmers, and SA men stormed into the farmyard, shouting, 'Mother, Mother! Mrs Alwin! Mother, Anna, Mrs Alwin, we've got him. Look, look, there next door at the Wurms', in the kennel, that's where he was sitting. And Max was in the fields with Karl. The fellow was wearing glasses; those are smashed now! He won't need them any more. They'll take him away in Algeier's car. Right next door at the Wurms', he was; too bad. Look, Mother, look!'

The younger woman woke from her daze; she went towards the gate with the expression of a person drawn irresistibly to the one sight forbidden to her. She got up on tiptoe. She took one look at the people crowding around Algeier's car. Then she turned away, crossed herself, and ran into the house. The older woman followed her, head wobbling, as if she'd suddenly turned into a much, much older woman. The laundry basket was left where it was. The farmyard was now quiet and empty.

'He had glasses!' George thought. 'Then it was Pelzer. Why did he come here?'

An hour later Fritz discovered the machine part, still in its wrapping, by the outer farmyard wall. His mother and grandmother and a few neighbours came to look too. They were surprised to find it there. From the company tag they reckoned that the machine part came from Oppenheim and was intended for the Darré School. Now one of the Alwins had to start up the car again. It was just a few minutes to the school by car. They asked him what his brother, who'd returned to work in the fields, had told them about taking the escapee back to Westhofen.

'Did they give him a thrashing there?' Fritz asked with shining eyes, hopping from one foot to the other. 'Thrashing?' Alwin said. 'You're the one who ought to be thoroughly thrashed. I was actually surprised that they treated the man so decently.'

They'd even helped him, Pelzer, get out of Algeier's car. Pelzer, expecting blows and kicks, relaxed when they took him under the arms and carefully led him inside. Without his glasses he couldn't tell from their faces what kind of carefulness it was. It was as if everything was filled with smoke. Now that all was lost for him, Pelzer was overtaken by an infinite exhaustion. He wasn't taken to the commandant's barracks, but into the room Overkamp had furnished for himself.

'Sit down, Pelzer,' Commissar Fischer said quite gently. His eyes and voice were those typical of people in such a profession, who usually have to prise things out of others: sick organs, confessions, admissions.

Overkamp sat to one side curled up in a chair, smoking. Evidently he was leaving Pelzer to his colleague.

'A short excursion,' Fischer said. He looked at Pelzer, whose upper body began to sway quietly. Then he looked down at his files. 'Pelzer, Eugene, born 1898 in Hanau. Right?'

'Yes,' Pelzer said softly, his first spoken word since his escape.

'But that you should stoop to such pranks, Pelzer, you of all people, and to let a man like Heisler of all people talk you into it. Look here, Pelzer, it's been exactly six hours and fifty-five minutes since Fuellgrabe started hitting people with that spade. Good heavens, for how long have you been planning this?'

Pelzer said nothing.

'Didn't you realise from the start, Pelzer, that it was a harebrained, suicidal idea? Did you try to talk the others out of it?'

Pelzer replied softly, for each syllable felt like a knife stab. 'But I didn't know anything.'

'My, my,' Fischer said, still speaking moderately and softly, 'Fuellgrabe gives the signal, and you run. So, why did you start running?'

Pelzer said, 'They all did.'

'Right. And you say you weren't in on it? Now really, Pelzer!'

Pelzer said, 'No.'

'Pelzer, Pelzer,' Fischer said.

Pelzer felt like a man who's dead tired when the alarm clock shrills and doesn't want to hear it.

Fischer said, 'When Fuellgrabe struck the first guard, the second guard was standing near you; that same second, as arranged, you threw yourself at the second guard.'

'No,' cried Pelzer.

'What did you say?' Fischer said.

'I didn't throw myself.'

'Yes, excuse me, Pelzer. The second guard was standing near *you*, Pelzer, you underlined, then they, plural, that is, Heisler, and – and – and yes, Wallau, in the same second threw themselves at the second guard who was standing near you, as agreed on beforehand.'

Pelzer said, 'No.'

'No what?'

'That it was agreed upon beforehand.'

'That what was agreed on?'

'That he was standing next to me. He came because, because—' He tried to remember, but he might just as well have tried to lift a leaden weight.

'Go on, you can lean back,' Fischer said. 'So then: nothing agreed upon. You were not in on anything. You simply ran off. When Fuellgrabe started striking the guard, Wallau and Heisler attacked the second guard who just happened to be standing next to *you*. You underlined, Pelzer! Correct?'

'Yes,' Pelzer said slowly.

Now Fischer called out, 'Overkamp!'

Overkamp got to his feet, as if their service ranking were reversed. Pelzer, who hadn't even noticed that there was a third man in the room, was startled. He even sat up and paid attention.

'Let's get George Heisler in right now to confront him.'

Overkamp lifted the receiver. 'Aha,' he said into it. Then he said to Fischer, 'Not quite ready to be interrogated yet.'

Fischer said, 'Either completely or not at all. What's that supposed to mean, not quite ready?'

Now Overkamp went over next to Pelzer. He said in a tone firmer than Fischer's, but not hostile, 'Pelzer, you have to pull yourself together now. Heisler just described all this quite differently. Please pull yourself together, Pelzer, your memory and whatever common sense is left.'

VII

George was lying in a furrow out on a farm field under the grey-blue sky. About a hundred yards away was the highway to Oppenheim. Just don't get stuck now, he told himself. To be in the city by evening! The city that was like a cave with its winding alleyways. His original plan was to get to Frankfurt that night, and go at once out to see

Leni. Once at Leni's place everything else seemed easy to him. A one-and-a-half-hour train ride between dying and living ought to be doable. Hadn't everything up to now gone according to plan? Except that he was about three hours late. Sure, the sky was still blue, but the mists were already coming in across the fields from the river. Soon the cars on the highway would be turning on their headlights in spite of the afternoon sun.

An uncontrollable wish, stronger than any fear, or hunger and thirst, and stronger than the damned thumping in his hand, which had long ago bled through the rag: to just keep lying there – after all, night would come soon. And the fog was already providing him with cover; the sun was just a pale disc behind the haze covering his face. They wouldn't be searching for him here during the night. He'd have some peace.

He tried to imagine what Wallau's advice would be. You could trust Wallau's advice. He could almost hear him say: If you want to die, just lie down and stay there. No, tear a piece of fabric off the jacket. Make a new bandage. Go to the city. Everything else is nonsense.

He turned over on to his stomach. Tears ran down his face as he pulled the crusted rag off his hand. Then he felt ill again, seeing his thumb: a stiff little black-and-blue lump. He turned on to his back as he tied a fresh knot with his teeth. Tomorrow he'd have to find someone who could take care of his hand. He suddenly expected all sorts of things from the coming day, as if time as it flowed were drawing him along.

The denser the mist over the fields, the more intense the blue of the meadow saffron. George noticed the flowers only now. Maybe he'd be able to get a message to Leni if he didn't get to Frankfurt before nightfall. Should he spend the mark he'd found in the jacket for that? He hadn't thought of Leni since his escape, or if he had thought of her it was at most the way he thought of a road sign, or the first grey stone. How much strength he'd wasted, so much valuable sleep for dreaming! Dreaming about the girl that luck had put in his path, exactly twenty-one days before his arrest. But I can't visualise her any more, he thought. Wallau and all the others, I can see. He saw Wallau quite clearly, but the others he saw only vaguely because they were now dim in the fog. Another day is done, one of the guards passes close by him, speaks to him: 'Well, Heisler, how long are we going to keep this up?' And he gives him a strange, sly look. George says nothing in reply. The realisation that everything is lost is mixed with these first vague thoughts of escape.

The first lights were passing on the highway. George climbed over the ditch. A sudden thought flashed through his head: You'll never catch me. With that same flash he was up in a brewery truck. He was dizzy with the pain from having grabbed on with his left hand in jumping aboard. Almost immediately, or so it seemed to him, they drove into a courtyard on a street in Oppenheim; actually, though, it was fifteen minutes later. The driver noticed only now that he had a passenger. He mumbled, 'Get going!' But something about the way George had jumped off, and his first wavering steps, caught his attention, and he turned round again and asked, 'Do you want a lift to Mainz maybe?'

'Yes,' George said.

'Wait here a moment,' the driver said.

George had put his wounded hand inside the jacket. He'd seen only the driver's back so far. And now he didn't see his face either, for the driver was holding his delivery book up against the wall and writing something in it. Then he drove his truck through the gate and across the courtyard.

George waited. The street outside the gate went slightly uphill. The fog had not reached here yet; the summer day seemed to be coming to a close, the light on the pavement was soft. Across the way was a spice dealer's shop, next to it a laundry, after that a butcher's shop. The bells on the shop doors tinkled. Two women with packages, a boy biting into a sausage. The power and splendour of everyday life, how he had despised it in the past. If only instead of having to wait out here, he could go inside to be the butcher's helper, a delivery boy for the spice dealer, a guest in one of these homes. In Westhofen he'd pictured a street here differently. He thought he would see a feeling of shame in every face, on every cobblestone, and that sorrow would mute the steps and voices and even the children's games. The street here was calm; the people looked happy.

'Hannes! Friedrich!' an old woman called from her window above the laundry to two young fellows in SA uniforms strolling with their girlfriends. 'Would you like to come upstairs? I'll make you some coffee.' Did Meissner and Dieterling also walk around like this with their fiancées when they were on leave? After a short whispered conversation, the four yelled up, 'Yes,' and burst into the house. The woman closed the window with a smile because it made her happy to have some good-looking young people, maybe they were her relatives, come to visit. George, witnessing this scene, was engulfed by a sadness such as he had never known before in his entire life. He might have wept if he hadn't been reassured by the voice that tells you even in your saddest dream that soon nothing will matter any more. But it *does* still matter, George thought. The driver returned, a robust man with small, black bird's eyes peering out from his fat face.

'Come on up,' he said brusquely.

It was already evening outside the city. The driver cursed at the fog. 'What are you going to do in Mainz?' he suddenly asked.

'Going to the hospital,' George said.

'Which one?'

'To my old one.'

'Seems you like sniffing chloroform,' the driver said. 'You couldn't drag me into a hospital with twenty horses. Last February on the ice...' They almost ran into two cars that had been stopped, one behind the other, by an SS patrol. The truck driver braked and cursed. Then the two cars in front of him were waved on. The patrolmen came up to the brewery truck. The driver handed them his papers, one of the men said, 'And you over there?'

The whole thing wasn't all that bad, George thought. I made two mistakes so far. Unfortunately you can't rehearse it all beforehand. He was having exactly the same feeling as he'd had back when he was first arrested; when the house was suddenly surrounded – a rapid adjustment of all feelings and thoughts, a lightning-fast jettisoning of all deadwood, a clean good-bye, and finally...

He was wearing a brown corduroy jacket; there was no doubt about that. The SS patrolman compared the jacket with his description. It was amazing how many corduroy jackets had turned up in the last three hours between Worms and Mainz, Captain Fischer had said when Berger had brought in a man in a corduroy jacket a while back. This item of clothing seemed to enjoy a certain popularity here among the locals. The Wanted poster had been based on the Westhofen intake records of December '34, with the exception of the description of the clothing. But except for the jacket, the guard thought, nothing about this man coincided with the specifications he'd been given. This fellow could have been the fugitive's father; the wanted man in the picture was his own age, a young fellow with a smooth, bold face, while this man here had a flat face with a thick nose and puffy lips. He waved them on. 'Heil Hitler!'

They drove on in silence for a few minutes at fifty miles per hour. Suddenly the brewery driver braked for the second time on the empty, open road. 'Get down,' he ordered. George wanted to say something. 'Get down!' the driver repeated threateningly when George hesitated. He made as if he were going to throw George off forcefully. George jumped down. Again he banged his bad hand and moaned softly. He floundered briefly as the lights of the beer truck receded, almost immediately swallowed up by the fog that had descended in the last few minutes. At short intervals cars whizzed by him; he didn't dare stop any of them. He didn't know whether he still had hours of walking ahead of him, or how many hours he already had behind him. He tried to work out just where he was between Oppenheim and Mainz – the road went through a little village with brightly lit windows. He didn't dare ask anyone to tell him the name of the village.

Occasionally someone passing him or leaning out of a window looked so directly at his face that he would wipe it with his hand. What kind of shoes had he stolen that they could carry him on and on, while he himself had lost the desire and the will to walk any farther? Then he heard bells ringing ahead of him, quite close by. A stretch of tram tracks came to an end before a small square that looked like a village green. He was now standing in a group waiting at the terminus of the electric tram. He paid thirty pfennig out of his mark. The tram, at first only moderately full, stopped after the third station at a factory. George sat with his eyes lowered. He looked at no one, just resigned himself to the warmth, the closeness, the crush of all these people; gradually he began to feel calm and almost secure. Still, whenever someone pushed into him or just looked at him even casually, he instantly felt a chill run down his spine.

He had to get off at the stop called Augustiner Strasse; he walked along the tracks towards the centre of the city. Suddenly he was wide awake. If it hadn't been for the pain in his hand, he would have felt lighthearted. It was the street that did this to him, the crowds, the city as a whole had that effect on him. The city that lets you be, or seems to let you be, to leave you alone. One of these thousands of doors would open for you, he thought, if only you could find it.

He bought two rolls in a bakery. The old and young women all around him were talking about the price and the quality of the bread, their children and husbands who'd be the ones eating it – had all that really never stopped in all the time he'd been gone? The things you imagine, George, he said to himself. All this never stopped; it would never, ever stop. He ate his rolls as he walked along. He brushed some flour off Helwig's jacket. Through a gate he could look into a courtyard where there was a well, and when he saw boys drinking from it using a cup hanging on a chain, he went inside and drank too. Then he continued on his way until he reached a very large open square that looked misty and empty in spite of the streetlamps and people. He would have liked to sit down. But he didn't dare to. Just then a bell began to toll, so close by and so loud, that the wall against which he'd been wearily leaning vibrated. As the square emptied, it seemed to him that the Rhine couldn't be far away. He asked a child, who at once answered, 'Do you want to drown yourself today?' At which point he noticed that this girl was no longer a child; it was just that she was slender, but otherwise she was quite forward and eager. She hesitated a moment, then asked if he would like her to accompany him down to the Rhine. But he had no intention of doing that. All this time his thoughts had been churning within him, but now he came to a decision. He was definitely not going to cross a major bridge to get to the other shore, but rather he would spend the night here in the city. The bridgeheads, especially, were bound to have twice as many guards as usual. The more difficult thing would be the more sensible; he would stay on the left bank of the river. Then he would look for another way to get to the other side farther down. Not going to his city directly but taking a detour. Preoccupied, he watched the girl walk off. Did something about her quick, irregular walk remind him of his own girl? Would any girl have reminded him of her? For a fraction of a second he could picture her. Of course only as she was leaving, but back then she had shrugged once more exactly like this girl. Meanwhile, the bells had stopped. And the sudden stillness in the square, as well as the fact that the trembling of the wall on which he was leaning stopped and that it seemed to be turning back into stone again, made him aware once more how strong and powerful the ringing had been. He even stepped back a few paces and looked up at the towers. He got dizzy even before he found the topmost of the spires, for above the two nearer towers there was another single spire rising up into the autumnal evening sky with such effortless boldness and ease that it hurt him.

Then it suddenly occurred to him that there must be many places to sit down in such a large building. He searched for an entrance, for a door, not the main gate. It surprised him when he actually got in. He dropped down into the nearer end of the closest pew. Here I can rest awhile, he thought. Only then did he look around him. He had never before felt so small, not even under the wide, open sky. When he saw the three or four women scattered here and there, as tiny as himself, and took in the distance between himself and the nearest column and the distance between the many individual columns and seeing no end to them from where he was sitting, neither above him or in front of him, but only space and more space, he was somewhat astonished. And perhaps what was the most astonishing thing about it all, was that for a moment he forgot himself.

However, the sacristan coming along with a firm step, since he was of course familiar with the place and was doing his professional duty, put an immediate end to his astonishment. He trotted along between the columns and announced in a loud and almost angry voice, 'The cathedral is closing,' and to the women who couldn't stop their prayers, he said more in the way of instructing than consoling them, 'The Good Lord will still be here tomorrow.'

George had jumped up with a start. The women walked slowly past the sacristan and out through another door closer to them. George went back to the door by which he had entered the church. But that door was already locked, and he had to hurry diagonally across the nave to catch up with the women. Then he had an idea. Instead of continuing towards that exit, he ducked behind a large baptismal font and waited until the sacristan had finished locking up.

Ernst the shepherd had driven his sheep inside their pen. He whistled for his little dog. Up here it wasn't yet night. The sky was still a pale yellow above the hills and trees, like linens that women have kept too long in their cupboards. The fog over the valley was so dense and so flat that one might have thought the plain had risen with its large and small clusters of light, and that the village of Schmiedtheim was at the edge of the plain rather than on the side of the hill. The clamour of the Hoechst sirens and the trains rose up out of the fog. Shift change at the plant. In the villages and towns the women were preparing the evening meal. Already he could hear the first bicycle bells on the road down below. Ernst climbed up as far as the ditch.

He put one leg forward, crossed his arms on his chest. He looked down to where the road began to climb upward by the Traube Inn, a superior mocking smile playing on his lips, meant no doubt for God and the world. He liked seeing all the workers down there having to get off their bikes and push them the rest of the way up the hill.

Ten minutes later the first men passed him, sweaty, grey, tired.

'Hi, Hannes!'

'Hi, Ernst! Heil Hitler!'

'You heil him! Hi, Paul!'

'Hey, Franz, wait up!'

'No time, Ernst,' Franz said. He pushed his bicycle up over the bumpy earth, down which he'd bounced so joyfully that morning.

Ernst turned round and watched him go. What's the matter with that guy, Ernst thought. Probably a girl. Suddenly he realised he didn't particularly like Franz. What does he need a girl for? he thought. If anyone needs a girl, it's me. He knocked on the Mangolds' kitchen window.

As soon as he got home, Franz went into the Marnets' kitchen. 'Hello!'

'Hello, Franz,' mumbled his aunt. The soup was already dished out, potato soup with sausages. Two little sausages for each of the men, one sausage for each of the women, and half a sausage for each of the children. The men were old Marnet, his oldest son, his son-in-law, and Franz; the women were Mrs Marnet and Augusta. The children, little Hans and little Gustav. There was milk for the children and beer for the grownups. And bread and salami because there wasn't all that much soup. During the war, in spite of all the regulations and prohibitions, Mrs Marnet had learned to milk the cows and to butcher pretty much everything the family needed.

The plates and glasses, the clothing and the faces, the little pictures on the walls, and the words spoken – they all revealed that the Marnets were neither poor nor rich, neither citified nor peasants, neither pious nor irreligious.

'And it's really a good thing that the young fellow didn't get his leave right away; he'll learn that he can't always get everything he wants with his pigheadedness,' Mrs Marnet said, referring to her youngest son, who was down in Mainz with the 144th, 'and on the whole it's good for the boy.'

Whereupon all those at the table, except for Franz, agreed that the young fellow deserved to be pushed really hard, and that, on the whole, it was a blessing that all those rascals were learning to follow orders.

'This is Monday,' Mrs Marnet said to Franz as he was getting up, having barely finished his soup. They were hoping Franz would help them take in the last of the apples.

But he left, leaving them still muttering. On the whole, though, they didn't really have any reason to complain about him. He'd always been helpful and decent except for that eternal chess game he had going with Hermann in Breilsheim. 'If only he had a decent girl,' Augusta said, 'then he wouldn't get involved in stuff like that.'

Franz got on his bike. This time he went in the opposite direction, taking the path through the fields down to Breilsheim. Breilsheim used to be an independent village, but because of the new development it had now grown together and been combined with Griesheim. Hermann had moved to the development when he got married for the second time not long ago because, as a railway worker, he was given preferential treatment there. In fact, he was surprised to learn that with this marriage he was entitled to a whole lot of things, all sorts of perks and credit possibilities. His new wife was Elsa Marnet, a very young cousin of the Marnets. She was one of the Schlossborn Marnets, and that also influenced the couple's standing in the Taunus and in the entire scattered family of Marnets dispersed over several villages. Hermann also said, when he was talking with his friends about the new amenities that came with his marriage, 'Yes, our Aunt Marnet, from the other Marnets, plans to give us a silver cake set. She's Elsa's godmother. For every name day she gave her a little silver spoon.'

'Every feast day she gets presents,' Hermann said. 'Of course, it's understood that Elsa has to go up and help during the harvest and with the laundry and the butchering because she's a member of the family.' Elsa, though, was happy with her cake set, with the entire arrangement. She was eighteen, had a round face and little round black eyes. Sometimes Hermann wondered if he'd done the right thing marrying the child. He'd been feeling unbearably lonely for the last three years, and she was so sweet and so young.

Now Elsa was singing in the kitchen. Her voice was neither especially strong nor especially pure, but it flowed along like a little brook, sometimes sad, sometimes joyful, depending on your own mood at the time.

Hermann frowned; he felt a little guilty. The two men set the chessboard up between them. Automatically, they made the same first three moves with which they usually started a game. Franz began to talk. He'd been waiting all day for just this moment. At last he could pour out his crazy tale. Now and then Hermann interrupted with a brief question. Yes, he also had heard some rumours. Nothing definite. In any case, they had to be ready. It was possible the rumour was true, and someone might turn up who needed help. Hermann didn't tell Franz that he had heard that the former district leader Wallau, a very good man whom he had known personally, had escaped from the Westhofen camp. He'd also heard that Mrs Wallau had played a role in the escape, a circumstance that deeply disturbed him. For, if that were really the case, then no one should have known about it. But this George, about whom Franz had asked, no, he, Hermann, hadn't heard anything about him. 'We have to give it some careful thought,' he said. 'A successful escape is a really big deal.'

VIII

Franz was certainly not the only one lying awake that autumn night thinking, what if my friend is one of them? He was surely not the only one worrying that one of the escapees from the camp might be someone he was concerned about. Franz twisted and turned in his bed in the little attic room he had asked them to give him now that he was paying for his keep there. Last evening they had hurriedly nailed a few boards on the wall for shelving because the apple harvest had been so abundant.

Franz got up again and stuck his head out of the window because the smell of the apples was overwhelming. Even though he really didn't feel like it and his belly was already full of them, he nevertheless took another apple and ate it quickly, throwing the core out into the garden. The glass garden globe on the pole, which glowed a beautiful blue above the pansies and wallflowers in the daytime, now had a silvery shimmer as if the moon had rolled down from the sky into the garden. Since the land sloped upward, the sky sparkling with stars in peaceful neighbourliness began right behind the tall fence of the Marnets' property.

Franz sighed and went back to bed. Why should George, of all people, be among them, he wondered for the hundredth time. This George was his friend from earlier years – Hmmm, he thought, but was he actually his friend? Of course he is. In fact he's my best friend, my only friend. The realisation disturbed him.

When did he first get to know George? In 1927 at the Fichte holiday camp. Oh, no, much earlier. He'd met him on the Eschenheim football pitch, shortly after they left school. He, Franz, was such a bad footballer that no team ever wanted him. And so he made fun of guys like George who thought of nothing but football. 'Hey you, George, you've got a football on your shoulders instead of a head.' George's eyes had narrowed. And Franz was sure it was no accident that a ball George had thrown struck his stomach the following afternoon. After that, Franz stayed away from the football pitch, though he was sorely tempted to go back. In fact, months and years later he still dreamed that he'd become the goalkeeper for the Eschenheim team.

Four years later he'd met George again in a course he, Franz, was teaching at the Fichte holiday camp. George had, so he said, come to Fichte because of the cheap jujitsu lessons and claimed that he'd signed up for Franz's course out of sheer boredom. He'd never thought that the Franz teaching the course was his old friend, the grungy Franz from the football pitch, and that here he was, teaching. Back then, George's eyes had narrowed again into slits and there were those tiny dots of hate as if he had something to revenge himself for, a curse or a humiliation. It seemed he had decided to spoil Franz's course. But then, when his troublemaking didn't seem to meet with approval from the class, but only resistance on the part of the others, he chose to stay away from the course after the second session. Franz never stopped watching him. There was often an expression of contempt on the handsome tanned face; his walk was almost too erect, as if he felt sorry for all those who were less handsome and less strong than he was. He forgot himself only when he was rowing or wrestling, and then his expression turned pleasant and happy, as if he'd escaped from himself. Franz, driven by some indefinable curiosity, decided to look up George's application form: George had trained as a car mechanic, but had been unemployed since he finished his apprenticeship.

The following winter he met George at the January demonstration. Again he had that rigid, almost contemptuous smile. His face didn't soften until they started the singing. Then later he met him at police headquarters after the demonstration had disbanded. George had a problem with one of his sneakers. The sole had separated in the slippery city snow. Franz had the impression that George was one of those who would have kept on going, even barefoot, from start to finish. He asked him his shoe size. But George's answer was, 'My mother's son fixes that himself.' Franz asked him if he'd like to see a couple of photographs from the holiday camp that had George in them too. Of course George wanted to see them if he was in them. Photos of the swimming contest and jujitsu. 'Yes, I guess I can find the time to come and look at them,' he said.

'Do you have something planned this evening?' Franz asked.

'What should I have planned?' George said. Both of them felt embarrassed for no apparent reason. They didn't say anything to each other during the walk back to the old town. Franz would have liked to find a pretence to ditch George. Why had he let himself in for a visit from this fellow? He'd wanted to spend the evening reading. He stopped at a shop and bought sausage, cheese, and oranges. George waited outside, standing in front of the shop window. His face didn't have its usual smile, but a rather dark expression that Franz didn't understand at all, though he kept watching him even from inside the store.

At that time Franz lived on Hirschgasse under one of those beautiful humpbacked slate roofs. His room was small with a slanting ceiling. The door led into the stairwell.

'You live here all by yourself?' George asked.

Franz laughed. 'I don't have a family yet.'

'So you live here all on your own,' George said again. 'Oh well.'

His face was now totally dark. Franz guessed that George lived crowded together with a large family. 'Oh well' meant, Oh well, if that's how you live, no wonder you're getting on in the world.

Franz asked, 'Would you like to move in here?'

George stared at him. There wasn't a trace of a smile on his face, no arrogance, as if he'd been taken by surprise before he could arm himself with his usual expression. 'Me? Move in here?'

'Well, yes.'

'Do you seriously mean it?' George asked softly.

Franz said, 'I always mean everything I say seriously.' But he really hadn't asked in total seriousness, it had just burst out of him spontaneously. But then it *had* become serious, bitterly serious.

George had turned pale. Franz realised only now that his accidental offer had taken on immeasurable importance for George, had become a turning point in his life. Franz grabbed his arm. 'So it's a deal.' George pulled away.

He instantly turned away from me, Franz thought up in his apple room. Then he went over to the window; he filled up my little window completely. It was evening, winter. I turned on the light. George sat down astride my chair. His beautiful brown hair fell down thickly; he peeled two oranges, one for himself and one for me.

I took the jug, Franz remembered, to get water from the tap in the stairwell. I stood in the doorway, and he watched me from where he was sitting on the chair. He had calm grey eyes, and those funny little dots of which I was always afraid as a boy were gone from his eyes. He said, 'I'll paint the whole place for us. And I'll make a shelf out of that box for your books and out of that good box over there, the one with the lock, I'll build a small wardrobe as good as new. Wait and see.'

Shortly after that Franz lost his job. They pooled their unemployment benefits and the money they earned from doing odd jobs. It was a unique winter that couldn't be compared to anything he'd experienced before or since. The small room with the slanting ceiling, now painted yellow. Patches of snow on the roofs. Back then they were probably hungry a lot of the time.

Like all those who really have thought about hunger, have actually struggled with it, they were less impressed by their own hunger than the hunger of the rest of the world. They worked, studied, and went together to demonstrations and meetings; both were called whenever two fellows like them were needed in the district. When they were by themselves, George would ask questions and Franz would answer them. And thus they created for themselves 'a common shared world', which grew the longer one lived in it and which expanded and increased the more one took from it.

That's how it seemed to Franz, at least. With time, George grew more silent and asked fewer questions. I must have hurt his feelings back then in some way, Franz thought. Why did I force him to read? I must have tormented him with it. George had admitted quite frankly that he couldn't remember everything he read, and that some of it just wasn't for him. And then he started staying overnight with his old football friend Paul occasionally. And he didn't mind Paul's laughing at him because he was acting stuck-up and constantly making speeches. George seemed to get bored when Franz went away. Sometimes George would spend the night with his relatives and often he would bring back his youngest brother, a tiny, skinny little devil with merry eyes. Franz thought: It all began back then already. He must have felt disappointed without knowing it. He probably thought that if he shared my room with me and if he had me ... But he got bored with the room pretty quickly; I was different from him. I probably made him feel there was a distance between us when in reality there wasn't any, for I had misjudged things.

Towards the end of the winter George got restless. He started going away a lot. He changed girlfriends frequently and for the strangest reasons. He suddenly ditched the most beautiful girl in his Fichte group and took up with a zany, somewhat deformed thing, a milliner from Tietz. At one point he took up with the baker's young wife until it came to a dustup with the baker. Then unexpectedly he went off for a weekend with a thin little comrade who wore glasses. 'She knows even more than you do, Franz,' he said later. Once he said, 'You're no friend, Franz. You never tell me anything about yourself. I introduce you to all my girls, one after the other and tell you everything. I'm sure there's something you're hiding from me, someone very lovely, someone steady.'

Franz said, 'That's because you just can't believe that a person can actually live alone for a while.'

I met Elli Mettenheimer, Franz thought, on the twentieth of March, 1928, at seven o'clock in the evening shortly before the post office closed. We were standing at the same window. She was wearing coral earrings. The second time I met her in the garden, and when I asked her to take off the earrings, she took them off and put them into her little purse. I told her only black women wore such things in their ears and through their noses. She laughed. Actually it was too bad because the coral looked nice with her brown hair.

He'd kept his friendship with Elli a secret from George. Then one evening he and Elli ran into him on the street by accident. Later George said, 'Oh well.' Whenever Franz came home on Sunday evenings, George would ask him with an oblique smile, 'How was it?' And the little dots in his eyes multiplied enormously.

Franz frowned. 'She's not like that,' he'd said.

Once Elli said she couldn't go out with him. He'd blamed it on her strict father, Mettenheimer the paperhanger. So he waited for Elli on Monday at her office. But she avoided him, calling out that she was in a hurry and jumping on to the next tram. The entire week he noticed that George kept watching him. He felt like throwing him out. When the weekend came, George cleaned himself up particularly well. As he left, he said to Franz, who was setting out his books on the windowsill to prepare for his course on Sunday, 'Have a good time, Franz.'

George came back on Sunday evening, tanned and happy. He said to Franz, who was sitting by the windowsill as if he'd never got up from there, 'That has to be learned too.'

A couple of days later, quite unexpectedly, Franz ran into Elli on the street. His heart leaped. Her face was red and hot. She said, 'Dear Franz, I'd better tell you myself. George and I – don't be angry with me. There's nothing anyone can do about it, you know; there's no cure for it.'

He'd said, 'That's all right,' and walked away. For hours he walked around in a profound darkness in which only two little red dots glowed, the coral earrings.

George was sitting on the bed when Franz came upstairs. Franz at once began to pack up his things. George watched him intently. His gaze was so intense that it forced Franz to turn towards him even though all he wanted was never to see George's face again for the rest of his life. George had the trace of a smile on his lips. Now Franz felt a burning desire to smack him right in the middle of his face, if possible in the eyes. The moment that followed was probably the first time in both their lives that they understood each other completely. Franz felt that all the desires that had governed his actions up to then had been obliterated, except for one.

Perhaps for the first time, George honestly wished to be relieved of all the chaos, to focus on one single goal outside his mixed-up, turbulent life. He said quietly, 'You don't have to move out on my account, Franz. If you don't like being with me any more – of course, I can understand that it was always difficult for you – I won't be living here any more anyway. Elli and I, we're going to get married right away.'

Franz hadn't wanted to say anything; but now it came out anyway, 'You? Elli?'

'Yes, why not?' George said. 'She's different from all the others. This time it's for always. And her father is going to find me a job.'

Since they were getting married no matter what, Elli's father, the paperhanger, who hadn't liked this son-in-law from the outset, insisted on a speedy wedding. He paid for a room for them because, as he said, he didn't want to see his favourite daughter being ruined.

Franz, lying on his narrow cot in his apple room, his arms crossed under his head, recalled every word that had been said back then, every change in George's expression. For many years he hadn't wanted to remember that time. If it did suddenly pop into his mind, he winced. Now he let everything pass slowly before his mind's eye. He felt nothing but surprise, astonishment. He thought: It doesn't hurt any more. It doesn't matter any more. Terrible things must have happened in the meantime for it not to hurt any more.

Three weeks later, Franz saw George from a distance in Bockenheim Park. He was with an incredibly fat woman and had put his arm around her waist, but couldn't reach all the way round. By that time, Elli had already moved back in with her parents to await the birth of the child. But Elli's father, Franz had found out from the neighbours, was forcing his daughter to return to her husband. The way he saw it: You married him, you're having a child with him, and now you have to make do with him. In the meantime George had lost his job again because he'd been running around, as his father-in-law put it. Elli went back to work at the office. Shortly before Franz left, he found out that, in the end, Elli had gone back to live with her parents.

There's a children's game that consists of putting different coloured panes of glass over a multicoloured drawing. You see a different picture with each colour of glass. Back then, Franz was looking through just one glass pane that his friend showed him and only during particular events. He never looked through any of the other glass panes. And soon he lost sight of George too. The city was now spoiled for Franz; he tried to find another place to move to. That's how far-ranging the consequences of this affair had been for Franz. For another man it might simply have ended in a fistfight. But for people like Franz, everything has consequences. So he looked up his mother, whom he hadn't seen for years. She had moved in with a married daughter who lived in northern Germany. Franz went there. This move led to a happy broadening of his life in all its aspects. Sometimes he even forgot the reason that had brought him there. He opened up in this new place among new companions. On the surface he was just one of the many unemployed who transferred from one city to another. But it was really more comparable to a student changing colleges. He might even have been happy had he been able to persuade himself that he really loved the quiet, decent girl with whom he was living for a while.

In '33, after his mother died, he came back to a place near the city where he used to live. There were three reasons for his return: he was too well known up north and things had got too hot for him there.

In the south the party needed someone like him who knew the people and conditions but had already been forgotten by the locals. He had room and board with his uncle Marnet. All the old acquaintances he accidentally encountered thought: He used to talk differently in the old days. Or: There's another one who's changed his spots.

One day Franz went to see Hermann, the one man in his immediate neighbourhood who knew him from before. Hermann worked for the railway. He told Franz calmly, even more calmly than usual, that the previous night there'd been a very nasty arrest. It was bad because, first of all, the person who'd been arrested had a list of all the contacts, and second, because he'd been appointed to that position only a short while before and only because the man who'd had the position previously had also been arrested. Hermann told it all calmly and reasonably, but clearly there was a possibility that this man who'd been arrested might reveal sensitive information, either because of weakness or inexperience. So even if this distrust was undeserved, it was still his duty to act as his doubts prescribed: to shuffle all the connections and contacts, to warn all the people whose names the arrested man knew. He suddenly broke off and asked Franz gruffly whether he knew the man from his earlier time when he had lived here. The man's name was George Heisler.

Franz barely managed to control himself, but not well enough, for Hermann saw the dismay in his face on hearing that name again after so many years. Franz tried, in a few sentences, to give Hermann a fair picture of George, something he probably wouldn't have been able to do any better even had he been calmer. Hermann interpreted his confusion in his own way. They made all the necessary provisions over the chessboard.

Franz thought: All our precautionary measures were superfluous. There was no need to change any connections, no need to warn any comrades. I didn't have to leave there with my heart pounding.

A few weeks later, Hermann arranged for Franz to meet a man who had been in protective custody in Westhofen and had been released. He told Franz about George: 'They wanted to use him as an example to show us all how they could knock down a man who was strong as a horse, one, two, three. But the opposite happened. They only managed to show us that there was no way they could break a man like him. And they kept on tormenting him. But now they wanted him dead. That face of his, the way it had been before, with a kind of smile that drove them mad, and he had such odd eyes with so many funny little spots in them. They beat his beautiful face to a pulp, and he's shrunk physically.'

Franz got up. He stuck his head as far as he could out of the little window. It was totally still outside. For the first time Franz felt no peace in this stillness – the world wasn't still – it was silenced. Involuntarily he pulled his hands back out of the moonlight, which could cling to surfaces and penetrate into the cracks like no other light. How could I have known, he thought, that he was the man he was? How could anyone have known that beforehand? Our honour, our good name and our safety were suddenly in his hands. All that stuff before, all his nonsense, all his escapades – that was all only nonsense, irrelevant stuff. But you couldn't have known this before- hand. Maybe if I'd been in his place I wouldn't have held out even though I was the one who . . .

Franz suddenly felt very tired. He went back to bed. He thought: Maybe he isn't one of the escapees. He must have been too weak for such an attempt. Still, whoever has escaped – Hermann was quite right: an escapee who's got away, that's really quite a big deal, that always churns things up. That always puts their omnipotence in doubt. It's a breach.

2

I

ONCE THE sacristan had left after locking the main door, and the last echoes of footsteps and voices had dissipated among the arches, George realised that he had been granted a grace period – such a grand respite that he almost mistook it for deliverance. For the first time since his escape – indeed, since his arrest – a warm feeling of security suffused his whole being. But the feeling, powerful though it was, lasted only briefly. 'It's damned cold in this hole,' he thought.

The dusk inside the cathedral was so profound that the colours in the windows became obscured, the walls receded, the ceiling vaults rose, and the columns aligned themselves into endless rows rising into an uncertainty that might have been nothing or perhaps infinity. George suddenly sensed he was being watched. He fought the sensation that was paralysing him, body and soul. Sticking his head out from beneath the baptismal font, his eyes met those of a man with a staff and mitre leaning against his memorial slab five yards away from him and from the nearest column. The twilight diminished the splendour of his flowing vestments, but not his facial features, which were clear, plain, and angry. The eyes followed George as he crept past him.

The twilight wasn't seeping in from the outside as it did on ordinary evenings. The cathedral itself seemed to be dissolving and losing its contours. The vines climbing the columns, the grimacing faces, and over there a pierced naked foot were all chimera and smoke; everything made of stone was evaporating, and it was George who was petrified with fear. He closed his eyes, took a couple of deep breaths; then it was over. For the twilight had deepened, become darker, and thus more calming. He darted from one column to another, looking for a place to hide, ducking as if he were still being watched. Not far from the column in front of which he was now crouching, a portly, healthy-looking man was leaning out of his grave slab imperturbably gazing past him. There was a bold smile of power on his full face. In each hand he held a crown with which, unnoticed by George, he was eternally crowning two dwarfs, the anti-kings of the interregnum. George sprang to the next column with one giant leap as if the spaces between them were being watched. He looked up at the man, whose opulent robes were so ample that he could have wrapped himself up in them. He gave a start when he saw a human face full of sadness and concern leaning over him. What more do you want, my son? Give up; even at the beginning you're already at the end. Your heart is pounding, your injured hand is throbbing.

George finally found a niche in the wall where he could conceal himself. Under the watchful eyes of six archchancellors of the Holy Roman Empire, he slipped across the side aisle with his hand held before him, like a dog who'd got his paw caught in a trap. He sat down and tried to get comfortable. He massaged the wrist of the bad hand; it had become stiff. He rubbed his knees, his ankles, and his toes.

He was feverish by now. But he hoped his injured hand wouldn't play any tricks on him before he got to Leni's. At Leni's he'd get it bandaged. And he'd have a chance to wash, to eat, drink, and sleep, to heal. Then he realised with a shock that he had to get this night, which he had so very much longed for, behind him as quickly as possible.

Again, he tried to picture Leni. A trick that sometimes worked and sometimes didn't, depending on the place and the time. This time it worked. He saw a slim nineteen-year-old girl with long, slender legs and blue eyes that were almost black under thick lashes in a lightly tanned face. This was the stuff of his dreams. In the course of their separation his memory of this girl – who in reality had at first seemed almost ugly to him and a bit ridiculous because her long arms and legs gave her walk a feeling of awkward flight – had become a kind of rare fairy-tale being. With each additional day of separation the image of her had become softer and more that of a flying creature. Now too, leaning against the ice-cold wall so that he wouldn't fall asleep, he lavished her with words of love. She *had* to wake up, he thought, and listen to him in the dark.

Countless such reaffirmations, unreal, far-ranging adventures, had followed the one time they had actually been together. Back then he had to leave the city the very next day. He could still hear her assurances, uniformly desperate: 'I'll wait here till you come back. If you have to flee, I'll go with you.'

From where he was, he could still see the man by the corner column. In spite of the darkness, the face was even more distinct from far away. On its curved lips the supreme offer: Peace in place of fear of death, mercy instead of justice.

Leni shared a small flat in Niederrad with an older sister who was usually away for work. The location of the flat made it convenient as a hiding place or a sanctuary for an escapee. Such considerations had followed him back then when he first crossed the threshold of the small room, even though he had forgotten everything else, his former love affairs, whole stretches of his past life. And even as the walls of the room closed in towards each other like impenetrable hedges, the idea that in an emergency this would prove a convenient hiding place never left him. When they had told him a while back in Westhofen that he had a visitor, he had been afraid for a moment that they meant Leni. He hadn't recognised the woman they brought in at all. They might just as well have put before him the first best farm girl from the nearest village, that's how strange this Elli was that they'd brought to see him.

He must have dozed off. He awoke with a start. The cathedral was full of noise. A bright light shone diagonally through the nave and fell on his foot. Should he try to get away? Was there still time? Where to? The gates and doors were all locked except for one, and that one was bathed in light. Perhaps he could make his way into one of the side chapels without being noticed. He supported himself on his injured hand, stifled a cry of pain, and collapsed. He didn't dare crawl across the strip of light now. Then he heard the voice of the sacristan: 'You slovenly women, every day it's something else!' The words resounded like a proclamations of the Last Judgement.

An old woman, the sacristan's mother, called out, 'Here it is. Here's your bag.'

And the voice of the sacristan's wife echoed from the walls and columns like a veritable cry of triumph, 'I knew I'd put it down between the pews while I was cleaning!'

The two women left. It sounded as if giantesses were shuffling across the floor. The gate was locked again. Only an echo remained, shattering against the walls, becoming loud once more, as if it didn't want to fade away, reverberating in the most distant corner, trembling still even as George had already stopped trembling.

He leaned back against his wall again. His eyelids were heavy. It was totally dark now. The shimmer of the various lamps floating somewhere in the darkness was so weak that it no longer lit up any of the arches, but proved instead that the darkness was impenetrable. Yet George, who just moments before had wished for nothing more, breathed heavily and uneasily. He resigned himself the way Wallau always had and was surprised to find that his exhaustion lessened even as he relaxed.

Wallau had been brought into the camp two months after him. 'So you are George.' Hearing the older man greet him with these four words, George had, for the first time, fully felt his own worth. A prisoner who'd been released had talked about him, George, on the outside. While he was being tortured nearly to death in Westhofen, people in the villages and towns where he had once lived had formed an impression of George, his indestructible monument. Even now, even here next to this ice-cold wall, George thought: If Westhofen were the only place I could see Wallau, I'd take it all on again ... For the first time and maybe for the last in his young life there had been a friendship that wasn't all about swagger and showing off or humbling yourself in order to cling to someone and giving yourself up completely, but rather just being the person you were and being loved for that.

By now his eyes no longer found the dark so impenetrable. The plaster on the wall gleamed dimly like freshly fallen snow. He felt that his body stood out in dark contrast. Should he change location once again? When would they open the place for mass? There were still countless minutes of safety before morning dawned. He had as many minutes ahead of him as, for example, the sacristan had weeks. For, after all, the sacristan wasn't eternally secure either.

Far off, towards the main altar, one single column was visible because the light ran along its grooves. This single bright column now seemed to be holding up the entire arched vault. But how cold it was! A world so icy cold it seemed no human hand, no human thought had ever touched it. It was as if he had landed on a glacier. He rubbed his feet and his joints with his healthy hand. This was a sanctuary in which you could freeze to death.

'A triple somersault. That's the most the human body can manage,' Belloni, his fellow prisoner, had explained to him. Belloni, whose everyday name was Anton Meier, had been arrested right as he came off the trapeze. They had found a couple of letters in his baggage sent him by his artists' lodge from France. He'd often been dragged out of bed to perform stunts. A dark, taciturn man, a good comrade, but very strange. 'Oh no, there are perhaps only three living performers who can do that. Sure, sometimes one or other will be lucky and pull it off, but never as a regular thing.' Belloni had approached Wallau of his own accord to tell him that he was going to attempt to escape no matter what. They were never going to get out of there any other way. He was depending on his physical skill and help from friends on the outside for this escape. He had given George an address where he was going to leave money and clothes for him in any case. He was probably a decent young fellow, but too strange to fathom. George didn't intend or want to use the address. He planned to send Leni to look up some old friends of his in Frankfurt on Thursday morning.

Then there was Pelzer. If, in addition to brains, Pelzer had had Belloni's tendons and muscles, he would probably have made it.

They must have caught Aldinger in the meantime. He was old

enough to be the father of all the boors who were no doubt tearing his hair out by now, spitting in the old peasant face that hadn't lost its dignity even after the man seemed no longer to be in his right mind. He'd been denounced by the mayor of the neighbouring village, who was motivated by an old family dispute.

Fuellgrabe was the only one of the seven whom he'd known from before. He'd often taken a mark out of the cash register in his shop for George's collection list. Even during his deepest despair he'd never quite got rid of the grudge he bore them. He felt he'd stumbled into it, that they had talked him into it and he just couldn't say no.

Beutler might already be dead. For weeks he'd put up with everything, always protesting that it had been only a minor violation, just some currency business: until he started raving and Zillich took him into the punishment squad. What dreadful beatings Beutler must have had to endure before the last spark was finally beaten out of his dulled heart.

I'm going to freeze to death here, George thought. They'll find me. And one day they'll point to this piece of wall and tell the children: 'This is where they found one of the escapees frozen to death one autumn night during those wild times.' What time was it now? Midnight soon. In the new, total darkness he wondered whether anyone from his earlier life would remember him. His mother? She used to complain unceasingly, waddling around on her bad feet on Schimmelgasse, a short, fat woman with very large, gently swaying breasts. I'll never see her again, George thought, even if I don't die. Of all her physical characteristics, it was always her eyes he was most aware of, young brown eyes, dark with reproach and bewilderment. Now he felt ashamed because he had been ashamed of his mother back then in front of Elli, who'd been his wife for three months – ashamed because of his mother's bosom and because she wore such a funny Sunday dress. He thought of his little friend and classmate, Paul Roeder. For ten years they'd played marbles on the same street and then, for another ten years, football. Then he'd lost track of him because he himself had changed, but little Roeder had stayed the same. He remembered Roeder's round, freckled face like a landscape forever closed off to him ... He also thought of Franz. Franz was good to me, George thought. He really tried hard. Thanks, Franz. We broke off with each other back then. I wonder why? I wonder what happened to him? Such a calm man, decent and loyal.

George held his breath. The reflection of one of the stained glass windows fell diagonally across the side aisle, probably from the light of a lamp in one of the houses on the other side of the cathedral square, or the headlights of a car. A tremendous carpet glowing in all colours was suddenly unrolled in the darkness. Night after night this rainbow-coloured carpet was cast over the tiles of the empty cathedral for no one to see; after all, even here night-time visitors such as George occurred only every thousand years.

This light from outside, by which someone was perhaps trying to calm a sick child or say good-bye to a man, also threw all the pictures of biblical life into relief as long as it was lit. Yes, over there, he thought, must be the two who were banned from paradise. And there, those must be the heads of the cows looking down into the crib of the child for whom there was no room anywhere else. And yes, that must be the Last Supper at which He already knew that He would be betrayed, and that must be the soldier who pierced Him with his spear when He was on the cross ... He, George, had forgotten many of those pictures. Many of them he'd never known, for back home they didn't heed all that any more. Anything that keeps one from feeling alone can be a consolation. Not only can what others are suffering be a consolation while we are suffering, but even knowing what others suffered long ago can be consoling.

Then the light coming from outside went out. It seemed even darker than before. George thought of his brothers, especially the youngest, whom he himself had raised with a tenderness that was more appropriate for a little kitten than a child. He thought of his own child, whom he had seen only once for a brief moment. Then he no longer thought of anything in particular. Faces came and went, sometimes blurry, sometimes clear. Some came with sections of streets, some with schoolyards and athletic fields, some with the river, and some with clouds and forests. They came to him of their own accord, and he wanted to hold on to all that had been dear to him. Then everything became more formless; he could no longer visualise his mother's face or any other. His eyes felt sore, as if he had really seen and gazed at all this. Far away – he didn't think the church even extended that far – something colourful gleamed. Outside a car drove past. When its light struck one of the windows its colours were reflected on the church floor. But there was only darkness when the beam of light hit a section of the wall.

George listened. The car engine kept running. He heard the squeals and laughter of men and women apparently squeezing into a much-too-small car. Then they drove off. The window colours were rapidly projected between the columns then drawn back, ever farther from George. His head dropped to his chest. He fell asleep. When he tipped over and on to his injured hand, the pain woke him up. The darkest time of night was already past. The plaster on the section of wall before him began to gleam. In reverse order from the previous evening the darkness began to fade. Then the columns and walls were seized by a constant trickling as if the cathedral had been built of sand. As the faintest, farthest early morning light hit the windows, the pictures in them began to take shape, not in glowing but rather in dull, dim colours. At the same time the trickling stopped, and everything began to solidify. The tremendous vaults of the main aisle solidified in accordance with the law that had guided its construction under the Hohenstaufen emperors, with the acumen of individual builders and the inexhaustible strength of the people. The vault into which George had crept solidified, a vault that had already been venerable in the time of the Hohenstaufen dynasty. The columns became solid and all the grimacing faces and animal heads in the capitals of the columns, and the bishops on the memorial slabs in front of the columns, became solid once more, proudly alert in death, along with the kings of whose coronations they had been excessively proud.

It's high time to get going, George thought. He crept out of his recess. He tied the little bundle together using his teeth and his good hand. Then he jammed it between a memorial plaque and a column.

With glowing eyes and all keyed up, he waited for the moment when the sacristan would unlock the doors.

II

Meanwhile, Ernst the shepherd greeted his Nelly in the deep chesty voice so familiar to the dog that she trembled with joy. 'Ah, Nelly,' Ernst said, 'Sophie didn't come after all, the stupid little thing. Oh, well, she doesn't know what's good for her. But then, Nelly, we slept anyway. So it did us no harm.'

Everything was still quiet at the Mangolds', but at the Marnets' someone was already clattering around in the barn. Ernst took his towel and the oilcloth bag in which he kept his toilet and shaving things and went over to Marnet's pump. Shivering with cold and pleasure he soaped himself, scrubbed his neck and chest, and brushed his teeth. Then he hung his pocket mirror on the garden fence and began to shave. 'Do you have a little hot water for me?' he asked Augusta when he saw her reflection with her milk pails in his mirror.

'Oh yes, come inside,' Augusta said.

'Marriage has really softened you, Augusta,' Ernst said. 'Before, you used to be rather brusque with me.'

'You must have drunk some sweet-talk water early this morning,' Augusta said.

'Haven't even had a drop of coffee,' Ernst said. 'My thermos is broken.'

In the distance, in the dense fog down by the Main River, the lights were going on amidst a lot of grumbling and yawning. A fifteen- or sixteen-year-old girl came out of the farmyard gate of the outermost house in Liebach. She had a handkerchief tied around her head. The handkerchief was so white that it contrasted with her fine eyebrows. She looked straight ahead out of the gate with an expression of calm expectation that brooked no doubt that the person she expected would turn up at any second, as on every other morning on the path behind the farm wall. She wasn't even looking in the direction from which she expected him to come. And now indeed young Helwig, Fritz Helwig from the Darré school, stepped out from behind the wall and came through the gate. Without a word, with barely a smile, the girl raised her arms. They embraced and kissed while the girl's grandmother and an elderly cousin watched from a kitchen window, showing neither displeasure nor approval, just the way you watch things that happen every day. For in spite of their youth, the two children were considered engaged. Today, after the kiss was over, Helwig took the girl's face in both his hands. They played 'who'll be the first to laugh', but neither felt much like laughing; they just gazed into each other's eyes. Since, like almost everyone in the village, they were distantly related, they both had eyes of the same transparent brown, lighter than was usual in the region. Both their eyes were deep and clear and, as they say, innocent. And it's probably true, for how better to express what was unique about these eyes. As yet no guilt had clouded their light, no inkling that under life's pressure the heart has to accept all sorts of things that later on you'll pretend you never understood – but why then beat so rapidly and fearfully? – No suffering yet, except for the fact that it was still such a long time before there'd be a wedding. So each looked into the other's clear eyes until they lost each other in them. Finally the girl blinked. 'Oh, Fritz,' she said, 'you'll be getting your jacket back now.'

'I certainly hope so,' the boy said.

'I hope it hasn't been ruined,' the girl said.

'You know, it was Alwin who nabbed him. That Alwin, he's a really tough guy.'

In the villages the night before they had talked about nothing except the fugitive who'd been caught in the Wurms' yard. When the Westhofen concentration camp was first set up, more than three years earlier, when the barracks and walls were erected, the barbed wire fences drawn, and the guards posted, the villagers had watched as the first column of prisoners was marched past, accompanied by laughter and kicks in which, already back then, Alwin and others like him had participated. And then at night they heard the screams and the jeering. And on three or four occasions when shots were fired, everyone felt uneasy and apprehensive. People in the villages crossed themselves at the thought of having such neighbours. Some, who had to take long detours on their way to work, had seen prisoners working outside the camp with guards standing over them. Many of them had thought, 'Poor devils.' And others wondered what it was they were digging there.

Once, back then, a young riverman had even publicly cursed the camp. He was immediately arrested and locked up in the camp for several weeks so that he saw firsthand what was going on inside there. When he got out, he looked strange and didn't answer a single question people asked him. He eventually found work on a barge, and later, his relatives said, he moved to Holland for good – a story that astounded the entire village back then.

Another time, two dozen prisoners had been marched through Liebach on the way to Westhofen; they looked in such bad shape even before being locked up that the onlookers were horrified and one woman in the village burst into tears. That evening the young mayor of the village had summoned that woman – she was his aunt – and explained to her that her blubbering might not only hurt herself, but it could also have long-term adverse effects on the lives of her sons, his cousins, one of whom was also his brother-in-law. In fact, now it was the young people in the village, the boys and girls, who were able to explain to their parents exactly why the camp was there and for whom it was intended. These young people always thought they knew everything better, but now they knew the worst. And there was nothing that could be done about the camp anyway. On the other hand, there had been quite a few new orders for vegetables and pickles and the sort of useful trade that results when you have a large number of people requiring food and shelter.

But when the sirens had howled early yesterday and guards suddenly appeared from nowhere on all the streets, when the rumours started to spread about the escape and then, when a fugitive was actually caught at midday in the neighbouring village, then suddenly it was as if the camp, which they'd all grown accustomed to long ago, had been built all over again, and they wondered why of all places it had been built here, where they lived. It was as if new walls had been constructed, new barbed wire fences erected all over again. Then there was the gang of prisoners that had recently been driven through the village street from the nearest train station – why, why, why? And then the woman who had been warned by her nephew, the mayor, almost three years ago, cried openly for the second time yesterday. Had it really been necessary to crush under one's heel a fugitive's fingers as he was trying to hold on to the edge of the car? After all, they'd already recaptured him. The Alwins, all of them, had always been very coarse, rough fellows. And now they were the ones who set the mood. How pale that poor devil looked, surrounded by all those robust, healthy farm boys...

Young Helwig had heard and seen all that. As long as he could remember, the camp had always been there and along with it all the reasons for its being there. He didn't know it any other way. The camp, after all, had been erected when he was still a boy. Now that he was almost a young man, it was as if it were being rebuilt for the second time.

The people said it wasn't possible that only scoundrels and fools were imprisoned there. That riverman who'd been inside once, he was no scoundrel. When Helwig's taciturn mother said no, young Helwig looked at her. He felt a little anxious. Why was everything cancelled tonight? He missed his usual companions, the noise, the war games and marches. He had grown up surrounded by the wild noise of trumpets, fanfares, shouts of 'Heil', and marching steps. Then suddenly this evening everything had stopped for two minutes, the music, the drums, and you could hear thin, faint sounds that would otherwise have been inaudible. Why had the old gardener looked at him so oddly today at midday? There were some, too, who praised him. They said it was because of the good, detailed description he'd given of his jacket that the fugitive had been found.

Young Helwig walked up the path through the fields and over a small hill. He saw the older Alwin in the beet field and called to him.

Alwin, already red in the face and sweaty from work, came over to the path. What a lot of things the man had already done today, Helwig thought, as if he had to stand up for Alwin. Alwin described it all to him, the way you describe a hunt. A moment ago he was just a farmer who went into his fields earlier than the others. Now, as he described the chase, he became Sturmführer Alwin, a man who could turn into a Zillich, if given the opportunity. After all, Zillich had been just another Alwin once, a farmer up near Wertheim by the Main. He, too, used to get up early; he, too, had sweated blood, even though it was all for nothing, because his tiny farm had been auctioned off back then. Helwig had got to know Zillich because he sometimes came over from Westhofen when he was off duty, sat down in the inn, and talked about village stuff. Helwig listened to Alwin describing the hunt for the escapee with downcast eyes. 'As to your jacket,' Alwin said at the end, 'I don't know about that. He wasn't wearing it. No, it must have been one of the other fugitives; you'll have to catch him yourself, Fritz. This guy, in any case, wasn't wearing a jacket.'

Helwig shrugged and, more relieved than disappointed, trudged off to his school, whose ochre-painted façade glowed across the fields.

III

Alfons Mettenheimer, a sixty-two-year-old master paperhanger, a longtime employee of the interior-decorating firm Heilbach in Frankfurt, had received a summons to appear before the Gestapo this Tuesday morning.

A person who suddenly finds himself involved in something totally unaccustomed, and incomprehensible, will usually try to find the one point where this incomprehensible thing comes close to touching his everyday life. And so Mettenheimer's first thought was to phone his firm to ask for the day off. He asked for the business manager, Siemsen, and told him that he had to have the day off. This request by their chief paperhanger did not suit Siemsen at all, because the Gerhardt house on Miquelstrasse was supposed to be ready for its occupants by the weekend. The new tenant, Mr Brandt, had asked them to get rid of everything that might be a reminder of the Jews who'd lived there before – a wish the Heilbach firm was happy to accommodate. Siemsen asked, 'What's happened?'

'I can't explain now,' Mettenheimer said.

'Will you at least come in after lunch?'

'I don't know.' After hanging up, he went out on to the streets crowded with people going to work. He felt apart from all these people although he was one of the most ordinary among them. Indeed, he could have stood in for any of them as a man who had grown old in an ordinary life, a man who had lived through the most ordinary joys and sorrows.

Any human being faced with the possibility of a calamity instantly thinks of his emergency reserves, the bedrock of his life. For one person this can be an idea, for another his faith; a third may think solely of his family. Some don't have anything. They have no fundamental principles to hold on to in emergencies; they have nothing to hold on to, just emptiness. Life outside with all its horrors can flow into them and fill them to bursting.

After he had hurriedly reassured himself that 'God' – of whom he seldom thought, having always left church attendance to his wife – was still there, Mettenheimer sat down on the bench at the tram stop where he'd been getting on recently to go to the western part of town for work.

His left hand began to tremble. But it was only an aftereffect. The initial dismay was already over. He was no longer thinking of his wife and his children; he was thinking only of himself now. And he felt locked into a fragile body that anyone for whatever reason could torment and torture.

He waited until his hand stopped shaking. Then he got up, intending to walk the rest of the way. After all, he had lots of time. The summons was for nine thirty. Still, he'd rather get there a bit early and wait. That showed he was brave in his own way.

So he walked along the street to Gestapo headquarters. It gave him a chance to think things over more calmly. The reason for the summons, after all, could only be in some way connected with George, the former husband of his middle daughter, Elli. But the man was in prison, had been for years already. Nothing new could have happened in that matter since late in 1933, when he himself, the former father-in-law, had been interrogated in that affair. And back then it had been clearly established that he had been stubbornly against the marriage, that he was in complete agreement with those who were questioning him about George Heisler. At the time they had advised him to persuade Elli to get a divorce. Of course, he hadn't done that. But that had nothing to do with this summons, Mettenheimer thought; this was something completely different.

He sat down on the first bench he came to. I once papered this house, number 8, he mused. How they had argued, the husband and wife: flowers or stripes. Blue or green for the front. I advised they do it in yellow. 'I hung your wallpaper, and I'll go on doing it for you. I'm a paperhanger,' he had told them.

It must have something to do with George; that's what they wanted to see him about. He'd never been one of those fathers who'd got involved in arguments with priests about religion. His youngest child was still in school, but only till Easter. And he didn't see young snub-nosed Liesel as a defender of the creed. He'd explained as much to the priest, who had discreetly raised the subject with him. The girl should go ahead and do everything the school asked her to do; she should go where all the other girls went. She shouldn't get involved in half-forbidden things, but simply do what all the others did. With the exception, of course, of the important holidays. He was confident that he and his wife – despite all the nonsense girls were now being taught – could raise their daughter Liesel to become a decent human being. He even believed that he could raise his daughter Elli's child, that fatherless child, to become a decent human being.

'You have been taking care of Alfons, the son of your second daughter, Elisabeth, called Elli by your family, in your flat full time from December

'33 until March '34, and from March '34 until today, during the day only. Is that right?'

'Yes, Herr Kommissar,' Mettenheimer said. He thought: What does he want with the child? He can't have summoned me here because of that. How does he even know all this?

The young man sitting in the armchair under the Hitler portrait must have been less than thirty years old. It was as if the room were divided into two climate zones, with the latitudinal line running across the desk – Mettenheimer was bathed in sweat, his breath came in short gasps; whereas the young man across from him looked fresh and cool; the air he was breathing certainly was cool.

'You have five grandchildren. Why are you taking care of this child in particular?'

'During the day my daughter works in an office.' What does he want from me, Mettenheimer thought. I'm not going to let a young fellow like him intimidate me. Here, in a room just like any other. A young man like any other... He wiped his face. The young police commissar watched him attentively with his grey eyes. The paperhanger kept his handkerchief crumpled in his hand.

'But there are children's homes for that purpose. Your daughter earns money. She has been earning one hundred and twenty-five marks since April the first this year. With that she can pay for the child's care.'

Mettenheimer switched the handkerchief to his other hand.

'Why are you supporting this daughter, when she can pay for herself?'

'She is alone,' Mettenheimer said. 'Her husband...'

The young person looked at him briefly. Then he said, 'Sit down, Mr Mettenheimer.'

Mettenheimer sat down. He suddenly had the feeling he would have fallen had he not sat down just then. He put his handkerchief in his jacket pocket.

'The husband of your daughter Elli was taken to Westhofen in January 1934.'

'Sir,' Mettenheimer cried, jumping halfway up from his chair.

Then he dropped back down. Calmly he explained, 'I never wanted to have anything to do with that man. I barred him from my house permanently. Towards the end, my daughter was no longer living with him.'

'In the spring of '32 your daughter was living with you. In June and July your daughter was living with her husband again. Then she moved back in with you. Your daughter is not divorced.'

'No. She isn't.'

'Why not?'

'Herr Kommissar,' Mettenheimer said, searching for his handkerchief in his trouser pockets, 'she married this man against our wishes, but...'

'Despite that, as her father, you didn't advise her to get a divorce?'

But the room was not an ordinary room. The thing that was really so frightening about this room was that it was quiet and bright and dappled with the soft shadows of the leaves of a tree, seemingly a completely ordinary room facing a garden. And the frightening thing was that this young person was a most ordinary person with grey eyes and blond hair and yet he was all-knowing and all-powerful.

'Are you Catholic?'

'Yes.'

'And were you against a divorce because of that?'

'No, but marriage is...'

'You think it is sacred? Yes? For you a marriage with a scoundrel is something sacred?'

'You can't tell beforehand whether a man will turn out to be a scoundrel,' Mettenheimer said softly.

The young man looked at him for a while, then he said, 'You put your handkerchief into your left jacket pocket.' Suddenly he slammed his hand down on the table. In a loud voice he said, 'What kind of upbringing did your daughter have that she would get involved with such a rogue?'

'Herr Kommissar, I raised five children. They all brought me honour. The husband of my oldest daughter is a Sturmbannführer. My oldest son—'

'I didn't ask you about your other children. I asked you about your daughter Elisabeth. You allowed your daughter to marry this Heisler. Towards the end of last year you yourself accompanied your daughter to Westhofen.'

At that instant Mettenheimer knew that he did have something in reserve, one last thing for an emergency. He answered quite calmly, 'That is a difficult path for a young woman to take.' He thought: This young man here is the same age as my youngest son. How dare he speak to me like that! How can you be so presumptuous? He must have had a hard time with his parents, and with his teachers too... The hand on his left knee began to tremble again. Despite that, he added equally calmly, 'It was my duty as her father.'

For a moment the room was quiet. Mettenheimer looked at his hand and frowned; it was still trembling.

'You won't have the opportunity to perform this duty any more, Mr Mettenheimer.'

At that Metttenheimer started. He cried out, 'Is he dead?'

If the interrogation had been leading up to this point, then this police commissar must have been disappointed. For the note of genuine relief in the voice of the master paperhanger was unmistakable. Indeed, the death of this fellow seemed suddenly to have settled everything: those strange duties the paperhanger had obligated himself to perform in a few but decisive moments of his life and his sometimes clever, sometimes tortuous attempts to escape those duties.

'Why do you think he is dead, Mr Mettenheimer?' The commissar jumped up. He leaned far across the tabletop. Now his voice was very gentle, 'Why, Mr Mettenheimer, are you assuming that your son-in-law is dead?'

The paperhanger grabbed his twitching left hand with his right. He answered, 'I'm not assuming anything.' His calm was gone. Thoughts of a different nature destroyed any hopes he might have had of being finally freed of that fellow George. It now occurred to him that, if the stories they told were true, such stubborn young fellows were tortured beyond all measure, and that his death must have been unimaginably hard. Compared with those stories, the compressed, clipped voice of this police commissar was the very ordinary voice of an unimportant man in a position of some power.

'You must have had some reason for assuming that this George Heisler was dead?' He suddenly shouted, 'Don't lie to me, Mr Mettenheimer!'

The paperhanger flinched. He clenched his teeth and looked at the commissar in silence.

'Your son-in-law was after all a strong young man without any illness. So you must have some reason for your allegation?'

'I didn't make any allegation.' The paperhanger had regained his composure. He had even let go of his left hand. And what if he hit this young man in the face with his right hand, what then? The man would shoot him down on the spot even as his face would redden and a white spot appear where the paperhanger's hand had struck him. For the first time since his youth, Mettenheimer's old worried head had thought up a daredevil act – one that could never be carried out. He thought: Ah, if I didn't have a family! He concealed a smile by fishing around in his moustache with his tongue.

The commissar stared at him. 'Now, you listen to me very carefully, Mr Mettenheimer. On the basis of your own statements in which you confirm our own observations, and on a few important points even complement them, we want to warn you. We want to warn you in your own interest, Mr Mettenheimer, in the interests of your entire family whose head you are. Do not take any steps or make any statements that are in any way connected with the former husband of your daughter Elisabeth Heisler. And should you have any doubts or require any advice, do not turn to your wife or any other member of your family, or ask for any help from a spiritual source, but rather come to our headquarters and ask to be directed to room 18. Do you understand what I am saying, Mr Mettenheimer?'

'Yes, Herr Kommissar,' Mettenheimer said. He hadn't understood a single word. What was he warned against doing? What was confirmed? What doubts might he have? The young face he had wanted to slap a moment ago had suddenly turned to granite, had become the impregnable image of power.

'You may leave now, Mr Mettenheimer. You reside at number 11 Hansagasse, and you work for the firm Heilbach, correct? Heil Hitler!'

A moment later he was outside on the street. Warm, soft autumn light bathed the city and lent the crowd a festive cheerfulness that it usually had only in the spring. The mass of people just pulled him along. What did they want from me? he wondered. Why did they summon me there? Maybe it was because of Elli's child? They can take away your right to – what do they call it – child custody. Suddenly he cheered up. He concluded that some authority or other had interrogated him because of some official matter. How could he have been so upset about that? He didn't feel like worrying about it any more. He longed for the smell of wallpaper paste, to get into his work clothes, to go back to his everyday life, to immerse himself so deeply in it that no one would find him. Just at that instant the number 29 tram came rolling up. He pushed people aside and jumped up into it. Now he was pushed in turn by a man jumping up behind him, a somewhat rotund fellow wearing a new felt hat that seemed to be resting on top of his head rather than pressed down on it. A man not much younger than he was. They were both breathing hard. 'At our age,' Mettenheimer said, 'this is pretty reckless.' The other replied angrily, 'Yes, exactly.'

When Mettenheimer arrived at the construction site, Siemsen greeted him. 'I wish I'd known that you'd be coming, Mettenheimer. I thought there was some emergency or that your wife had fallen into the Main.'

'Just an official thing. What time is it?'

'Ten thirty.'

Mettenheimer slipped into his overalls. He immediately started scolding his helpers, 'You've pasted the border first again. That doesn't look good at all! It doesn't stand out that way. You're afraid that the wallpaper will smear? You just have to be careful. Take it down, nothing can be done about it.' He mumbled, 'A lucky thing I came back in time.' He was hopping around on the ladder like a squirrel.

IV

George had succeeded. He'd transformed himself into an early morning churchgoer by the time the cathedral was opened to the public. Now he was just one of a few men among a large number of women. Dornberger, the sacristan, saw him and recognised him from the night before. Well, he thought with satisfaction, there's another one who was converted three minutes before closing time ... It took George a few moments to get up. Laboriously, he dragged himself outside. That man won't last another two days, the sacristan thought. He'll collapse outside on the street. George's face looked grey as if from some fatal illness.

If only he hadn't had the bad luck with his hand! It's always the small stupid things that ruin everything. Where and when was it that I hurt my hand? It was that wall set with glass fragments about twenty-four hours ago ... People were pushing him through the door out of the cathedral into a short, narrow alley. Walking between some low houses in which the shops already had their lights on, he came to a large square that seemed to stretch out endlessly because of the fog. Yet in spite of the fog, the square and all the little side streets were teeming with people. Market stalls were opening. From the cathedral doorway he had smelled the strong aroma of coffee and fresh-baked cake, for right next door was the Cathedral Pastry Shop Café. The apple and streusel cakes in the shop window were attracting the gaze of all those now coming from mass.

The cool, damp air that hit his face was no longer of any help. His legs slid out from under him, and he found himself sitting on the cobblestones. Just then two old women came out of the cathedral, unmarried sisters. One forced five pfennig into his hand while the other scolded her, 'You know that it's forbidden.' The younger one bit her lip. For fifty long years she'd had to put up with being scolded.

George couldn't help but smile. How much he had loved life. He liked everything about it, the sweet clumps of sugar on the streusel cake and even the chaff they baked into the bread during the war. The cities and the rivers, the entire country and all its people, Elli, his wife, and Lotte and Leni and little Katherine and his mother and his little brother. The slogans with which they roused the people; the battle songs; the sentences Franz had read to him that expressed great thoughts and ideas and that had turned his life upside down, and even old wives' gossip. How good all of it had been; it was only isolated parts that had been bad. Even now he held it all dear. He managed to get up and, leaning against a wall, he pulled himself together. Hungry and miserable, he looked towards the market, where the stalls were just then being set up in the fog under the streetlamps, and a sudden warm feeling shot through his heart. It was as if, in spite of everything, he were loved in return by everyone and everything with a painful, helpless love, although perhaps for the last time. He walked the few steps to the bakery café. He had to keep fifty pfennig as his emergency capital. He put the rest of the pfennigs on the counter. The woman poured a plateful of crumbs and pieces of zwieback and burned cake rims on to a piece of paper for him. She glanced briefly at his jacket; it seemed too good for such a meal.

Her glance brought George to his senses. Once outside the shop, he stuffed the crumbs into his mouth. Chewing slowly, he dragged himself towards the edge of the square. The streetlamps were still on, although they had become superfluous. You could already see the row of houses on the far side through the autumn morning mist. George walked on and on through a maze of streets that wound like a skein of yarn around the market square to which he eventually returned. Then he saw a sign: Dr Herbert Loewenstein. There might be the man who'd help him, he thought. He went up the stairs.

The first ordinary stairwell in how many months? He cringed at the creaking of the floorboards as if he were intending to commit a burglary. Here too, it smelled of coffee. Behind the flat doors a normal day was beginning with yawning, waking the children, and the grinding of coffee mills.

For a moment there was silence as he stepped into the doctor's surgery. Two groups of patients. They all looked at him. On a sofa near the window a woman with a child and a young man in a raincoat – at the table an old farmer and an elderly city man with a boy, and now George. The farmer went on with what he had been saying: 'I'm here for the fifth time. He hasn't helped me, but there's been a degree of relief, some relief. If only it keeps up till our Martin comes home from the army and gets married.' You could hear in his monotonous voice how painful it was for him to talk. But he accepted the pain in exchange for the pleasure he got from talking about it. He added, 'And what about you?'

'I'm not here on my own account,' the other man said, 'but because of the boy there. He's my only sister's only child. The child's father forbade her to go to Loewenstein. So *I* brought the boy here.'

The old farmer said (he had both hands on his stomach, probably where the pain was), 'It's not as if he were the only doctor in town.'

The other man said unperturbed, 'You're here too, aren't you?'

'Me? But I've already been to see all the others: Doctor Schmidt, Doctor Wagenseil, Doctor Reisinger, Doctor Hartlaub.' He suddenly turned to George, 'Why are you here?'

'Because of my hand.'

'He's not a doctor for hands; he's for the insides.'

'I have an internal problem too.'

'A car accident?'

The office door opened. The old farmer, blinded by his pain, got up, supporting himself with one hand on the table and the other on George's shoulder. George experienced not just fear, but the same uncontrollable childish anxiety he used to experience in doctors' surgeries when he was the same age as the jaundiced boy sitting at the table. As he had back then, he now kept tugging at the fringes of the armchair upholstery.

The hall doorbell rang. George started. But it was just the next patient arriving. She stepped into the room and walked past the table, a half-grown, dark-haired girl.

Finally it was George's turn. He was asked for his name, address, profession. He made up something. The walls were already swaying; he was sliding down into an abyss of whiteness, glass, chrome – a totally clean abyss. As he was slipping down, he was informed that the doctor was Jewish. The smell in the place reminded him of the aftermath of all his interrogations, when they would douse you with iodine and bandage you.

'Please sit down,' the doctor said to George. Already, walking through the door, he could tell this patient was in bad shape. He was familiar with the symptoms: no open wounds, no swellings, the slightest dark tinge under and above the eyes; but with this man it had already turned to a dense blackish shadow. What could be wrong with him? He was used to patients coming to see him very early in the morning so that the neighbours wouldn't see, or very late at night, like people in the old days when they used to go to consult a witch.

He began to unwrap the tattered bandage. An accident? Yes. In spite of the powerful spell that every injury and every sickness cast over him because he was a physician through and through, he again felt that same trepidation at the mere sight of the man, and it was even more powerful now than before. What kind of bandage was this? Made from the lining of a jacket. He unrolled it very slowly. What sort of man was this? Old? Young? His trepidation increased, constricting his throat, as if he'd never been this close to death before in all the nineteen years he'd been healing the sick.

He looked down at the hand now lying exposed before him. It was certainly in bad shape, but not so bad that it would justify the symptoms in the man's face and eyes. What had caused the man's exhaustion? He had come because of the hand, but he probably had some other illness that he perhaps didn't even know about. First, he had to take out the glass splinters. The man had to be given an injection; otherwise he'd slip away. He had said he was a car mechanic. 'You'll be able to go back to work again in fourteen days,' he told him. The man made no reply.

The doctor wondered if the patient would be able to tolerate the injection. But the heart of this strange man wasn't in such bad shape, although it wasn't in top-notch condition either. So what was the matter with him? Why, as a doctor, not give in to the urge to find out what illness the man was suffering from?

Why hadn't he gone immediately to the nearest hospital after his accident? The dirt had been in the wound at least overnight. He wanted to ask, also to distract the man while he got to work on the hand with the tweezers. But the look the man gave him kept him from asking. He stopped. Looked at the hand again very carefully, and then briefly at the man's face, at his jacket, at the man as a whole. The man moved his lips and looked at him sideways but intently.

Slowly the doctor turned away, feeling himself turn pale. He went over to the sink, and when he looked at himself in the mirror, there was already a blackish shadow on his own face. He closed his eyes. He soaped his hands and washed them with infinite slowness, letting the water run. I have a wife and children. Why did this person come to me? I tremble every time the bell rings. All the things I have to put up with . . .

George stared at the doctor's white back. He thought: You're not the only one.

The doctor held his hands under the water, making it splash. Unbearable, all the things I have to bear. And now this on top of everything else. It's impossible that one should have to suffer like this.

But you're not the only one, George thought again, frowning, while the water flowed like a fountain.

Then the doctor turned off the tap. He dried his hands on a fresh towel. For the first time he smelled the chloroform the way his patients usually smelled it. Why did this man come to me of all people? To me in particular? Why?

He turned the tap back on and washed his hands for the second time. It's none of your business, he thought. In your consulting room it's his hand, an injured hand, that should be your concern. It shouldn't matter to you at all whether the hand dangles from the arm of a rogue or from beneath the wing of an archangel. Once more he turned the tap off and dried his hands. Then he prepared the injection. When he pushed up the patient's sleeve, he saw that the man wasn't wearing a shirt under the jacket. That's none of my business either, he told himself. My concern is his hand.

When it was done, George slipped his freshly bandaged hand into his jacket and said, 'Thank you very much.'

The doctor had wanted to ask him for money, but the man thanked him in a way that sounded as if he assumed he had been treated for nothing. Even though he was weaving a little as he went out, it now seemed to the doctor that his illness had been entirely due to the hand.

As George was coming down the stairs, a short man in shirtsleeves planted himself on the bottommost landing and asked, 'Are you coming from the third floor?'

George lied, because he had no time to think whether it was better to tell the truth or to tell a lie. 'From the fourth.'

'Oh,' the short man who was the caretaker said, 'I thought you were coming from Loewenstein.'

Once George was on the street outside, he saw the old farmer from the doctor's surgery standing on the doorstep of a house farther on. He was staring towards the market. The fog had lifted. The autumn sunlight fell on the market umbrellas set up like mushrooms over the stalls. The fruits and vegetables lay there, luscious and artless as though arrayed in simple, fairly neat garden beds. It looked as if the farm women had brought entire sections of their own fields and gardens to the markct. He didn't see the cathedral. It was as if it had vanished behind the four- and five-storey houses, market umbrellas, horses, trucks, and womenfolk.

Not until George lifted his head and looked up did he see the topmost spire, a golden pinnacle by which the city could be lifted up. Once he had walked a few steps farther on, past the farmer who was now staring after him, he saw, high above the roofs, Saint Martin on his horse, cutting up his cloak. George pushed his way in among the market crowd. Apples, grapes, and heads of cauliflower danced before his eyes. At first he felt so ravenous that he would have liked nothing better than to dunk his face into the displays and bite into the produce. But then all he felt was disgust and revulsion. He was now in such bad shape that it had become dangerous. Dizzy from exhaustion and too weak to think clearly, he staggered around among the market stalls. Finally he arrived at the fishmongers' stands. Leaning against an advertising column, he watched one of the vendors scaling and eviscerating a huge carp. Once done, the man wrapped it in a piece of newspaper and handed it to a young woman. Then with a ladle he searched in the tub for some small fish and, making a tiny cut on each, threw a handful of them on the scale. Although it revolted him, George felt compelled to watch it all carefully.

The old farmer from the doctor's surgery watched George walking off until he was out of sight. He stayed there a while longer, watching the people milling about in the autumn sun. The whole market was darkened for him by the pain he felt. His upper body swayed. And for this the louse had demanded ten marks, he thought, not a pfennig less than Reisinger! You couldn't bargain with Reisinger. He was going to send his son to take care of the Jew. He dragged himself across to the other corner of the market square and went into an automat. When he looked out of the window, he saw George again with his newly bandaged hand, leaning against an advertising column. He kept staring at him until George, feeling uneasy, turned his head towards the window. From where he stood he couldn't really see much behind the window; nevertheless, he tore himself away and walked past the fish stalls and on towards the Rhine.

By this time Franz had already punched out a hundred little plates. Instead of Woodchip, who'd been arrested, a very young boy came to vacuum up the dust. Everyone was taken aback at first because they were so used to Woodchip. But the boy was such a cheeky, cheerful rascal that they immediately gave him a nickname too: Peppernut. Now instead of Woodchip everyone was saying Peppernut, Peppernut.

Last night while they were all changing out of their work clothes in the locker room, they had been less upset by Woodchip's arrest than by the sudden increase in the number of punched-out aluminium plates produced. None of them could quite understand this. They realised what was happening only as the day wore on. One of the men had worked out that some part on the machines had been altered so that you could raise the lever four times a minute instead of just three times. And furthermore, the little plates, once they were put in, turned by themselves after each punch instead of having to be rotated by hand each time. One man said that for him the pay increase to be expected on the first of the month was what mattered, whereupon a third man, an older worker, said that he'd never felt so exhausted as yesterday at the end of the workday, and then the second said that they were always exhausted Monday evenings.

Usually conversations like this, the reasons for them, and the mood of the men would have given Franz enough food for thought for a long time: the fact that this basic underlying process triggered a long series of other processes, each one in its own way more important than the process before, the exposure of people's character, the sudden revelation of their true natures. But this time Franz was disappointed, even distressed, that the news preoccupying him day and night wouldn't sink into the arid ground of his daily life.

If only I could go to see Elli and ask her, Franz thought. I wonder whether she's living with her parents again. No, I can't risk that. Only if I were to run into her by accident.

He decided to enquire discreetly on her street whether Elli had moved back in with her family. Maybe she didn't even live in the city any more. So the ache was still there. The injury George and Elli had inflicted on him back then, either out of stupidity or playfulness, still hurt. It was real and would be for the rest of his life.

Oh, it's all nonsense, Franz told himself. Elli's probably got fat and ugly by now. If I saw her again, maybe I'd even be grateful to George that he got me out of it back then. Besides, she's none of my business at all.

He decided to bicycle to Frankfurt after his shift. There was something he wanted to buy at a shop on Hansagasse, and while he was there he could ask about the Mettenheimer family.

Just then little Peppernut came over and grabbed him by the elbow; Franz raised his arms a little and because of that, one of the plates was spoiled, the next one too, and the third was not cleanly cut. Franz's face turned beet red; he would have liked to take hold of the boy and shake him, but the boy pulled a long face. In the glaring light young Peppernut's round face had turned mealy white, and there were dark blue circles of weariness around his sparkling, cheeky eyes.

Franz suddenly saw and heard the entire department the way he'd seen it five weeks ago, that first moment after he'd been assigned to work there. He heard the humming of the belts that cuts through one's brain, right through all one's thoughts, but without drowning out the subtle sound the metal band makes rubbing in the tracks. He saw the men's faces, bleak in that unremitting light and twitching every three seconds when the levers were pushed down. That's the only time they twitch, Franz thought. He forgot that he had just wanted to pounce on Peppernut for spoiling one of his pieces.

Not all that far from where Franz was working, maybe half an hour away by bike, a large crowd had gathered on a busy street near the main railway terminal in Frankfurt. They were all craning their necks trying to see what was happening. The police had been chasing a man who had climbed up a building façade in a housing complex in which there was also a large hotel. No one was surprised that SS men had been deployed along with a large contingent of police officers. The word was that this façade climber had escaped several times before, and this time the thief had been caught in a hotel room in the act of helping himself to a couple of rings and pearl necklaces. 'Just like a movie,' the people said. 'All that's missing is Greta Garbo.' Many of the faces smiled in surprise and amusement. A girl cried out. She'd seen something, or thought she had, way up on the edge of the hotel roof. The crowd grew denser; the excitement increased. They were expecting to see some extraordinary spectacle any moment, something halfway between a ghost and a bird. Now the fire department arrived with ladders and nets. At the same moment there was a lot of confusion at the back of the Hotel Savoy. A young man had jumped off a small cellar door and tried to elbow his way through the crowd. But the crowd, in the course of the long wait and all the fuss about the dangerous thief, had become so wild and eager to see someone caught, that they encircled the young fellow, beat him up pretty badly, and dragged him to the nearest policeman, who established that he was just a substitute waiter who wanted to go to the train station.

The real target of the pursuit was already sitting on top of the Hotel Savoy roof, on the other side of the chimney. It was Belloni. In his ordinary, everyday life, he'd been Anton Meier; ah, but where had that vanished to, his ordinary life? This Belloni was an acrobat, an artist; George and his comrades in Westhofen hadn't got to know him till the end. He was probably quite a decent fellow. In any case, Belloni was aware that George didn't know him. To have gained his trust, they would have had to spend more time together. From his place of concealment, Belloni couldn't see anything nearby, couldn't see the streets packed with people intently following the chase and burning to join in. Over the low iron railing of the downward-sloping roof he could see only the farthest edge of the plain. Towards the west he could see the sky, a calm pale blue, with not a single bird or cloud. While the crowd waited down below, he waited on his rooftop with the audacious cool that had been trained into him as a child, that same cool calm he had used in his profession to enrapture the masses without their quite understanding what it was about the simple stunts he performed that enthralled them so. Belloni felt as if he had been waiting up on that roof for a long time, such a long time that his pursuers, if they were actually on his trail, should already have discovered him.

Three hours earlier they had come to arrest him in the flat of a former friend's mother. The friend had been a member of his troupe until he had been disabled by an accident. But the police, among other things, had made lists of all the troupes in which he'd ever worked. It wasn't any more difficult for them to keep an eye on these connections than it would have been to encircle a couple of blocks. Belloni had jumped out of a window, run along a few streets, and fled in the direction of the main train station. In the course of his flight he'd almost been caught twice. When he came to the hotel, he went in through the revolving door. He was wearing the new clothes he'd acquired the day before, and his manner was so calm and elegant that he'd walked right through the lobby without being bothered by anyone. He had a bit of cash on him and hoped he'd be able to get away on a train. That was scarcely half an hour ago. He no longer had any hopes, but even on this last hopeless stretch of the way he was going to fight for his freedom. And for that he now had to climb down to the roof of the adjacent building. Carefully and calmly he made it down the slanting roof for a few yards until he reached a small bricked-up chimney close to the iron roof railing. He didn't think they'd discovered him yet. As he looked out from under the railing, he saw the dark throng of people below surrounding the block of houses. The crowd had even pushed out into the streets to prevent the fugitive from escaping. Belloni could now see all the way across the city, across to the Main River and the Hoechst factories and the Taunus foothills. In the overall pattern of the city's streets and alleys, the circle around the block of houses was merely a small black whorl of people. The infinite glimmering space seemed to be inviting an artistic stunt he was not able to perform. Should he try to climb down? Or should he simply wait it out? Neither made any sense. A move out of fear was as senseless as one inspired by courage. Still, he wouldn't have been Belloni if he hadn't chosen the second of the two senseless alternatives. He extended his legs from their crouching position until his feet touched the railing.

Belloni had already been discovered by the time he hid behind the second chimney. 'Aim for his feet,' said one of the two fellows behind one of the advertising signs at the edge of the roof of the adjacent building. Overcoming a slight feeling of nausea, or maybe it was excitement, the other, as ordered, aimed, fired, and hit the target. Then they both clambered skilfully and bravely up on to the hotel roof in pursuit of Belloni. Despite the intense pain from his wound, Belloni had not let go but was holding on even more tightly. He even managed to go a bit farther between the two chimneys and then diagonally across one corner of the roof. Then he rolled down to the railing. Once more he gathered all his strength and tumbled over the low railing before they could catch up with him.

He had plunged into one of the hotel courtyards, and in the end all the spectators on the street had to leave without actually having seen anything happen. But in the speculations of the idlers and excited reports of the women, he was still floating for hours over the roofs, half spook, half bird. When he died in the hospital sometime around midday (for he didn't die immediately), there also were two there deliberating about him. 'All you have to do is to fill out the death certificate,' the younger doctor said to the older one, 'so why are you concerned about his feet? That injury wasn't the cause of his death.' Overcoming a slight feeling of nausea, the older doctor did as the younger had suggested.

V

By now it was ten thirty. The sacristan's wife was in charge of a flock of cleaning women who did their chores according to a prescribed housekeeping plan set up long ago for the Mainz Cathedral. In accordance with this plan the entire cathedral would be cleaned in the course of the year. The ordinary cleaning women, of course, were assigned only to certain areas: tiles, walls, stairs, and pews. The sacristan's womenfolk, on the other hand, his mother and his wife, with their more delicate brooms, brushes, and specialised cleaning tools, cared for the national shrines of the German people.

And that is how the sacristan's wife came to find the little bundle wedged in behind the archbishop's memorial slab. It would have been better if George had shoved it under one of the pews. 'Look at this,' the woman said to Sacristan Dornberger, who was just then coming out of the sacristy.

The sacristan looked at what his wife had found, thought about the find for a moment, then said, 'Get back to your work! Go on!' He went with the little bundle through a courtyard into the diocesan museum. 'Father Seitz,' he said, 'take a look at this.' Father Seitz, like his sacristan in his sixties, spread out the little bundle on top of a glass case in which a collection of numbered and dated baptismal crosses were displayed on a layer of velvet. Just a dirty scrap of cotton twill... The priest raised his head. They looked at each other. 'Why did you bring me this dirty rag, Dornberger?'

'My wife,' the sacristan said slowly so that Father Seitz would have time to think about it, 'found it behind Bishop Siegfried von Epstein.'

The priest looked at him in surprise. 'I wonder, Dornberger,' he said, 'are we a lost and found office or a diocesan museum?'

The sacristan went up quite close to him. In a low voice he said, 'Do you think I ought to take it to the police?'

'To the police?' the priest asked Dornberger in astonishment. 'Come now, do you take every wool glove you find under a pew to the police?'

The sacristan muttered, 'This morning they were saying things.'

'Saying things, saying things. Don't you hear enough stories? Do you think that maybe tomorrow we should tell them that people dress and undress here in our cathedral? This thing really smells bad. You know, Dornberger, you could catch something from it. I'd burn it. On the other hand, I wouldn't want it in my kitchen stove; it's disgusting. You know what? I'll put it in here.'

The little cast-iron stove had been in use since the first of October. Dornberger stuffed the bundle into it. Then he walked off. There was a smell of burning rags. Father Seitz opened the window a crack. The merriment left his face, his expression turned serious, even dark. Again something had happened that could easily escape and vanish through a crack in the window or it could turn into a terrible stink that might suffocate them in the end.

While the rags in which he had sweated blood turned into a little plume of foul-smelling smoke escaping much too slowly through the crack in Father Seitz's window, George had made his way down to the Rhine. He was now plodding along on the sandy walkway situated somewhat above the paved road heading downstream along the river. Years ago, as a boy, he had sometimes come here on outings. He knew that there were innumerable ways of crossing the river by boat or ferry from the villages and small towns to the west of Mainz. Every time he had thought about it, especially at night, it had all seemed senseless, a futile hope dependent on thousands of contingencies. But now that he was walking on his own two legs and thinking about these coincidences and possibilities, even surrounded by danger as he was, it all seemed a bit less hopeless. The river, the tugboats lowering their smokestacks so as to be able to pass under the bridges, the shore on the far side with its bright strip of sand and above that the row of low houses, the mountains of the Taunus range in the background – for George all this had the same excessive clarity as a landscape in a battle zone in the midst of great danger when all contours stand out and sharpen until they seem be to quivering. At the market he had been afraid he would not have enough strength left to reach the riverbank. But now that he was resolved to get out of the city as quickly as possible – walking downstream would take him at least three hours – he no longer felt quite so weak, and the ground under his feet seemed to be getting firmer. He thought back over the last hours. Who saw me? Who can give them a description of me? Once he got lost in this vicious cycle, he was half lost. Fear is a state of mind in which one thought starts to overwhelm everything else. This fresh attack of fear had hit him out of the blue, here on this quiet path where no one was even looking at him! Fear – it was like an intermittent fever that kept breaking out periodically, though at ever-longer intervals. He stopped and leaned on the railing. For several seconds the sky and the water darkened. Then the attack passed, as if by itself; and as a reward for its passing, George now saw the world not darkly or in a super-real light, but in its everyday glory, calm water and squawking seagulls that did not so much disturb the stillness as complement it. After all, it was autumn, he thought, and the seagulls are here.

Someone was leaning over the railing next to him. He looked at the fellow, a boatman wearing a dark blue sweater. No one leaning on that railing would be alone for long. A kind of human chain forms, a riverman on leave, some fishermen who for the moment don't feel like fishing, elderly people. For all of this: the flowing water, the gulls, the loading and unloading of the ships, everything in motion was there for them to watch and observe. Next to the boatman there were already five or six others. 'What does a jacket like that cost?' the boatman asked George.

'Twenty marks,' George said. He was ready to move on, but the question had jarred something loose in his head.

A fat, nearly bald boatman came walking across the paved road below the place where they were standing.

'Hello! Hey there!' someone from up above yelled down at his bald pate.

He looked up and laughed. Grabbing the legs of the boatman above him, he hoisted himself up. One, two, three ... and there he was in spite of his obesity. His great big bald head came up between the legs of the boatman. 'How are things? What's new?' they greeted him.

'All right,' said the newcomer, who was obviously Dutch from the sound of it.

Now a short little fellow came along from the direction of the city with fishing tackle and a little pail like those that children use for playing in the sand.

'Here's Pikestail,' the fat man said. He laughed because for him Pikestail with his fishing rod and child's pail was as much a part of the city pier as the wheel in the municipal coat of arms.

'Heil Hitler!' Pikestail said.

'Heil, Pikestail!' the Dutchman called out.

'Now we've caught you,' said a fellow whose nose had been temporarily rearranged by a blow and might soon return to its original position. 'Now we know you buy your little fish at the market.'

Looking at the Dutchman, the fellow said, 'What's new in the great world?'

'Well, there's always something,' the Dutchman said. 'Quite a lot's happened in your country too.'

'Yes, here everything's running like clockwork,' said the fellow with the crooked nose. 'Everything's coming along nicely. We really don't need a leader any more.'

They all stared at him.

'We already have one for whom the whole world envies us.'

They all laughed except for the fellow himself, who pushed at his nose with his thumb.

'Eighteen marks?' the boatman said to George.

'I said twenty,' George said. He had half closed his eyes because he thought the gleam in them might give him away.

The boatman fingered the material. 'Does it wear well?' he asked.

'Yes,' George said. 'Except it's not very warm. A wool sweater like yours is warmer.'

'My fiancée knits me one every season.'

'Ah, then it comes from the heart,' George said.

'Want to do a swap?'

George shut his eyes as if thinking it over.

'OK. Hand it over!'

'Let's go over to the privy,' George said. The others could laugh as much as they wanted, but he didn't want them to see that he wasn't wearing a shirt under the jacket. Once the exchange had been completed, he went on his way along the Rhine, almost at a run.

The boatman coming from the toilet marched proudly back to the railing, his broad face smug in the knowledge that he'd once again bamboozled someone in an exchange. One hand on his hip, he raised the other in greeting.

George had reckoned that continuing to wear the jacket would be risky; the exchange was risky too. But what's done is done. Suddenly someone coming up behind him called out, 'Hey!'

Pikestail had come skipping after him with his pail and fishing rod, light-footed as a boy. 'Where are you headed?' he asked.

George pointed straight ahead. 'Right along the Rhine.'

'Aren't you from around here?'

'No,' George replied. 'I was in a hospital here. I'm going to visit relatives.'

Pikestail said, 'Would you like company? I'm a right companionable chap.'

George didn't say anything. He looked at him sideways briefly. From the time he was little, George had always had to fight a strong feeling of discomfort when something or other wasn't quite right with a man, if, say, he had some mental tic or some physical defect.

It wasn't until he met Wallau in the camp that he'd been completely cured of such spells. The present encounter made George think again of Wallau. 'Here's an example, George,' Wallau would have said, 'of how a man can come to have something like that.' George was gripped by an uncontrollable despondency. I owe him my life, everything, he thought, yes, even if I die today.

And all the while Pikestail just kept chattering on. 'Were you here not too long ago when they had the big celebration? It all seems so strange now. Were you here during the occupation? When they rode through the city on their little white horses, the Moroccans in their red coats, the Bettkult Indians? It all seems so strange. The French, they gave a different atmosphere to the city, a sort of greyish-blue fog. Why are you walking so fast, if I may ask? Do you want to make it all the way to Holland today?'

'Can you get to Holland from here?'

'Well, first you have to go to Mombach where they grow asparagus. Do your relatives live there?'

'Farther on.'

'In Budenheim? In Heidesheim? Are they farmers?'

'In a way.'

'In a way,' Pikestail repeated.

George wondered, should I try to shake him off? But how the devil am I going to do that? No, it's always better when there are two of you. Then you're more a part of the landscape. They passed the little swing bridge across Flosshafen.

'My, oh my, how time passes when you have company,' Pikestail said as if he had been asked by someone to make the time pass.

George looked across the Rhine. Just over there, quite nearby, on an island, three low white houses standing close together were reflected in the water. Something about these houses seemed familiar to him, inviting, as if someone he liked lived there. The middle house looked like a mill. Beyond the island towards the farther shore he could see the railway bridge. They passed a bridgehead with a guard on duty.

'Looks good,' Pikestail said.

George followed the little man away from the path and down over the meadow. Once the fellow stopped and sniffed the air. 'A nut tree!' He bent down and picked up two or three nuts and put them into his little pail.

George hastily picked some up too and in a frenzy cracked them on a stone with his heel.

Pikestail started to laugh. 'You must really be crazy about nuts!'

George calmed down. He was sweating and exhausted. Damn, this Pikestail fellow couldn't keep trailing along with him for ever. 'Aren't you going to try to catch a fish at some point?' George asked him.

'Let's wait and see,' he said in answer to George's gentle question. Willow bushes were beginning to line their path. They reminded him of Westhofen. His discomfort grew.

'There,' Pikestail said.

George stared straight ahead. They were standing on the point of the peninsula. Before them and to the right and left was the Rhine. There was no 'farther'. When Pikestail saw George's dismayed expression, he started to laugh. 'Oh, my. I really fooled you, oh my I really played a trick on you. Because you were in such a hurry. You didn't know, did you?'

He had put down his pail and fishing rod and started rubbing his thighs. 'Well, at least I had company.' The little fellow had no idea how close to his end he had come a second earlier.

George turned away, covering his face with his good hand. He said with incredible effort, 'Well, then, good-bye.'

'Heil Hitler!' said Pikestail. But just then the willows were pushed aside, and a police officer with a little moustache on his upper lip and one strand of hair over his forehead said cheerfully, 'Heil Hitler, Pikestail. Come now, show me your fishing licence.'

Pikestail said, 'Oh, well, I'm not going fishing.'

'And your fishing rod?'

'Oh, that, I always take it with me, like a soldier his rifle.'

'And the little pail?'

'Look inside. Three little nuts.'

'Pikestail, Pikestail!' the policeman said and turneds towards George. 'Well, and you? Do you have your identification card?'

'He's my friend,' Pikestail said.

'Well, then especially,' the policeman said or was going to say, for George, who had at first taken a couple of slow steps in the direction of the willows, was now walking faster, bending the branches apart, then running, running.

'Stop!' the policeman called out, not cheerfully any more, not at all affably any more. Quite like a policeman he called, 'Stop! Stop!'

Suddenly both of them were running after him, the policeman and Pikestail. George let them run past him. It all was so much like Westhofen: shimmering puddles and willows and now the police whistle and his heart pounding as if it would betray him, give him away. Over there on the nearby shore he saw a swimming area, piles washed over by water and between them, a float.

'There he is!' Pikestail screamed. Now the whistling started along the river shore too; all that was missing was the siren. Worst of all was the damned falling down; his knees felt like papier-mâché. On top of that he was having trouble holding on to reality. All this couldn't be happening to him. It was all a dream, and in the dream you run and run and run. Then he fell down flat, and he realised there were rails under him. He had run inland from the shore and to a factory area. Behind a wall he could make out a regular, even, purring sound, but no more whistles, and no human voices.

'Finished,' he said without knowing what he meant with the word, whether he meant his strength had given out or whether his fit of weakness was finished. He waited a while, without thinking, for some outside help or just to wake up, or for some miracle. But there was no miracle, or any outside help. He got up and continued walking. He came to a wide street with two sets of rails, but the street was deserted; there were no houses, just several factories. He told himself that the riverbank was probably being watched now, and so he walked on in the direction of the city. So many hours lost, wasted! She must be waiting for him, he thought, until it occurred to him how foolish it was of him: Leni couldn't be waiting for him, because she didn't know about any of this. He could not expect help from anyone; no one was waiting. Was there really no one here who would be waiting, no one who would help him? His hand hurt again because he had fallen on it; the new gauze bandage was soiled.

In a small square, an annexe to the big market, some of the market stalls were being dismantled. A caravan of trucks had stopped outside an inn. He went inside, sat down, and used his fifty-pfennig coin to order a glass of beer. His heart leaped as if there were a lot of room inside his chest. But with each leap it crashed hard against the chest wall. This couldn't go on much longer, he thought. A few hours maybe, but not for days.

A man at a neighbouring table was looking intently at him. Didn't I come across this fellow earlier today? George wondered. I'd better get cracking right now, keep running like a mad dog. No help for it, nothing to be done. Up with you, George!

Both inside the inn and outside there were quite a lot of people, visitors and market people. He took a good look. There was a young fellow who was helping an older woman loading up her produce. George walked over to him as he went back and forth between the truck and the baskets. 'You there. What's the name of that woman over there?'

'The one with the bun? That's Mrs Binder.'

'Yes, right,' George said, 'I have a message for her.'

He waited next to the baskets until the woman started the engine. Then he went over to the truck. Looking up he asked, 'Are you Mrs Binder?'

'What is it? What do you want?' the woman asked, suspicious and surprised.

George looked at her fixedly. 'Please let me get up there with you for a minute,' he said. 'I'll explain while we're driving, I'm headed in that direction too.' The truck got under way. George held on tight. Very slowly, in great detail, he began to make up a story, about the hospital, about distant relatives. Meantime back at the inn, a man from the adjacent table went out to the young fellow with whom George had talked before. 'What did he ask you just now?' he asked.

'Whether that woman was Mrs Binder,' the boy said, slightly bewildered.

VI

Mettenheimer the paperhanger usually went home for lunch if his
current work site wasn't too far away. Today he went to a restaurant
and ordered pork ribs and a beer. He treated his little apprentice to
a plate of pea soup. Afterwards he ordered a beer for the boy too and,
in the way of a man who's raised a couple of sons of his own, asked
him all sorts of questions. Someone came through the door, sat down,
and ordered a light beer. Mettenheimer recognised the man by his
new felt hat. They'd both been on the number 29 that morning. For
an instant he felt a slight discomfort but was scarcely aware of it. He
stopped chatting with his apprentice and finished the last bite. He
hurried back to the construction site to catch up on what he thought
he'd neglected to do because of his late arrival that morning. He
hadn't told his wife anything about having been summoned. Now
he resolved not to tell her anything about it after the fact either. He
wanted to totally forget the interrogation, the crazy summons. He
couldn't work out what it all meant. Most likely it had no significance
at all. They probably just picked on people from time to time. No
doubt there were others like him among all the many in the city,
people who'd been selected. Except nobody told anyone else. Now,
from the top of the ladder, Mettenheimer complained because they'd
pasted the border all the way around the bay. He was about to climb
down to make sure that it was done right on the ground floor, but
suddenly became so dizzy that he had to crouch on the top rung. The
laughter of the painters teasing the apprentice, the high voice of the
quick-witted apprentice rang through the empty, breezy house, far
more clearly than the voices of its past and future occupants ever did
or would, voices that had or would be damped by all the usual house-
hold stuff, furniture, carpets. The paperhanger swayed on his ladder.
Just then a voice yelled in the stairwell: 'Workday's over!'

The paperhanger yelled back, 'I'm the one to say when the workday's
over!'

At the stop for the number 29 he again met the short man with
the felt hat who'd been on the tram with him and then had a drink

in the same pub that morning. He must work around here too, Mettenheimer thought. When the 29 came, they both got on.

Mettenheimer nodded to the man. Then it occurred to him that he had again left the package of wool for his wife with the porter. She'd scolded him about it yesterday already. So he got off again and went back to get it. Then he hurried with the little package so as to be able to catch the next 29. He was pretty tired by now and looking forward to supper, and to being at home. Suddenly his heart contracted with an unusually cold, sick feeling. The man with the new felt hat, whom he thought he'd left on the last 29, was suddenly there too, waiting on the platform for the next 29. The paperhanger changed to another spot because he didn't trust his own eyes. But he hadn't been wrong. He knew the hat by now, the clean-shaven nape, the short arms. Mettenheimer hadn't intended to change trams, but to stay on this one to the end of the line and then walk the last bit. Now he changed at the stop in front of police headquarters to the number 17. He heaved a sigh of relief when he saw he was by himself. But hardly had he stepped on to the platform of the number 17 when he heard behind him a couple of hurried footsteps, and a brief snorting as someone jumped up. The felt-hatted man casually glanced at him, then he turned his back to him since Mettenheimer would have to push past him anyway when he got off. And now Mettenheimer knew that this man would be getting off right behind him, that there was no possibility of escape. His heart pounded with fear. His shirt, which had dried on his body long before, became soaking wet again. What does he want from me, Mettenheimer wondered. What did I do? What might I do? He couldn't resist the temptation to turn around again. Among the many hats of the evening crowd – leftover summer hats, premature felt hats – he could see the one he expected to see, following at a measured pace, as if he already knew that the paperhanger had no hankering any more tonight for any unexpected dashes. He crossed the street. Before stepping inside his front door, he turned around quickly in a sudden access of courage that can come to people who in a corner of their hearts are ready in certain circumstances to take a stand. The face of his pursuer was close behind him, a plump, phlegmatic face with bad teeth. His clothes were pretty shabby, with the exception of the new hat. Maybe the hat wasn't new either, just a bit less shabby. There was actually nothing about the man that was worrisome. What was worrisome for Mettenheimer was the inexplicable contradiction between the man's stubborn pursuit and his utter ordinariness.

Once Mettenheimer had arrived inside his front hall, he put the package of wool on the stairs and went back to lock the front door, which during the day was held open by means of a hook attached to the hallway wall.

'Why are you locking the door?' asked his daughter Elli, who was just then coming down the stairs.

'There's a draught,' Mettenheimer called back to her.

'That won't bother you upstairs in the flat,' Elli said. 'They'll lock it at eight o'clock anyway.'

The paperhanger stared at her. His skin crawled with the feeling that the man standing just on the other side of the narrow street was watching him and his daughter.

She was in secret his favourite daughter. Maybe the man who was keeping watch outside there knew that. What clandestine moves did he hope to catch him in? What public misdeed? Wasn't there some fairy tale in which the father promises the devil the first person to come out of the house to greet him? Up to now he had hidden from the rest of the family, even from himself, the fact that this child was dearest to him. Why was she? He didn't know. Perhaps for two contradictory reasons: because she was beautiful and because she had always caused him grief. He was glad whenever his grown children came to see him. But when Elli came, his heart gave a leap of genuine happiness. In his imagination he had papered quite a few magnificent houses for this daughter – he'd imagined her walking through quite a few suites of rooms and acting no less demanding than those cold, curt womenfolk who let their husbands show them their future homes. Elli touched his arm. Her face, framed by her thick, curly hair, looked small, like a child's face; it held an expression of sadness and affection. She was remembering the day on a bench in a pub in Westhofen when he'd held her close and told her to go ahead and cry. They'd never again spoken about that day. But probably they both thought of it whenever they saw each other. 'I'll take the package of wool with me so I can start to work on it,' Elli said.

The paperhanger, who sensed the man on the other side of the street staring at the little package, now felt that his daughter was putting something malignant into her shopping bag, even though he knew there was nothing inside it except a few colourful hanks of wool. Her face had turned cheerful again. A warm glow spread from her eyes, golden brown like her hair, over her entire face. Didn't that guy George have eyes in his head when he walked out on her? Her cheerfulness cut him to the heart. He tried to block anyone else's view of her by standing in front of her. Even if someone were trying to trap him, he thought again – this child was innocent. But Elli was tall and strong, and he was short and shrunken in stature. He couldn't hide her. He watched tensely as she went out into the street, walking with a light step, head held high, and swinging her shopping bag. He breathed a sigh of relief. His pursuer had just turned to face the display window of the soap shop. The paperhanger did not notice the nimble young fellow with a little moustache who had come out of the pub next to the soap shop, in the process lightly nudging the felt-hatted man with his elbow. Their eyes met in the reflecting glass of the shop window. Like fishermen staring into the same water, at the same fish, they both saw the other side of the street reflected in the glass: the paperhanger's front door and the man himself.

Mettenheimer thought: You want me to involve my family in a calamity, but you can't force me to. He went up the stairs, suddenly at peace with himself. The man in the felt hat went into the pub from which the young fellow with the moustache had come. He sat down by a window. The other one, with long, bouncing strides, easily caught up to Elli, whose legs and hips promised to make his boring job a lot easier.

Mettenheimer almost tripped over Elli's child playing on the floor with blocks. Elli had left him with them for the night. Why? His wife shrugged. He could tell from her face that something was troubling her, but he didn't ask what it was. Every other evening he would have been happy to have the child here. Now he asked, 'What does Elli have a room of her own for?' The child grabbed his index finger and laughed. He didn't feel like laughing at all. He pushed the child away. He recalled every word said that morning during the interrogation. He no longer had the feeling that he had dreamed it all. His heart felt heavy as lead. He stepped over to the window. The soap shop across the way had lowered its roller shutters. Mettenheimer refused to be misled. He knew that one of those blurry shadows in the pub window had his eyes fixed on his house. His wife called him for supper. At the table she took up her old refrain, 'I'd like to know when you'll finally get around to wallpapering your own flat.'

In the meantime, Franz on his way home from work had got off his bike just before he reached Hansagasse. He pushed the bike along, not sure whether to ask in one of the shops about the Mettenheimers. Then what he had hoped for and, perhaps, had also been afraid of, happened. He accidentally ran into Elli. He tightened his grip on his bike. Elli, deep in thought, didn't see him. She hadn't changed. A melancholy mood seemed to dampen her calm movements – but this had already been the case back then when there was as yet no reason for it. She was still wearing the earrings. That was good. He liked the way they looked against her thick brown hair. If Franz had been the sort of man who was good at expressing his feelings in words, he would probably have said that the Elli of this evening was more herself than the Elli he remembered. She walked right past him and he felt hurt even though she hadn't seen him, in fact shouldn't see him. Just as that first time at the post office, he would have liked to simply take her in his arms and kiss her lips. Why shouldn't I have what was meant for me? he thought. He forgot himself. Forgot that he was a homely man with plain features, lacking a lively temperament, that he was poor and awkward. This time he let Elli walk past him – as well as the young man with the moustache, not even realising that there was some sort of connection between the fellow and Elli.

Then he got back on his bicycle and pedalled along behind her for about ten minutes, until she went into the house where she was subletting a room for herself and her child.

He looked at the house that had swallowed her up. Then he looked at the surroundings. Diagonally across from Elli's front door was a pastry shop. He went inside and sat down.

There was only one other client in the place; it was the slender, fairly well-dressed man with the little moustache. He was sitting by the window, looking out. Franz paid no attention to him. He had enough sense left not to simply rush into the house behind Elli. But the day wasn't over yet. Maybe Elli would come out again. In any case he would sit here for a while and wait.

Upstairs in her room, Elli had changed, combed and brushed her hair, had done all the things she thought necessary in case the guest she expected this evening actually did turn up and stay for supper, and maybe stay – Elli didn't even totally dismiss this possibility – till the following morning. Then she put an apron on over her clean dress, went into her landlady's kitchen, and pounded and salted two veal cutlets so that they'd be ready to set on the stove as soon as the bell rang.

Her landlady, a woman of about fifty, not a bad sort, who loved children and had no objections to any strong expressions of vitality, was watching her with a smile. 'You're quite right, Mrs Heisler,' she said, 'we're only young once.'

'Right about what?' Elli asked. Her face had suddenly changed.

'To have supper with other people and not always with your own family.'

Elli was about to say, I'd much prefer to eat by myself. But she didn't say anything. She realised she was waiting to hear the front door slam shut and firm steps on the stairs. Yes, of course she was waiting, but maybe she was also hoping that something might come up, that there might be a hitch. I'll make a pudding too, she thought. She put some milk on the stove and gradually poured in the pudding mix. If he comes, good, she thought; if he doesn't come, that's all right too.

She waited a little longer, but what a sad waiting this was compared with her waiting in the past . . .

Back then, when she waited for George's footsteps, week after week, night after night, she had still dared to set her young life against the empty night. Today she knew that that waiting hadn't been senseless or ridiculous, but something far better, prouder than her current existence, now that she had lost the actual strength to wait. Now I'm just like all the others, she thought sadly; nothing is particularly important to me any more. No, she was sure she wouldn't be spending the coming night awake and waiting for her friend to come. And if he didn't, she'd yawn and fall asleep.

The first time George had told her she no longer needed to wait for him, she didn't believe a word of it. She had moved back in with her parents, but by doing that, she had only changed the place of her waiting. If waiting could have resulted in bringing him back to her, George would have come back to her then. But there's no magic in waiting, it has no power over the other person, it affects only the person who's doing the waiting, and for that reason, it requires courage. Nor had it been useful in any way to Elli, except for the silent, never-discussed sadness that had now and then unexpectedly made her pretty, young face more beautiful. This is what the landlady was thinking as she watched Elli cook. 'By the time you've eaten the veal cutlet,' she assured Elli, 'your pudding will have cooled off.'

The last time George had told her that she shouldn't wait for him any more – not unkindly but firmly and decisively, because her waiting bothered him – when George explained in quiet, intelligent words that marriage was no sacrament, and even the child she was expecting was not an inevitable fate, Elli had given up their joint room for which she'd been paying in secret.

But she continued to wait, even the night her child was born. What night would have been better suited for his sudden return?

After a few days of searching, the paperhanger had succeeded in dragging his son-in-law, that rascal, to see Elli. But later he regretted having done it when he saw his daughter after the fellow had left. He had, from the start, advised Elli against marrying this man, and then

THE SEVENTH CROSS · 109

later against getting a divorce. But now he had to admit that his daughter ought not to wait any longer. So at the end of the second year he went to the authorities to find out where his son-in-law was. For not even the fellow's parents knew his whereabouts. The year 1932, the second year, was coming to an end. Elli hushed the child who'd been awakened by the fireworks and the boisterous toasts to the year 1933. George still could not be found. Whether they were afraid to search too thoroughly, or because the child brought joy into Elli's life and she became more resigned – the whole affair sort of petered out. She could still remember the morning when she had stopped waiting. She had been awakened towards dawn by a car horn. She had heard footsteps in the street, which might have been George's. But they had passed by the house. With the fading away of the foot- steps, Elli's waiting faded away too. At the last echo, Elli was done with waiting. It wasn't that she'd had a sudden insight; she had made no decision. It was just that her mother and all the older people were right. Time heals everything, and even the hottest iron cools off. Back then she fell asleep again quickly. The next day was a Sunday, and she slept until noon. Pink cheeked and fresh, she appeared at lunchtime in the family living room, a new, healthy Elli.

Early in 1934 Elli was summoned by the authorities. Her husband, she was told, had been arrested and taken to Westhofen concentration camp. Now at last, she said to her father, she knew where he was and could hand in the papers for a divorce. Her father looked at her amazed, the way you look at a beautiful, precious thing after you suddenly see that it has a flaw. 'Now?' was all he said.

'Why not now?'

'Inside that place it would come to him as a blow.'

'I've suffered some blows too,' Elli said.

'But he's your husband after all.'

'That's over and done with for ever,' Elli said.

'No need for you to stay in the kitchen,' her landlady said. 'I'll put the veal cutlets on the stove when the doorbell rings.'

Elli went to her room. The cot stood at the foot of her bed, but it was empty tonight. Her guest should have been here by now, but Elli decided not to wait any longer. She opened the package, fingered the wool, and cast on the first stitches.

She had met the man she was now expecting, Heinrich Kuebler, by chance. Chance, if you let it take over, is not blind at all, as they say, but clever, even witty. You just have to trust in it completely. If you interfere and try to help it along, then things get bungled and chance mistakenly gets the blame. If you just leave everything to it and yield to it completely, then it usually arrives at the right outcome quickly, unpredictably, and directly.

A friend from the office had convinced Elli to go to a dance. At first she regretted having agreed to go. But then at the dance a waiter behind her dropped a glass. She turned round to look, and at the same time Kuebler, who just happened to be walking through the room, turned round too. He was tall and dark haired with good teeth. Seeing a slight resemblance to George in his posture and smile, Elli felt her face become animated; it became more beautiful. Kuebler noticed. He stopped and approached her. They danced into the early hours of the morning. From close up he didn't resemble George at all, of course. He was a decent young man. After that, he frequently picked her up to go dancing, and on Sundays they went on outings into the Taunus Mountains. They kissed and were happy.

She had casually told him about her first husband. 'I had bad luck there' – that's how she described it to him. Heinrich encouraged Elli to get rid of George once and for all. And she decided to take care of the matter on her own.

Then, unexpectedly one day, she received a permit to visit the Westhofen concentration camp. She went to see her father. She hadn't asked him for advice in a long time.

'You have to go,' the paperhanger said. 'I'll come along.'

Elli hadn't applied for this visitor's permit; she actually found it unwelcome. The permit had been issued for a different reason.

Since the people at Westhofen had been unable to get anything out of their prisoner by beating and kicking him, or by withholding food and keeping him confined in the dark, it had occurred to them to get his wife to come to see him. Wife and child – that usually made an impression on a man.

So Elli and her father asked for a day off from their respective jobs. They hadn't told anyone else in the family about this distressing trip. During the train ride Elli wished she were lying on a Taunus meadow with Heinrich. Mettenheimer longed to be hanging wallpaper. After they got off the train they walked side by side along a country road, passing through a couple of grape-growing villages. Elli felt as if she'd shrunk back into a little girl and sought her father's hand. It was soft and dry. Both of them felt apprehensive.

As they came to the first houses of the village of Westhofen, people watched them with a sort of abstract, vague pity, as if they were on their way to a hospital or a cemetery. Oh, how painful it was to walk through the bustle and cheerful excitement in the wine-growing villages. Why couldn't she just be one of these villagers? Why couldn't she be the one rolling that vat diagonally across the street to the tinsmith? Why couldn't she be the woman scrubbing the sieve on her windowsill? Why couldn't she help wash the yard where the wine press was to be set up? Instead she and her father, with unbearable feelings of foreboding, had to walk through all this everyday life on their strange errand. A young fellow with a broad head, shorn bald in a summer haircut, and looking more like a riverman than a farmer, approached them and said seriously and calmly, 'You have to go around up there, across the field, all the way to the wall.'

An elderly woman, who could have been his mother, was watching from a window and nodded.

Does she want to console me? Elli wondered. George doesn't concern me any more. They climbed up the field. Walked along a wall studded with pieces of glass. To the left was a small factory: Matthias Frank & Sons. Now they could already see the camp gate with the guards. The country road passed right by the gate, taking a sharp turn whose two sides were formed by the walls of the so-called interior camp. The inner camp gate was thus the only part abutting the country road. It was obvious that the Rhine was somewhere back there, but it couldn't be seen from here. Dead, stagnant water glittered here and there on the brown, damp soil.

Mettenheimer decided to stop in the garden of an inn they came to and wait there for Elli. From this point on she had to make her way by herself. Elli was afraid. But she told herself that George didn't concern her any more. She wasn't going to let herself be swayed by his special situation, or by his familiar face, his eyes, his smile.

Back then George had already been in Westhofen for a long time. He had gone through dozens of interrogations, and suffering and torment enough for a whole generation engulfed by war or some other disaster. And the torments would go on for him, tomorrow or perhaps even the next minute. By then George already knew that only death could help him. He knew the terrible power that had overwhelmed his young life, and he also knew his own power. He knew now who he was.

That first moment Elli thought they'd brought in the wrong man. She raised her hands to her ears – a characteristic gesture with which she used to make sure that her earrings were still in place. Then her arms dropped. She stared at the strange man standing between two SA guards. George had been a tall man; this man was almost as short as her father, with buckling knees. Then she recognised his smile. It was the old smile, unmistakable, the same half-joyful, half-scornful smile with which he'd taken her measure at their first encounter. Of course it now was not intended to beguile a young woman away from one's dear friend.

In his tortured mind George tried to form a thought. Why had they brought this woman here? What was their purpose? In his state of exhaustion and physical suffering, he was afraid he would overlook something important, some trap.

He stared at Elli. To him she was just as strange a creature as he was to her: the little upturned felt hat, the curly hair, the earrings. He kept watching her. Bit by bit he began to remember how she had been involved with him before, not much after all. Five, six pairs of eyes were observing every change in his face, still disfigured by the most recent punches.

I have to say something to this man, Elli thought. She said, 'The child is doing well.'

He perked up. His gaze focused. What could she have meant by that? She must have meant something special; maybe she was bringing him a message. He was afraid he was too weak to work out what it meant. He said, 'Yes?'

She could have recognised him by that look he gave her. His eyes were fixed as intensely and fervently on her half-open lips as they had been the first time they met. What information would come out of that mouth now to fill his life once more with strength and excitement?

After a long, agonising silence, during which she was probably searching for the right words, she said, 'He'll be going to kindergarten soon.'

'Yes,' George said. How agonising it was to have to think so quickly and clearly with his disintegrating mind. What did she mean by 'going to kindergarten'? He's doing well and starts kindergarten? Probably it had something to do with the reorganisation Hagenauer had talked about when he was brought in here four months ago after the most recent party leaders were arrested. His smile became brighter.

'Do you want to see a picture of him?' Elli asked, searching in her little purse, which the eyes of the guards were now fixed on too. She took out a small photograph pasted on cardboard: a child playing with a rattle.

George bent over the picture, frowning with the effort of trying to make out something important. He looked up, looked at Elli, looked back at the picture. He shrugged. He glowered at Elli as if she were making fun of him.

A guard shouted, 'Visiting time is over.'

They both flinched. George asked quickly, 'How's my mother?'

Elli said, 'She's well.' She hadn't seen the woman, who had always behaved strangely, almost disagreeably to her, for a year and a half.

George called out, 'And my little brother?' He seemed suddenly to come alive, to wake up. His entire body twitched.

It seemed no less dreadful to Elli that from one second to the next he was suddenly taking on a more human appearance.

George called out, 'How is—' But he was grabbed from both sides, turned around, and led out of the room.

Elli couldn't remember how she'd got back to where her father was waiting. She knew only that he had pressed her to him and that the innkeeper and his wife and two other women had stood there watching and that she didn't care. One of the women had patted her shoulder and the other had touched her hair. The innkeeper's wife had picked her hat up off the floor and brushed the dust off it. No one had said a word. For that the concentration camp wall was too close. Their consolation had been as mute as her sorrow.

Once she was back home, Elli sat down and wrote a letter to Heinrich, asking him not to pick her up at the office any more; in fact, asking him not to come to see her at all any more.

But in spite of the letter, Heinrich came to wait for her at the office. He asked her all sorts of questions about whether George had made an impression on her again, whether she loved him again, whether she felt sorry for him, whether she wanted him back once he got out. Elli had listened to all his questions in amazement – these vague and senseless ideas of his about a matter that she alone knew about.

She replied calmly that no, she didn't love George any more. She didn't want to ever return to him, not even once he was released. That it was over with for ever. Nevertheless, now that she had seen George, she no longer found any pleasure in being with Heinrich; she simply didn't feel like it any more. That was all.

But Heinrich stopped her on her way home, just as Franz had done a few years ago when George had suddenly taken her away from him. For Heinrich, not being too serious himself, didn't really believe in the serious finality of her rejection. It didn't make any sense. Fine, if she still loved George. But to stop seeing him just like that! What good would it do George for her to stay alone? He'd never know, probably wouldn't believe it even if she did have occasion at some point later on to tell him. She was just creating artificial difficulties . . .

All that had happened almost a year ago. Today she had invited Heinrich for supper. The veal cutlets were prepared, the pudding was ready. She had made herself pretty for him. How did this all come about? Elli wondered. Why am I starting things up again with him now? It hadn't required a firm resolve, nor was it a difficult decision to make. Nothing in particular had happened, except that a year is a long time. Spending every evening alone was boring. Elli wasn't cut out for that. She was like most girls. Heinrich had been right. Why do all that for a man from whom she was estranged? In the course of the year, her memory of the terrible face so dreadfully disfigured by blows and punches had faded somewhat. Her mother and the other older people had been right: time heals everything; even a hot iron cools down.

Deep in her heart Elli still held a small hope that Heinrich wouldn't come for some reason. She couldn't have said how that would change anything since she herself had invited him.

Downstairs in the pastry shop Franz was sitting at a table looking out at the street. The streetlamps were on. Although the day had been warm, it was finally obvious that summer was long behind them. The little café was only dimly lit. The owner was clattering around at the cash register, probably wishing her two stubborn guests would leave. Suddenly Franz grabbed the edge of the little table with both his hands. He couldn't believe his eyes. Walking under the streetlamps, with a few flowers in his hand, was George. Franz's insides whirled round and round in a raging vortex. There was everything in that vortex: shock and joy, rage and fear, happiness and jealousy. Then as the man came closer, it was over. Franz calmed down and cursed himself. The man bore only the weakest resemblance to George, and only from far away, and even that only if one just happened to be thinking of George.

Meanwhile, the pastry shop owner was rid of at least one of her customers. The young man had thrown a coin down on the table and walked out. Franz ordered another coffee and another piece of streusel cake.

When the downstairs doorbell rang, Elli's face beamed in spite of everything. A moment later Heinrich was standing in her room, holding a bunch of carnations. He looked in dismay at the young woman sitting on the edge of her bed. It seemed she hadn't been expecting him. Nor, because of the colourful ball of wool in her lap, did she jump up to greet him. Then Elli raised her face. She reached for her bag and stuffed all the knitting things into it with an exaggerated slowness inspired by her embarrassment. She got up and took the carnations from Heinrich's hand. The smell of sautéing meat was already coming from the kitchen. Dear Mrs Merkler. The thought made Elli smile. But Heinrich's face was so grave that she stopped smiling. She turned her face away from his fixed gaze. He took her by the shoulders, holding her tight until she lifted her head again and looked at him. Forgetting everything else, Elli could think only how lucky it was that he had come after all. At that instant there were voices and steps on the stairs and at the hall door. Had someone actually called out 'Gestapo!' or had she only imagined it?

Heinrich's hands dropped; his face froze, and Elli's face, which only a moment before had been warm and happy, looked as if it had never smiled and could never, ever smile again.

Even though Franz was not a quick thinker or good at putting two and two together, he more or less worked out what it was that he saw happening in the next few minutes from his seat in the pastry shop.

For a little while there was a good deal of activity on the small quiet street, although not enough to be conspicuous. A large, dark blue sedan stopped at the nearest street corner. At the same time, a taxicab stopped in front of the door to Elli's house. Almost simultaneously a second taxi came, not passing the first, but coming to a stop close behind it.

Meanwhile, three young men in street clothes had got out of the first cab and after a brief time inside the house had climbed back inside the cab with a fourth person. Franz couldn't have sworn for certain that the fourth person was the man he had momentarily mistaken for George because his escorts blocked him from view on the way from the house door to the cab, either cleverly on purpose or by accident. But he did notice that the fourth person wasn't just quietly and meekly going along between his escorts but that he acted as if he was drunk or sick. After they drove off without the motor ever having been turned off, the second cab also drove slowly past Elli's front door, making just the briefest stop. Two passengers ran into the house, coming back with a woman between them.

A couple of passersby stopped momentarily. And maybe some people watched from their windows. But the little stretch of roadway outside the front door under the streetlamps was undamaged and clean, not the site of an accident; no blood was smeared on the pavement. If passersby formed any conjectures, they took them back with them to their immediate families.

Franz expected to be stopped at any moment too. But he managed to get away safely on his bike.

So George was one of the escapees, Franz mused, and they're watching his relatives, his alleged wife, probably his mother too. They suspect he's here in the city. Maybe he really *is* hiding here. How's he going to get away?

In spite of the stories George's fellow inmates had told him, Franz had never formed an image of George the way he looked now, the way Elli had seen him. But a recollection of the old George suddenly came back to him with great clarity, and he wanted to cry out to him. That's probably what happened to people long ago, in centuries gone by, too. That's why they had suddenly cried out in equally dark times when, on a bustling street or at noisy party, they thought they'd caught sight of the one man conjured up by a forbidden memory or their conscience. He now saw George's youthful face, his fresh, sad look, his dark hair, so thick and beautiful. He saw George holding his head in his hands; then the image morphed into George's head on his shoulders, to the head as a thing, and finally he saw the head as a prize. Franz raced off as if he himself were threatened and in danger.

He arrived at Hermann's place in a state of confused distraction. Luckily it wasn't obvious on his somewhat coarse, heavy features. But he couldn't pour out all that was in his full heart just then because Hermann hadn't yet come home from work. 'He's at a meeting,' Elsa said, gazing at the distraught Franz with her round, innocent, but also curious eyes.

Sensing that he needed consolation, she offered him some pieces of liquorice from a box. Hermann often bought her sweets because he had been so touched the first time he had brought her a present and seen how such a trifle could light up her face. Franz also saw her as a mere child and stroked her hair, but immediately regretted it because she was startled by the gesture and blushed. 'So, he's not here,' Franz said, almost in despair and so lost in thought that a groan escaped his chest.

She watched him as he left, pushing his bike up the street; and like a child she felt a deep sadness, although it was a sadness she couldn't explain.

The Marnets waited for a while for Franz, but then they started eating without him. Although Ernst, the shepherd, was already seated at the table, he got up again and went outside to get a bone for his Nelly. As he stepped out of the hot, stuffy kitchen into the fresh air, a change came over his face, and he sighed with relief. The fog wasn't thick today. You could see the lights of many villages and of a city in the distance far away, the lights of the train lines and the factories, of the Hoechst Dye Works, and of Opel in Rüsselsheim. With one hand on his hip, the other holding the bone, he gazed calmly about him. His face had a happy, proud expression, as if he'd moved in today at the head of his people from a dark time immemorial, as if he were now gazing at the land they had conquered, its rivers, its millions of lights. Like a conqueror surveying what he has conquered. And hadn't he indeed marched at the head of his people from a dark time immemorial and subjugated this land, its wilderness and its rivers?

Ernst stirred; he had heard something squeaking on the other side of the field. It was the bicycle Franz was pushing up the road. Cunning curiosity now showed in the shepherd's face, which only a moment before had been clear and almost sublime. Why was Franz coming home so late, and why from that direction? 'Everything's been eaten,' Ernst told him. He saw with his sharp, impudent eyes that Franz wasn't exactly cheerful. He didn't feel sorry for him, only curious, and the expression on his face meant, Oh, little Franz, how small must be the flea that's bitten you.

Although no words were exchanged, Franz felt put off by this Ernst, by his scornful coldness that used to amuse him, by the fellow's indifference. Even before he went inside he was already repelled by the indifference of the people with whom he would now be eating his soup as well as the indifference of the stars that had just appeared in the sky above him.

VII

George kept walking on into the night, which was so foggy, so still, that it seemed impossible that anyone would ever find him. With each step he told himself the next would be his last. But every new step was always merely the one before the next one. He'd had to get off the market truck shortly after Mombach. There were no more bridges here, but each village had a docking place for boats. George had passed one after another. The moment had not yet come to cross the river. When all a man's powers are focused on one thing, everything, both instinct and reason, will send him a warning.

He lost all sense of time, just as on the previous evening. Foghorns were blowing on the Rhine. Occasional lights rumbled past at ever-longer intervals on the road built on the low embankment running along the river. A nearby wooded island blocked his view of the water. On the other side of the willows he could see the lights of a farmstead gleaming, but they neither frightened nor reassured him. The area was so deserted that these lights seemed like mere will-o'-the-wisps. The island that had been blocking his view had moved or he had passed it. Maybe the lights were from a ship or from the opposite shore that was now no longer blocked from sight by the wooded island, only by fog. It would be easy to perish here from plain exhaustion. If only he could spend a few minutes with Wallau, in whatever hell...

There was hope that if Wallau managed to get to a certain Rhine city they could get him out of the country from there. There were people waiting for him there who had already prepared the next stage of the escape.

When they locked up Wallau for the second time, it became clear to his wife that she would never see her husband again. When her requests for permission to visit him were brusquely, even threateningly, denied, she had come to Westhofen from Mannheim, where she was now living – for she had decided she would try to rescue her husband no matter what the cost. She acted on this decision with the determination of someone under a spell: the way women approach impossible undertakings by first switching off their minds, or at least that part of them that exists to test whether something is feasible or not. Wallau's wife didn't depend on experience, or information from sources around her, but rather on the legends of two or three successful escapes. Beimler's escape from Dachau, and Seger's from Oranienburg. Legends do provide certain information, certain experiences. But she also knew that her husband was totally aware and focused on going on with his life, and that he would grasp at the tiniest lead and follow it. Her general refusal to distinguish between what was possible and what was not didn't keep her from skilfully investigating and following up on the many details. She used her two sons to set up connections and deliver messages, especially since the older one had been thoroughly taught by his father in times past. Now having been initiated into his mother's secret plan, he too acted as if under a spell. A tough, dark-eyed boy in a Hitler Youth uniform, he had been burned rather than enlightened by a flame that seemed almost too strong for his heart to take.

By now, on the evening of the second day, Mrs Wallau knew that the escape from the concentration camp itself had been successful. She had no way of knowing when her husband would get to Worms and to the summer house where money and clothes had been readied for him, or whether perhaps he had already arrived there the previous night. The summer house belonged to the Bachmann family. Mr Bachmann was a tram conductor. Mrs Bachmann and Mrs Wallau had been schoolmates thirty years ago; their fathers had been friends and later their husbands as well. Both women had shared with their husbands the troubles and burdens of ordinary everyday life, and in the last three years, the troubles of a not-so-ordinary life too. Bachmann had been briefly arrested early in '33. But he got off scot-free and went back to his job.

At the same time that Mrs Wallau was waiting for her husband, Mrs Bachmann was waiting for hers, the tram conductor, to come home. She was quite distraught, and it showed in the tiny random twitching movements of her hands. Her husband usually took only ten minutes to get to his city flat from the tram depot. But maybe he'd had to fill in for someone; in that case, he wouldn't be home before eleven. Mrs Bachmann went to take care of her children, and in the process she herself calmed down somewhat.

Nothing can happen, she told herself over and over; there can't have been any leaks. And even if information gets out, no one can prove we're involved in any way. Wallau could just as well have stolen the money and the clothes. We live here in the city; neither of us has been at the summer house for weeks. If only someone could check to see if the stuff was still there, she thought. It's really hard to wait like this. I just hope Wallau's wife manages it all right!

She, Mrs Bachmann, had said to Mrs Wallau back then, 'You know, Hilde, this has completely changed all the men, ours too.'

Mrs Wallau had said, 'Nothing's changed my husband.'

She had replied, 'If you've ever really looked death in the face…'

Mrs Wallau had said, 'Nonsense. And how about us? And me? I almost died when my oldest son was born. And the next year I had another one.'

She had said, 'Those people at the Gestapo, they know everything about a person.'

Mrs Wallau had said, 'That's all exaggeration. They only know what they've been told.'

Now that Mrs Bachmann was again sitting there alone, the twitching of her hands started again. She got some sewing to work on. That calmed her. Nobody can prove anything. It was a break-in.

She heard her husband coming up the stairs. At last. She got up and prepared supper for him. He entered the kitchen without saying a word. Even before his wife turned to look at him, she had a feeling, not just in her heart but all over her skin, that the temperature in the room had dropped a few degrees with his entry. 'Is something wrong?' she asked, seeing his face. Her husband didn't answer. She put the plate with the food between his elbows on the table. Steam from the soup rose to his face. 'Otto,' she said, 'are you ill?'

He still didn't say anything.

Now his wife really was afraid. But it couldn't have anything to do with the summer house, because he's here after all. He's probably depressed by it all. If only this whole affair were over. 'Don't you want to eat something?' she asked.

Her husband didn't reply.

'Don't keep thinking about it,' his wife said. 'If you keep thinking about it, you'll go crazy.'

Rays of torment streamed from the man's half-closed eyes. But his wife had gone back to her sewing. When she looked up, her husband had closed his eyes. 'Is something the matter with you?' she asked. 'Have you got something, are you ill?'

'Nothing,' her husband said.

But the way he said it! As if she'd asked him whether he had nothing left in the world, and he had answered truthfully, Nothing.

'Otto,' she said, and went on sewing, 'maybe you *do* have something.'

But her husband answered unemotionally and calmly, 'No, nothing, nothing at all.'

When she looked at his face, lifting her eyes briefly from her sewing and looking into his, she knew that he really had nothing. Everything he'd ever had was lost, gone.

She felt ice cold. With hunched shoulders she bent over her sewing, as if her husband weren't sitting at the end of the table, but rather . . . She sewed and sewed, thinking of nothing, asking nothing, because otherwise the answer might come, and it would destroy her life.

And what a life! Certainly an ordinary life with the ordinary struggles for bread and children's socks. But also a strong, spirited life participating in everything that was worth living for. If she added to that what she and her friend had heard from their fathers, she and Hilde Wallau – when they were two little girls with braids living on the same street: there was nothing that hadn't resounded within their four walls, fights for a ten-, nine-, eight-hour workday. Speeches that were even read to the womenfolk while they were darning really devilish holes in all the socks, speeches by people ranging from Bebel to Liebknecht, and from Liebknecht to Dimitroff. Even before that, their grandfathers, the parents had proudly told the children, had been put in prison because they participated in strikes and demonstrations. Of course back then they didn't kill off and murder people for doing that. What a bold, clear-cut, straightforward life it had been. Is all that over and betrayed because of one single question; indeed, because of one idea? But there's the thought already. What's the matter with the man? Mrs Bachmann, a simple woman, was devoted to her husband. They had once been lovers; they'd been together for a long time. She wasn't like Hilde Wallau, who had added a lot to her knowledge over the years. But this man there at the end of the table wasn't her husband at all. He was an uninvited guest, strange and eerie.

Where was he coming from? Why so late? He was upset. He'd been different for a long time already. Ever since he was suddenly released from prison back then, he'd been different. How happy she was then, shouting with joy, but his face had been empty and tired. An inner voice asked, Do you want the same thing to happen to him that happened to Wallau? No! Mrs Bachmann wanted to think. But a voice that was much, much older than hers and at the same time younger, had already answered: Yes, it would be better that way. I can't bear his face, the wife thought. And as if her husband had heard the thought, he got up and went over to the window, standing there with his back to the room, even though the blind was down.

George had probably stumbled past several sheds similar to the one he finally chose. Inside, nothing but stacks of wicker baskets that smelled mildewed and unused.

Now all he wanted to do was sleep. That was all. To sleep and never to wake up. He crept into a corner; at some point in his sleep he accidentally bumped against a stack of baskets; they toppled over and he woke with a start. The fog had lifted. Moonlight was falling through the empty doorframe on to the worn floor, as still as snow. It was easy to see his own fresh footprints as well as old ones.

George didn't really sleep. Maybe he did, for two minutes. He dreamed he had arrived. He buried his fingers in Leni's strong hair and it crackled. He pressed his face down into it and breathed deep and knew that now at last it wasn't a dream any more but cold reality. He twisted her hair around his wrist so that she couldn't get away from him. Then his foot struck something; glass shattered. He woke again with a start. Yes, it was true, he thought, deeply moved, because awake he had never thought of it: back then I *did* knock down something – a lamp. Her laughter had been a bit coarse and her voice too, the same voice that had kept reassuring him back then with the insistence of someone inebriated that it would bring them good luck: It will bring us good luck, George.

He had such a sharp and sharply defined pain in his head that he automatically reached up with his hand to see if he was bleeding. Sleep was out of the question now. I really thought, he mused, that I could already have been with her by now. Wherever he directed his thoughts, they helplessly came back to her. The emptiness in his head soon turned into sheer despair.

Far in the distance something was prowling across the field, man or animal. Gradually it came closer over the soft soil without getting any louder; there were light, quick footfalls. George dragged some things over and stacked them in front of himself, sacks, baskets. It was already too late. A figure filled the doorway and darkened the interior. The shadow of a woman, he could tell from the hem of the skirt. She asked softly, 'George?'

George felt like shouting. But he couldn't breathe.

'George,' the girl said, sounding disappointed. She sat down then inside the shed on the floor in front of the door. George could see her clogs and heavy stockings and her hands between her knees on a skirt made of some coarse fabric. His heart pounded so loudly he thought she would hear it and jump up. But she was listening to something else. Firm footsteps were coming across the field. She said joyfully, 'George.' And she put her knees together and smoothed her skirt over her knees, and now George saw her face too. It seemed beautiful. But wouldn't any face have seemed beautiful in this light and in the expectation of love?

The other George stooped to go through the doorway and sat down next to her. 'Aha, there you are, you're here,' he said. And contentedly he added, 'And I'm here.' She embraced him calmly. She put her face next to his without kissing him, yes, maybe without any wish to kiss him. They spoke together so softly that the real George couldn't hear what they said. Then after a while the other George laughed. Then it was once more so quiet that the real George could tell when the other George was passing his hand through her hair and when across and over her dress, murmuring, 'My dearest.' He also said, 'My all.' The girl said, 'That isn't true at all.' He kissed her hard. The baskets scattered except for those that George was holding on to in front of himself. The girl began in a changed, brighter voice, 'If you knew how much I love you.'

'Yes, really?' the other George said.

'Yes, I love you more than anything...No!' she suddenly cried.

The other George laughed. The girl said angrily, 'No, George, go now.'

'I'm leaving,' the other George said, 'you'll soon be rid of me.'

The girl asked in dismay, 'How come?'

'Well, next month I have to join the army.'

'Oh, my God.'

'Why? It isn't such a bad thing. It'll finally put an end to all that drilling every evening and never having a free minute.'

'But then you'll really be put through the mill.'

'That's different,' the other George said. 'Then you're a real soldier and that's different from playing at being a soldier. Algeier says so too. Say, last winter, didn't you go dancing once with Algeier in Heidesheim?'

'And why not?' the girl said. 'I didn't know you then, after all. Anyway, it wasn't the same thing as now.'

The other George laughed. 'Not like this?' he said. He held her tight and the girl said nothing any more. Much later she said with sadness in her voice as if she had lost her lover in a storm or in the dark, 'George.'

He answered cheerfully, 'Yes.'

Then they sat as they had at first, the girl with her knees drawn up, one of the man's hands between both of hers. At one with each other, they gazed out at the fields and the quiet night. 'See, over there, that's where we walked,' the other George said. 'I have to go home now.'

The girl said, 'I'll be afraid when you leave.'

'But I'm not going away to fight in a war,' the man said, 'only to be with the soldiers.'

'That's not what I mean,' the girl said. 'I mean, when you leave me, right now.'

The other George laughed. 'You're a silly little ninny. I can come back tomorrow. Don't go starting to cry now.' He kissed her on the eyes and on her face. 'There, see? Now you're laughing,' he said.

The girl said, 'With me laughing and crying are pretty close.'

Then when the other George walked away across the field, and the girl watched him go in the pale light that was no longer silvery, the real George realised that she wasn't pretty at all, but had a round, flat face, and he was afraid for the girl and wondered whether the other George would come back tomorrow. Ah yes, if he had been permitted, he, the real George, he would have come back. There was a trace of fear on her face. She tried to stifle it, as if she wanted to find a stable point far away from where she was. She sighed and got to her feet. George moved slightly. There was now only the thinnest bit of moonlight on the ground outside the door, and already it was gone from there. A new day was dawning.

3

I

THAT NIGHT after his arrest Heinrich Kuebler was taken to Westhofen for interrogation. Numb at first, he had allowed himself to be led from Elli's flat without saying a word. Then, on the way, he suddenly went berserk, striking out wildly like any normal young man would when attacked by bandits.

Half conscious from the terrible blows with which they'd instantly overpowered him, his wrists bound together, and unable to find any explanation for his present predicament, he rolled and pitched over the knees and arms of his captors like a sack during the rest of the ride. When they reached the concentration camp, the SA, alerted to his arrival, saw that the captive had already been beaten and knew that the order of the police commissars not to touch the prisoner before his interrogation no longer applied here, since it was applicable only to those who arrived unharmed. For an instant there was complete stillness, then came the brief deep humming like an insect's that always came before, then one man's shrill scream, then minutes of mad turmoil, then perhaps stillness again – 'perhaps' because there hadn't ever been anyone present who could describe it exactly without describing also the unremitting wild noise made by his own heart pounding.

Heinrich Kuebler, having been beaten beyond recognition, was at last taken away, unconscious. Fahrenberg was notified: 'Fourth fugitive recaptured – George Heisler.'

Ever since this misfortune had come into his life two days ago,

Commandant Fahrenberg had slept as little as the fugitives. His hair had started to turn grey, his face to shrink. Just thinking about all that was at stake for him, realising all the things lost to him, made him double up groaning even as he found himself inextricably entangled in a maze of intertwined electric wiring, tangled telephone cables, and now useless switching circuits.

Between the two windows in the office hung a picture of the Führer; it was he who had made him powerful, Fahrenberg told himself. Made him almost but not quite all-powerful, a master over men, able to rule them body and soul, with power over life and death, no less. Having full-grown strong men brought before you, and having the power to break them, quickly or slowly; bodies that moments before were erect, going down on all fours; men, a moment before still bold and brazen, turning grey and stammering with the fear of death. Some you finished off utterly, some you turned into traitors, and some you set free with bowed necks and broken wills. Most of the time the taste of power was quite perfect; sometimes, in a few interrogations, there were hitches; as for instance in the case of this George Heisler. There was this soft, slippery thing that can rob you of your taste for it all because it simply slips through your fingers, a thing you can't touch, can't capture, can't kill, that's invulnerable – a little beast as slick as a little lizard. During all the Heisler interrogations the look and smile on the man's face had persisted, a faint glint, even when he was struck over and over again. Now, with the report of the arrest before him, Fahrenberg could see with that precision the visions of deranged people sometimes have, the smile on George's face being slowly extinguished and covered with a few shovelfuls of soil.

Zillich entered the room. 'Commandant, sir...' He could hardly catch his breath, such was his consternation.

'What?'

'They've dragged in the wrong man.' He stiffened because Fahrenberg came towards him. But Zillich probably would not have moved even if Fahrenberg had begun to strike him. Up to this moment Fahrenberg had never reproached him for any reason whatsoever. But even without reproof, a dull feeling of guilt and despair permeated Zillich's squat, powerful body. He struggled to breathe. 'That man they picked up last night over in Frankfurt at the flat of Heisler's wife wasn't our Heisler; it was a mistake.'

'Mistake,' repeated Fahrenberg.

'Yes, mistake, a mistake,' Zillich repeated as if their two tongues were revelling in the word. 'He was just some chap the wife was consoling herself with. I looked at him. Even if his face may now be gone for the rest of his life, I know my man.'

'A mistake,' Fahrenberg repeated. He seemed to be pondering something.

Zillich, motionless, watched him from under heavy lids.

Then Fahrenberg flew into a rage. He bellowed, 'What kind of lighting is this in here anyway? Do I have to butt my head against everything? It seems there's not a single man here capable of replacing a lightbulb, is there? And look outside! What time is it? What sort of fog is this anyway? Good God, every morning the same thing.'

'That's how it is in the autumn, Commandant, sir.'

'Autumn? Those shitty trees out there. Their crowns have to be clipped off. Prune those things; Make it snappy!'

Five minutes later there was a general hustle and bustle inside and outside the commandant's barracks. A couple of prisoners cut the tops off the plane trees growing along the length of Barracks III. Another prisoner, a professional electrician, meanwhile replaced some of the lightbulbs, also under supervision. He lay on his stomach in the barracks and fiddled around with the circuit breakers, while from the outside came the sound of saws screeching and sawn-off branches crashing to the ground. Looking up once from his position on the floor, the prisoner saw the look in Fahrenberg's eyes. 'I've never before in all my life seen such a look,' he would say two years later. 'I thought at any moment the guy was going to start dancing around on top of me cracking my vertebrae. But he just kicked me in the butt and said, "Make it snappy, hurry up." Finally they tested the lamps I'd fixed and they worked. Then they turned them off again, for by now it was quite light inside because all the branches had been cut off the plane trees, and anyway it was daytime by then.'

Meanwhile Heinrich Kuebler, still unconscious, was handed over to the camp physician. Commissars Fischer and Overkamp were now convinced that Zillich was right, that this man was not George Heisler. But there were some others, who, after looking at the fellow beaten beyond recognition, just shrugged, still not sure. Commissar Overkamp was constantly giving off his little whistles, not much more than puffs of air; it was what he did when curses no longer sufficed. Fischer waited, the phone clamped between his head and shoulder, until Overkamp had finished puffing and wheezing. Overkamp didn't need additional light. It was still night in their office, the shutters still closed; an ordinary desk lamp provided sufficient light, and for certain interrogations there was always the portable hundred-watt lamp if needed. Fischer repressed a desire to flash the lamp into the face of his superior so that he'd finally stop his puffing and wheezing. Then came a phone call from Worms, and that put an end to the puffing. Fischer shouted, 'They've got Wallau!'

Overkamp took up the receiver and scribbled something on a pad. 'Yes, all four of them,' he said. Then he said, 'Seal off the flat.' Then, 'Bring them here.' Then he read aloud to Fischer what he'd written:

When they went through the lists in the various cities the day before yesterday, the names of quite a number of people came up who were involved, in addition to Wallau's relatives. These individuals were again taken in for questioning yesterday. Of the five selected (all those who were pulled out of the last series from the second interrogation have to be ruled out of course), there was a certain Bachmann who seemed suspicious; a tram conductor by profession, thirty-three years old, two months in a concentration camp, released so his contacts could be observed. If you remember, last year in the Wieland matter, we tracked down Arlsberg's cover address by observing such contacts – anyway, he hasn't been politically active since then; during his first and second interrogation he denied everything, but when he was put under pressure yesterday he softened up.

Wallau's wife had stored things in his summer house near Worms, but he says he didn't know what or for what purpose, and he was then allowed to go home again under continued surveillance with the objective of observing any additional contacts. Wallau was arrested at this summer house property but has refused to make any statements up to now. Bachmann has not left his house so far. Did not report for duty at six o'clock. Possibility of suicide exists, no news about his family so far.

'That's it for now,' Overkamp said.

He had Fischer release the information to the press and radio in time for the morning news reports. Overkamp had at first fought those who were in favour of the immediate release of the information to enlist the help of the public. He felt that releasing it to the public would have been useful had they been dealing with just two, or at most three escapees – an exact, a reasonable number, adaptable to the circumstances of the escape – and in such a case the details if they were released would enlist popular support. However, he thought it would hardly encourage public confidence to hear that the number of escapees was as high as seven, or even six or five, and that in a breakout of such magnitude the citizenry would not aid them in the recapture of the escaped prisoners. It might even encourage speculation, doubts, and give rise to rumours about the number of escapees being even higher. However, in the meantime all these arguments no longer applied, because with Wallau's recapture a plausible number had been reached.

'Did you hear the news, Fritz?' the girl asked without even a hello as soon as the boy walked through the farmyard gate. She had tied a freshly bleached white kerchief about her head.

'What news?' the boy said.

'A little while ago,' the girl said, 'on the radio.'

The boy said, 'Oh, the radio. I'm in too much of a rush in the mornings. With Paul going to the vineyard with Father, and Mother delivering the milk, I have to do the stable for Mother. And it all has to be done before seven thirty. So I have no time for the fool radio.'

'Yes, but today there was a story about Westhofen,' the girl said. 'Those three fugitives; they were saying that they killed that SA man Dieterling with a spade, and that they broke in somewhere in Worms, and that after that they separated and went off in three different directions.'

The youth said, 'Hmm. Odd. Yesterday at the inn, Lohmeier from the camp and Mathes were saying that the guy who was hit with the spade was lucky because he just got a cut above the eye and all he needed was an adhesive bandage. You said three...'

'Too bad that they still haven't caught your guy,' the girl said.

'Oh, he probably got rid of my jacket a long time ago. My guy isn't going to walk around in the same clothes for very long. My guy probably guessed that there's a description out about what he's wearing. He must have sold it somewhere by now; it's probably hanging on a hanger in a strange closet in a strange shop. Or maybe he filled the pockets with stones and threw it in the Rhine...'

The girl looked at him in surprise.

He explained, 'At first I really felt awful about it, but by now I've got over it.' He came up close to her. He was going to catch up on something he hadn't yet done today. He took hold of her shoulders, shook her a little, and kissed her lightly. He held on to her for a moment longer. He thought: That guy knows that he's never going to get out of this alive if they catch him. He was thinking of the one fugitive with whom he had a connection. He had dreamed the night before that he was walking past Algeier's garden. And he saw a scarecrow among the fruit trees on the other side of the fence: a few sticks with an old black hat on top and wearing his corduroy jacket. That dream, which seemed pretty funny now in broad daylight, had scared him half to death during the night. Now too his arms slackened. The delicate, cool smell of freshly bleached laundry emanated from the girl's headscarf. He smelled it for the first time now; it was as if something had come into his world that differentiated its various parts more clearly from each other, the rough from the gentle. Then he went on his way.

Ten minutes later, when he ran into the gardener at the school, the man also asked, 'Had any news yet?'

'News about what?'

'About the jacket. They mentioned it on the radio.'

'My jacket?' Fritz Helwig asked, surprised, because the girl hadn't said anything about that.

'"He was seen last wearing the following items of clothing,"' the gardener quoted. 'It'll be all sweaty under the arms by now.'

'Oh, leave me alone,' the boy mumbled.

Ernst the shepherd was sitting by the kitchen stove in the Marnets' kitchen spreading jam on his bread when Franz came in to have a quick coffee before going off to work on his bicycle. He said, 'Franz, have you heard?'

'Heard what?'

'The guy from here who's one of those involved—'

'Who? Involved in what?' Franz asked.

'If you don't listen to the radio, you're not going to be up on the latest news.' He turned to the rest of the family sitting around the kitchen table with their second cups of coffee – they'd been working for several hours already, sorting apples, because two wholesale buyers were coming to the market hall in Frankfurt the next day. 'What are you going to do if you suddenly find this guy hiding inside your shed back there?'

'Lock the shed,' the son-in-law said, 'and bike down to the telephone to call the police.'

'You don't need the police for that,' the brother-in-law said, 'there are enough of us to take care of him; we'd club him and then drive him over to Hoechst. Right, Ernst?'

Ernst the shepherd was spreading the jam so thick on his bread that it was more like jam with bread than bread with jam. 'I won't be here by tomorrow,' he said. 'I'll be over at Messers' place.'

'He could just as well be sitting in the Messers' shed,' the son-in-law said. Franz was listening intently.

'Sure, he could be sitting anywhere,' Ernst said, 'In any hollow tree, in any old shed. But he won't be sitting in any of the places I'll be looking.'

'Why?'

'Because I won't look,' Ernst said. 'This wouldn't be something I'd want to find.'

Silence. They all looked at Ernst with the jammy bread halfway into his mouth like a bridle.

'You can afford to do that sort of thing, Ernst,' Mrs Marnet said, 'because you don't have a farmstead or anything of your own. But on the other hand, if the poor devil gets himself captured tomorrow and he tells them where he spent the previous night, then you' – she turned to her husband – 'could end up in jail.'

'In jail?' old Marnet said. He was a taciturn little farmer, who'd got skinny on the same diet that had plumped up his wife.

'Yes, you'll be put in jail and you'll never get out. What's going to happen then with all your stuff? The whole family will end up in misery.'

'I can't say much about that,' Ernst said. He licked his lips with his incredibly long, supple tongue while the children looked on in amazement. 'I only have a few sticks of furniture from my mother in Oberursel and my little savings bank book. In that respect I'm like our Führer, I have neither wife nor child. I only have my Nelly. But the Führer used to have a housekeeper; I read that he himself actually went to her funeral.'

Suddenly Augusta said, 'But there's one thing I want you to know, Ernst. I told Marnet's Sophie the truth about you. How can you lie to her like that, telling her you were engaged to little Marie from Botzenbach? Didn't you propose to Ella the Sunday before last?'

Ernst said, 'That kind of proposal really has nothing at all to do with the way I feel about little Marie.'

'It's pure bigamy,' Augusta said.

'It's not bigamy,' Ernst said, 'it's my nature.'

'He got that from his father,' Mrs Marnet explained. 'When he died in the war, all his girls came and cried together with Ernst's mother.'

Ernst said, 'Did you cry too, Mrs Marnet?'

Mrs Marnet glanced at her skinny little farmer. She said, 'Oh sure, I held back a couple of tears too.'

Franz was listening as breathlessly as if he thought the ideas and conversation of the people in the Marnets' kitchen would of their own accord eventually get round to dwelling on the subject his own heart was indicating to them. But no. Their ideas and words flowed merrily right over that subject, going in all sorts of other directions. Franz dragged his bike out of the shed. This time he didn't notice how he got down to Hoechst; the other bicycles around him and the noise in the narrow streets were only a vague reverberation.

'You knew him, didn't you?' one chap in the locker room asked. 'After all, you used to live there in that neighbourhood?'

'Why that particular guy?' Franz said. 'I don't recognise the name.'

'Look, here's a picture of him,' another said, holding the newspaper under his nose.

Franz looked down at the pictures of three men. Although seeing George again was like a punch in the gut – for he was seeing him again, because this George on the picture of the Wanted poster, this actual George, seemed only half as real as the George he remembered; he was also struck by the Wanted pictures to the right and left, and they made him feel ashamed for always thinking only of George.

'No,' he said, 'this picture doesn't mean anything to me. Good God, just think of the many people you come across in the course of a day.'

The paper was passed from hand to hand; about a dozen of them looked at it.

'Don't know him,' they said, and, 'Good Heavens, three at one time – maybe even more.' – 'Why did they escape?' – 'Ask yourself why.' – 'Killed with a shovel.' – 'It's hopeless, after all.' – 'Why? But they got out.' – 'For how long?' – 'I wouldn't want to be in their shoes.' – 'Look how old that one is!' – 'That one looks familiar.' – 'They were done for in any case; they had nothing to lose.'

One man calmly asked in a voice that sounded a bit muffled, maybe because he was bent over a locker or tying his shoelaces, 'What's going to happen to the concentration camps once there's a war?'

The men all felt a cold chill come over them, and they quickly finished dressing.

The same man added in the same tone, 'What will it take then to be safe at home?'

Who'd said that? They couldn't see his face because the man was bent over. But they all knew the voice. What was he actually saying? Nothing that was forbidden. A short silence followed, and there wasn't anyone who didn't flinch when the siren sounded again. As they were running across the yard, Franz heard someone behind him ask, 'Is Beutler still inside?' and another one answering, 'I think so.'

Ever since he'd come back from Mainz, Binder, the old farmer who'd been in Dr Loewenstein's office, had been twisting and turning on his oilcloth-covered sofa feeling sicker than before, or so he thought. He was just about to yell to his wife to turn off the radio, but then he pricked up his ears. He listened open mouthed. He forgot the life-and-death struggle inside him. He shouted to his wife to hurry up and help him get his jacket and shoes on. He started up his son's car. Was it that he wanted to get his revenge on the doctor who couldn't help him, or on that patient who had simply gone on his way yesterday with his bandaged hand even though by rights he ought to be the one to die, as it turned out? Or did Binder simply think that by doing this thing he'd be joining in more thoroughly with the living?

II

In the meantime, George had crawled out of the shed where he'd been hiding, afraid that someone might discover him there. He felt so miserable that it seemed futile even to put one foot in front of the other. But the momentum of a new day, more powerful than any night-time horrors, was enough to pull along someone who had been waiting for the dawn. Wet asparagus fronds swiped at his legs. There was a breeze, but barely strong enough to dispel the fog. Even though, because of the fog, George couldn't see much, he could feel the new day sweeping over him and everything around him. Soon the small round seeds hanging in the asparagus fronds began to sparkle in the low sun. Then he saw a glow. At first he thought it was the sun gleaming on the other side of the fogged-in shore, but getting closer he realised it was a fire burning on a spit of land. Then gradually but noticeably the fog lifted, and he could see a couple of low-lying buildings on the peninsula. At its end, which was bare of trees and surrounded by boats, he could see the open water. In front of him, in the middle of the field, on the road that led from the highway to the shore, he saw the house from which the pair of night-time lovers might have come. Suddenly from the peninsula came the sound of drums that made his teeth chatter. Since it was too late to hide, he walked on stiffly, ready for anything. But the field around him remained still. Nothing moved in the farmhouse, all he could hear was the voices of boys coming from the peninsula, and they sounded beautiful and angelically clear to him simply because they weren't the voices of men. And now he heard the splash of oars coming towards the shore even as the fire on the peninsula was being extinguished.

Wallau had told him: If you can no longer avoid people, you have to walk towards them purposefully, right into their midst.

These people whom he could no longer avoid turned out to be some two dozen boys jumping out of the boats, yelling wildly like Indians invading the hunting preserves of an enemy tribe. They brought their backpacks ashore along with cooking utensils, ground-sheets, and flags. Then the tumult subsided and the tangle of boys separated quickly into two groups in response to orders given by a skinny, pale blond boy who, tight-lipped but with a still quite boyish voice, issued a lot of sensible, curt instructions. Two of the boys strung dishes and pails on a rod by their rings and handles and marched off with it towards the farmhouse, escorted by two of their comrades, also with heavy loads, and two drummers, led by a ninth boy carrying their little flag. George sat down on the ground and watched them, not as if he had outgrown his childhood, but rather as if it had been stolen from him. 'Get moving,' the scrawny boy ordered the rest of the boys, who, meanwhile, had had to line up and count off. The scrawny leader had just noticed George. Some of the boys were searching for flat pebbles, and you could already hear them counting the number of skips on the water's surface. The others sat down half a yard away from George on a plot of grass around a small bushy-haired boy who was carving something in his lap. Listening to the boys giving their appraisals and advice, George almost forgot himself. Several of the boys took up stances and spoke the way children do when they feel an adult whom they're unconsciously attracted to is observing them.

The brown-haired boy jumped up, and running past George drew his arm way back and with a serious, tense face threw the thing he'd been carving up into the air. It came down again in front of him the way things do in accordance with the law of gravity. Still, the boy seemed inordinately disappointed. He picked up the object, examined it with a frown, sat back down, and continued to whittle away at it – his comrades' curiosity turning into mockery.

George, having watched it all, said to the boy with a smile, 'You're trying to make a boomerang, aren't you?'

The boy looked at George. George liked his direct, calm gaze. 'I can't help you because my hand is hurt,' he said, 'but maybe I can explain it to you.' Then his face darkened. Hadn't some boys just like these discovered Pelzer in Buchenau yesterday? That boy there with the calm, beautiful eyes, was he one of those who had banged on the courtyard gate? The boy lowered his eyes. The others were now crowding around George rather than the wood-carver. Without having encouraged it, he was almost completely surrounded by the horde of boys. He didn't even have to play a pipe like the pied piper. The group could sense that something hung over this man, an adventure or some terrible misfortune or fateful destiny. Of course they had no clear notion of this. They moved closer to George, talking and stealing sidelong glances at his bandaged hand.

By now, at Westhofen, Overkamp already had the report in front of him. It said that although George Heisler himself had not yet fallen into the hands of the state, they did have the jacket he had worn most recently, a brown corduroy jacket with zip. A riverman had got the jacket by swapping it for a sweater and had taken it to a secondhand shop intending to get money to buy himself some liquor. His girlfriend knit him lots of sweaters, and the swap had been like found money for him. But the old clothes dealer, having been strongly cautioned after getting caught several times selling suspicious items, immediately informed the police and gave them a description of the jacket. At first the riverman complained about having to hand over this fine specimen to the officers; but he calmed down when he was promised compensation. He had no problem proving his identity since he had some half-dozen witnesses to the swap. His witnesses all had the impression that the man with whom he had swapped had then walked on in the direction of Petersau in the company of another person. During the questioning, the name of this other person came out: it was Pikestail.

Pikestail was easy to get hold of. As a result of the information provided by the riverman, Overkamp issued some instructions. He felt as if some fresh air were finally blowing into this matter, which until just a moment ago had been a wholly muddled affair. Among the reports that had come in, there was a bit of significant testimony by a man named Binder from Waisenau. He claimed he had seen a suspicious-looking man in the surgery of Dr Loewenstein the morning before, a man who fit the description on the Wanted poster. And he saw the same man again with his freshly bandaged hand walking towards the Rhine. Overkamp ordered all these people to be brought in for questioning. From their testimony it was possible to trace Heisler's escape route up until midday yesterday, and from that they could surmise where he would have gone from there.

*

The boys had moved imperceptibly from their grassy plot over to the sand, forming a tight knot around George. The shaggy-haired boomerang carver was left sitting to one side of the circle. Then at the sound of a boat coming from the peninsula, they all turned their heads. A man with a backpack got off as well as a tall boy with a longish face and regular, bold features that could no longer be considered boyish. 'Give me that,' the boy said right off to the carver, and taking a step forward, he threw the thing up into the air with a relaxed singular movement that caused it to spin and made his body turn on its axis.

Meanwhile, the second group of boys came back from the farmhouse. The teacher praised the skinny one who had arranged everything so quickly. Then they again lined up and counted off before getting ready to leave. George also got up. 'You have some good boys there, sir,' he said to the teacher.

'Heil Hitler,' the teacher said belatedly. He had a tanned, very young face. But it seemed a bit rigid because of the effort made to retain its youthfulness. 'Yes, this is a good class.' Even though George said nothing else, the teacher added, 'They come of good stock. I made what I could of them. Luckily I moved on with the same class at Eastertime.'

It seemed to George that his having kept the same class played a big role in the man's life. It wasn't hard for him to speak calmly with the man. Suddenly, the previous night lay far behind him. The stream of ordinary, everyday life was flowing along in such a relaxed manner that it carried along everyone who put his foot in it. 'Is it far to the dock where the boats come in?'

'Scarcely twenty minutes,' the teacher said. 'We're all going there.'

He'll take me to the other shore, George thought; he has to take me along.

'Forward, march,' the teacher said to the boys, not aware of the strong spell emanating from the stranger because he himself had already come under it. The tall fellow who had come with him on the boat was still walking along beside him. The teacher put a hand on his shoulder, but George, had he been able to choose a companion for this hike from among all these young boys, would not have picked this handsome fellow walking next to the teacher, nor the clever skinny one, but rather the little boomerang carver. The boy's clear, direct look was often directed at him, as if he saw more in this stranger than the other boys did.

'Did you spend the night out in the open?'

'Yes,' the teacher said, 'we have a hostel, on the meadow. But we spent the night outside the house for the experience. Last night and early this morning we cooked over a campfire. Last night we studied how one would occupy the heights over there nowadays, comparing it with how they did it back in historical times, you see. In other words, how an army of knights in armour went about it, how the Romans did it...'

'You're the sort of teacher one would have wanted to have in school,' George said. 'You're a good teacher.'

'If you like what you're doing, you do it well,' the man said.

By now they had walked the whole length of the peninsula. Right next to them was the open water. You could see that the meadow, which had obscured everything with its bushes and groves of trees, was actually only a narrow triangle among countless shore projections and meadows. George thought: If I can get across I can still get to Leni's today.

'Were you in the war?' the teacher asked.

George realised that this man, who was probably the same age he was, thought him to be much older. He said, 'No.'

'Too bad, had you been you could have told my boys about it. I use every opportunity that comes along.'

'I would have disappointed them,' George said. 'I'm a bad storyteller.'

'My father too; he never told us anything about the war.'

'I hope the boys keep their healthy limbs.'

The teacher said, 'I hope they'll keep them. What I mean to say is, I hope they'll keep their limbs but not by shirking the duty they have to take part in the action.'

George's heart was pounding because he could see the piles and stairs of the docking place ahead of him. And yet the urge, his habit of trying to have an effect on people, was so strong in him that he answered even now, 'You take part with all your body and soul as a teacher, and that is taking part in the action too.'

'I'm not talking about that sort of engagement now,' the man said. His words were also directed at the boy who was walking very erect next to him. 'I'm talking about committing everything, risking life and death. We have to go through that – how did we get on the subject anyway?' He looked again at the stranger next to him. If their road together had been longer, he would have liked to reveal more of his thoughts to this man. How many confessions are offered the reserved person on the road! 'Here we are. Tell me, would you mind taking a couple of the boys across?'

'No, not at all,' George said, his heart beating in his throat.

'My colleague promised that he would take the boys into his class while the rest of us go collecting in the sand; we'll wait till the next boat gets here.'

Maybe little Boomerang will come with me, George thought . . .

But then, when they lined up for the third time and counted off, little Boomerang unfortunately was part of the teacher's group.

They brought Pikestail to Westhofen for questioning. It turned out that he was good at giving a description. His information was detailed, precise, and witty. Idlers like him were usually very good at observing things around them. Since they never take part in the action, their observations stay in their heads like an unexploited treasure. For that reason they often turn out to be of incomparable help to the police. Pikestail gave the police commissars a detailed report about how the man with whom he was walking yesterday was frightened to death when they arrived at the point of Petersau. 'He had a fresh bandage on his hand,' he said. 'The gauze was as white as snow, could have been an ad for a laundry detergent. The man must have had at least five teeth missing, probably three on top and two on the bottom, because the gap on top was bigger than the one on the bottom. And on one side,' Pikestail pointed into his own mouth with his bent forefinger, 'there was a kind of rip, or whatever you call that, as if someone had tried to extend his mouth all the way up to his left ear.'

They thanked Pikestail and released him. Now they had to identify the jacket. Then they could send out new descriptions of the fugitive over the information network that covered the entire country, to all the train stations and bridgeheads, to all the police stations, to all the docking places and hostels and inns.

At the Darré school they were shouting, 'Fritz, Fritz, they've found your jacket!' When Fritz heard that, he was dizzy with joy. He ran outside. They had finished checking things out behind the shed. Fritz looked inside the greenhouse. Gueltscher the gardener was collecting the seeds of the double begonias himself so that he could sort them right away. 'They found my jacket,' Fritz told him.

Without turning round, the man said, 'Well, then they must be very close on his heels. You must be glad.'

'Glad? To get my jacket back from somebody like that? All sweaty, dirty, and stained?'

'Well, at least take a look at it; maybe it isn't even yours.'

'It's coming,' the boys shouted. You could already hear the engine exhaust in the still air. The wake of the boat as it crossed the river was slightly lighter than the rest of the water, and took about as long as the boat to reach the shore. The rays of the morning sun picked out the boatman's bandana, a bird in flight, the white wall of the riverbank, a church spire far away in the hills, as if these few things especially were worth remembering for ever. They climbed down the stone steps to the dock. It was still a little early, for the boat wasn't that close yet. And then something in a person that always wants to keep moving, flowing, never standing still, separated from the part of his nature that wants to stay in a place for ever and never leave. And the one part moved on with the big river and the other part stayed close to the shore, clinging with all the fibres of its being to these villages, river walls, and vineyards. The boys had become quiet too. For once quiet is able to reign, it goes deeper than drumbeats and whistles.

George saw the guard on the dock on the opposite shore. Had there always been a guard posted there? Or was he posted there now because of him? The boys surrounded him, pulled him down the steps, pushing forward on to the boat. But George had his eyes fixed on the guard.

'Move aside, boys, let me through, I'm jumping overboard. Not the worst outcome if something goes wrong.' Such were the thoughts racing through his mind. He looked up. He could see the Taunus region far in the distance. He'd often gone there in the past, once to pick apples during apple harvest time with someone ... with whom? Ah, with Franz. There must be apples again now, because, well, it's autumn. Is there anything more beautiful on earth? And the sky was no longer hazy, it was a cloudless grey blue.

The boys stopped their chatter and turned to look in the direction the man was gazing at so intently, but they couldn't see anything special; maybe the bird he'd seen was already gone. The wife of the skipper came to collect the fares. They were already halfway across the river. The guard kept watching the approaching boat without moving. George dipped his hand into the water without taking his eyes off the guard. The boys all dipped their hands into the water too. Oh, it's probably all my imagination – but if they take you away, hand you over, and torture you, then you'll regret you didn't take this easy way out.

It was barely five minutes by car from the Darré school to Westhofen. Fritz had imagined Westhofen to be something hellish. But what he saw were clean barracks, a large, clean-swept square, some guards, a few clipped plane trees, calm autumn sunshine.

'Are you Fritz Helwig? Heil Hitler! Your jacket has been found. There it is.'

Fritz cast a sideways glance at the table. There was his jacket, brown and fresh, not at all dirty and bloodied the way he had imagined. Only on one of the sleeve hems was there a dark spot. He looked at the police commissar questioningly. The man nodded and smiled. Fritz went over to the table; he pointed at the sleeve. Then he pulled back his hand.

'So, there is your jacket,' Fischer said. 'Well, put it on,' he said with a smile since Fritz was still hesitating. 'Go on,' he said in a loud voice. 'Isn't it yours?'

Fritz lowered his eyes. He said softly, 'No.'

'No?' Fischer said.

Fritz shook his head vigorously in spite of the shock his answer caused.

'Look at it carefully,' Fischer said. 'Why wouldn't that be your jacket? Does it look any different?'

Fritz, with downcast eyes, began at first hesitantly, then laboriously to explain why it wasn't his jacket. His jacket had a zip in the breast pocket too; this one had a button. Here his jacket had a little hole from a pencil, and this lining did not have a hole. This jacket had a tape with the firm's name on it to hang it up by, and his jacket had two ribbons on the sleeves to hang it up by that his mother had put on because the original loop always used to tear. And the more he said, the more differences he noticed and the better he described them. In the end they interrupted him brusquely and sent him away. When he got back to the school, he said, 'It wasn't my jacket after all.' They all laughed in surprise.

In the meantime George had got off the boat and, still surrounded by his boys, walked past the guard. After he had said good-bye to them all, he walked on along the highway that led from Eltville to Wiesbaden.

Overkamp kept whistling to himself softly until Fischer, sitting across from him, felt his hands begin to tremble. That young rascal would have gleefully grabbed his jacket after all the complaining he had done. But luckily he was honest and rejected the jacket. And so, since this jacket hadn't been the one that was stolen, the man who had swapped it wasn't the man they were looking for. Consequently their arrest of Dr Loewenstein was futile too. Even if it was true that the man he had bandaged yesterday had been the man who'd swapped the jacket.

Overkamp might have kept on whistling for hours more if the whole concentration camp hadn't suddenly been brought up short with a jolt. Someone rushed in to say, 'They're bringing in Wallau!'

Much later someone described that morning:

Wallau's capture made the same impression on us prisoners that the fall of Barcelona or Franco's invasion of Madrid or some similar event might have. An event that makes you think that the enemy is all-powerful. The escape of the seven men had had terrible consequences for the rest of us prisoners. In spite of that we endured with equanimity being deprived of food and blankets, being subjected to even harder forced labour, many hours of interrogations, beatings, and threats, sometimes even mockery. Our feelings and attitudes, which we couldn't hide, incited our torturers to ever greater excesses. Most of us considered the escapees so much a part of ourselves that we felt as if we had urged them to get out. Even though we hadn't known about the escape plan, it seemed to us as if we had accomplished something very special. To many of us the enemy seemed all-powerful. Strong men can make mistakes without losing anything, because even the strongest of men are, after all, only human – indeed, their mistakes make them more human. Yet someone who represents himself as omnipotent can never make a mistake because he's either omnipotent or he's nothing. Thus, if even a tiny escapade is successful against the omnipotence of the enemy, then it's been a total success. This feeling turned to shock, and soon into despair, as they brought back one after another of the escaped prisoners relatively quickly and, as it seemed to us, with a ridiculous lack of effort. The first two days and nights we wondered whether they'd catch Wallau too. We scarcely knew the man. He had been put in with us for only a few hours after he'd been brought in; then almost immediately they'd taken him away for questioning. We'd seen him two or three times after these interrogations, weaving slightly, one hand pressed to his stomach. With the other he made a small gesture towards us as if to tell us that in the end none of it really meant anything and we should take comfort in that. When Wallau was recaptured and brought back to Westhofen, some of us cried like children. Now we were all lost, we thought. They'd kill Wallau now, the way they'd murdered all the others. In the first month after Hitler took power they'd murdered hundreds of our leaders in all parts of the country. Every month more were killed. Some were publicly executed; some tortured to death in the concentration camps. They exterminated an entire generation. That's what we were thinking about on that terrible morning. And we said it out loud then for the first time, that if we were all exterminated and cut down in such great numbers, we would perish without leaving any who could follow in our footsteps. Something that had almost never happened before in history, except once before among our people – the most terrible thing that can ever happen to a people, this is what was about to happen to us now: there was to be a no man's land between the generations through which none of the old experiences could be passed down. If you're fighting and are killed, another takes up the banner and he fights and is killed too, and the next one takes up the flag and dies too. That's the natural sequence of events, for you don't get anything for nothing. But what if there's no one there who wants to take up the flag because no one knows its meaning?

We pitied those fellows who were lined up when Wallau came back, spitting at him and gloating. They were destroying the best of what this country produced because they had been taught as children that such men were like weeds. All those boys and girls out there, once they'd passed through the Hitler Youth and the Labour Service and the army, they were like the children in the saga, children who'd been raised by wild animals to rip apart and devour their own mothers.

III

That morning, as on every other morning, Mettenheimer had gone to work punctually. Deep down he was resolved that, come what might, he would concentrate on his work and not think about anything else. He wasn't going to let yesterday's questioning, or his daughter Elli, or the stiff-hatted shadow that had attached itself to his heels – today again – keep him from doing his work well. Threatened, stalked, and spied on everywhere he went, in constant danger of being torn away from his wallpapering, he now saw his craft in a totally new light, almost as a noble calling, assigned to him in this disorderly world by whoever or whatever assigns men to their trades.

Because of his zeal to arrive early after yesterday's missed time, he had not heard or read anything this morning, nor did he see the glances the whitewashers exchanged among themselves upon his arrival. In his silent haste, broken only by curt, grumbled orders, he didn't even notice that they were helping him more willingly today than ever before. Of course, these people had no idea that his zealous efforts were inspired by lofty thoughts about the meaning of the work. They saw only the natural dignity of an old man whose family had been hit by a terrible stroke of bad luck. His best worker, Schultz, who was lending him a hand, suddenly said after a sidelong look at the old man's face, 'Such a thing can happen to anyone, Mettenheimer.'

'What thing?' Mettenheimer asked.

In the somewhat affected but sincere tone of voice that people use for condolences because they haven't yet found the proper words to express their feelings, only the conventional ones, Schultz added, 'Things like that can happen in any German family these days.'

'What can happen in any German family?' Mettenheimer asked.

That was too much for Schultz; it made him angry. At the moment there were a good dozen people busy with the interior finishing at the construction site. Half of them had been working regularly with the firm for many years, and Schultz was one of them. In such a group the lives of individuals can't really be kept secret for any length of time. They all knew that Mettenheimer had a couple of pretty daughters, that the prettiest of them had got married against old Mettenheimer's wishes, and that the marriage had failed. Back then it had been difficult to work with the old man. They also knew that the divorced son-in-law had landed in a concentration camp. And the radio and the newspaper reports this morning made them recall several things that the serious expression of the old man seemed to confirm. As far as Schultz was concerned, Mettenheimer didn't have to put up a pretence in front of him. It didn't occur to Schultz that Mettenheimer knew less about what had happened than the rest of them.

When lunch hour came, a couple of the men went downstairs to the caretaker's flat to warm up their food. With exaggerated urgency they invited Mettenheimer to join them. Mettenheimer didn't register the tone of the invitation and accepted. He thought he'd forgotten to take his sandwiches in his haste this morning and didn't want to go to a restaurant. The dark shadow didn't reach up here. He felt safe here in the stairwell niche that this familiar group of young and old whitewashers had chosen for their lunch break. They teased the little apprentice boy, sending him on errands, first to the caretaker to get salt, then down to the inn to get beer.

'Come on, let the poor boy eat his lunch,' Mettenheimer said.

There were a couple among the dozen or so men for whom the state was a kind of business firm, like Heilbach, for instance. They didn't care about anything so long as they could feel that their solid, honest work was properly appreciated and they received what they thought were just wages. What concerned these people was not that they were papering elegant flats in exchange for meagre wages. They were more concerned with individual, sometimes outlandish questions such as religious questions. The man Schultz, though, who had tried to console

Mettenheimer, was from the outset and had always been against the state. He knew when it came to professional competition and similar things how to differentiate between what was just humbug and what was purposeful. He also knew that what was expedient was good for the trade and for those who made a living at it. And that the best way to tempt people was with a dish they would most likely take a bite of. Those who felt that Schultz had remained, so to speak, constant in his heart stuck with him. Actually you couldn't really call it remaining constant any more; rather, the biggest difference possible was whether people revealed what was most important to them in the way they acted or whether they concealed it. Among the workers there was also a fellow named Stimbert who was a rabid Nazi. Everyone thought he was a spy and an informer. But this worried them less than you might have thought. They were careful and avoided him, even those who might have shared his views. They all saw him the way people see the odd or different individuals – such as a pathological tattletale, or simply a terribly fat person – who invariably turn up in any sort of social group, starting with the first year in school.

But all the men eating there in the stairwell would have mobbed this Stimbert fellow and soundly beaten him if they'd seen his mean, sick face at that moment and the way he was watching Mettenheimer. However, they were all looking at Mettenheimer, several of them having stopped eating and drinking. For Mettenheimer had just got hold of a newspaper that was lying around and was staring at one particular spot in it. His face had turned pale. They could all see that he had only now found out what had happened. They held their breaths. Slowly Mettenheimer raised his face. He looked devastated. In his eyes an expression as if he'd been cast down into hell. He saw the whitewashers and paperhangers around him. Even the little apprentice was there, having finally found a chance to eat but stopping now mid-bite. Stimbert in his ruthless way was smiling scornfully. But all the other faces showed sorrow and respect. Mettenheimer took a breath. He had not been banished to hell – he was still a man among men.

*

At the same time, Franz was standing in the factory canteen listening. One man was saying, 'I'm going to Frankfurt to the Olympia cinema.'

'What are they showing?'

'*Queen Christina.*'

'I prefer my little sweetie to your Greta Garbo any time,' a third one said.

The first one said, 'Those are two completely different things, necking and gawking.'

'How can you still enjoy such stuff?' another said. 'As for me, all I want is to go home.'

'You're struggling like crazy, and all you can afford is a movie ticket.'

Franz was listening, outwardly sleepy, but inwardly he was bursting. Again, or so it seemed, everything had gone to pot. That morning there'd been a moment, an opening. Suddenly he gave a start. The mention of the Olympia cinema gave him an idea; it was something he'd been mulling over all morning. The only way he could get in touch with Elli safely was through her parents' flat. Go up there himself? Weren't they watching the front door? And letters too? I'll bike over to the cinema after my shift, he thought, and buy two movie tickets; maybe my plan will work. And if it doesn't, it won't hurt anyone.

George continued walking along the Wiesbaden highway. He resolved to go as far as the next viaduct. He wasn't expecting anything in particular of that goal. Nevertheless, he had to set himself a goal every ten minutes. He allowed quite a few cars to drive past him. Trucks loaded with goods, others carrying soldiers, a disassembled aeroplane, private cars from Bonn, Cologne, Wiesbaden, an Opel, a new model he hadn't seen before. Which one should he hail? That one? None of them? He walked on, swallowing dust. A foreign car with a man, fairly young, at the wheel. George raised his hand. The car stopped instantly. The driver had already seen George walking along the road several seconds before. He felt that mixture of boredom and loneliness that can make you think you've been drawn to someone by fate; it was almost as if he'd actually expected George's wave of the hand. He cleared the seat next to him of blankets, raincoats, and other stuff. He asked, 'Where to?'

They glanced at each other briefly, intently. The foreigner was tall, thin, and pale; even his hair was pale. His calm blue eyes under colourless eyelashes had no particular expression, neither serious nor amused.

George said, 'Towards Hoechst.' Once he'd said it he was frightened.

'Oh,' the foreigner said, 'I'm headed for Wiesbaden. But doesn't matter at all. Are you cold?' He stopped again and put one of the plaid blankets over George's shoulders. George wrapped himself in it. They smiled at each other. The foreigner drove on. George looked away from the half of the face he could see and the bulge in the cheek made by chewing gum and turned his gaze to the pale hands on the steering wheel. These were more expressive than the face. On the left one there were two rings; he thought one was a wedding ring until he noticed when the man gestured with the hand that the ring was only turned around and that on the inside there glittered a flat yellowish stone. It bothered George that he was taking note of all these small details, but he felt compelled to do so.

'Here, up, farther around,' the foreigner said, 'but more beautiful.'

'What?'

'Up, there forest, here nearby, dust.'

'Up, up,' George said. They turned off, driving upward, at first climbing almost imperceptibly between the fields. But soon George could see with a sort of shock that the hills were getting closer. The air already smelled of forest.

'The day is turning out nice,' the foreigner said. 'What German names of trees? No, there all forest. All red?'

'Beeches,' George said.

'Beeches. Good. Beeches. You know the monastery Eberbach, Rüdesheim, Bingen, Loreley? Very beautiful.'

George said, 'We like this part here better.'

'Ah so, good. You want to drink?' He stopped for the second time, rummaged in his baggage, and unscrewed a bottle. George took a swallow, made a face. The foreigner laughed. His teeth were so large and white that if his gums hadn't been receding, you might have thought they were false.

For ten minutes the car climbed upward. George closed his eyes in the overwhelming forest smell. Up at the edge of the forest, they came to a clearing. The foreigner turned around, said 'Ah,' and 'Oh,' and asked George to look at the view. George turned his head, but kept his eyes shut. He just couldn't endure looking across the river, at the fields and forests, just now. They drove a bit farther on into the forest clearing and turned. The morning light filtered through the beech trees in golden flakes. Sometimes the flakes of light rustled for, after all, it was autumn and the leaves were dropping. George braced himself. He was close to tears and very weak. They drove inland away from the water along the edge of the forest. The foreigner said, 'Your country very beautiful.'

'Yes, the country is,' George said.

'What? – Much forest, streets good. People too. Very clean. Much order.'

George was silent. Now and then the foreigner looked at him because, as strangers often do, he viewed the man as a representative of his people, his country. George stopped looking at the foreigner, focused only on the man's hands; those powerful but pale hands stirred a faint feeling of repugnance in him.

They left the forest behind them and drove through a mowed field and then through vineyards. The total silence, the seeming absence of people gave the landscape a note of wilderness even though it was planted everywhere with crops. The foreigner looked at George sideways. He noticed George was looking fixedly at his hands. George was startled. But the foreigner, that oddball, actually stopped the car now just to turn his ring right-side up with the stone on top. He showed it to George. 'You like much?'

'Yes,' George said hesitantly.

'You take if you like,' the foreigner said calmly with a smile that was no more than a pulling back of the lips.

George said emphatically, 'No,' and since the foreigner didn't immediately draw back his hand, he repeated firmly, as if someone were trying to force him to take something, 'No, no.' Hmm, I could have pawned it, nobody would have known where it came from, he thought then. But it was too late.

His heart was pounding harder and harder. For the last few minutes, ever since they had left the forest edge above the valley and were driving through this stillness, one thought had been passing through his head, actually the seed of an idea he hadn't quite got hold of yet. But his heart, as if it understood better than his mind, was pounding, pounding.

'Good sun,' the foreigner said. He was going only fifty kilometres per hour.

If I were going to do it, what would be the best thing to use? George wondered. Those hands of his, they're not cardboard; he'd defend himself. Slowly, slowly George moved his shoulders downward. He could already touch the crank next to his right shoe with his fingers. Hit him over the head with it and then push him out of the car. He'd be lying there for a long time. Just his bad luck that he picked me up. These are the times . . . One life is worth that of another. By the time they find him, I'll be out of the country with this beautiful car. He drew back his arm, kicked the iron to one side with his shoe.

'What is the wine called here?'

George replied, 'Hochheimer.'

Don't get so excited, George said to his heart, in much the way Ernst the shepherd talked to his little dog. I'm not really going to do any of it. Go on, calm down. All right, if you absolutely want me to, I'll get out here.

Over where the road from the vineyards joined the highway, there was a sign giving the distances: Hoechst, two kilometres.

Heinrich Kuebler was still in no shape to be interrogated, but now that he had been bandaged and revived, they could look at him more closely. They now got all the witnesses they had picked up for this

purpose to walk by him, staring at him. He stared back at them, all
of them – he wouldn't have recognised any of them even if he had
been fully conscious: Gingersnap; Binder, the farmer; Dr Loewenstein;
the riverman; Pikestail; and lots of other people who would never
ever have crossed his path in the natural course of events. Gingersnap
said cheerfully, 'Might be him, or it might not.'

Pikestail said the same thing, even though he knew very well that
it wasn't George. But uninvolved people are always sorry when things
aren't carried to extremes. Binder said, almost darkly, 'It's not him.
Only looks like him.' Dr Loewenstein provided definite evidence.
'There's nothing the matter with his hand,' he said. And actually, his
hand was the only part of the man that had remained uninjured.

After that, all the witnesses except for Dr Loewenstein were taken
back to where they had come from at the state's expense. Gingersnap
had them drop him off at the vinegar factory. Binder was driven
through a world clouded over by pain, back to Waisenau, to his oilcloth-
covered sofa; it had all been futile, just as before his departure, he was
going to die anyway. Pikestail and the riverman had themselves
dropped off at the dock in Mainz where the swap had taken place
the day before.

Shortly after that, instructions were issued for Elli to be released, but
observation of her person and her house were to continue. There was
still a possibility that the real Heisler might try to get in touch with
her. Kuebler for the time being, because of the condition he was in,
could not be released.

At first Elli had simply sat in her cell as if turned to stone. Towards
evening, though, once she was permitted to stretch out on the cot,
her torpor dissolved and she tried to make some sense out of what
had happened. Heinrich, she knew, was a good fellow, the son of good
parents, who hadn't tried to pull the wool over her eyes. Would he
have done the sort of thing George had done? Oh sure, sometimes
he grumbled about taxes, but not any more than everyone else. After
all, her father grumbled when he didn't like something, or when he

felt something ought to be done away with, and her SS brother-in-law grumbled about the very same thing because he thought it was a good thing that hadn't been properly carried out. Possibly Heinrich had listened to a forbidden radio station at somebody's house, or maybe somebody had lent him a forbidden book. But Heinrich wasn't keen on either radio or books. He'd always said that a person who was in public life had to be twice as careful, whereby he was referring to his father's fur business in which he was a partner.

George had left Elli several years ago with not only the child, who was growing up healthy, and a few memories, of which some had already healed and some were still smarting, but also with a couple of vague ideas about what was important to him in life back then.

In contrast to most other people during their first night in jail, Elli fell asleep quickly. She was as exhausted as a child that has experienced more than its share. The next day, too, she wasn't worried except when she thought of her father. She hadn't yet come to her senses, everything was still too incomprehensible for that; rather, she found herself in an unreal state, half expectation, half remembering. She wasn't afraid. And she knew her child was well cared for by the family. Thinking about this, she was, without being conscious of it, prepared for anything that might come.

When they came to fetch her from her cell early in the afternoon, she was ready with a sort of courage that was perhaps only melancholy in disguise.

According to statements made by her father and her landlady, Elli's circumstances were fairly clear. Her release had already been ordered since she would be much more useful as a free person in case the escapee should try to contact her. Moreover, she certainly wouldn't protect a man she wanted to be rid of in order to marry another. As a result there was only a brief questioning. Elli answered all the questions about the past, about her former husband's old relationships, lamely and hesitantly, not out of cleverness, but rather because that was her nature and because she remembered little about that part of their life together. In the beginning friends probably came to visit them, but they all just called each other by their first names. Soon these visits, which she wasn't much interested in, stopped altogether. Heisler spent his evenings out of the house. In answer to the question where she had met Heisler, she replied, 'On the street.' Franz's name never even came to mind.

They told Elli that she could go home now, but they warned her that if she were arrested a second time because she had been foolish enough to do anything whatever in connection with the escaped Heisler without knowledge of the authorities or failed to report anything having to do with him, she ran the risk of never seeing her child or her parents again.

When she heard this, Elli opened her mouth and raised her hands to her ears. Right after that, standing outside in the sun, she felt as if she had been away from her home for years and years.

Her landlady, Mrs Merkler, received her in silence. Her room was in dreadful disorder. Balls of wool lay around on the floor, children's things and pillows were scattered everywhere; and over it all, the strong smell coming from Heinrich's bouquet of carnations still standing fresh in a glass. Elli sat down on her bed. Her landlady came in looking grim; she gave Elli notice for the first of November. Elli said nothing, only looked at the woman, who had always been kind to her. Admittedly, Mrs Merkler had decided to give Elli notice only after brooding over it for a long time, after severe threats, bitter self-recriminations, and agonising consideration for her only son, whom she supported, and finally resigning herself to it.

Meanwhile the afternoon was passing. George had reached Hoechst and had waited in desperation for the shift change that would fill the streets and pubs. Now he was standing, surrounded by people, on one of the first crowded trams coming out of Hoechst.

Mrs Merkler, the landlady, stood undecided in Elli's room, as if she were waiting for words to come to her by themselves, words to console, to soothe the young woman, whom she'd always liked, but not words that were too kind, words that might remind her to observe the laws of common decency.

'Miss Elli,' she finally said, 'please don't hold it against me. It's just the way life is. If you only knew how I feel in my heart...'

Elli still didn't say anything.

The doorbell rang. Both women were startled and stared wild eyed at each other. Both expected to hear shouts, noise, the breaking down of the door. But all that happened was that it rang a second time, nice and orderly. Mrs Merkler pulled herself together and went to open the door. Then she called from the entrance hall in relief, 'It's only your father, Miss Elli.'

Mettenheimer had never before visited Elli in this flat. It seemed to him a less-than-suitable place for his daughter even though his own place was in no way magnificent or roomy. Since he had heard vague rumours about Elli's arrest in the meantime, he turned pale with joy when he saw her standing, hale and hearty, before him. He took her hand in both of his, squeezed and stroked it, something else he had never done before. 'What are we going to do now?' he said. 'What are we going to do now?'

'Nothing at all,' his daughter said. 'There's nothing we can do.'

'But what if he comes?'

'Who?'

'That man, your former husband.'

'Oh, I'm sure he won't come to see us,' Elli said. She was both sad and calm. 'He won't even think of us.' The joy she had felt at seeing her father because it meant she wasn't completely alone in the world dissolved now as she saw that her father was even more perplexed than she was.

'Oh, I think he will,' Mettenheimer said. 'A man faced with an emergency thinks of every possibility.'

Elli shook her head.

'But what if he does come, Elli, what if he comes upstairs into my flat because you were last living at my place? They're watching my flat and yours too. What if at some point I'm standing at my living room window and I see him coming, Elli, what then? Should I just let him come on up, let him walk right into the trap? Or should I signal him?'

Elli looked at her father, who seemed to be beside himself. 'No, I'm sure he'll never come again,' she said sadly.

The paperhanger said nothing; his face clearly showed the distress he was feeling. Elli was astonished; she looked at him affectionately.

'Dear God in heaven' – the way the paperhanger said these four words, they sounded like a prayer – 'if only he doesn't come! If he comes we're lost either way.'

'Why lost either way, Father?'

'You still don't understand, do you. Just imagine that he's coming here, I signal him, to warn him. What's going to happen to me, to us then? Or imagine that he's coming. I see him coming, but I don't signal him. He isn't my son after all, only a stranger, worse than a stranger. So then, I don't signal him to warn him. They grab him. Could anyone do such a thing?'

Elli said, 'Father, dear, please don't worry; he won't come.'

'But what if he comes to find you, Elli? What if he somehow found out where you live now?'

Elli wanted to tell her father what had become obvious to her but only after his question; namely, that she would help George, come what may. But to spare her father she only repeated, 'He won't come.'

The paperhanger thought about it all, brooding. May the calamity, may the man walk right past his door. I hope he succeeds in his escape soon. What if he's caught before he gets away? No, he didn't wish that even on his worst enemy. But why did he have to be faced with such insoluble problems? All of it had happened because of a foolish young girl's infatuation. He rose to his feet and said in a changed voice, 'That fellow who was in your room yesterday evening, what's his name?'

In the hall he turned round once more. 'There's a letter for you here.'

The letter had been pushed under the kitchen door a little while before. Elli looked at the handwriting: 'For Elli', it said. She opened it after her father had left. Inside was a movie ticket enclosed in a blank piece of paper. Maybe it was from Elsa. Her girlfriend sometimes got her cheap tickets. This little green ticket had dropped down like manna from heaven. If it hadn't, she might have just sat on the edge of her bed all night, with her hands in her lap. Is this even permitted? she wondered. Is it all right for someone stuck as deep in misfortune as I am to go to the movies? Maybe it's not the right thing to do. Oh, nonsense. That's exactly what movies are for. At times like this especially.

'There are still two cold veal cutlets left from last night,' the land-lady said.

Especially at times like this, Elli repeated to herself. They'll be tough as leather, but at least they're not poisoned.

Mrs Merkler looked perplexedly at the delicate, sad young woman sitting at the kitchen table eating the two cold veal cutlets one after the other.

Especially now, Elli thought again. She went across to her room, took off the clothes she was wearing, washed herself from top to bottom, brushed her hair until it was shiny and fluffy. Life seemed a tiny bit more bearable now for this pretty, curly-haired Elli looking back at her from the mirror with sad brown eyes. If they're really watching me as Father claims, she thought, then all right, I just won't let on that anything's wrong.

'It was all just talk,' Mettenheimer said to his worried wife once he was back at home. 'Elli is sitting in her room. She's fine.'

'Why didn't you bring her here?' The few members of the Mettenheimer family still living under the old people's roof were just sitting down for supper. Father and mother; Elli's younger sister, snub-nosed Liesel, who, in her father's opinion, didn't seem to be a suitable protagonist in matters of faith, for which reason she was now sitting dressed for an evening at home, soft and pretty like all her sisters; Elli's child, their grandson, an oilcloth bib over his tummy, feeling a little glum because of the silence around the table, and play-ing around with his big spoon in the steam coming off his bowl.

Mettenheimer ate slowly, his eyes on his plate to keep his wife from asking any more questions. He thanked God she didn't have brains enough to comprehend the extent of the calamity looming over them.

George was actually just half an hour's walk away from where the Mettenheimers were eating. He got off the tram and took another one to Niederrad. The closer he came to his destination, the stronger his feeling that he was expected there, that they were preparing his bed, fixing him food; at this moment his girl was already listening for his step on the stairs. As he got off the tram, the tension he felt was almost like despair; as if his heart were balking at actually taking the path he'd walked countless times in his dreams.

He walked through the few quiet streets with their front gardens as if walking through memories. His awareness of the present was extinguished and along with it any awareness of danger. Hadn't the leaves at the kerb rustled back then, he wondered, without realising that he himself was pushing the leaves ahead of him with his shoes. How his heart balked at entering the house! This wasn't a simple heartbeat any more, it had turned into a furious rattling – he leaned out of the staircase window, the gardens and yards of many houses came together here: wall ledges and balconies were covered with the perpetually dropping leaves of a chestnut tree. Several windows were already lighted from inside. The sight had calmed his heart sufficiently for him to be able to continue on up the stairs. The old sign on the door with the name of Leni's sister was still there, and under it a new one, a small intarsia sign with a strange name. Should he knock or ring the doorbell? Wasn't that a children's game they used to play? He knocked softly.

'Yes?' a young person in a striped, long-sleeved pinafore asked. She opened the door only a crack.

'Is Miss Leni home?' George asked, not quite as softly as he intended because his voice was so hoarse. The woman stared at him. An expression of dismay came into her wholesome face with the round, blue eyes shiny as glass marbles. She tried to close the door, but he put his foot into the crack. 'Is Miss Leni home?'

'Doesn't live here,' the woman said in a husky voice. 'Go away, right now.'

'Leni,' he said calmly and firmly, as if he wanted to conjure his own former Leni from the past, to get her to leave this sturdy, aproned woman into whom she'd been bewitched. But it didn't work. The person stared at him with the shameless fear with which a woman under a spell stares at those who haven't changed. He pushed the door open, pushed the woman backward into the entrance hall, and pulled the door closed behind him. The woman ran back through the open kitchen door. She had a shoe brush in her hand.

'Leni, listen to me, it's me. Don't you know me?'

'No,' the woman said.

'Then why were you so shocked?'

'If you don't leave this flat immediately,' the woman said, suddenly bold and brusque, 'you'll regret it. My husband will be here any moment.'

'Are those his?' George asked. On a little bench were two tall, shiny black boots, and next to them a pair of women's shoes. Next to them, a tin of shoe polish, a few rags.

'Yes,' she said, having moved behind the kitchen table as if it were a fortification. She said out loud, 'I'm going to count to three. On three you'll be gone, otherwise—'

He laughed. 'Otherwise, what?' He pulled the sock off his hand; a black, matted sock he had found somewhere on the way and pulled on over his hand like a glove to hide the bandage. She watched open mouthed. He came around the table. She raised her arm up to her face. He grabbed her hair with one hand; with the other he pulled down her arm. He said in the tone of voice you might use to address a toad you knew had once been a human being, 'Stop it, Leni, admit that you know me; I'm George.'

Her eyes widened. He held her tight, at the same time trying to wrest the shoe brush out of her hand, despite the pain it caused his injured hand.

She said, pleading, 'But I don't know you at all.'

He let her go. He took a step back, said, 'All right. Hand over the money and some clothes.'

She said nothing for a moment, then she said, again quite bold and brusque, 'We don't give anything to strangers. We only contribute direct to the Winter Aid.'

He stared at her, but differently than before. The pain in his hand was letting up and along with it his awareness that all this was happening to him. He was barely aware that his hand was bleeding again.

On the kitchen table, on the blue-checked tablecloth, were two place settings. Swastikas had been ineptly carved into the wooden napkin rings – a child's handiwork. Slices of sausage, radishes, and cheese had been arranged nicely with parsley; and with it a few open little boxes of pumpernickel and crispbread, the kind you buy in health food shops. With his good hand he grabbed whatever he could from the table and stuffed it into his pockets. The marble eyes followed his every move.

With his hand on the door handle, he turned round once more.

'You wouldn't be willing to rebandage my hand, would you?'

She shook her head twice, emphatically.

Going downstairs he stopped again at the same stairwell window. He supported his elbow on the sill and pulled the sock back over his hand. She won't tell her husband anything because she's afraid. She can't admit she ever knew me. Now there were lights on behind all the windows. All those leaves from just one chestnut tree, he thought. As if autumn resided within the tree, a tree mighty enough to cover a whole town with its foliage.

As he shuffled slowly along by the side of the road, he tried to imagine Leni walking towards him from the other end of the street with her long flying steps. Only then did it become clear to him that he could never go back to Leni, and what was even worse, he could never even dream about going to see Leni again. That dream had been totally destroyed. He sat down on a bench and absently started chewing a piece of zwieback. Because it was cool and dim and he was much too conspicuous sitting there, he got up again almost immediately and walked on, following the tram tracks, for he didn't have enough money left for the fare. Where to now before night fell?

IV

Overkamp closed his door so he could have a few minutes alone before interrogating Wallau. He straightened out his papers, looked through a few notes and statements, sorted them, underlined and connected items using his own special system of lines. His interrogations were famous. Overkamp could elicit useful information from a corpse, according to Fischer. His outlines for interrogations could be compared only to musical scores.

On the other side of his door, Overkamp heard the abrupt, jerky sounds produced by men saluting. Fischer entered and closed the door behind him. Anger and amusement were battling in his face. He sat down at once very close to Overkamp. Overkamp warned him with a mere lift of his eyebrows about the presence of guards outside the door and the slightly open window.

'Something wrong again?'

Fischer spoke softly, 'This affair has gone to Fahrenberg's head. He's about to go crazy because of it. He is already. He's got to be fired in any case. We have to get things rolling on that. Let me tell you what just happened.

'We can't build a steel strongroom here just for the three recaptured escapees. I thought we had an agreement with the fellow that he wouldn't lay a hand on the three until we have all of them back. After that, for all we care, he can fill sausage casings with them. Yet he had the three brought before him again. There are those trees there in front of his barracks. I mean those things that aren't trees any more. He had them all topped this morning. Then he had them stand the three men up against the trees like this' – Fischer spread out his arms – 'he had the things studded with nails so that the men couldn't lean against them, and he had all the other prisoners line up and then

he made a speech. You should have heard it, Overkamp. He vowed
that all seven trees would be occupied before the week was over. And
you know what he said to me? He said, "You see that I'm keeping my
word, not a single blow.'"

'How long is he planning to let them stand there like that?'

'That's why all the ruckus started just now. Are those men going
to be fit to be questioned after an hour, an hour and a half of that?
All right. So he'll only lead them before the camp once a day. This
caper is going to be his last in Westhofen. I think he imagines that
if he gets all seven back, they'll let him stay.'

Overkamp said, 'If Fahrenberg topples off the ladder now, he'll
land with such a hefty bounce that he'll bounce right up a few rungs
of a new ladder.'

'I plucked that fellow Wallau off the third tree,' Fischer said. He
got up suddenly and opened the window. 'They're already bringing
Wallau. Forgive me if I give you some advice now, Overkamp.'

'That would be?'

'Have them bring you a raw beefsteak from the canteen.'

'What for?'

'Because you're more likely to pound answers out of that steak
than out of the man they're bringing before you now.'

Fischer was right. Overkamp knew it as soon as the man was standing
in front of him. He might just as well have torn up the slips of paper
on his desk. This stronghold was impregnable. A short, exhausted
man, a small, ugly face, dark hair growing to a triangular point on
the forehead, strong eyebrows with a vertical line between them that
divided his forehead. Eyes so inflamed they were almost shut, a broad,
somewhat lumpy nose, the lower lip bitten all the way through.

Overkamp looked fixedly at the face, the site of the coming action.
This was the fortress he now had to penetrate. If, as they claimed, it
was impervious to fear and all threats, then there were always other
means to take a fortress that was starved and worn out with exhaustion.
Overkamp knew all those means. He knew how to handle such cases.

As for Wallau, he knew that the man before him knew all those means. He's going to start now with his questions. At first he'll test the weak places of the fortress with his questions, starting with the simplest. He'll ask you when you were born, and already you'll be revealing the stars governing your birth.

Overkamp was observing the man's face the way you study an unknown territory. He had already forgotten his initial feeling when they'd first brought Wallau in. He came back to his basic belief that no fortress was impregnable. He turned his gaze from the man to one of his slips of paper. Then he made a little dot with his pencil next to a word; then he looked back at Wallau. Politely he said, 'Your name is Ernst Wallau?'

Wallau replied, 'From now on I will not answer any more questions.'

Overkamp said, 'So, your name is Wallau? I'd like to point out to you that I shall take your silence as an affirmative answer. You were born in Mannheim on October the eighth, eighteen hundred and forty-nine.'

Wallau was silent. He had said his last word. If you were to hold a mirror in front of his mouth, not a breath would mist its surface.

Overkamp didn't take his eyes off Wallau. He was almost as motionless as the prisoner. Wallau's face had turned a shade paler, the vertical line splitting his forehead had become darker. The man's eyes faced straight ahead, looking right through the things of this world that had suddenly turned transparent, right through to the core that was not transparent and could withstand the eyes of the dying. Fischer, who was also there, motionless, watching the questioning, turned his head in the direction of Wallau's gaze. But he saw nothing except the lush, bounteous earth, which isn't transparent and is without a core.

'Your father's name was Franz Wallau; your mother's, Elizabeth Wallau, maiden name, Enders.'

Instead of an answer, only silence from the bitten-through lips. — There was once a man whose name was Wallau. That man is dead. You were just now a witness to his last words. He had parents by that name. Now one can place the tombstone of the son next to that of the father. If it's true that they can force answers from corpses, I am more dead than all your dead people.

'Your mother lives in Mannheim, 8 Mariengaesschen, with her daughter Margarete Wolf, née Wallau. No, wait, she used to live . . . This morning she was transferred to the old-age home at Bleiche 6. After the arrest of her daughter and her son-in-law on suspicion of aiding in your escape, the flat on Mariengaesschen was sealed.'

When I was still alive, I had a mother and a sister. Later I had a friend who married my sister. As long as a man is alive he has all sorts of connections, all sorts of attachments. But this man is dead. And whatever remarkable things happened after my death to all these people in this remarkable world, they don't concern me any more.

'You have a wife, Hilde Wallau, née Berger. The marriage produced two children: Karl and Hans. May I remind you that I shall take your silence for an affirmative answer.' Fischer stretched out his hand and pushed aside the lampshade covering the hundred-watt bulb so that it was now shining into Wallau's face. The face remained the same as it had been in the dusky evening light. Not even a thousand-watt lamp could reveal any traces of torment or fear or hope in those blank final faces of the dead. Fischer pushed the shade back over the bulb.

When I was still alive, I had a wife. We had children together. We raised them in the belief we shared. There was great joy for husband and wife when their teachings took hold. What long strides their boys' little legs took marching in those first demonstrations! And the pride, the fear in the little faces that they might drop the heavy flags they were holding in their fists. When I was still alive in those first years of Hitler's rise to power, when I still did all those things that I considered worth living for, I could let my boys know about my hiding places without worry, this in a time when other sons betrayed their fathers to their teachers. Now I am dead. May their mother manage to scrape along with the fatherless orphans.

'Your wife was arrested yesterday at the same time as your sister for helping in your escape – your sons were transferred to Oberndorf Reformatory, to be educated in the spirit of the National Socialist state.'

When the man whose sons they're speaking of here was still alive, he tried in his own way to take care of his family. Now we'll soon find out what my care was worth. Some men who were much stronger than those two simple children broke down here. And the lies were so juicy, and the truth was so dry. Strong men have forsworn their lives. Bachmann betrayed me. But those two young boys – and that can happen too – they didn't swerve a smidgen. Fatherhood for me at any rate is over, whatever the outcome may be.

'You fought on the front lines during the World War.'

I went to war when I was still alive. I was wounded three times, at the Somme, in Romania, and in the Carpathians. My wounds healed, and I finally returned from the war in good health. Although now I'm dead, I didn't die in the World War.

'You joined the Spartacus League the month it was founded.'

The man who was still alive in October 1918 joined the Spartacus League. But what does that mean now? They could just as well summon Karl Liebknecht for an interrogation, he'd answer just as loud. Let the dead bury their dead.

'Well now, tell me, Wallau, are you still committed to your old ideas?'

They should have asked me that yesterday. Today I can't answer them any more. Yesterday I would have had to shout out, Yes! Today I can be silent. Today others will answer for me: the songs of my people, the judgement of those who come after me—

It turned cold around him. Fischer shuddered. He would have liked to signal Overkamp to break off this useless interrogation.

'So, Wallau, ever since you were transferred to the special punishment squad you were busy with escape plans?'

In my life I often had to flee from my enemies. Sometimes the escape succeeded, sometimes it failed. Once, for example, it had a bad outcome. That was when I wanted to escape from Westhofen. But now it has succeeded. Now I have escaped. The dogs sniff in vain at my tracks, which have been lost in infinity.

'And then you told your plan to your friend George Heisler?'

When I was still a living man in the life that I lived, I met a young fellow. His name was George. I latched on to him. We shared our pain and joy. He was much younger than I was. I valued everything about young George. In that young man I found again everything I prized in life. Now he has as little to do with me as a living man does with a dead one. May he think of me from time to time, if he has the time for it. I know that the living are very busy.

'You first got to know Heisler in the camp?'

No flood of words, just an icy stream of silence broke from the man's lips. Even the guards outside the door who were listening shrugged uneasily. Was this still an interrogation? Are there still three of them inside there? – The man's face was no longer pale; it had turned bright. Overkamp abruptly turned away. He made another dot with his pencil, whereupon the point broke off.

'You have only yourself to blame for the consequences, Wallau.'

What consequences can there be for a dead man they throw from one grave into another? Not even a tombstone as tall as a house on his final resting place would be of any consequence to the dead man.

Wallau was led off. His silence remained inside the four walls and would not go away. Fischer sat motionless on his chair as if the prisoner were still there, and continued to look at the spot where Wallau had been standing. Overkamp sharpened his pencil.

In the meantime George had reached the Rossmarkt. Even though the soles of his feet were burning, he kept walking. He couldn't afford to become separated from the crowd; he couldn't risk sitting down anywhere. He cursed the city.

Before he had finished mentally reviewing all the pros and cons, he was standing in a side street off Schiller Strasse. He'd never been here before. On the spur of the moment he decided to make use of Belloni's offer. He could hear Wallau's voice advising him to do it. Now the little artist with the serious face no longer seemed so impenetrable. The people walking past him were those who were impenetrable! How familiar that hell had been compared with this city!

Then, standing in the flat Belloni had described to him, he felt his old distrust return – what a strange smell! In all his life he'd never smelled anything like this. The elderly sallow-faced woman with her shoe-polish-black hair looked him up and down silently. George wondered if she might be Belloni's grandmother. However, the resemblance didn't stem from any familial relationship, but rather from a shared occupation.

'Belloni sent me,' George said.

Mrs Marelli nodded. She didn't seem to find that unusual. She said, 'Please wait here a moment.' The room was full of clothes in all shapes and colours spread out everywhere. The smell, even stronger here than in the hallway, was almost numbing. Mrs Marelli cleared off a chair for him. Then she went into the adjacent room.

George looked around. His gaze went from a jacket glittering with black sequins to a wreath of artificial flowers, from a white hooded coat with rabbit ears to a little flag of violet silk. He was too exhausted to make sense of his surroundings. He looked down at his hand in the sock. He started at the sounds of whispering in the next room. Expecting hands to grab him, the clinking of handcuffs, he jumped up.

Just then Mrs Marelli came back with clothes and linens on both arms. She said, 'Here you are; now go and change your clothes.'

He said hesitantly, 'I don't have a shirt.'

'Here's a shirt,' the woman said. 'What's the matter with your hand?' she suddenly asked. 'Oh, that's why you can't work.'

George said, 'It's bleeding through. No, I don't want to open the bandage. Just give me a rag.'

Mrs Marelli brought out a handkerchief. She looked him up and down. 'Yes, Belloni gave me your measurements. He has the eye of a tailor. You have a real friend in him. A good man.'

'Yes.'

'You were working together?'

'Yes.'

'If only Belloni can keep going. He didn't look so good to me this time. And you, what's the matter with you?' Shaking her head, she looked at his emaciated body but with no other curiosity than that of a mother who'd borne a lot of sons so that she had comparisons ready for almost anything that might happen, whether it affected the body or the soul. A woman like that can calm even the devil. She helped George get dressed in the new clothes. Even though her black, sequin-like eyes remained opaque to him, he no longer mistrusted her.

'Heaven has denied me children,' Mrs Marelli said, 'that's why I worry so much more about all of you when I sew your things. You have to take care of yourself so that you can hold out. What a couple of good friends you are. Do you want to take a look at yourself in the mirror?' She led him into the adjacent room, where there was a bed and her sewing machine. Here too odd items of clothing were strewn everywhere. She shifted the wings of the large, rather ostentatious three-part mirror.

George, now wearing a stiff felt hat and a yellowish overcoat, looked at himself from all angles, from the side, from the front, and from the back. His heart, which had behaved quite sensibly for many hours up to now, started to pound rapidly at the sight.

'Now you can appear in public. If you don't make a decent appearance, you won't get anywhere. We have a little saying: "Where one little dog has relieved himself, all the others will too." Now I have to pack up your old rags.'

He followed her back into the other room. 'I made up a bill,' Mrs Marelli said, 'even though Belloni thought that unnecessary. Billing goes against the grain for me. For example, look at this hood, almost three hours' work. Tell me, though, can I ask someone who needs a rabbit costume for just one evening to pay me a quarter of his salary in exchange for my sewing it for him? Belloni gave me twenty marks. I didn't want to take on the work at all. I work on street clothes only in exceptional cases. I think twelve marks isn't too much. So here are eight marks back. Give my regards to Belloni when you see him.'

'Thank you,' George said. In the stairwell he again suspected that the front door might be watched. He was almost at the bottom, when Mrs Marelli called to him that he'd left the little package of old clothes. 'Mister, mister,' she called. But he didn't go back up, but rather hurried out into the street, which was empty and quiet.

'It looks as if Franz isn't coming home today,' Mrs Marnet was saying. 'Divide his pancake among the children.'

'Franz isn't the same as he used to be,' Augusta said, 'ever since he's been working down in Hoechst. He doesn't lift a finger for us any more.'

'He's tired,' Mrs Marnet said; she really liked Franz.

'Tired,' her husband, the little shrunken farmer, said. 'I'm tired too. If only my work were limited to an eight-hour day! For me it's eighteen hours every day.'

'Well, just remember,' Mrs Marnet said, 'when you used to go to work at the brick factory, you'd come home at night all crooked.'

'But with Franz, the reason he isn't coming isn't because he's worked until he's crooked,' Augusta said. 'Quite the opposite, there's probably something or someone drawing him either to Frankfurt or to Hoechst.' All eyes turned to Augusta, who, bursting with gossip, was sugaring the last pancake.

Her mother asked, 'Has he dropped any hints?'

'Not to me.'

'I always thought,' the brother said, 'that Sophie liked Franz. He could really have had everything handed to him on a silver platter there.'

'Sophie likes Franz?' Augusta said. 'She's got too much fire.'

'Fire!' All the others were amazed. It was twenty-two years ago that Sophie Mangold's nappies had hung on the line in the neighbour's garden. The same Sophie who, her friend Augusta now claimed, had fire in her.

'If she has a spark of fire in her,' the little farmer said, his eyes flashing, 'it needs a bit of kindling.'

Yes, right, kindling just like you, Mrs Marnet thought, who never really liked her husband. Actually, this hadn't made her unhappy for a single moment of her married life. As she had explained to her daughter before the girl's wedding, it's only when you like someone that you can be made unhappy.

Just about the time his cousin Augusta was dividing his pancake into two equal halves, Franz was entering the Olympia. It was already dark outside. People grumbled as he awkwardly pushed his way along the row of seats, because he was keeping them from seeing all of the newsreel.

As he came to his seat Franz saw that the one next to it was occupied. Then he caught sight of Elli's face, white and staring wide eyed at the screen. His eyes on the newsreel, he drew his elbows in close, for the arm on the shared armrest was Elli's.

Why couldn't the years be erased? Why couldn't he just wrap his hand around her wrist? His eyes moved from her arm to her shoulder and up to her neck. Why couldn't he stroke her thick brown hair, which looked as if it needed exactly that. A little red dot glowed in her ear. In all that time, had no one given her another pair of earrings? He frowned. He felt he had to watch every word he said, every thought. Later, during the intermission, there wouldn't be anything special or suspicious about his speaking to the pretty young thing who happened by chance to be sitting in the seat next to his, even if she was being spied on here in the middle of the cinema. He was suddenly ashamed of the turmoil in his mind and in his heart. On any other evening, this section of the newsreel, which threw pictures of the world at you like a door suddenly being flung open and then just as suddenly being slammed shut again, would have sufficed to occupy his mind. But then the next item, George's escape, blocked out everything else on that particular evening, in the same way you can block out, with just one hand, the sun. Even if everything else was a world shaken by wars that shook him too. But maybe those two dead men lying there on top of each other on the village street, maybe they had once been a Franz and a George.

I'll go and buy some burnt almonds now, he thought as the lights went on in the auditorium. He made his way past Elli and out of the row of seats. She looked at him without recognising him, even at this close range. So Elsa hadn't come after all, Elli thought; she wondered if the man's ticket had been Elsa's. Or maybe the old woman sitting on the other side of me is Elsa's mother. In any case, I'm glad to be here in the cinema. I hope the intermission is over soon and they put the lights out so it's dark again.

She looked at Franz when he came back. Her expression changed; a glimmer of recognition. Vague memories, she didn't know whether they were happy or sad.

'Elli,' Franz said.

She looked at him in surprise. She felt comforted, even before she fully remembered who he was.

'How are you?' Franz asked.

Her face darkened. She didn't answer his question.

He said, 'I already heard. I know everything. Don't look at me now, Elli, but listen to me, listen to what I'm saying. Just keep taking almonds out of the bag and keep chewing. I was outside your house yesterday – now look at me and laugh . . .'

She acted quite cleverly. 'Eat, eat,' he urged. He spoke rapidly and softly. 'Just say yes or no. Try to recall who his friends were. Maybe you know someone I don't know about? Try to remember whom he knew here. Maybe he'll come here to the city. Look at me now and laugh. After the movie we can't be seen together. Tomorrow, very early, go to the market hall. I'm helping my aunt there. Order some apples; I can deliver the apples to you and we can talk then. Do you understand?'

'Yes.'

'Look at me.'

There was almost too much trust in her young eyes. Franz told himself: just stay calm; it could have been something else too. She gave a forced laugh. When the movie was dark, she looked at him again briefly with a genuine, serious expression on her face. Perhaps she would have liked to take his hand, if only because of a feeling of apprehension.

Franz crumpled the empty bag in his hand. Then it occurred to him that there couldn't be anything between him and Elli as long as George, one way or another, was still in the country. He should simply be happy that he could see her again without endangering either of them.

But here she was, sitting next to him. She was alive and so was he. The ripple of joy, weak and fragile though it might be, was stronger than any of the concerns weighing on him just then. He wondered whether she was really seeing the film her wide-open eyes were staring at. He would have been disappointed had he known that Elli, forgetting herself and everything else, was actually wholeheartedly following the wild ride through snow-covered country that was taking place on-screen. Franz had stopped watching the screen. He was looking down at Elli's arm, now and then snatching quick glances at her face. He was startled when the film was over and the lights went back on. Before being separated by the crowd leaving the cinema, their hands touched fleetingly like the hands of children who've been forbidden to play with each other.

V

George in this yellowish coat felt like a different man now, more relaxed. I owe you some apologies, Belloni...What next? The streets would soon be empty as the people leaving the cafés and movies went home. The night stretched before him, an abyss where he had expected a house. He walked on, faint with weariness, a dressed-up mannequin, propelled forward as if by a spring. He had intended to ask Leni to go to one of his old friends, to Boland. Now he'd have to go there himself. There was no other way. A good thing that he had these new clothes at least. He tried to remember the shortest way there. Mentally working out the streets he would have to take was as much of a torment as plodding through the actual streets. He got there shortly before ten thirty. The house door was open because two neighbour women were just saying good-bye. The lighted window on the fourth floor was Boland's. So far, so good. The house, still unlocked; the people, still awake. He had no doubt that Boland was the right one – the best of all the possibilities. By far the best; no need to worry about that. He's the right one, George repeated to himself on the stairs going up. His heart beat calmly, maybe because it wasn't paying attention any more to useless warnings, maybe because this time there was really nothing to warn him about.

He recognised Boland's wife. She was no longer young, neither beautiful nor ugly. George remembered that once, when there had been all the strikes, she had taken in someone else's child to care for along with her own. The child, without parents, maybe because the father was sitting in jail, had been brought to the tavern one evening. And Boland had led it by the hand up into his own flat to ask his wife to take care of it, and he'd come down again without the child. The evening continued with discussions and preparations for some rally or other. Meanwhile the child had interim parents, sisters and brothers, and supper. 'My husband isn't here,' Boland's wife said. 'You can go over to talk to him; he's across the street in the tavern.'

She was a little surprised, but not suspicious. 'Would it be all right if I wait for him here?'

'I'm sorry but that really isn't possible,' the woman said, not angry, but firm. 'It's late already and I have a sick child in the house.'

I'll have to watch for him, George thought. He went down a flight and sat down on the stairs. What if they lock the house door now? Someone could come in and find me here and ask me questions before Boland gets back. Boland might also come back with someone else. Maybe I should wait downstairs on the street, maybe go into the tavern. His wife didn't recognise me; the boys' teacher this morning thought I was his father's age. He slipped past the two neighbour women still saying good-bye to each other and went outside.

Maybe it was the same tavern they had brought the child to back then. The whole company was getting ready to leave, a little tipsy, their laughter so loud that people were shushing them from the windows. Almost all of them SA, only two men in street clothes, one of them Boland. He was laughing too, but in a noiseless, easy way that suited him. He looked the same as he used to. He and two others, SA people, separated from the rest of the group. The three of them weren't laughing any more, just grinning. Evidently they all lived in the same building, for one of them unlocked the house door, which had been locked only moments before, and the other two followed him in.

George knew that the company Boland was in didn't necessarily prove anything. He also knew that the shirts Boland's companions wore didn't prove anything either. He'd heard enough in the camp and knew about such things. He knew that peoples' lives had changed, their outer behaviour, their acquaintances, the kinds of battles they had to fight. He knew it, the way Boland knew it, if he really was still the same as before. George knew all that, but he didn't feel it.

George felt the way he'd felt these last few years; he felt the way people felt in Westhofen. He had no time now to explain to himself why these brown shirts were indispensable to Boland's companions and why these companions were indispensable to Boland. Looking at them he only felt the way he had felt in Westhofen. And Boland had no mark on his forehead that identified him as trustworthy. He might be trustworthy. George had no feeling about that. He might be, and then again, he might not be.

What am I going to do now? George wondered. By then he'd already done something: he'd left Boland's street. The city was coming to life again; it was the last general burst of boisterousness before the night-time quiet descended.

'They had to arrest the Bachmann woman in Worms too.'

'Why?' Overkamp asked brusquely. He had told them he was opposed to arresting her, for it would only arouse curiosity and tension among the populace, and overtly considerate treatment of the Bachmann family by the police would be more effective in isolating them.

'When they took Bachmann down from the attic where he'd hanged himself, his wife had yelled that he should have done it a day earlier, before the questioning, and it was a shame about her clothesline. Nor did she calm down after they had taken her husband away. She roiled up the whole neighbourhood, screaming that she was innocent and so on and so on.'

'How did the neighbours react?'

'Some one way, some another. Should I ask for the reports?'

'No, no,' Overkamp said. 'It has nothing to do with us any more. It's in the hands of our colleagues in Worms now. We have enough to do here.'

George couldn't very well disappear into thin air. So he thought, I'll take up with the first woman to come along…

But then when she came out from behind the shed and stood in the middle of Forbachstrasse, behind the freight terminal, she, the first one to come along, was worse than he could possibly have dreamed. He didn't want to touch her, not even with the tip of his finger. The flesh seemed to be melting off her longish head. In the weak lamplight he couldn't tell whether the tan bush grew out of her skull or was sewn on as a decoration. He started to laugh. 'Is that your hair by any chance?'

'My hair, yes.' She looked at him questioningly, and a touch of humanity came into her death mask.

'Doesn't matter,' he said quite loud.

She gave him another sideways glance. She stopped at the corner of Tormannstrasse, hesitated, but then only touched up her face and hair. It failed to improve anything, couldn't help but fail. She sighed.

George thought: She must have a place she's heading for now. There'll be four walls there. A door that closes. He linked his arm in hers with a pretence at heartiness. They went off rapidly. She was the first to see the policeman on the corner of Dahlmannstrasse and pulled George into a doorway. 'All the controls have been tightened,' she said. After a while, they walked on, arm in arm, through a few more streets, carefully avoiding the police guards. At last they arrived. A small open square, neither quite circular nor square, more as if a child had drawn a circle. And the place and the overlapping slate roofs seemed strangely familiar to George. I must have lived around here once with Franz, he thought.

On the stairs going up, they had to squeeze past a small group, two young men, two girls. One of the girls was tying a kerchief around the neck of one of the guys; he was almost two heads shorter than she was. After tying the knot, she pulled the ends upward. The young fellow immediately pulled them down, and the girl pulled them up again. The other fellow had a smooth-shaven face, was a little bit cross-eyed, and very well dressed. The second girl, wearing a long black dress, was amazingly beautiful; her pale face was surrounded by a cloud of flaming light golden hair. But switching girls now was impossible for George. Unthinkable. Besides, it didn't matter. And the girl's incredible beauty would probably prove to be an illusion. He turned round again. All four were just then looking at him. And indeed, the girl was suddenly much less beautiful. Her nose was too pointy. One of the boys cried out, 'Good night, Sweetie.'

George's female companion called back, 'Good night, Squinty.' As she was unlocking her door, the short one called out, 'Take care.'

She called back, 'Shut up, Shorty.'

'Is that supposed to be a bed?' George said.

But now she started to get angry. 'Why don't you go to the Englischer Hof hotel, to the Kaiserstrasse—'

'Oh, be quiet for a moment and listen,' George said. 'Something happened to me and it really doesn't concern you what it was. But it was a big problem for me, and I haven't had a wink of sleep since then. If you can arrange it so I can get some sleep, I'll take care of you. I've got some cash, and I can spend it.'

She looked at him in surprise. Her eyes glowed as if a light had been placed inside a skull. She said, 'It's a deal.'

There was another knock at the door. The short fellow stuck his head in. Looked around as if he'd left something there. She went over to him and cursed him out, but stopped in midsentence because he was signalling with his eyebrows for her to come outside.

George heard all five of them whispering together on the other side of the door, trying hard to keep the sound down, but quite distinct. In spite of that he didn't understand a single word, just a hissing that suddenly broke off. His hand went up to his neck. Had the room shrunk, were its four walls, ceiling, and floor closing in? He thought, I've got to get away from here.

Then she came back. She said, 'Don't look at me like that. What are you upset about?' She touched his chin. He brushed her hand away.

But then, wonder of wonders, he really was able to sleep. For hours, minutes? Had Loewenstein turned on the tap a third time in his desperate indecision? George came awake very slowly. And as he became fully conscious he expected the crazy pain to come back in five, six places of his body. But he continued to feel amazingly refreshed and well. So he really had slept. I'll give her everything I have, he thought. What had caused him to wake up? he wondered. The light hadn't been turned on. Only some lamplight from the courtyard came through the little window above the head of the bed. When he sat up, he cast a huge shadow on the opposite wall. He was by himself. He listened and waited. He thought he heard a noise on the stairs, the faint creaking of bare feet or cat's paws. He felt unbelievably anxious facing his huge shadow that extended up to the ceiling. Suddenly the shadow jerked as if it were about to pounce on him. A thought flashed through his mind: the four pairs of eyes at his back as he was going up the stairs earlier. The short guy's head in the doorway. Gesturing with his eyebrows. Whispering on the stairs. He got up on the bed and jumped out through the window into the courtyard below. He fell on to a pile of cabbages. Getting up, he plunged on, broke a windowpane, although it proved unnecessary because the bolt would have been quicker to slide open. He knocked down something that got in his way. At first he didn't realise that it was a woman. He bumped into a face, two eyes staring at his, a mouth yelling at him. The two of them twisted and turned on the pavement as if clinging to each other in fear and horror. He zigzagged across the square into one of the narrow streets that unexpectedly turned

out to be the same one where he had lived happily years ago. As if in
a dream he recognised the paving stones, and even the birdcage above
the shoemaker's shop, and here was the door into the courtyard that
led to other courtyards and from there to Baldwingaesschen. But
what if the door is locked, he thought, then it's all over with me. The
door was locked. But what did a locked door matter if what was
coming after him gave him the strength to throw himself against it?
No sense in measuring things by the old forces; they were no longer
applicable and had lost their strength. He ran on through many
courtyards. Then turning into a doorway, he caught his breath and
listened. Everything was still quiet here. He shoved the bolt back and
stepped out into little Baldwingaesschen. The sound of whistles was
still coming from Anton's Square. He walked through another maze
of streets. Again it was as if it were a dream; a few places were still
the same; others completely changed. There was still a picture of
Mary, Mother of God, over the gate, but next to it, the street stopped
and there was a strange new square he didn't know. He crossed the
unfamiliar square into another maze of streets, came to a different
section of the city. Here it smelled of earth and gardens. He climbed
over a low fence into a little nook formed by yew hedges. He sat down
and took a breather. He crept a bit farther and then he just lay down
because his strength had suddenly given out.

Yet he had never thought more clearly. He was just now regaining
all his wits. Not merely since his escape through the window, but
since the very beginning of his escape. How terribly bare everything
was now, how cold, and how clearly predictable the impossibility of
it all. Up to now he had been walking along its edge, propelled by an
urge he no longer understood, like a sleepwalker. Now at last, he was
fully awake and could see where he was. He felt dizzy and clung to
tree branches. Up to now he had come through safely, guided by
powers granted only to sleepwalkers that vanish on awakening. He
might perhaps even have ultimately succeeded with his escape if he
had continued that way. But unfortunately he was now wide awake,
and sheer willpower was not enough to recapture his previous state.
He felt a chill of fear. But he pulled himself together, even though

he was alone. From now on I shall control myself and behave decently to the end, he told himself. The branches slipped through his fingers and he was left holding something sticky. He looked and saw it was a large flower, unlike any he had seen before. The dizzying feeling that the earth was moving under his feet was so powerful that he had to grab for the branches again.

How wide awake he was! How awful to be fully awake like this. And awakening to find himself abjectly forsaken by his good spirits.

They'd probably figured out his escape route by now and broadcast an exact description. Possibly both radio and newspapers were already imprinting his facial features and characteristics on people's minds. This city was more dangerous for him than any other; here he was close to losing his life for the most ridiculous of reasons, for the most ordinary one imaginable, because he had put his faith in a girl. Now he saw Leni the way she'd really been back then, neither romantic nor trite, but ready to go through fire, cook soups, or distribute flyers for the lover of the moment. Had he been a Turk back then, she would for his sake have gone to help him proclaim a holy war in Niederrad.

He heard footsteps coming along the road next to the fence. A man with a walking stick went past. The Main River must be close by. This wasn't a garden; he was on the riverbank. Now he recognised the smooth-surfaced, white houses of Obermain Quai on the other side of the trees. He could hear the rumbling of trains, and for the first time, even though it was still pretty dark, the bell of a tram clanging.

He had to get away from there. He was sure they would be watching his mother. And the woman, Elli, who carried his name, was without a doubt being watched. Anybody in that city who'd ever added even a small stone to the mosaic of his life was probably being watched. His few friends and his former teachers might be watched, as well as his brothers and those dearest to him. The entire city, a dragnet. And he was already in it. He had to slip through its meshes. But by now he was really done in. He had barely enough strength to climb over the fence. How could he possibly make it out of the city, retracing the way he had come yesterday, and then twenty times farther than that, all the way to the border? He might just as well sit here till they found him. At the thought he rebelled in anger, as if it had come as a suggestion from someone else. Even if he had only enough strength left to take one tiny step towards freedom, no matter how ridiculous and useless the step might be, he was going to take it.

Not far away, close to the next bridge, they were already beginning dredging operations. My mother must be able to hear it, he thought. And my little brother too.

4

I

PETER Wurz, who had been the mayor of Oberbuchenbach but was now the mayor of the combined villages of Ober- und Unterbuchenbach, got up from his bed of torment even before the sleepless night was over and tiptoed through the yard to the barn. There he took the milking stool and sat down in the darkest corner. He wiped the sweat from his forehead. Ever since they had reported the names of the escapees on the radio yesterday, the men, women, and children of the village had been trying to get hold of him. Is the fellow's face really green? they asked. Did he really have the gout? Had he really shrivelled up?

Buchenbach was situated up the Main River, a couple of hours' walking distance from Wertheim, but also some distance from both the highway and the river, as if it wished to withdraw from all traffic. In the past it had consisted of two villages, Oberbuchenbach and Unterbuchenbach; they bordered on a common road that was crossed in the exact middle by a path that led into the fields on either side. The previous year this crossroad had been turned into a village square shared by both villages. Here, in the presence of assorted dignitaries and authorities and with all sorts of festive presentations and speeches, they had planted a Hitler oak. And thus Ober- und Unterbuchenbach were combined through various administrative reforms and the consolidation of arable land.

When an earthquake destroys a flourishing town, a few rotten walls, already in bad shape, will always collapse anyway. Since the same ruthless fist that had suppressed justice had also suppressed a few useless old customs, the sons of old Wurz and their SA comrades felt emboldened and rebellious towards all those farmers who had opposed the consolidation of the villages.

Wurz, sitting on his milking stool, wrung his hands till the joints cracked. The cows remained calm and unmoved since it wasn't milking time and their udders were not yet distended. Every few moments he would slump and then pull himself upright only to slump down again. He thought: The fellow could slip in here and ambush me. The man he was so terribly afraid of was Aldinger, the old farmer George and his comrades in Westhofen had considered not quite right in the head any more.

The oldest of Wurz's sons had once been as good as engaged to Aldinger's youngest daughter. They were just going to wait a few more years before getting married. The fields of the two clans were adjoining, as were the two little vineyards on the other side of the Main that could be used for something else later, when it no longer paid to grow grapes. In those days Aldinger was the mayor of Unterbuchenbach. Then, in 1930, his daughter fell in love with a fellow who worked on the Wertheim road-construction projects. Aldinger gave his approval to the couple. The marriage had its advantages, one of which was that the fellow had a steady income. The couple moved to the city. In February '33, the son-in-law made a brief appearance in the village without anyone giving it much thought. Like many workers in small towns whose political orientation was only too well known, he preferred staying in the country with relatives during that early period of arrests and persecutions. He had already left when Wurz, on the advice of his sons, told the state police about the fellow's visit to the village. Meanwhile, since the merger of the villages was imminent, Aldinger had gathered together a group of people who felt that if Aldinger could not retain his post as mayor, then Wurz should not stay in office either. Instead a third party should be appointed to head the combined communities. The group's resolve was strengthened by the priest who lived and preached in Unterbuchenbach, since the church and parsonage had been built there.

Now they were actually searching for the son-in-law since he had for many years collected funds for his union group, as well as a small workers' newspaper. No Buchenbach residents, even though there was a great deal of prejudice in the village against outsiders, had ever noticed anything unusual about this quiet man who helped the Aldingers at harvest time in exchange for bread and sausage for his family of five. It was just that he had had arguments at the inn with Wurz's sons, who were already at that time favouring the SA. This is what led them later on to give the advice to their father.

Wurz, having acted on his sons' advice, was taken aback at the quick results. Aldinger had actually been picked up. Wurz had only wanted to get Aldinger out of the way until he himself was officially in office. He would have enjoyed gloating over Aldinger's frustration. But it didn't work out quite that way. For some inexplicable reason, Aldinger had not come back. In the first months Wurz had a hard time of it. The people of Unterbuchenbach had avoided him, had managed to make every one of his official acts miserable for him, even his attendance at church. But his sons and their friends consoled him: The 'new' men, the Führer, as well as Wurz, they said, had to persevere in performing their duties in spite of the difficulties and hostility they faced at the outset.

It is a joy to see Buchenbach from an aeroplane: with its church steeple and small fields and forests, all neat and tidy. But driving through, you get a different picture, yet only if you have the time and inclination to look closely. True, all the streets and roads are very clean, and the school has been freshly painted, but why does that cow have to pull a wagon even though she's pregnant? Why is that child who has filled her apron with grass looking around in fear? And, of course, if you're driving through or looking down from an aeroplane, you can't see farmer Wurz sitting on his milking stool in the dark barn. You can't see that there aren't more than four cows in any of the barns, that there are only two horses in the combined villages. And neither driving through nor flying over can you see that one of the horses belongs to one of Wurz's sons and the other came into the possession of its owner about five years ago in a rather dubious way after a fire insurance claim payment. (A request was presented recently at a meeting of the farm community council that the trial be reopened.) This quiet, clean village is poor; it's as miserably poor as a village can be.

They said at first that Hitler would never be able to change the geography. He can't move us any closer to the vineyard, they said. And Alois Wurz would never lend us his horse to pull our machines and carts. Buying a thresher for the village on the instalment plan? That wasn't a new idea; they'd been planning to do that anyway.

A harvest festival? Hadn't there always been carousels and stalls every autumn? But when the young people came back from Wertheim Monday evening, they said there had never been anything like it. Had anyone ever in all their lives seen three thousand farmers assembled in one place? Seen such fireworks? Heard such music? And who was it in the end who was allowed to present the bouquet of flowers to the man representing the leader of the Reich Farmers? It wasn't Alois Wurz's Agathe; it was little Hanni Schultz III from Unterbuchenbach who didn't have a penny to her name.

The village couldn't be moved closer to the city, and they still didn't have a regular market. But the city could come out to the village: every week a truck arrived with a movie reel. And on the screen in the school they saw the Führer in Berlin, and they saw the whole world – China and Japan, Italy and Spain.

Wurz, sitting on his stool in the barn, thought: Aldinger was done for anyway. Where had he been staying at the end? Nobody thought about him any more. They'd forgotten about him.

What most perplexed the people in Buchenbach was the affair with the domain, the estate. It had always been an estate. Now they were putting up a sort of model village there. Thirty families from all the villages in the area were to be housed there, primarily farmers who also had knowledge of some trade or handicraft and who had many children. They had brought in a blacksmith from Berblingen, and a shoemaker from Weilerbach. And they had selected one family from each of the many different villages round about and settled them there. Next year they would bring in more people to be settled there. Farmers in all the villages were hoping they'd be chosen. It was like a big lottery. Everybody knew at least one family from a neighbouring village who'd been picked. Gradually some people who had been against Wurz earlier because of the Aldinger affair were beginning to realise that Wurz had been backing the right horse back then when he had allowed his sons to join the SA. If you wanted to have a chance of being picked for this estate village, if you wanted to have even the slightest hope of going to the estate village, you had to hide your dislike of or opposition to Wurz, for all the files of the villagers passed through his hands. Indeed, you couldn't let yourself be seen visiting the Aldingers too often. And so, bit by bit, Aldinger's family became more isolated. People stopped asking about them. Maybe he was already dead. Aldinger's wife always wore black and went to church a lot, something she'd always been inclined to do anyway. His sons never went to the tavern at the inn.

Then yesterday morning, when the news about the escape was first announced on the radio, something changed. Nobody wanted to be in Wurz's shoes any more. Aldinger had been a strong man, and he'd get himself a gun if he ever came back to the village. What Wurz had done, bearing false witness against your neighbour, was wrong. Because of him the whole village was now surrounded by guards.

The SA storm troop to which Wurz's sons belonged was guarding the Wurz farm. But all the guards wouldn't be able to help him. Aldinger knew the area, and he'd turn up unexpectedly. And without warning Wurz would get his bullet, and none of it would surprise the villagers. The guards wouldn't be able to prevent it. Someday he'd have to go to the other side of the Main. Or into the woods... someday.

Wurz started. Someone was coming. It was his oldest daughter-in-law, Alois's wife; he could tell by the clatter of the milk pails.

'What are you doing here?' she said. 'Mother is looking for you.' She watched him through the barn door as he stole across the farmyard as if *he* were the intruder. Ever since she'd married into the family, Wurz had always ordered her around; now it was his turn; he deserved this.

II

Even though Belloni's file, as far as Westhofen was concerned, had been closed by his death, there were still a few open files on him that concerned other departments. His files weren't dust covered and decaying. It was only Belloni who was decaying; the files on him had remained fresh. Who had helped him? Who had spoken with him? Who were these people? They must still be living here in the city. As early as Wednesday night they got Mrs Marelli's name by asking around in places frequented by performers. And the night wasn't yet over. In fact, Wurz, the mayor of Buchenbach, was still sitting on his milking stool when the secret police went up to Mrs Marelli's flat. She wasn't in bed but was sitting by the lamp sewing metal sequins on a little skirt that belonged to a woman who had appeared on stage at the Schumann Theatre that evening and wanted to leave on the early-morning train to get to her Thursday engagement. When they arrived and informed Mrs Marelli that she had to come with them at once for questioning on an urgent matter, she was dismayed, but only because she had promised the dancer that she would have her skirt ready by seven o'clock. She felt no apprehension about the questioning itself. She'd already experienced quite a few of them. Besides, an SA or SS uniform left her as cold as the flash of a secret policeman's badge of identity. Either because she was one of those few without a guilty conscience, or as a result of professional experience, she'd learned that outward appearances and a change in costume can produce amazing effects. She put the little bag of metal sequins and her sewing things next to the half-finished skirt, wrote a note, and hung the little package on the handle of the outer door. Then she calmly went off with the two secret police officers. She did not ask them any questions about where they were going, since her thoughts were still on the skirt hanging on the door handle. But she was surprised when they stopped at a hospital.

'Do you know this man?' one of the two officers asked. She drew back the sheet. Belloni's regular, almost beautiful features were only slightly disfigured; you might say they were blurry. The officers were expecting the customary eruption of simulated or genuine emotion that the living think they owe the dead on such occasions. But the woman only uttered a soft 'Oh!' Much as if she were saying, What a shame!

'So, you recognise him?' the officer said.

'Of course,' the woman said. 'It's little Belloni!'

'When was the last time you spoke with this man?'

'Yesterday – no, the day before yesterday, in the morning,' she said. 'I was surprised because he'd come so early in the morning. I still had to sew a few more stitches on his jacket. He was just coming through . . .'

Involuntarily, she turned to look for the jacket. The officers were watching her, and they nodded to each other. They both felt the woman was probably being honest, although they couldn't be absolutely certain. The officers waited calmly until she slowly, bit by bit, finished what she was saying. She kept adding a phrase here, a question there. 'Did it happen during a rehearsal? Did they rehearse here? Did he do another performance here? I thought they intended to leave for Cologne on the midday train.'

The officers said nothing.

'He told me,' the woman continued, 'that he had an engagement in Cologne. And I asked him whether he was in tip-top shape again. How did this happen?'

'Mrs Marelli,' one of the officers shouted at her. The woman looked up in surprise, but not in fear. 'Mrs Marelli,' the police officer repeated, speaking with the rough, unnatural seriousness that criminal police use to impart such information since only its effect and not its content is important to them. 'Belloni did not lose his life during a professional performance; the accident happened as he was escaping.'

'Escaping? Escaping from what?'

'Escaping from Westhofen concentration camp, Mrs Marelli.'

'What? When? – He was in a concentration camp two years ago. Wasn't he released a long time ago?'

'He was still in the camp. He escaped. You say you didn't know?'

'No,' was all she said, but in a tone of voice that convinced the officers that she hadn't known anything about this business.

'Yes, he was escaping. He lied to you yesterday.'

'Oh, the poor man,' the woman said.

'Poor?'

'Well, he wasn't rich, was he?' Mrs Marelli said.

'Don't talk nonsense!' the officer said.

The woman frowned.

'Come now, just sit down. Wait, we'll have them bring you some coffee. You haven't had anything to eat yet.'

'That doesn't matter,' she said with quiet dignity. 'I can wait until I'm back home.'

The officer said, 'Please tell us now exactly all the circumstances surrounding Belloni's visit to you. When he got there, what he wanted from you. Everything he said to you, every word. Wait, before you say anything further: Belloni is dead, but that doesn't keep you from falling under suspicion. It all depends on you.'

'Young man,' the woman said, 'you probably have no idea how old I am. My hair is dyed. I'm sixty-five. I've worked hard all my life, although many people don't know anything about my profession and have a mistaken idea about our work. I work very hard, even at my age. What are you threatening me with?'

'With prison,' the man said.

Mrs Marelli's eyes opened wide.

'Your little friend whom you might have helped in his escape has quite a record, you see. If he hadn't broken his neck himself, then . . . probably . . .' He made a gesture with the palm of his hand in the air.

Mrs Marinelli started. It seemed that something had just occurred to her. Then, with an expression indicating she thought that with all their talking they had forgotten the most important thing, she went over to where Belloni was lying and pulled the sheet back up over the dead man's face. You could tell that this wasn't the first time she was performing this service for someone.

But then her knees gave way; she sat down and said calmly, 'If you don't mind, I'll have some coffee after all.'

The officers were getting impatient because, for them, every second counted. They took up positions on either side of her chair and alternately fired their questions at her.

'Just exactly when did he arrive here? How was he dressed? Why did he come? What did he want? How did he ask for it, what were the words he used? How did he pay you? Do you still have the bill you gave him change for?'

Yes, she even had it with her in her handbag. They wrote down the number of the bill; they counted the money she'd given him back in change and compared it to the amount of money they'd found on the dead man. Quite a bit was missing. Did Belloni buy something before his excursion over the rooftops?

'No,' the woman replied, 'he had left some cash with me; he owed it to somebody.'

'Did you spend it already?'

'Do you think that I would steal the money of a dead man?' Mrs Marelli asked.

'Did someone pick it up?'

'Pick it up?' she asked, no longer so sure of herself, for she realised that she had said a bit more than she'd intended to.

The officers stopped. 'Thank you, Mrs Marelli. We'll take you home by car now. And we'll make use of the opportunity to have a look around your place.'

Overkamp didn't know whether to whistle or puff when the report came in to Westhofen that the sweater the escaped prisoner George Heisler had got from a riverman in exchange for the corduroy jacket had been found in Mrs Marelli's flat. They might already have recaptured Heisler by now if they hadn't believed the garden apprentice, that stupid boy. Not able to recognise his own jacket! Was that possible? Was something not right there? What? So Heisler had gone back to his home town after all. The question was, did he plan to hide there until he could find a safe way to get out of the country? Or maybe he was already up and gone in the new clothes and maybe even with new funds. The search was intensified. All roads that led out of the city, all crossroads, train stations, bridges, and ferries were now being as keenly monitored as if war had broken out. The sum of five thousand marks was offered on the latest Wanted posters for information leading to the capture of each of the escapees.

As George had anticipated that night, his home town, along with all the people who had ever had any connection to his life, the community that supports and surrounds every person – his blood relatives, lovers, teachers, bosses, and friends – had been turned into a network of living traps. With every hour of police activity, the net around him was tightening and becoming more intricate.

'This little tree has been growing there just for Heisler,' Fahrenberg said. 'If the horizontal plank's set a little lower, he'll have to stoop. My inner voice tells me he'll be resting up there from all his exertions this weekend.'

'Aha, your inner voice,' Overkamp echoed. He looked at Fahrenberg the way he looked at people professionally. The man was pretty much done for.

Fahrenberg had married of necessity during the war when he was still very young. His somewhat older wife and two almost grown daughters lived with his parents in the house on the market square, the same house in which the plumbing supply shop was located. It was expected that he would one day join the business, for his older brother, a plumber, had been killed in the war. The plan had been that he, Fahrenberg, would study law. But the war, the generally unsettled times had prevented him from doing well by mere hard work in a subject that his mind couldn't easily master. Rather than helping his old father laying pipe in Seeligenstadt, he wanted to build up a new Germany, to win over little towns with his SA storm troopers, especially his home town, where he had earlier been considered a ne'er-do-well. He wanted to go around shooting off his gun in the workers' districts and beating up Jews. Then he was going to refute all his father's gloomy prophecies and the neighbours' lies by coming back home on leave with epaulettes on his shoulders, money in his pocket, with followers, and power.

Of all the spectres that had been haunting Fahrenberg the last three nights, the spookiest was a Fahrenberg double wearing a plumber's blue overalls blowing out a clogged pipe. His eyes were smarting from lack of sleep. The latest report about the discovery of the sweater seemed to be an answer to all his night-time prayers to the powers-that-be to stand by him in his time of need, that the escapees be found and brought back to the camp, and not to visit upon him the worst of all punishments: the loss of power.

Right now the most important thing of all for me is to eat as much as possible, George thought; otherwise I won't even manage the next hundred steps. Wasn't there an automat a few minutes from here? Where the tram stop was. He felt a pain in his chest. It was almost as if he'd been stung, were falling over, and everything had turned black before his eyes. That had happened to him a couple of times before in the camp after some very rough days. Afterwards he'd been disappointed because it went away, as if the sharp stinger hadn't got embedded but rather had been pulled all the way through. Now he was angry. He had imagined his demise somewhat differently, had wanted to fight it, shouting his defiance at his pursuers.

What was the use of it all? he wondered. Then he was up and walking once more. He shook out his coat; it was damp and wrinkled. He crossed the Upper Main section of the city. Wouldn't that be a great joke on them, if he had been lying dead behind the fence all the time they were searching for him all over the city.

How young the city suddenly seemed, so quiet and clean. It emerged from the fog, dappled with the softest light, and not only the trees and lawns, but also the bridges and houses, even the pavements were morning fresh. He concluded, coolly and clearly, that getting out of the camp had been worthwhile, no matter how it would end. Maybe Wallau has already got out of the country, he thought; Belloni must have for sure. He seems to have had connections here. What was it I did wrong to have got stuck here? The outer streets were still empty. Behind the theatre, life was already beginning, as if the new day were spreading outward from the inner city. When George entered the automat and smelled the coffee and soup and saw the bread and bowls of food displayed behind the glass, hunger made him forget his fears and hopes. He changed one of Belloni's marks at the cashier's. The sandwich turned towards the opening with agonising slowness. Waiting for the cup to fill under the thin stream of coffee was no doubt easier for people who had lots of time to wait.

The place was pretty full. Two young fellows wearing gas company caps had taken their cups and plates to a table where their tool bags were lying. They ate and talked; then one of them suddenly stopped mid-sentence. At first his friend looked at him in surprise, but then he turned round to find out what his companion had been looking at.

Meanwhile, George had eaten his fill. He'd left the automat without looking to the right or left. In the process he'd brushed against the fellow who had just a moment before started at the sight of him.

'Do you know him?' the other fellow asked his companion.

'Fritz,' the first one said, 'you know him too. At least you used to know him.'

The other one looked at him questioningly.

'I'm sure that was George,' the first one went on, quite beside himself. 'Yes, George Heisler, the one who escaped.'

'God, you could have earned yourself some money!' the other one said with a half smile and a sideways glance.

'Could I really have done something like that? Could *you*?'

They suddenly looked directly into each other's eyes with the terrible look of deaf-and-dumb people or of very smart animals, creatures whose intelligence is imprisoned during their lifetimes and remains incommunicable. Then there was a flash in the eyes of the second one, and he said, 'No, I couldn't have done it either.'

They packed up their bags. They used to be good friends, these two; then came the years during which they no longer talked about anything meaningful with each other for fear of giving themselves away, in case the other had changed. Now it turned out that they were both still the same; neither one had changed. They left the automat, friends again.

III

Elli had been under surveillance day and night ever since her release; so, if her former husband, in the event he was still in the city, tried to get in touch with his old family, she would be leading him to his doom. The evening before, she'd gone to the movies, and there wasn't a moment when she hadn't been watched. Her front door was under surveillance all through the night. The net they'd thrown over her pretty head couldn't have been tighter. But even the tightest net, so they say, consists mainly of holes. They may have observed Elli as she engaged in conversation during the intermission with the man sitting next to her, but she had met half a dozen acquaintances on her way to and in the movie itself. In the end, one of them had even waited for her at the exit, to walk her home. It turned out he was harmless, one of the innkeeper's sons.

The Marnets were surprised when Franz offered, early that morning, to drive his cousin and aunt along with the baskets of apples to the market hall before he started his shift. This was quite a change from his habitual behaviour recently.

Franz was already busy loading the baskets when they came down. 'You have time for some coffee,' Augusta said, mollified.

The moon and stars were still in the sky as they were driving down the hill in their rattling truck.

Franz had been racking his brains the entire night in his attic room, which still smelled of apples although they'd all been packed the day before. If I were in George's shoes, if he were actually here, to whom could I turn for help? Just as the police had spread an ever-tightening net over the city using all their files, card indexes, all the records and knowledge of the escapee's previous life, just so Franz had been spreading his own net, which became tighter from hour to hour because of all the people emerging from his memory, people with whom George had once been connected in some way. Some of them had never left their names or any trace on any report or form or any other official record. It required knowledge of a different kind to dig them up. And, of course, there were some whom the police knew about too.

I hope he doesn't go to Brand, Franz thought. Supposedly he worked here four years ago. And not to Schumacher either. That guy might even report him. —So who else was there? The fat cashier whom he'd seen George sitting on a bench with after the affair with Elli was over? Stegreif, the teacher he used to visit occasionally? Little Roeder, whom he'd liked, and who had been his friend in school and on the football pitch. One of his brothers? – They were unknown quantities, and besides they were certainly being watched by the police.

The Marnets sold their produce at a street market in Hoechst at irregular intervals. In the spring, when there was usually only green-house produce on sale, they would bring their vegetables to be sold in the large market hall in Frankfurt, and in the autumn, they took the better varieties of their apples there. They were well enough off that they didn't have to find takers for every last thing. Their motto was 'take care of your own family first'. If they didn't have enough cash one year, one of the children could earn some additional money working at the factory.

Augusta, who was quite strong, helped Franz unload. Then Mrs Marnet set up her wares. Holding a little knife in one hand and a cut-up apple in the other as a tasting sample, she waited for the expected head buyer.

If Elli really does come, Franz thought, it would have to be now. A little while before he'd caught sight of a shoulder, a hat, a part of someone that could have turned out to be Elli if only the person it belonged to had decided to approach him. Over there he saw, or thought he saw, her face, small and pale with weariness. It disappeared again immediately behind a pyramid of baskets. He was afraid he'd been mistaken, then it suddenly came nearer, as if hesitantly fulfilling his deepest wish.

She acknowledged him with her eyebrows only. He marvelled at how quickly she had taken his hint, how cleverly she pretended to be merely buying some apples. As if she didn't know that Franz was with the Marnets, she stubbornly turned her back on him. Thoughtfully she tasted a slice of apple. She bargained down the price with Mrs Marnet for the pile of apples that would be left after the expected wholesaler's order was filled. Like all good deceptions this pretended transaction succeeded because Elli was acting it out with all her heart: she had really liked the sample of apple she'd tasted, and she didn't want to be fleeced in her purchase. There was no way she could have dissembled better, even if she had known how closely she was being watched.

In place of the young man with the moustache, whom Elli might already have noticed, there was now a fat female who looked like a nurse or needlework teacher. But the man with the moustache was still on duty, still a member of the surveillance team. Only now he was stationed in the pastry shop. On the way over Elli had been on the lookout for anyone following her. She thought that there would be someone tailing her and that it would probably be a man. But so far she hadn't noticed anyone except the nice, roly-poly woman, and pretty soon she was gone too because at a previously agreed-upon spot she changed places, handing Elli over to an approaching agent. But everything was still going smoothly; no one had so far paid any attention to Franz. For Elli proceeded so calmly with her apple buying that it couldn't possibly be concealing anything. She didn't speak to Franz at all. The few words Franz spoke were directed to Mrs Marnet. 'We can store the baskets at the Behrends'; I'll take them up there after I'm finished at work. I have to come back here anyway.'

Augusta had her own ideas about his readiness to do this, but it never occurred to her that the buyer of the apples was the very girl who had drawn Franz into the city twice in one day. Of course she had already formed an opinion of Elli: thin as an asparagus stalk, a hat like a little mushroom – an asparagus stalk with a head of curls. What does she wear on Sundays if she walks around on a workday wearing a blouse like that! After Elli had left, she said to Franz, 'One advantage of being so skinny is that she doesn't need a lot of material for a skirt.'

Franz suppressed his feelings and said, 'Not every girl can have a behind like Sophie Mangold's.'

George was waiting by the theatre for the number 23. All he wanted was to get out of the city. He felt his throat tightening. Belloni's coat, in which he had felt safe yesterday, seemed burning hot this morning. Should he take it off? Stuff it under the bench? There's a village two hours on the other side of Eschersheim, he mused. We used to ride the trolley to the last stop, up the Eschersheim highway. What was the name of the village? That's where the old people lived with whom I once spent a summer holiday from school during the war; then later on I used to go back to visit them from time to time. What was their name? My God, what was the name of the village? Oh God, what was their name? I've forgotten everything. If only I knew the name of that village. That's where I'd like to go. I can rest up there. Old people like that, they don't know about any of this. You dear people, what was your name? I've got to catch my breath at your place. My God, their name has vanished.

He got on the 23 when it came. I have to go there, no matter what. But I've got to get off before the last stop. The terminals are always watched. He had picked up a newspaper someone left behind, folding it so as to hide his face. The headlines jumped out at him, and here and there a phrase, a picture.

The electrified barbed wire fences, the cordons and the machine guns hadn't succeeded in keeping news of the events occurring in the outside world from penetrating into Westhofen. The sort of people imprisoned in Westhofen knew as much about many remote happenings if not more than the people living in the many scattered villages of the countryside and in many city flats. By some law of nature, through some secret circuitry, this little bunch of chained, miserable human beings seemed to be connected with the hot spots of the world. And so, when George looked at the newspaper – the fourth morning of his flight happened to be during the week in October when they were fighting for Teruel in Spain, and Japanese troops were invading China – he thought briefly, without being very surprised: So that's what's happened. These were the headlines of the old stories that had tugged at his heart and shaken his soul. But now he was only concerned with the current moment. When he turned the page, his gaze fell on three pictures. The faces were painfully familiar. He quickly looked away. But the pictures remained before his eyes: Fuellgrabe, Aldinger, and himself. He folded up the newspaper until it was a small packet and put it in his pocket. He glanced briefly to his right and his left. An old man standing next to him looked at him, too closely he felt, and he abruptly jumped off the tram.

I'd better not get on again, he thought. I'd be shut inside a closed car. I'll walk the rest of the way. As he came to police headquarters, he put his hand to his chest, felt his heart miss a beat, but then it went back to beating quite regularly. He walked on at an even pace, without fear, without hope. What's the matter with my mind? I'm lost if I can't think of the name of that village, and what if I do think of it, then maybe I'll really be lost. Maybe the people there already know about everything and won't want to take any risks. He walked past the museum, through a small street market. He walked through Eschenheimer Gasse, past the *Frankfurter Zeitung* building. He walked all the way to the Eschenheim Tower, then he crossed the street. He was walking more quickly now because for some minutes he'd had a tingly feeling of danger all over his skin. One thought permeated his brain: I'm being watched. He wasn't afraid, but actually calmer, and relieved because his enemy was becoming visible. He felt a pair of eyes at the back of his neck constantly following him from the little traffic island at the foot of the tower; it was as if his skin were feeling things more keenly, even as his mind became more dull. Instead of following the tram tracks he walked towards the small park. Suddenly he stopped. Something forced him to turn round. A man stepped out from a group of people at the trolley stop in front of the tower. He walked over to George. They grinned at each other; shook hands. The man was Fuellgrabe – the fifth of the seven escapees. He looked as dapper as a window mannequin. How could Belloni's yellow coat compare with that? What was going on! Fuellgrabe had sworn he'd never go back to the city. The devil only knew why he hadn't stuck to that. He had always kept an escape door open. They were still standing there as if they couldn't finish with the process of greeting each other. Face to face, with bent elbows. Finally George said, 'Let's go into the park.'

They sat down on a sunny bench amidst the greenery. Fuellgrabe scraped in the soil with the tip of his shoe. His shoes were no less elegant than his suit. How quickly he'd managed to get all that, George mused.

Fuellgrabe said, 'Do you know where I was headed just now?'

'Well?'

'Mainzer Landstrasse!'

'Why?' George asked. He pulled his coat tight around him so that it wouldn't touch Fuellgrabe's. Was this really Fuellgrabe, he suddenly wondered.

Fuellgrabe did the same with his coat. Then he said, 'Have you forgotten what's on Mainzer Landstrasse?'

George said wearily, 'What's supposed to be there?'

'The Gestapo,' Fuellgrabe said.

George was silent. He was waiting for this strange apparition to vanish.

Fuellgrabe went on, 'George, do you have any idea what's happening in Westhofen? Did you know that they've caught all of them already, except for you and me and Aldinger!'

In front of them, their shadows melded in the bright sun. George said, 'How do you know?' He moved farther away from his companion so that there were now two cleanly separated shadows.

'Maybe you haven't seen a newspaper,' Fuellgrabe replied.

'Actually, yes, here . . .'

'Well, take a look,' Fuellgrabe said.

'Whom are they looking for?'

'You, me, and grandpa. He must have had a heart attack by now and be lying somewhere in a ditch. He can't have lasted long. So it's just the two of us left.' He quickly rubbed his head on George's shoulder. George closed his eyes. 'If there were another one they were looking for, there would have been a description of him. No, no, they've got all the others. They've got Wallau, Pelzer, and – what's his name – Belloni. I even heard the guy screaming.'

George almost said, 'I did too'; his mouth opened but nothing came out. What Fuellgrabe said was true, crazy but true. He cried out, 'No!'

'Shhh,' Fuellgrabe hissed.

'It's not true,' George said. 'It isn't possible. They can't have caught Wallau; he'd never let them capture him. Not Wallau.'

Fuellgrabe laughed. 'Well, then how is it that he was in Westhofen in the first place? Dear, dear George! We were all crazy, and Wallau was the craziest.' He added, 'And I've had enough.'

George said, 'Enough of what?'

'Of the craziness – for my part, I'm cured. I'm turning myself in.'

'Turning yourself in? Where?'

'I'm turning myself in!' Fuellgrabe said stubbornly. 'At Mainzer Landstrasse. I'm giving up, that's the sensible thing to do. I want to keep my head on my shoulders; I can't stand this foolish, crazy running around any more, and in the end you get caught anyway. We're no match for them.' He was speaking ever more calmly, putting one word after the other in a simple monotone. 'It's the only way out. You'll never get across the border; it's impossible. The whole world is against you. It's a miracle that the two of us are still free. We should end the miracle voluntarily before they catch us, because once they do, there'll be no more miracles. Then it'll be: Good night! You can imagine what Fahrenberg is doing with the ones who got caught. Do you remember Zillich? Do you remember Bunsen? Do you remember the Dance Ground?'

George began to feel a horror that he couldn't fight; he was paralysed. Fuellgrabe's face was clean-shaven. His thin hair was combed and still smelled of the barbershop. Was this really Fuellgrabe?

Fuellgrabe went on, 'You still remember, don't you, what they did with Koerber, who, they said, was planning to escape? And he wasn't planning to at all. *We* were the ones.'

George began to tremble. Fuellgrabe looked at him for a moment, then he continued. 'Believe me, George, I'm going there this instant. I'm sure it's the best thing to do. And you'll come along. I was just on my way there. It was God himself who brought us together. No doubt about it!' His voice faded out. He nodded twice. 'No doubt about it!' he said again, and nodded once more.

Suddenly George recoiled. 'You're crazy,' he said.

'We'll see which one of us is the crazy one!' Fuellgrabe said in that cool, deliberate way that had garnered him a reputation as an agreeable, sensible fellow who never raised his voice. 'Good heavens, man! Use what little brains you have. Look around you. If you don't come along with me, my friend, you'll crack up in no time and end up dead. For sure! Come on!'

'You're completely mad,' George said. 'They'll die laughing when you show up there. What in the world are you thinking!'

'Laugh? Let them laugh. Just so long as they let me live. Look around you, my friend. You have no other choice. If they don't catch you today, they will tomorrow, and nobody will care. My boy, this world has changed quite a bit. Nobody cares about us any more. Come along with me. It's the very smartest thing to do. It's the only way to save ourselves. Come on, George.'

'You're quite insane.'

They'd been sitting on the bench up to this point, just the two of them. But now a woman wearing a nurse's cap sat down at the unoccupied end. She was gently rocking a perambulator with one practised hand. It was an impressive perambulator full of pillows and lace and light blue ribbons and a tiny sleeping child who was obviously not yet fast asleep. She set the pram diagonally against the sun and took out her sewing kit. She cast a brief look at the two men. She was neither old nor young, neither beautiful nor ugly. Fuellgrabe returned her look, not just with his eyes, but with a crooked smile, a terrible, forced contortion of his face. George saw it. He started to feel queasy.

'Come!' Fuellgrabe said, getting up.

George grabbed his arm, but Fuellgrabe broke free with a move more powerful than George's grip, so that his arm hit George in the face. He leaned down to George and said, 'A man who won't accept advice can't be helped. Good-bye, George.'

'No, hold on a moment,' George said.

Fuellgrabe actually did sit back down.

George said, 'Please don't do it. It's madness! Voluntarily walking into the trap! They'll break you. They've never shown any pity. Nothing makes any impression on them. Oh, Fuellgrabe, don't do it. Don't do it!'

Having moved very close to George, Fuellgrabe said in a changed, saddened tone of voice, 'Dear, dear George, come with me! You were always a decent human being. Come with me. It's horrible going there all by myself.'

George looked at the mouth from which these words were coming, at the teeth that seemed too large because of the gaps between them – the teeth of a skull. Fuellgrabe's days were certainly numbered. Probably even his hours. He's already insane, George thought. He very much wished Fuellgrabe would go quickly and leave him behind, alone and healthy. In the same instant Fuellgrabe had probably been thinking the same about George. He looked at George in dismay, as if he realised now for the first time with whom he was actually dealing. He got up and left, disappearing on the other side of the bushes so quickly that George had the feeling he had dreamed the entire encounter.

Then he was overcome by an attack of fear, as sudden and wild as during that first hour when he was stuck in the willow thicket at the perimeter of the camp. A cold fever convulsed his body and soul with a couple of quick tremors. An attack that lasted three minutes, the kind that turns one's hair grey. But back then he was wearing prison clothes and the sirens were howling. This was worse. Death was just as close, but not behind him; it was everywhere. It was inescapable; he felt death's physical presence – as if death itself were something alive. Like in the old pictures, a creature that can hide behind a bed of asters or behind a pram and can come out and touch you.

Then suddenly the attack was over. He wiped the sweat off his brow; it was as if he'd survived a battle. And he had, even though he only thought he had suffered. What had been the matter with him?

What was I just told? Can it be true that they've got you, Wallau? What are they doing to you?

Calm down, George. Do you think you'd be better off somewhere else?

Would you have gone to Spain if you could have? Do you think they'd go easy on us there? Do you think getting caught on barbed wire or being shot in the stomach would be any better?

And this city that is afraid to shelter you today – once the grenades rain down from the sky, it won't have anything more to fear.

But Wallau, I'm all alone here. In Spain you're never this alone, not even in Westhofen. Nobody is as alone as I am here.

Stay calm, George. You have a lot of good company. A little scattered at the moment; that doesn't matter. Heaps of company – dead and living.

On the other side of the big bed of asters, behind the lawn, behind the brown and green bushes, maybe on a playground or in a garden, he could indistinctly hear a swing going back and forth. George thought, I have to start from the beginning again, think it all through. First of all, I really have to get out of the city. What use is it to me? That village – aha, it's called Botzenbach. Those people, oh, yes, Schmitthammer was their name. Are they safe? Safe – no way. And even if they were, what then? How am I going to go on from there? Across the border without any help? I could be picked up a thousand times over. My cash is almost gone. I'm too weak now to be shifting for myself from one coincidence to another. Here in the city at least I know some people. All right, one girl refused to take me in. What does that mean after all? There must be others. My family, my mother, my brother? Impossible – all of them under surveillance. Elli, who came to see me once? Impossible – they're sure to be watching her. Werner, who was with me in the camp? Also being watched. The Reverend Seitz, who, they said, helped Werner when he got out? Impossible, almost sure to be watched. Who else of my friends is left?

In the time before he was imprisoned, in his life before death, there had been people on whom one could depend completely. Franz was one of them – but Franz was far away, he reckoned. But he thought about him for another moment. Wasting the few minutes he now had in which to think things over. It was a consolation to tell yourself that somewhere there was the sort of man he needed now. If such a man existed, then his being alone here was only an accident. Yes, Franz would have been the right man. But the others? He considered them, one by one. It was surprisingly easy; astonishingly rapid the first selection, as if the danger in which he now found himself were a kind of catalyst, a chemical means that could reveal the secret composition of the stuff a man is made of. A couple of dozen people went through his head who were probably just then working at their jobs or picking at their food – with no idea of the terrible scale on which they were being weighed at that moment. A Last Judgement on a bright autumn morning without trumpet blasts. In the end George had picked four.

He firmly believed that any of these four would put him up, would shelter him. But how to get to them? Suddenly, at that very instant, a mental image came to him of guards being posted outside each of their four doors. I can't go there myself, he thought. Someone has to go there for me. Someone who would never come under suspicion, who has no connection with me and yet would do anything for me. He began again to review the possibilities. Again he felt as if he were all alone, as if he had no parents, hadn't grown up with brothers, as if he had never played with other boys, or fought with his friends. Swarms of faces, old and young, flew through his head. Exhausted, he peered into this crowd that he had conjured, half of them followers, half of them hounds. Suddenly he saw a face dotted all over with freckles, neither old nor young; for sitting on a classroom bench Paul Roeder had really looked like a little man, and when he got married he'd looked like a boy at his confirmation. When they were twelve years old, they'd got their first football partly through trickery, partly in exchange for work. They'd been inseparable, until ... until other ideas, friendships of a different nature had taken over George's life. The entire year he'd lived together with Franz he couldn't get rid of his feelings of guilt about little Paul Roeder. He was never able to explain to Franz why he felt so ashamed for being able to understand ideas that Roeder would never have understood. Sometimes he felt as if he wanted to shrink and to unlearn everything so he could return to his little classmate's level. A confused tangle of memories that quickly turned into one smooth thread and a decision. I'll go to Bockenheim at four o'clock. I'll look up the Roeders.

IV

It was noon now. Work was easier for Ernst the shepherd in this new pasture on this side of the highway. The sheep stayed closer together. On the other hand, though, he couldn't see as far into the distance. Messer's fields ran along the highway at their lower boundaries. On the other side of the highway, the farm buildings of the Mangolds and the Marnets blocked Ernst's view. Higher up, the fields bordered on a long tongue of beech woods. This wooded stretch belonged to Messer too. It was separated from the rest of the large forest by a wire fence. Behind the tongue of wooded land there was more land that also belonged to Messer.

The smell of sauerbraten was coming from the Messers' kitchen. Eugenia herself had brought a little pot of it to him in the field. Ernst lifted the cover and the two of them, Ernst and Nelly, looked inside. 'Isn't it strange,' the shepherd said to his bitch, 'that pea soup should smell like sauerbraten?' Eugenia turned round again. She was half and half: half the Messers' cousin and half their housekeeper. 'At our house the leftovers are eaten too, my friend.'

'But Nelly and I, we don't eat slop from a trough,' Ernst said.

The woman looked at him briefly and laughed. 'Hey, don't get on my bad side, Ernst,' she said. 'Here we have two courses at a meal. When you've finished this, bring your plate to the kitchen window.' She walked off quickly. Though she could almost be considered fat and was no longer very young, she had a nice, easy walk. Ernst had heard people say that her hair used to be as black and shiny as the wings of a blackbird. She was the child of decent people; could even have married old Messer himself if she hadn't been cut out of it all when General Mangin of the Allied Commission had decided to bring two regiments up here in 1920. A grey-blue cloud winding up the road, portioned out among the valleys and villages, and in the hills, some here, some there. The sharp foreign music that cut through everything. A foreign soldier's jacket on a hook in the hall, a foreign smell in the stairwell, foreign wine poured by a foreign hand, foreign words of endearment, until all the foreignness became familiar and the old familiar things were no longer so familiar. Then, almost eight years later, when the grey-blue cloud was moving off down the road again, and the catchy foreign march music was no longer in the air but only a memory in the ear, Eugenia leaned far out of the Messers' attic window. This was where she had come to live when the woman of the house had died after giving birth to her fifth child. Eugenia's own parents – who'd thrown her out with her French child – were dead. The little occupation-army boy was going to school in Kronberg. The boy's father was long gone, drinking his aperitifs on Boulevard Sébastopol by now. Nobody mentioned any of this any more. People had got used to it. And Eugenia had also got used to it. Her face was paler but still beautiful. A dry sound had come from deep down in her chest when she realised that the greyish blue that she was staring at was not an occupation army but genuine fog. That was years ago already. Ernst thought that Eugenia had been an undeserved godsend for fat old Messer. I wonder if she made up that business with the two courses or only invented it on the spur of the moment, he mused.

Franz was so tired by this time that it felt as if the fan belt were whirring through his head. In spite of that, he wasn't making any mistakes, probably because, for the first time, he wasn't afraid of making one. All he was thinking of was whether later, in the course of the apple delivery, he'd have a chance to talk to Elli alone.

Thinking that he'd be seeing Elli again in a few hours, the very same Elli he'd been longing for all this time, he suddenly realised that his dreams might all come true. They weren't meeting to help

George, but for their own sakes. He, Franz, wasn't delivering apples so he could slip through a net of spies and informers; nothing threatened them, no one was in danger. Franz tried to imagine that he had just bought two baskets of apples for the first winter of their life together, the way hundreds of other people did. Was it impossible for them to have a normal life together? Or would this dark shadow always hover over everything?

Franz wondered for one moment, one single moment, whether such simple happiness wasn't worth more than everything else. Just a little ordinary happiness now at this moment, instead of the dreadful, relentless fight for the ultimate happiness of humanity in general, which by that time, he, Franz, would perhaps not even be part of any more. 'So now we can bake some apples in our oven,' he'd say. They'd have a wedding in November with pipes and flutes, and then they'd furnish their two little rooms out in the Griesheim development. In the mornings when he went to work, he'd know all day long that Elli would be home in the evening waiting for him. Aggravation? Wage deductions? Working like a slave? At home in the evening in his clean little rooms he'd be able to shed all that. When he would be standing here, as he was now, stamping out piece after piece, he would be constantly thinking of being with Elli in the evening. Hang out the flags? Swastika badge in the buttonhole? Give unto Hitler what is his? Never mind all that... Elli and he would have fun doing things together – making love and decorating the Christmas tree, the Sunday roast and the workday sandwiches, the small privileges of newlyweds, their little garden and the workers' excursions. They would have a son, they would be happy. Then, of course, they would have to put something aside and postpone the Kraft durch Freude* cruise until the following year. They would be content with the new wage scale. Clever what those in charge thought up – that total production would go up in spite of lower pay. Gradually the constant hustle at work would get a little much. Just don't grumble out loud, Elli would tell

*Kraft durch Freude, translated as 'Strength Through Joy,' was a Nazi-state operated leisure organisation, part of the German Labour Front. —*Trans.*

him. Don't get into any hassles, Franz – especially not just now. For by now they would be expecting their second child. But luckily, Franz would have been appointed foreman, and they would be able to pay back the money they'd had to borrow from Elli's father. If only Elli wouldn't be afraid that she'd get pregnant again. Franz said, As long as they don't turn out to be war babies. This time Elli cried. They would add and subtract, figuring back and forth, calculating all their expenses against all the compensations for people having lots of children. But even while he was doing all this figuring, Franz would be feeling a strange heaviness in his chest. He didn't know the cause. It was as if he were aware deep down that such calculations were unseemly, not allowed. Then Elli got some good advice, and this time the problem passed them by. Now they could reserve places on the cruise after all, since Elli's mother would take the older child and Elli's sister the younger one during the time they were gone. The sister would teach the little one to do the Hitler salute. Elli would still be quite pretty and young looking. All that day at work, Franz would keep thinking: If only she puts some delicious food on the table tonight, instead of another cobbled-together stew.

Then one day Franz arrived at the factory, and instead of Woodchip there had been a new boy sweeping up the scraps and dust. So Franz asked, 'Where's Woodchip?'

And one man said, 'Woodchip was arrested.'

'Woodchip arrested?' Franz asked. 'But why?'

'Because he spread rumours,' one of the punchers said.

'What kind of rumours?' Franz asked.

'About Westhofen. You know, some guys escaped from there on Monday.'

'What? From Westhofen?' Franz asked. 'Are there any people still alive there?'

Then one of the punchers, a tall, quiet man with sleepy-looking features to whom Franz had never paid much attention, said, 'Did you think that everybody gets killed there?'

Franz flinched; he stuttered, 'No, no – I'm just surprised that there are still some men in there.'

The puncher smiled vaguely and turned away.

If only I didn't have to go home tonight, Franz thought. If I could just talk with someone like that fellow. Franz suddenly remembered that he knew the puncher from before. Somewhere in the past he'd had something to do with this man. He knew him long before he met Elli. Before . . .

Franz started. Now he'd really made a mistake, ruined one of his pieces. But he couldn't blame the new boy, little Peppernut they all called him, praising him because after only three days he'd learned to sweep the dust out between their arms as well as Woodchip, who'd been doing it for a whole year before his arrest.

George, waiting on the platform for the number 3, wondered if it wouldn't have been better to go there on foot. To take the long way there, walking around the outer fringes of the city. Wasn't he more conspicuous this way? You mustn't brood about things you didn't do, Wallau had advised – it's a futile waste of energy. And don't suddenly jump off, trying this, trying that. Just act calm and sure of yourself.

What use is all this advice if it hasn't helped you? He had lost Wallau's voice, couldn't hear it any more in his head. He'd been able to recall the sound of it any time he wanted to, and now suddenly it was gone. And the noise of an entire city couldn't drown out what had been silenced. The tram had gone in a loop towards the outskirts of the city. Suddenly he couldn't believe that he was riding through this place, alive, in bright daylight. It seemed to go counter to all probability, counter to all calculations. Either he wasn't himself or— He felt an icy, cutting draught at his temples as if the number 3 had entered a different zone. He was sure he was being watched by now. Why should he, of all people, have run into Fuellgrabe just now? Probably they'd been leading Fuellgrabe on a leash. Fuellgrabe's look, his movements, his avowed intention – only a crazy man or one who's already being led on a leash behaves like that. Why didn't they grab me right then and there? Simple: because they wanted to wait and see where I was going. They wanted to see who'd take me in.

And at that point he tried to work out who his pursuer might be. The man with the little beard and glasses who looked like a teacher? The fellow in the blue mechanic's overalls? Or the old man carrying a carefully wrapped little tree maybe to plant in his little garden?

In the last few moments the music of a march had become distinct above the general noise of the city. It was approaching rapidly, getting louder, overpowering all other noises and all movement with its sharp rhythm. Windows opened and children came running out of their houses; suddenly the street was lined with people. The tram driver stepped on the brake.

The tarmac was vibrating. You could hear jubilant shouts from the end of the street. For the last few weeks the Sixty-Sixth Infantry Regiment had been quartered in their new barracks, and whenever they marched through a section of the city, they were given a fresh reception. And finally here they came: trumpeters and drummers, a drum major tossing up his stick, a little horse prancing. There they were! Finally. The people raised their arms to salute. The old man raised his arm, supporting his little tree with his knees. His eyebrows twitched in time to the march. His eyes glittered. Was his son among the marchers? This was a march that roiled up the people, made their spines tingle and their eyes glow. What magic was this, composed in equal parts of ancient memory and total forgetting? From the way they acted you might think that the last war these people had fought was the happiest of undertakings and had brought them only joy and prosperity. The women and girls smiled as if their sons and sweethearts were invulnerable.

How well the young fellows had learned to march in just those few weeks! Mothers, justifiably fearful for every pfennig and always asking, What's it for? willingly gave up their sons and parts of their sons as long as they kept on playing this march. Once the music had faded away, they'd ask softly, What for? What for? Then the driver would start up his motor again; the old man would see that a little branch on his tree had been bent, and he would grumble. The spy, his tail, if there really was one among these people, would come to with a start.

For George had climbed down from the tram platform. He was going to walk to Bockenheim. Paul lived at number 12 Brunnengasse. Neither the beatings nor the kicks had knocked that out of his head – he even remembered the name of Paul's wife: it was Liesel, née Enders.

He had walked off confidently and quickly during the last few minutes, and without once turning round. He stopped after a while to catch his breath in front of a shop window on a street that joined Brunnengasse. When he caught sight of himself in the mirror behind the displayed merchandise, he had to hold on to the crossbar. How pale was the face of that man just then reaching with one hand for the bar – and that strange yellowish coat dragging him down – and the stiff felt hat on his head!

Should I even go up to Roeder's place? he asked himself. What right do I have to assume that I've got rid of my tail, if I was actually being tailed? And Paul, why should he, of all people, put everything at risk for me? How come I was sitting on that bench a while ago?

V

On the fourth floor, left, Roeder's name had been delicately and precisely inscribed on a small piece of cardboard, inside a circle resembling a coat of arms. George leaned against the wall staring at the name as if it had light blue eyes and freckles, short arms and legs, common sense and a good heart. While he was devouring the little sign with his eyes, he realised that the loud unidentifiable noise he'd heard already downstairs was coming from this flat. He could hear a child's toy being rolled back and forth across the floor, a child calling out train stations and another one calling, 'All aboard,' and, accompanying that, the hum of a sewing machine. Above it all, the sound of a woman singing the Habanera from *Carmen*: 'Love is a gypsy child; he has never, ever, known the law,' in a voice so strong and powerful that George thought it was coming from the radio, until it unexpectedly broke on a high note.

Liesel Roeder had always been what you would call cheerful. The gulf that had suddenly sprung up to separate him from Roeder when he first moved in with Franz, this unintentional but fateful gulf, became evident to him only in the behaviour of Roeder's wife. Moving in with Franz had meant not only learning to accept certain ideas, and taking part in the struggle, it also meant behaving differently, dressing differently, hanging up different pictures, and considering different things beautiful. How could Paul stand his waddling Liesel; why did the Roeders have all those knickknacks standing around? Why had they been saving two years for a sofa? George had found the couple boring and had stopped going there. Until Franz started to bore him too, until the room he shared with him seemed too bare.

George, who was himself still very young back then, with a mind filled with a jumble of half-formed ideas and confused emotions, would frequently wrench himself loose from erstwhile friendships. This gave him a reputation for being unpredictable. At the time he had reckoned you could cancel one thing with another, that you could eliminate one feeling with an opposite feeling.

George had already put his thumb on the doorbell, still listening to the sounds coming from inside the flat. Not even in Westhofen had he felt such a longing to see someone. But abruptly he pulled his hand back. Could he really go in there, where they would probably accept him quite without suspicion? Might not one push on their doorbell scatter this family to the winds? Bring them prison, reform school, death?

In his head he felt a burning brightness. It was his exhaustion that had given him the idea to come here, he told himself. Hadn't he felt half an hour ago already that he was being followed? Did he really think that somebody like him could shake off his pursuers this easily?

He shrugged, and walked back down a couple of steps. Just then someone came up the stairs. George turned his face to the wall; he let the man – it was Paul Roeder – go past him. He dragged himself to the nearest stairwell window, leaned his elbow on it, and listened. But Roeder hadn't entered his flat; he, too, had stopped and was listening. Suddenly Roeder turned round and went back down the stairs. George went on down. Roeder leaned over the banister and called out, 'George!'

George didn't answer him, just kept on going. But in two jumps Roeder was behind him. Grabbing his arm, he said, 'George, is it you or isn't it?' He laughed and shook his head. 'Have you already been upstairs to our place? Didn't you recognise me just now? I was wondering if it was you. But you've changed . . .' He suddenly felt hurt. 'It took you three years before you thought of your friend Paul again. No, come on up with me.'

George hadn't said a word all this time; he followed Roeder up the stairs in silence. They stopped in front of the large stairwell window. Roeder looked George up and down. If he had any dark thoughts, his small face was too heavily freckled to reveal them. He said, 'You look green around the gills. Are you still the same George?'

George moved his dry lips. No sound came out.

'It *is* you, isn't it?' Roeder asked, utterly serious.

George had to laugh.

'Come on! It's really a miracle that I recognised you in the stairwell,' Roeder said.

'I've been ill for a while,' George said calmly. 'My hand hasn't healed yet.'

'What's the matter? Did you lose some fingers?'

'No. I was lucky.'

'Where did it happen? Have you been here all this time?'

'I was a driver in Kassel,' George said. Still speaking very calmly, he briefly described the place and circumstances as he knew them from the stories a fellow prisoner had told.

'Just wait till you see Liesel's face when she catches sight of you!' Roeder said.

Then he pressed the doorbell. George heard the high shrilling tone and then a storm of slamming doors and children's screams and Liesel's voice: 'Well, I'll be flabbergasted.'

Clouds whirled off flowered dresses and wallpaper with little pictures, and faces with thousands of freckles, and wide, surprised little eyes – then all was dark and still. The first thing George heard when he came to was Roeder's voice angrily ordering, 'Coffee, you hear, and none of your usual dishwater!' George sat up on the sofa. It took great effort to come back from his unconscious state where he'd felt so safe and to come back into the Roeders' kitchen. 'This keeps happening to me from time to time,' he explained. 'It was really nothing. Liesel shouldn't be bothering now with grinding coffee.'

He put his legs under the kitchen table, and put his bandaged hand on the oilcloth between the plates. Liesel Roeder had turned into a stout woman. She wouldn't have fit into a page's trousers any more. The warm, somewhat heavy gaze from her eyes rested briefly on George's face. She said, 'All right. The best thing for you now is to eat; we'll have coffee later.' She set the table and got dinner ready. Roeder seated his three oldest children around the table. 'Wait, I'll cut it up for you, George, or can you pick it up with your fork? We have "one-pot Sundays" every day here. Want some mustard? Salt? Eating well and drinking well keeps body and soul together.'

George said, 'What day is today?'

The Roeders laughed. 'Thursday.'

'You gave me your sausages, Liesel,' George said. It had taken as much willpower for him to adjust to this ordinary evening as it would have to adjust to the most extreme danger. While he was eating with his good hand and as the others were eating too, Liesel and Paul kept giving him brief looks. He realised that he was fond of them and they were still fond of him.

Suddenly he heard steps coming up the stairs – he listened.

'What are you listening for?' Paul asked him.

The footsteps continued on up the stairs. On the oilcloth next to his injured hand there was a circle where someone had once put down a very hot cup. George took his beer glass and pushed it like a stamp on to the discoloured spot.

'Well, whatever is coming will come.' Paul, who'd interpreted George's movements in his own way, opened a bottle of beer and poured. They ate their meal slowly to the end. Then Paul said, 'Are you living at home again with your parents?'

'Temporarily.'

'How about your wife, or have you completely separated?'

'From which wife?'

The Roeders laughed.

George shrugged.

'From Elli!'

George shrugged again. 'We're permanently separated.'

He pulled himself together and looked around him. At all those astonished little eyes. He said, 'You've accomplished quite a bit in the meantime.'

'Didn't you know that the German people are supposed to quadruple themselves?' Paul asked with laughing eyes. 'You probably don't listen when the Führer speaks.'

'Oh yes, I listen,' George said. 'But he didn't say that little Paul Roeder from Bockenheim has to do it all by himself.'

'It really isn't so hard to have children any more,' Liesel Roeder said.

'It never was.'

'Oh, George,' Liesel said, 'your spirits are returning.'

'No, it's true. We were five at home, and you?' Paul asked.

'Fritz, Ernst, me, and Heini – four,' George said.

'No one ever gave a hoot about us,' Liesel said. 'But now things are different.'

Paul said with a smile, 'Liesel got an official congratulatory letter.'

'I did indeed. Me!'

'Are you to be congratulated for your great achievement?'

'All joking aside, George, all the perks and benefits and allowances, seven pfennig per hour; it makes a difference. Being exempt from deductions from your wages, and a great big stack of the best-quality nappies!'

'As if the Nazi welfare had known that the old ones were all worn out by the dirty behinds of our three older kids.'

'Don't listen to him,' Liesel said. 'Believe me, Paul's eyes sparkled on our summer holiday last August, and he was as happy as when we were first married . . .'

'Where did you go?'

'To Thuringia, and we went to see the Wartburg and Martin Luther and the contest of the minnesingers and the Venusberg. That was a kind of reward too. Really, there's never been anything like it before.'

'Never,' George said. He thought: What a lot of lies. Never before. He said, 'And you, Paul? How do you feel about things? Are you satisfied?'

'Can't complain,' Paul said. 'Two hundred and ten a month, that's fifteen marks more than I made in my best year after the war, in '29, and then it was only for two months – but now – it's permanent.'

'You can see on the street that things are running at top capacity,' George said. His throat tightened and his heart ached.

Paul said, 'Oh well, what do you expect – it's the war.'

George said, 'Doesn't it give you an odd feeling?'

'What?'

'What you just said; you're manufacturing things that will kill thousands of people over there?'

Paul said, 'Oh well, one man's owl is another's nightingale. If you want to start bothering your head about that . . . Now this, Liesel, this is good coffee. George has to come here more often and pass out.'

George said, 'This is the best coffee I've had in three years.' He patted Liesel's hand. To himself he thought, I've got to get out of here, but where to . . . ?

Paul said, 'You always used to be one for worrying about things, George, my friend. So? You're done with that now. You're quieter. In the old days you would have told me all the things I should feel guilty about.' He laughed. 'You still remember, George, how you came to see me once, all upset? I was unemployed at the time. But I absolutely had to buy something from you, something from the Chinese. Me of all people! Of all things, a little book! And of all people, from the Chinese!

'And don't come to me now about the Spanish,' he said angrily, even though George hadn't said anything. 'Don't even mention them. They're done for, even without Paul Roeder. They defended themselves, and now, in spite of that, they're done for! My few percussion caps won't make any difference to them.'

George still said nothing.

'You always came to me with such crazy, far-fetched things.'

George said, 'But if you're making the caps, then that's not far-fetched at all.'

In the meantime Liesel had fed all the children and cleared the table. Now she told them, 'Say good night to your father. And say good night to George too.

'I'm going to put the children to bed now,' Liesel said. 'You don't need to put the light on yet for your conversation.'

George thought, I have no choice; do I have a choice? He said, quite casually, 'Listen, Paul, would you mind if I slept here overnight?'

Roeder looked at him in surprise. 'No, why should I mind?'

'I got into an argument back home, I want to let it blow over.'

'You're welcome to join our family,' Roeder said.

George put his head in his hands. Between his fingers he watched Roeder. He probably would have looked serious if his face hadn't been covered with so many jolly freckles.

Paul said, 'Are you still getting into arguments about things? What a lot of schemes you had back then! I asked you back then to leave me out of things. I couldn't abide all that useless stuff; I'd rather have my potato soup. And those Spaniards are all like you. I mean, the way you used to be, George. Now it seems you're taking things easier. And look at your Russia – they didn't accomplish anything either. At first it looked as if they'd succeed, and sometimes you even thought, Well, maybe, who knows? But now...'

'Now?' George said. He quickly covered his eyes.

In spite of that, Paul had caught a sharp glance from between two fingers. He faltered. 'Now, well... Oh, you know.'

'Know what?'

'How everything's in a mess over there.'

'What? Who?'

'I don't know; I can't remember all those tongue-twister names.'

Liesel came back. 'It's time you went to bed, Paul. Don't hold it against us, George, but...'

'George wants to spend the night here, Liesel. He got into an argument at home.'

'You're quite something!' Liesel said. 'What about?'

'It's a long story,' George said. 'I'll tell you tomorrow.'

'Yes, enough talk for one day. Otherwise Paul will be too worn out at work tomorrow.'

'I can imagine that they don't make things easy for him,' George said.

'I'd rather work a little harder and make a few more marks,' Paul said. 'I'd rather do overtime any day than air-raid drill.'

George said, 'And get older a little sooner.'

'With another war we'll be getting older quicker anyway. And it's not at all so great and wonderful that you'd want to have it last for ever, George. OK, Liesel, I'm coming.' He turned round and said, 'Only thing is, George. What are we going to cover you with?'

'Give me my coat, Paul.'

'What a funny coat that is. Put the pillow on top of your feet, and don't step on Liesel's roses.' Suddenly he asked, 'Just between the two of us, what were you arguing about at home – was it about a girl?'

'Ah, well,' George said, 'it was because of the little one, because of Heini. You know how attached he's always been to me.'

'Oh, because of that! I ran into him recently, your Heini, he's almost sixteen, seventeen years old. You Heisler boys are all pretty good-looking fellows, but Heini's really turned into something! They put a bug in his ear about joining the SS later on.'

'Heini?'

'But you should know more about that than I do,' Roeder said. He'd sat down again at the kitchen table. Seeing George's face now directly in front of him, he wondered again, just as he had on the staircase, whether this was really George. Just now George's face had changed completely. Roeder couldn't have put his finger on exactly what the change was, since George's face had remained quite still. But it was there, like the change in a clock that suddenly has stopped. 'You used to have arguments in the old days because Heini kept following you and was always on your side; now...'

'Is this thing true about Heini?' George asked.

'Didn't you know?' Roeder asked. 'Weren't you coming from home?'

Suddenly Roeder's heart began to pound wildly. He started to scold George. 'That's just what we needed. You're lying to me. For three years we don't see hide nor hair of you, and then you come here and lie to me. You were always like that – you're still like that. Lying to your friend Paul. Aren't you ashamed of yourself? What were you doing all that time? You must have been up to something, don't take me for stupid. So, you're not coming from home at all. Where were you all this time? You seem to be in a pretty pickle. Running away? What's really the matter with you?'

'Have you got a few marks for me?' George said. 'I have to get away from here. Don't let Liesel know.'

'What's wrong with you?'

'Don't you have a radio?'

'No,' Paul said. 'With Liesel's voice and the constant noise in our flat...'

'My name's been on the radio,' George said. 'I escaped.' He looked directly into his friend's eyes.

Roeder paled, turned so pale that his freckles seemed to glimmer in his face. 'Where did you escape from, George?'

'I escaped from Westhofen; I...I...'

'You from Westhofen?...All that time you were in Westhofen? What a character you are! They'll kill you when they catch you.'

'Yes,' George said.

'And you want to leave here now? You're out of your mind.'

George was still looking into Paul's face, which seemed to him like heaven itself, dotted with little stars. He said calmly, 'Dear, dear Paul, I can't do this to you – to you and all your family. You're all so happy, and now I... Do you have any idea what you're saying? What would happen if they came up here now? They may already be on my trail.'

Roeder said, 'Then it's too late anyway. If they come, we'll have to say that I knew nothing about it. You and I, we two simply didn't say these last few sentences to each other. You understand? We didn't say them at all. An old acquaintance can turn up any time. How was I to know where you've been all this time?'

George said, 'When did we see each other last?'

'The last time you were here was in December '32, on the second day of Christmas. You ate up all our cinnamon star cookies that time.'

George said, 'They'll ask you – interrogate you. You have no idea, the means they've invented to get people to talk.' In his eyes were all the tiny sharp little sparks that Franz had been afraid of as a child.

'Don't speak of the devil or he'll show up. Why should they pick on our flat? They didn't see you go in, or they'd already be up here. Think, my friend, where do we go from here? How will you get out from these four walls— Don't hold it against me, George, but I like you better on the outside than in here.'

George said, 'I have to get out of the city, out of this country! I have to find my people!'

Paul laughed, 'Your people? First find all the holes into which they've crawled.'

George said, 'Later, when we have time, I can show you a couple of holes into which they've crawled. Out there in Westhofen there are a couple of dozen men nobody knows anything about. If the two of us haven't crawled into holes like that by then.'

'Look here, George,' Paul said. 'I've been thinking about a man – Karl Hahn from Eschersheim. Back then—'

George interrupted, 'Never mind!' He was also thinking of a certain man. Was Wallau dead already? Dead in a world that went on spinning all the more frantically the more motionless he lay there? He heard him say again 'George,' one single syllable that not only travelled across space but also elapsed time.

'George!' Roeder called to him. George started. Paul gave him a worried look. For a moment George's face had turned strange again. And like a stranger he asked, 'Yes, Paul?'

Paul said, 'I could go to see those people early tomorrow morning so that I can be rid of you.'

George said, 'Let me try to remember who else lives in the city here. It's been more than two years.'

'You'd never have got involved in all this mess if you hadn't been so crazy about Franz back then. Do you still remember?' Paul asked. 'Back then he got you deeply involved, because before that – well, we all went to a meeting now and then, or we'd participate in a demonstration. We were all angry once. And we were all hopeful once. But your Franz – it was all his fault.'

'It wasn't Franz,' George said. 'It was something bigger, more powerful than anything else ...'

'What's that supposed to mean, more powerful than what?' Paul said, as he was folding down the side arm of the kitchen sofa to get it ready for George to spend the night there.

VI

That evening Elli's nieces and nephews were all hanging out of the window to watch for the arrival of the apple delivery. These were the children of the SS troop leader, the son-in-law old Mettenheimer had boasted about at the interrogation. Elli knew that Franz wouldn't get there with the apples until the family had all gone to their various meetings, activities, or homes – her brother-in-law to his SS division, her nieces and nephews to their home, and her sister, probably but not for sure, to her women's group.

The sister, a few years older than Elli, had a fuller bosom and less delicate, more cheerful features than Elli. Her husband, Otto Reiners, was a bank employee during the day, but in the evenings he was an SS man, and at night, if he was at home, a mixture of both. In the dark hallway Elli hadn't noticed when she arrived that her sister's face, so much like hers, looked dismayed and perplexed.

As the children ran from the window over to greet Elli, whom they all liked very much, Mrs Reiners made a resigned gesture with her arm as if acknowledging that it was too late to keep her children away from a calamity. She mumbled, 'Why did you come, Elli?'

When Elli had first told her on the telephone about the apple delivery, Reiners had ordered his wife either to send the apples away or to pay for them herself. For the time being he wouldn't allow Elli to come inside their home any more. When his wife asked him if he'd lost his senses, he took her by the hand and explained to her why she had no alternative but to choose between her own family and Elli.

Of all the Mettenheimer daughters, Mrs Reiners had made the best match. She had been and continued to be sensible. She accepted it as part of Reiners's nature that he had turned from being a Stahlhelmer – a member of a postwar paramilitary organisation – into a passionate follower of the New State; he was a Jew baiter, and spoke out against the church. She attended the women's group meetings and air-raid practice evenings even though they bored her. She thought she owed it to her marriage, by which she meant her life with Reiners and with her children, an entirely controllable matter of balance and mixing. She was also sensible enough to keep some of the things she enjoyed to herself, so that Reiners could not raise any objection when it came to his children receiving communion and following religious observances on important holidays. Such matters seemed to be a little chancy to him and so he thought it prudent to seek some form of insurance.

Now, as she saw Elli standing there surrounded by the children, who were helping her take her hat off, tugging at her earrings, pulling her arms out of their sockets, it became clear to her just what had happened these last few days and what momentous consequences her husband's order would have. To have to choose between Elli and my children, what nonsense! Why in the world should I have to choose at all? Is such a choice even possible? She suddenly told her children to leave Elli alone and to go away.

When the children were gone, she asked Elli about the price of the apples. Then she counted the money out on the table. When Elli resisted, she pressed the money into her hand and held Elli's folded hand in her own two hands. Then she carefully began to explain the problem. At the end she said, 'So you can understand my situation. We can see each other at our parents' home. By the way, they mentioned him on the radio again today. Oh, Elli dear, if only you'd accepted my brother-in-law! He was so very much in love with you. But you can't help any of that now. You know Reiners. Do you have any idea what could still happen to you?'

At any other time Elli's heart would have stopped on hearing such words from her sister. Oh no, she thought now, if only she doesn't throw me out before Franz comes with the apples. She said quite calmly, 'What could happen to me?'

'Reiners says it's possible that they would put you in prison again. Did that ever occur to you?'

'Yes,' Elli said.

'And in spite of that, you act so calm and go right ahead and buy winter apples?'

'Do you think it's less likely they'll lock me up if I don't buy any?'

Her sister thought: Elli's always walking around in a half daze with her eyes cast down, her long eyelashes like curtains before her eyes. Aloud she said, 'You don't have to wait for the apples.'

Elli quickly said, 'Yes, I do; I ordered the apples, and we don't want them to cheat us. You can't let Reiners drive you crazy. I'm not going to pollute your flat in the few minutes that I'm here. Anyway, I've already polluted it.'

'You know what,' her sister said after pondering it briefly, 'here's the attic key. Go upstairs, dust off the shelves, and put the jars of preserves on top of the cupboard. Afterwards put the key under the mat.' She felt quite cheerful now that she'd found a solution to get Elli out of the flat without sending her away. She drew her sister close and was about to kiss her, something she usually did only on her name day. But Elli turned her face aside and the kiss landed on her hair.

Once the door shut behind Elli, her sister went over to the window. This was already the fifteenth year they'd been living on this small, quiet street. This evening the familiar, ordinary houses looked to her sober eyes like houses seen from a moving train. In her cool heart there now rose one slight doubt, although in the habitual form of a housewifely calculation: What was it all worth . . .

In the meantime, Elli had opened the attic window to get rid of the stale, stuffy air. On the little labels of the jars of preserves, her sister had written in a neat hand the names and varieties of the fruits and the year. My poor sister. Elli felt a strange, inexplicable pity for her older sister, even though she had been blessed by fortune. Then she sat down on a suitcase to wait, hands in her lap, eyelids lowered, head down, the same position she had been waiting in yesterday on the Gestapo cot, and as she would be waiting tomorrow, God only knew where.

Franz came lumbering up the stairs with his apple baskets. He really is a friend, Elli told herself, and not everything's gone down the drain. Hurriedly the two of them emptied the baskets, their hands reaching over each other. Elli looked sideways at Franz. He was silent, listening. At least they'd managed to meet up here under this pretence. Hermann would probably not be too happy if he heard about their meeting, even if everything went smoothly. Franz said, 'Have you thought it over? Do you believe he's here somewhere in the city?'

'Yes,' Elli said. 'I think he is.'

'Why do you think so? This would really have been a long way for him to travel. And everyone knows him here.'

'Yes, but he also knows a lot of people here. Maybe he has some girl here that he's counting on for help.' Her expression turned a little stiff. 'About three years ago, shortly before he was arrested, I saw him once from far away, in Niederrad. He didn't see me. He was walking with a girl. And not just arm in arm, but holding hands; maybe a girl like that...'

'Maybe, but how can you be so certain?'

'Well, I am certain. He has somebody here. A girl like that, or a friend. And the Gestapo think so too. Because they're still following me and above all...'

'Above all?'

'Because I can feel it,' Elli said. 'I can feel it here, and here.'

Franz shook his head. 'Elli, dear, not even the Gestapo would pay any heed to something like that.'

They sat down on a trunk. For the first time Franz really looked at Elli. For a brief moment out of the little time they had, of the dreadfully short time that was theirs, he looked at her from head to toe. Elli lowered her eyes. Even though she had up to now completely forgotten Franz and was feeling her way along as if on a tightrope with nothing but air beneath her, even though what led them to meet here in this apple room was a matter of life and death, could Elli help it if her heart fluttered a few beats in the expectation of love? Franz took her hand in his; he said, 'Elli dear, I'd love to pack you into one of these two empty apple baskets now and carry you down the stairs and put you on my truck and drive off with you. God knows, that's what I'd like more than anything else. But it's not possible. Believe me, Elli, all these years I wanted and hoped to be able to see you again. But we can't meet again, for the time being.'

Elli thought: All kinds of people seem to be telling me how much they like me and that they can't see me any more.

Franz continued, 'Has it occurred to you that they might arrest you again, as they often do with the wives of escaped prisoners?'

'Yes,' she said.

'Are you afraid?'

'No, why should I be?'

Why isn't she afraid? Franz wondered. He had a very faint suspicion that she still liked being in some way involved with George. He asked her, seemingly out of the blue, 'Who was the man they arrested at your place last evening?'

'Oh, he was an acquaintance of mine,' Elli replied. To her shame, she'd almost forgotten Heinz. She hoped he was back home by now with his parents. From what she knew of him, he wouldn't ever come back to see her after such an unpleasant experience. That's not the stuff he was made of.

The two of them, still holding hands, looked straight ahead. Both choked by a sadness for which there was no remedy.

In a changed, matter-of-fact tone of voice Franz said, 'So Elli, have you thought of anyone he knew back when he still lived in this city who might possibly take him in?'

THE SEVENTH CROSS · 229

She mentioned a few names; among them were two or three friends Franz knew from before. It was unlikely that George, if he still had his wits about him, would go to any of them directly. Two or three names, totally unknown to Franz, made him feel uneasy. Then Elli mentioned a friend from their school days, little Paul Roeder, whose name had already occurred to Franz. And there was also an old teacher, but he'd long ago retired and left the city.

Franz thought: So there are two possibilities. Either George is done for and can't think any more at all, in which case all our efforts would be futile because then everything would be unpredictable. Or he *is* thinking – and if so then he must think as I do, and in that case – besides, Hermann must know with whom he was just before he was arrested. But I shouldn't go to see Hermann right after seeing Elli. That means more time will be lost. Almost forgetting about Elli, he jumped up, causing her hand to slide off his knee. Quickly he stacked the empty basket in which he'd wanted to hide Elli inside the other empty one. Elli paid for the apples, and he gave her change. Suddenly a thought occurred to him, 'If they ask about us, tell them you gave me fifty pfennig as a tip.' He was half expecting to be stopped as he left the house.

But once the suspense was over and he had safely left the house and driven off in the empty, rattling truck, he realised that he hadn't even said good-bye to Elli. And that he hadn't mentioned the possibility of seeing her again sometime.

Back at the Marnets, he settled the account, not forgetting the tip. 'That's yours,' Mrs Marnet said, considering herself most generous. After Franz had a bite to eat and returned to his room, Augusta said, 'He was turned down by a woman today, you can tell.'

Her husband said, 'He'll go back to Sophie eventually.'

Whenever Bunsen entered a room, people felt they had to apologise for the room being too small and the ceiling too low. Then his keen, handsome face would take on an expression of placating reassurance, as if to say he wouldn't be staying long and it was really quite all right.

'I saw that your light was still on,' he said. 'We all had quite a day.'

'Yes. Please sit down,' Overkamp said. He was certainly not enchanted by his visitor. Fischer cleared off the chair on which he usually sat during interrogations and went over to sit on the little bench by the wall. Both men were dog-tired.

Bunsen said, 'You know, I happen to have some schnapps in my room.' He jumped up again, opened the door, and called out into the night, 'Hey, hey.' There was the sound of heels scraping. Fog rolled like steam over the threshold as if the world outside had been extinguished. 'I was happy to see your light still on,' Bunsen continued. 'Quite frankly, I can't stand what's going on here any more.'

Good heavens, Overkamp mused, now this on top of everything else! Problems of conscience take at least an hour and a half to deal with. Aloud he said, 'My dear friend, this world – the way it is – gives us relatively few alternatives. Either we keep a certain type of people here behind barbed wire so we can keep an eye on them and do it all better than before by making certain they all stay inside, or we'll be the ones inside and they'll be guarding us. And because the first situation is the more sensible, we have to take certain measures, sometimes unpleasant ones, to make sure it remains the way it is.'

'You're echoing my sentiments,' Bunsen replied. 'But what I can't stand any more is old man Fahrenberg's drivel ...'

'My dear Bunsen,' Overkamp said, 'that's your problem.'

'He's absolutely convinced, that now that they brought Fuellgrabe back this afternoon, he'll get all the others too. What do you think, Overkamp?'

'My name is Overkamp, not Habakkuk. I'm no prophet, not even a minor one. I work hard here.' But to himself he thought, This fellow really thinks a lot of himself just because last Monday morning he issued a couple of routine orders all on his own that were required by his job.

Just then they brought in a tray with the schnapps and little glasses. Bunsen poured; he tossed one down, then a second, then a third. Overkamp watched him with a professional eye. The schnapps had an odd effect on the man. He probably never got really drunk, but after the third little glass, his posture and speech were already slightly altered. Even the skin of his face had slackened.

Bunsen said, 'Still, I don't think those four fellows feel anything by now, and the fifth one, Belloni, he certainly doesn't feel anything any more, because it's just his hat and his old dress coat that are hanging out there. But the other prisoners when they're led to the Dance Ground to watch, they'll feel it – that'll be something to see when they're all lined up on the Dance Ground – they won't want to watch and yet they'll have to. But the other four prisoners who already have an idea of what's in store for them – I've heard that when you know what's in store for you, then nothing matters any more and you don't feel anything. Besides it's just uncomfortable for them, the way they have to stand there; the nails don't hurt them; only Fuellgrabe moaned in disappointment. Will he have another turn tonight? Hmm, if so, I'd like to be there!'

'No, my dear fellow.'

'Why not?'

'It's a matter of official regulations – a ticklish matter, my friend.'

'Yes, for you,' Bunsen said. His eyes flashed. 'Leave Fuellgrabe to me for five minutes, and I'll tell you whether or not it was a coincidence that he met Heisler.'

'It's possible that he'll tell you that he had a date with Heisler if you give him a kick in the stomach. But even after that I'd still say it was a coincidence. Why? Because all you have to do is shake Fuellgrabe and the answers will come dropping down like plums. Because I know what sort of person Fuellgrabe is, and Heisler too. Because the Heisler I know would never make an appointment to meet Fuellgrabe in a city, in the middle of the day.'

'If he was sitting on that bench, the way Fuellgrabe told you, then he must have been waiting for someone. Was his picture distributed to all the house and block wardens?'

'My dear Bunsen,' Overkamp said, 'be grateful for all the trouble other people are taking.'

'Cheers!' They clinked glasses.

'If you could take Wallau's head apart, bit by bit, then you'd no doubt find out who his friend Heisler was waiting for. Why don't you take Fuellgrabe and Wallau on together?'

'My dear Bunsen, your idea, like Maria Stuart, is beautiful but unhappy. But if you're interested, we've interrogated Wallau thoroughly; here's the file on his interrogation.'

He handed a sheet of white paper over to Bunsen who stared at it. He smiled. His teeth, little mouse teeth, were a bit too small for his bold face. 'Let me have Wallau until tomorrow morning.'

'You can take the piece of paper,' Overkamp said, 'and let him spit blood on it.' He poured another drink for Bunsen. Bunsen, much like anyone three-quarters drunk, was keeping his eyes fixed on one single face. He paid no attention to Fischer. Fischer on his little bench, since he never drank, was holding his full glass in his fist, careful not to spill anything on his trousers. Overkamp now signalled to him with one eyebrow. Fischer got up, carefully walked around Bunsen over to the table, and took one of the receivers off the hook.

'Excuse me,' Overkamp said, 'but duty calls.'

'And looks like an armed archangel, like a Saint Michael,' Fischer said as soon as Bunsen was safely outside.

Overkamp picked up the small riding crop next to his chair, looked at it briefly, the way he looked at hundreds of such things, holding it carefully so as not to destroy any fingerprints. He said, 'Your Saint Michael left his sword behind.' He called to the guard at the door, 'Clean up here! We're finished for today! Guards will stay at their posts!'

It was already the third time that evening that Hermann asked his Elsa whether Franz had given her a message. And for the third time Elsa told him that Franz had asked for him the day before yesterday but that he hadn't come back since then. What's going on there? Hermann thought. At first he's all crazy about the escape and doesn't talk about anything else, and now suddenly he doesn't show up any more. If only he doesn't do something on his own. Could something have happened to him?

Elsa was humming in the kitchen in her deep, slightly rough voice; sometimes it sounded as if a little bee were humming 'Heidenröslein'. Her humming allayed any pangs of conscience Hermann might have felt for having married this child who knew nothing about him or about anything else for that matter. In fact Hermann was thinking tonight about how difficult it would be for him to bear this life in isolation and a constant state of tension without the child. Hermann had already heard of Wallau's recapture. He tried to tear himself away from the image of a bleeding body lying on the ground and men trying to break it with kicks and blows because there was something unbreakable within. He tore himself away from these introspective thoughts, the involuntary image of his own fragile body, which, he hoped, also had something unbreakable at its core, and turned his thoughts to those escaped prisoners who hadn't been caught. Above all this George Heisler, because he came from this area, because it was still possible that he might be trying to find a hiding place here. The things Franz had told him about George were too much a muddle of only half-clear perceptions for his taste. Hermann had already formed an impression of Heisler, whom he'd never met, from what he had known previously about him: a man who doesn't spare himself, who can give up things in order to win. Whatever he still lacked, his fellow prisoner Wallau may have contributed, Hermann thought. He knew Wallau slightly. Now there was a man you had to think yourself into. Money and identity documents must be obtained and held in readiness, Hermann thought. For the second time his thoughts suddenly tore themselves away from this image of one single man being pursued who might turn up almost anywhere. He wondered whether he'd be able to go tomorrow to the one place where papers and such things could be obtained in the event of an urgent need. That's all I can do for the present, and that's what I will do. He felt reassured, calmer.

His little bee was now humming 'Mühlenrad' in the kitchen. I'd probably be a lot less calm without my Elsa, he mused. Everything has its benefits.

Franz threw himself down on his bed. He was so tired that he fell asleep fully dressed. Suddenly he was back in the attic room with Elli, making up for not having said good-bye. Then out of the blue, it seemed, Elli had lost an earring; it had fallen in among the apples. They began to search for it. He was worried because they were wasting time, but the earring had to be found, and there were so many apples, all the apples in the world. 'Here it is,' Elli screamed, but the earring slipped away like a little bug, and their rummaging in the apples continued. No longer was it just the two of them searching; everyone was helping. Mrs Marnet rummaged around in the apples, and Augusta and her children, and the old teacher who had retired, and little freckled Roeder. Ernst the shepherd in his red neckerchief and his Nelly were rummaging around too. Anton Greiner and his SS cousin Messer; even Hermann himself was looking in the apples, as well as the district leader from the year '29. Whatever happened to him? Sophie Mangold was searching and little Woodchip. And also the fat cashier Franz had seen George with right after he left Elli; she was rummaging around in the apples, too, panting. The thought flashed through his mind that George might be at her place. She was awfully fat but quite decent. Then the apples were done and gone. He was already sitting on his bicycle pedalling along on the road down to Hoechst. Just as expected, the cashier was standing inside the soda shack wearing Elli's earrings. But George was nowhere to be seen. Franz flew onward on his bike in ever greater terror, feeling sought-after rather than seeking. Until it occurred to him that George would of course be at home, in the room they shared. Where else? What an ordeal, going up there again! But Franz pulled himself together, went upstairs, and entered the room. And of course, there was George, sitting in their room, astride his chair, his hands held in front of his face. Franz began to pack up his things; after all that had happened, their life together was over. A bitter memory. George's eyes followed him; his every movement hurt, but the packing had to be done. In the end he had to turn round. At that George took his hands away from his face. His face had no features. Blood was running out of his nostrils and out of his mouth and even out of his eyes. Franz's scream got stuck in his throat, but George said calmly, 'No need for you to move out on my account, Franz.'

5

I

THE LAW that governs human emotions – what ignites them, causing them to flare up or to cool down – did not apply to the fifty-four-year-old woman sitting by the window in a room on Schimmelgaesschen with her aching legs stretched out in front of her on a second chair. For the woman was George's mother.

Since the death of her husband, Mrs Heisler had been sharing the flat with the family of her second-oldest son. With the passing years she'd grown ever more obese. In her brown eyes there was an expression of fear and reproach, the same expression you find in the eyes of people who are drowning. Because her sons were used to this, as well as the short sighs that issued from her open mouth like vaporized thoughts, they assumed that their mother didn't quite understand what she was being told, or at least not its significance.

'If he comes, he won't come walking up the stairs,' her second-oldest son said. 'He'll come through the courtyards. He'll climb up on to the balcony the way he used to. He doesn't know that you're not sleeping in the same room any more. The best thing for you to do is just to stay where you are and go to sleep.'

The woman shrugged and her legs twitched; she was too heavy to get up by herself. The youngest son said eagerly, 'Just go to bed, take some valerian, and bolt the door, all right, Mother?'

Her second son agreed, 'That would be best.' He was a heavily built man who looked older than he was. His large head was shaved, and his eyebrows and eyelashes had recently been singed by a welding torch flame, giving his face a dull expression. He'd been a good-looking fellow, like all the Heisler sons. Now he was a regular lout of an SA man. Everything about him had coarsened, thickened. But Heini, the youngest, he was just as Roeder had described him. His physique, his head, his hair, his teeth – all were as if his parents had created him according to the racial textbook. So now the older one, putting the best face on it and with a forced smile, got ready to take his mother together with both her chairs over to the bed. He stopped short when he caught the look in his mother's eyes; the message contained in that look seemed to be costing her an enormous effort. He let go of the chairs and bowed his head.

Heini said, 'You did understand what I said, Mother, didn't you? How about it? What do you say?'

She said nothing at all; she just looked at her youngest son, then at the older one, then back at the youngest. What a tough hide the youngest must have had to withstand that look! The older son went over to the window. He looked out at the night-time street. But the younger son had no trouble withstanding his mother's look; he hadn't even noticed it.

'Well now, do lie down,' he said. 'Put the cup next to your bed. You don't have to worry about whether he's coming or not. Don't even think about him. After all, you have the three of us.'

The older one listened to him, still looking out at the street. He was astonished at the language Heini, George's favourite little brother, had acquired. He was participating in the hunt as if it didn't mean anything to him at all. Wants to prove to the Hitler Youths on the street and the men, too, that George means nothing to him, even though in the old days he'd clung to George like a burr. *They* had turned the young one upside down and inside out in a way quite different from him, and he himself felt thoroughly upended and turned inside out. He'd gone to the SA a year and a half ago because he shuddered in revulsion at the five years he'd been unemployed. This revulsion was one of the few mental exercises of his dull, not very enterprising mind. He was the least mature and stupidest of the Heisler boys. They said to him, You'll lose your job tomorrow if you don't sign up today. There was still the faint idea in his clunky, dull head that all this business about a New State, a New Order was only partly valid. That the real thing was not yet in sight. All this about a New State was only a fantasy that would pass. How? Through whom? When? He didn't know. His insides churned listening to Heini talking so brashly, so coldly to his mother. This same Heini whom George used to take on his shoulders to all his demonstrations now had his head filled with all sorts of fancy ideas about Nazi leadership schools, the SS, and the motorised SS. He felt his heart turn over deep inside him. Turning away from the window, he stared at his youngest brother.

The latter now announced, 'I'm going down to Breitbach's, and you should go to bed, Mother. You understood everything we said, yes?'

Their mother, to both their surprise, answered, 'Yes.'

And she was really all done with thinking. She said, quite cheerfully, 'Please bring me my valerian.' I'll drink it, she thought, so that my heart won't play any tricks on me. And I'll lie down too, so that they'll leave the room. Then I'll go over and sit by the door and when I hear George arrive in the courtyard, I'll yell down to him: Gestapo!

For the last three days they'd all been telling her, especially her second-oldest son's wife and Heini, what a big family they were, even without George – three sons, six grandchildren. And how much she could be destroying by any thoughtless behaviour on her part. She had listened to them in silence. In the past George had been just one among her four sons. He'd given her a lot of trouble. There'd been constant complaints from teachers and neighbours. He'd argued with his father and his two older brothers. He quarrelled with the second-oldest because he didn't seem to care about anything, and that upset George; and he quarrelled with the oldest one because although he was upset by this too, his opinions on the subject were quite different from George's.

This oldest brother was now living with his own family at the other end of town. He knew about George's escape from the radio and newspaper reports. Not a day had gone by since George had been imprisoned that he hadn't thought about his younger brother; but now he could hardly think of anything else. If only he knew of some way to help him – he wouldn't hesitate to sacrifice himself or his family. They'd asked him ten times at work whether he was related to this Heisler who'd escaped. And ten times he'd answered in the same tone of voice, as silence fell around him, 'He's my brother!'

Their mother used to favour the oldest brother, and from time to time the youngest. She was also quite fond of the second oldest because he was good to her, maybe better than all of the others in his dull, simple way.

None of that counted any more. For, contrary to what you might have expected, the longer George was away, the less they heard from him and the less anyone asked about him, the clearer his features became in her mind, the clearer her memories of him. Her heart withdrew from the plans and hopes of the three sons who were living their lives around her. It gradually became full of the plans and hopes of her absent, all-but-vanished son. She would sit in bed at night recalling all the details of his life that she hadn't thought about for ages: George's birth, the little accidents during his early years, the serious illness to which she almost lost him, the time during the war when she was employed making grenades and shifting for herself and her sons, the time when George was denounced because he'd stolen something, the small triumphs she could cling to, the meagre rewards – a teacher's praise, a boss who thought he was clever at his work, a victory in an athletic event. She remembered half proudly and half vexed his first girlfriend and all the girls he'd had later on. Elli, who had remained a total stranger to her, who hadn't even brought the child over, and then – the sudden change in his life! Not that he would ever have brought something foreign into the family! Except that the sort of things that might have been considered just an isolated rebellious occurrence in her husband and her other sons – a spoken word, sometimes a strike, sometimes a flyer – were for George a decisive and all-important fight involving his entire being.

It was as if she were inventing a thousand counterarguments to refute someone trying to prove to her that she had only three sons, that the fourth one had never been born, had never existed.

How often had Heini told her that the street was closed off, that the flat was under surveillance, that the Gestapo was on the alert and that she had to think of the sons still left to her.

Now she was giving up on these three sons. They had to take care of themselves. The only one she would never give up on was George. The second-oldest son was watching his mother; her lips moved constantly. She was thinking, Dear God, You have to help him. If You really exist, You must help him. If You don't exist . . . She turned away from this uncertain helper. She now addressed her prayers to all living existence as she knew it and also to the most uncertain, the darkest realms, of which she knew nothing, but where, perhaps, there were people who would or could help her son. Maybe somewhere there was someone whose heart could be reached by her prayers.

Her second-oldest son came over to her chair. He said, 'I didn't want to tell you so long as Heini was here because you never know with him how he'll take it. I talked with Zweilein, the plumber.'

His mother looked at him, fully alert now. Quickly and without much effort she put both her feet down.

'Zweilein lives in a convenient spot; from his place he has a view of two streets. If George is going to come here, he's sure to be coming from the Main. Of course I didn't really say it in words, only with gestures and with my eyes.' And he showed his mother how he'd used his thumbs and his eyes to communicate with Zweilein. 'And then Zweilein did this with his eyes and his thumb indicating he'd be staying awake tonight and that he'd be on the lookout for George and keep him from coming into our street.'

Her eyes lit up when she heard these words, and her face, which just a moment before had been as limp as dough, became firm and strong as if reanimated. She grabbed her son's arm to pull herself upright. Then she said, 'And what if he comes from the direction of the city?'

Her son shrugged.

His mother continued almost to herself, 'But if he goes up to see Lore, she's on Alfred's side; they'll denounce him.'

Her son said, 'I wouldn't be so sure that those two would denounce him. But he'll be coming from the Main. Zweilein will be waiting for him.'

His mother said, 'He's lost if he comes here.'

Her son said, 'Even if he does, he's not totally lost.'

II

A new day had dawned, even though you couldn't tell in the villages along the marshy banks of the river because of the dense fog. The light was still on in the kitchen of the house on the edge of Liebach as the girl came out into the farmyard with her pails. She shuddered. Walking over to the gate, she set her pails down. Her face looked calm and relaxed; she was waiting for her fiancé, Fritz.

She shivered in the cold. The fog penetrated her clothes; everything was turning grey, even the kerchief she'd tied over her hair. She thought she heard the young fellow's footsteps. He ought to be coming by now. She was already raising her arms. But no one came through the gate. Still, she wasn't worried, only a bit puzzled. She continued to wait, crossing her arms over her chest to warm up. She stepped to the gate and peered out. The fog was thick enough to cut with a knife. Will it lift soon? Now she was able to make out two shadowy forms coming up the path, one of them had to be Fritz. It's got to be him . . . but it wasn't. The two shadows entered a shadowy house. The girl turned away. For the first time her face expressed momentary dismay over this futile waiting. Oh, he'll probably come this afternoon, she thought. And she lifted her pails and carried them into the barn. After they'd been emptied, she took the pails into the house. They tried three times turning off the light in the kitchen but had to turn it back on each time. Without the light her grandmother couldn't sort the lentils, not even with her glasses on. Her older cousin was grinding beets; the younger one was sweeping the dirt out through the door. Her mother quickly filled both the pails the girl brought. Not one of the four women noticed that Fritz hadn't come. The girl thought: They really don't notice anything.

'Watch out,' her mother said, for the swill was spilling from the ladle.

As the girl walked through the courtyard for the second time with her pails, a shop doorbell rang in the distance. It was ringing because Gueltscher had gone into the shop to buy tobacco. Fritz was waiting outside the shop door. He'd got a new summons yesterday. They wanted to see him again and ask him some more questions about the jacket. 'Yes, but it wasn't yours, was it?' his mother had asked. And he had told her quite emphatically that no, it wasn't his.

He worried all night about what they'd ask him this time. That morning he'd turned on the radio to get the news. There were descriptions of the escaped prisoners – only two of the seven were still at large. It made him feel hot all over. Maybe they'd already caught the one he'd come to think of as his own guy. His guy might have said, 'Yes, that was the jacket!'

Why did he suddenly feel so alone? He couldn't ask his father and mother or any of his favourite mates for advice. He couldn't even ask his squad leader, Albert, whom he trusted implicitly. Last week everything had still been fine, his mind cool and calm, the entire world all right. Last week if Albert had ordered him to fire at the escapee, he would have shot him. If his squad leader had ordered him to lie in wait in the shed with a dagger until the escapee sneaked in to steal the jacket, he would have stabbed him to death before he could steal it.

When he saw Gueltscher, the gardener, a man old enough to be his father, coming along, he ran after him. He was a crusty old man who smoked a pipe. You could talk about things with him.

'They've summoned me again.'

Gueltscher looked at the boy. He said nothing. They walked to the shop in silence. Gueltscher went in, and Fritz waited for him outside.

When he came out, the old man filled his pipe and they walked on. Fritz had completely forgotten his girl; it was as if he'd never had one. He said, 'I wonder why they've asked me to come back again.'

'If it really wasn't your jacket . . .'

'I explained to them all the things that were different about my jacket. What if they've caught the man whose jacket it was! They're only looking for two guys now!'

Gueltscher was silent. You get more complete answers by not asking any questions.

'What if that guy now says: "Yes, that's my jacket . . ."'

Gueltscher said, 'It's possible. They might have tortured him until he gave in.' He'd squeezed his eyes almost shut, but he could still see the boy. He'd been watching him for two days.

Fritz frowned, 'Well – do you think? And what about me?'

'Oh, Fritz, there are hundreds of jackets like that.'

They walked on up towards the school, sure of where they were going in spite of the dense fog. A whole storm of thoughts swirled in the old man's head. He couldn't have said in exactly which way the boy at his side was different from the other boys. He wasn't even sure that he was. But still there was something he couldn't quite work out. He had as little doubt as did Overkamp that there was something odd, something not quite right about this jacket mix-up. He thought of his own sons. They were half his and half the property of the New State. At home they were his. At home they said he was right, that the top in the state was still the top and the bottom was the bottom. But outside home they both wore the regulation shirts and shouted 'Heil' whenever they were supposed to. Had he done everything he could to encourage their resistance? Not really! It would have meant breaking up the family – jail – sacrificing his sons. He had to choose, and there was the breach. Not just for him, but for many others too. But how could a person come to such a decision, how could one bridge such a breach? Still, in spite of that, there *were* some people here in this country, and especially abroad. All those people in Spain who, so they said, were defeated, and who were obviously not defeated. And all of them had taken this leap. Hundreds of thousands! All of

them former Gueltschers, people like him! What if one of his sons
had his jacket stolen, what would he have advised him to do? Was it
right to give advice to Fritz? The son of other parents? What a decision to have to make! What a weird world! He said, 'I'm sure that all
the many jackets delivered from the factory are the same. All the
Gestapo has to do is to call them up. The zips are all the same down
to the millimetre. The pockets are all alike. But if, for instance, a key
or a pencil has made a hole in the lining, then that's something the
Gestapo can't prove or disprove, and that's what makes the difference.
That's the point you have to stick to.'

III

In Westhofen Fuellgrabe had been shaken awake five times during
the night to be interrogated, always just at the point when, utterly
exhausted, he had fallen asleep. Since, by his return, he had proved
that fear had been the driving force behind his actions, he had given
them the means whereby they could cure him, in case he still had a
stubborn streak left in him. At last Overkamp had come into possession of a juicy piece of evidence about Heisler himself, having previously
had only dubious traces of the man and only alleged articles of clothing. True, Fuellgrabe still balked even at his fifth interrogation session
when he was asked about their encounter, even though he himself
had given them this information when they forced him, with dire
threats, to describe his own escape, hour by hour.

Fuellgrabe twitched and fidgeted in his chair. Then suddenly
something seemed to be clogging the interrogation machinery, which
up to that moment had been running so smoothly. Some useless
item seemed to have got mixed in with the fear that had up to then
lubricated all the little parts of his brain. However, all Fischer had
to do was take the receiver off the hook and ask Zillich to come in.
The mere name worked to clear the impediment. The feeling of fear
separated itself from all the other feelings; the vision of a painful
death separated from one of being alive. The grey and trembling

Fuellgrabe of the present separated himself from the long forgotten one who actually used to have spells of courage, who had known the contagion of hope. Lies and evasions separated themselves from the real record.

> Thursday afternoon, a little before twelve, I ran into George Heisler near the Eschenheim Tower. He led me over to a bench in the garden, on the first path to the left in front of the large round flowerbed of asters. I urged him to come with me so we could turn ourselves in. But he didn't want to hear anything about that. He was wearing a yellow coat, a stiff hat, low shoes with laces, not new, but not worn out. I don't know whether he had any money. I don't know why he was in Eschenheim Park. I don't know if he was waiting for someone. He was still sitting on the bench when I left. I think now that he was expecting someone there, because he was the one who led me there and because he went on sitting there. Yes, after I left him, I turned round once; he was still sitting there.

By the time Paul Roeder left his flat early that morning, orders had already been issued to the municipal authorities on the basis of this deposition. And some of the block wardens had already received these orders, but they had not yet passed them on to the caretakers in charge of each house. For as soon as they leave the radio transmitters and telegraph lines, all these events fall again into the hands of human beings.

The caretaker's wife at Roeder's house wondered why their tenant had gone to work so much earlier than usual. She told her husband about it when he came into the hall with a bucket of green soap. He was going to give her some for her laundry. Neither of them had any particular feelings, either for or against the Roeders. Sometimes there were complaints about Mrs Roeder singing at inappropriate hours, but otherwise they were cheerful, easy-to-get-along-with tenants.

Roeder was walking along the misty streets to the tram stop, whistling to himself. It would take him fifteen minutes to get into the city and fifteen minutes to get back, so he had half an hour, enough for a second visit, in case the first one didn't work out. He'd explained to Liesel that he had to get up early to catch his friend Melzer; he was the Bockenheim goalkeeper. He admonished her as he was leaving, 'Take good care of George till I get back.' He'd lain awake, unmoving, long into the night, next to Liesel, until finally he did fall asleep for a little while.

Roeder stopped whistling. He'd left without having his coffee. His mouth was dry. The early morning hour, his thirst, the pavement itself, all seemed still to be full of night-time darkness, of unremitting threat: Be careful, just think what you're letting yourself in for. Roeder repeated to himself, Schenk, number twelve Moselgasse, Sauer, number twenty-four Taunusstrasse. These were the two men he now had to look up before he went to work. George felt that both of them had remained steadfast, safe, and would help him with advice and shelter, with identification papers and money. Schenk had worked at the cement works, at least when George knew him. He remembered him as a calm, clear-eyed man, with nothing about him that was in any way conspicuous. He was neither particularly daring nor clever, for his wit was an inherent aspect of all his thinking and his bravery was an integral part of his entire life. On the other hand, Schenk symbolised for George everything that represented the movement, the very essence of his life. Indeed if, because of some terrible misfortune, the movement bled to death and were condemned to come to a standstill, then Schenk alone would be the one who had it in him to resuscitate and lead it onward. If there was still a shadow of the movement left, Schenk would have his hand on that shadow. If there were any in the leadership left, then Schenk would know where one might find them. So at least it had seemed to George the previous night.

Roeder would probably have understood very little of all that if George had had the time to explain it to him. But time or no time, understood or not, Roeder was helping. Indeed, from that morning on, all three of them were in Roeder's hands. Not just George, but Schenk and Sauer too...

Sauer had been hired by the Municipal Street Construction Office after five years of being unemployed. That was just a month before George's arrest. He was still a young man, and being quite talented in his profession, the years of inactivity had made him rather desperate. After reading several hundred books, attending several hundred meetings, hearing several hundred slogans, sermons, and talks, and in the course of several hundred discussions, he had eventually met George. George considered Sauer, in his own way, just as dependable as Schenk. Sauer followed his mind in everything, and his mind never let go of anything it had learned. On top of that he was incorruptible and dependable, even if his heart sometimes encouraged him to give in a little and follow an easier path, so that afterwards he could rest and then get up again, ready with all sorts of justifications.

Paul kept thinking: Sauer, twenty-four Taunusstrasse. Schenk, twelve Moselgasse.

Then he saw Melzer coming round the corner, right on cue. The same Melzer he had told Liesel so much about. 'Hey, Melzer, what luck to run into you. Do you have two free tickets for Sunday's game for us?'

'It can be arranged,' Melzer said.

Do you really think, Paul, a small little voice inside Roeder whispered, that you'll be able to use two free tickets on Sunday? That you'll need them?

'Yes,' Paul said aloud. 'I need them.'

Melzer talked about the probable outcome of the game between Niederrad and Westend. Then he suddenly broke off. He had to get home, had to get home immediately before his mother woke up. He was coming from seeing his fiancée, who worked for Cassella, and his mother, who owned a tiny stationery shop, couldn't stand her future daughter-in-law.

Paul knew the little stationery shop; he knew the girl, knew the mother; the knowledge made him feel at home and safe. He smiled at Melzer. Then the little voice came back, small and clever: You might never see this Melzer again. Nonsense, a thousand times nonsense! Roeder thought angrily. He'll even invite me to his wedding.

Fifteen minutes later he was whistling again as he walked down Moselgasse. He stopped at number 12. Luckily the front door was open. He rapidly climbed up to the fifth floor. A stranger's name on the door – Roeder grimaced. An old woman wearing a bed jacket opened the door across the way. She asked who he was looking for.

'Don't the Schenks live here any more?'

'The Schenks?' asked the old woman. She called into her flat in an odd tone of voice, 'There's somebody here asking about the Schenks.'

A younger woman leaned over the railing on the floor above; the old woman called up to her. 'He's asking about the Schenks.'

An expression of dismay spread over the younger woman's tired, swollen face. She was wearing a flowered dressing gown and had a large, wobbly bosom. A lot like Liesel, Paul thought. In fact, this stairway resembled his own. His next-door neighbour Stuembert was also a nearly bald elderly SA man like that one there with his uniform unbuttoned and still in his socks because he'd just thrown himself on his bed when he came home after the evening drill. 'Who is it you want to see?' he asked Roeder as if he didn't trust his ears.

Paul said, 'The Schenks owe my sister money for some dress fabric. I'm collecting for my sister. I picked this time of day because you usually find people at home early in the morning.'

'Mrs Schenk hasn't been living here for the last three months,' the old woman said.

The man said, 'You'll have to go to Westhofen if you want to collect the money.' He suddenly looked quite cheerful. He'd had a hard time actually catching the Schenks while they were listening to the forbidden radio station. But in the end, using all sorts of tricks, he'd succeeded. All along they'd acted so demure and innocent. Heil Hitler! every time you met them. But there's nothing you can teach me about people living next door to me.

'Good heavens!' Roeder said. 'Well, Heil Hitler!'

'Heil Hitler!' the other man, standing there in his socks, replied with a hint of raising his arm, his eyes still shiny at the memory.

Walking back downstairs, Paul could hear him laughing. He wiped his forehead, surprised to find it so damp. For the first time since he'd seen George again, indeed maybe since his childhood, he had an icy feeling in the pit of his stomach, which even now he refused to admit was fear. Rather, he imagined that he, who had been healthy his entire life, was coming down with some contagious disease. This feeling bothered him and he fought it. He stamped hard on the stairs to rid himself of the slack feeling in his knees. The caretaker's wife was standing on the lowest landing. 'Whom did you want to see?' she asked.

'I was looking for the Schenks,' Roeder said. 'I collect money owed to my sister. The Schenks still owe her money for some dress fabric.'

Now the woman from the top floor came down with her rubbish bin. She said to the caretaker's wife, 'He was asking for the Schenks.'

The caretaker's wife looked Roeder up and down. He could hear her calling into her flat, 'There's somebody here who asked about the Schenks.'

Roeder stepped out into the street. He wiped his face on his sleeve. He'd never been given such strange looks as these people had given him. What devil had advised George to send him to Schenk? How was it that George didn't know that Schenk was in Westhofen? Curse that George, it'll make you feel better, the little voice inside him whispered. Curse him; he'll destroy you.

George can't help that, Roeder thought; it wasn't his fault. He walked on, whistling. Then he reached Metzergasse and his face brightened. He stepped into one of the open entryways. In the large courtyard surrounded by the tall houses was the garage that was part of his Aunt Catherine's haulage firm. She was standing in the middle of the courtyard, shouting at the drivers. The talk in the family had it that she'd met Grabber, a haulage entrepreneur, when she was young. He was a drunken fellow, and she'd learned to drink too and had become coarse and ill humoured. There was another story as well that the family told. About a child that Aunt Catherine had had during the war, eleven months after her haulage entrepreneur's first home leave. Everyone in the family wondered what he'd say when he came home on his second home leave. But he never did get a second home leave, for he was killed in action. And the child probably didn't live to grow up, for Paul had never seen it.

He'd always felt drawn to this aunt, half out of curiosity and half against his will. Because he enjoyed life, he liked looking at her big, angry face, which showed the wear and tear of the hard life she'd lived. For several minutes he now forgot George and himself, listening with a smile to the woman, to her curses, which were new even to him. She's the last person I'd like to work for, he thought. And yet he'd come to talk to her about one of Liesel's brothers, to ask that she hire him, an unlucky fellow who'd had his driving licence taken away after an accident. But, Paul thought, I can talk to her about that later on tonight just as well. Terribly thirsty and unable to master his thirst, he entered the local tavern through the back door that opened on to the courtyard. He waved to his aunt, uncertain whether, with all her shouting and cursing, she even noticed his greeting.

A little old man with a red nose who was still – or again – tippling in the back room, raised his little glass. 'Cheers, little Paul!'

I'll come back and have a couple myself tonight, once I finish that other business, Paul thought.

The little bit of brandy he'd had lay in his empty stomach like a small hot ball. By now the streets were filling with people. He didn't have much time left. Inside Paul, the little mousy voice squeaked, crafty and thin: Well then! Get the other thing settled first! You're the right fellow to do this! Yesterday at this time you were happy.

At this time yesterday he'd run to the baker to get two pounds of flour for his wife. But, Paul mused, she never did bake the sweet yeast dumplings yesterday. I hope she'll bake them today. He stood now in front of 24 Taunusstrasse. He looked around the stairwell in surprise, for it was well kept, with brass railings and carpet runners on the stairs. He felt a stirring of suspicion and wondered if people living in such a house would help someone like him.

Paul breathed a sigh of relief as he saw, while still on the stairs, the name embossed in gothic letters on a metal plate. He touched it in amazement before he rang the bell. 'Sauer, Architect', it said. Paul was annoyed that his heart was pounding. A good-looking blond woman in a white apron answered the door, not the lady of the house but only a servant. Right afterwards the wife appeared. She was also young and good looking, without an apron. Her hair was brown.

'What's that? Now? You want to see my husband?'

'On business; it will only take two minutes.' His heart had stopped pounding. He thought: This man Sauer lives quite well ...

'Come in,' the woman said.

'In here!' her husband called out. Roeder glanced to the right and to the left. He was curious by nature. Even now he was intrigued by the glass tube on the wall that gave off light, as well as the bedframe made of chrome. A feeling that everything in life was worth being felt, admired and tasted, hindered him from dwelling on any one object. He followed the voice and went through a second door. Even though his heart was heavy, he marvelled at the sunken tub, which you didn't climb into but rather plopped into, and the three-part mirror above the sink.

'Heil Hitler!' the man said without turning round. A mirror reflected the man's face above a towel tied around his neck. Thick lather covered the unfamiliar features like a mask. Only the eyes examined him in the mirror with a keen look that revealed nothing but intelligence.

Roeder searched for words.

'Please,' the man said. He stropped his razor with infinite care. Roeder's heart was pounding, but Sauer's heart pounded no less hard. He'd never seen this man before in all his life. He had never seen him at the Municipal Street Construction Office. These days unfamiliar visitors at unusual times could mean anything. Just don't admit you know anything, or that you know anyone. 'Well?' he said again. His voice was rough, but then Roeder wasn't familiar with his customary voice.

'I'm bringing you regards from a mutual friend,' Paul said. 'Do you still remember him? He went on that nice canoeing trip with you on the Nidda some time back.'

The test will be, Sauer thought, whether I'm going to cut myself or not. He started to shave with a slack wrist. He didn't cut himself and his hand didn't tremble.

So now he's done, Paul thought. Why doesn't he wipe his face off and speak reasonably with me? I'm sure he doesn't usually scrape around on his face that long. I should think he'd be rather quick.

Sauer said, 'I don't understand you at all. What do you want from me? Whose regards are you bringing me?'

'From your canoeing friend,' Paul repeated. 'On the little *Annemarie*.' He caught the sideways look of the other man over the mirror and around the corner. Sauer got some lather on his eyelashes and wiped it off with a corner of the towel. Then he continued shaving. Without really opening his mouth, he said, 'I still don't understand a word you're saying. Excuse me, please. And I'm also in a hurry. You must have made a mistake in looking up the address.'

Roeder had taken one step towards the man; he was much shorter than Sauer. Now he could see the left side of Sauer's face in the side mirror. He tried to see something under all the foam but saw only the lean neck, the forward-thrust chin.

Sauer thought: He's hovering around me, watching, but I won't let him see my face. No matter how long he waits around. Why have they picked on me? So there is some suspicion. —I am being watched. —The way he's sniffing all around me! The little rat! —Aloud he said, 'Well, it seems your friend got the wrong address. I'm in a great hurry. Please don't bother me any longer. —Heidi!'

Roeder flinched. He hadn't noticed that there were now three of them in the room. A child stood by the door, pulling a necklace between her teeth. She'd probably been watching him all this time in silence.

'Show him to the stairs!'

As he walked out into the hall behind the child, Roeder was thinking, Bastard! He understood every word I said. Just doesn't want to take any risks, maybe because of that brat there. Don't I have children too?

After he'd slammed the door shut, Sauer wiped his face in one swipe, just as Roeder had thought he would. Then he rushed over to the bedroom window; breathlessly he pulled open the blind. He saw Roeder down below crossing the street. Did I do the right thing? What will he tell them about me? Calm down; I'm certainly not the only one. They're probably grilling a couple of dozen suspects today. What a funny pretence to use! Of all things, this escape. Not a bad pretence at all, actually! Something must have made them realise that I used to have a connection with Heisler. Or are they asking everybody the same things?

Suddenly he felt an icy chill running down his spine. What if it was for real, and not a Gestapo ploy? What if it was really George who sent him! What if he wasn't a Gestapo informer? No! If it wasn't just a rumour that George Heisler was here, walking around the city, they could have found other ways of getting in touch with him. That funny little fellow was just spying on me. Clumsy, a bungler. He took a deep breath and stepped back to the mirror to comb his hair. His face had turned pale the way tanned faces turn pale, as if the skin were wilting. Light grey eyes stared back at him from the mirror, looking deeper inside him than a stranger's eyes ever could. Stuffy air! That damned window, always plastered shut! He lathered his face anew. Still, they must have had a reason for sending that stool pigeon up here. Should I try to get away? Can I even ask whether I should try to get away without endangering others? He started shaving again, but his hands were trembling now. He cut himself, and he swore.

Oh well, I still have time to go to the barber – People's Court and it'll all be over – two days after being arrested. Don't make such a fuss, darling. Just imagine I'd gone down in a plane crash, my love.

He put on his tie, a healthy, lean, trust-inspiring man of around forty. He bared his teeth in the mirror. Last week I was telling Hermann: Those guys with their flags and brass bands will lose their jobs long before we lose ours, and I'll build you a couple of decent roads right through the new republic.

He went back to the bedroom window. Looked down at the empty street that the little fellow had walked along before. He felt cold. The fellow didn't look like a spy. He didn't have any of the mannerisms. He sounded honest, upright. How else could George have reached me? He's the one who sent the man to see me.

He was just about certain now. But what should he have done? The man had shown him no proof that he'd come from George. He had to send him away if there was even the slightest doubt. I'm not to blame, he told himself.

He would have done anything humanly possible for George. He not only wanted to be the sort of person who would have done everything, he really was such a person. Where, inside what four walls, was George waiting for an answer? Please understand me, George, just on the off chance, I couldn't have done anything anyway.

Then he thought again, maybe the fellow was a spy after all. The name of the boat? They could have easily found that out. They didn't need to know my name for that. And George, I'm sure, didn't give away anything.

There was a knock on the door. 'Mr Sauer, the coffee is ready.'

'What?'

'The coffee is ready.'

He shrugged, slipped into his jacket with the party insignia in the buttonhole and the Iron Cross ribbon. He looked around, as if searching for something. There are moments when the most familiar of rooms, the most tasteful furnishings are transformed into a sort of dump with a lot of stuff lying around that nobody could possibly use any more. He fished out his briefcase with an expression of distaste.

When the door to the hallway slammed shut for the second time, Mrs Sauer, who was sitting with the child at the coffee table, asked, 'Who was that?'

'Probably Mr Sauer,' the maid said as she poured the coffee.

'That's impossible,' Mrs Sauer said.

'Yes, it was Mr Sauer.'

But that's impossible, his wife thought. Leaving without his coffee, without saying good-bye. She tried to pull herself together.

The child was looking at her, not saying anything. She had immediately sensed the icy draught that came off the little freckled man.

*

Roeder had jumped up on a tram and made it to work just in time. He kept cursing Sauer under his breath until, towards the end of the first hour, he ended up burning his arm. Such a thing hadn't happened to him in ages.

'Quick, go to the doctor!' Fiedler said. 'Otherwise if it gets worse they won't pay. I'll take over for you meanwhile.'

'Shut your trap!' Roeder said.

Fiedler looked at him in surprise from behind his safety glasses.

Moeller turned round. 'Whoa there, you two.'

Paul went on with his work, gritting his teeth. Why did that bastard have to call out to him? How did he ever get to be the foreman? He's ten years younger than me.

George would have said, Well, he got old a little sooner. George was waiting back home now, waiting and waiting. If only Liesel bakes a few yeast dumplings. Just a few dumplings, Paul thought while, with compressed lips and closely watching the indicator, he let the melted metal pour into the pipe. Once Fiedler gave him the signal that the plug caps had been pressed in place, he would open the pipe, at the same time quickly raising his left leg – a habitual but superfluous movement he had acquired long ago. Paul was like a small, quick, ageless elf among all those half-naked, strong, mature men. They all liked him because he told jokes and had no objection to the practical jokes they played on him. For twenty years you've liked me, Paul thought grimly. But you can forget about me now. Find yourself another butt for your jokes. —I'll go mad if I can't have a drink soon. Is it really only ten o'clock? Suddenly Werner came up to him and incredibly quickly put a bit of salve on his wound and a piece of gauze on top of that. Paul said, 'Thanks, Werner.'

'No need to thank me!'

Fiedler told him to do it, Paul thought. They're all of them good chaps. And I don't want to leave the place. I'll be standing here again tomorrow. That damned Moeller, what if he knows something about me? And Werner? What if he knew who's sitting in my flat? – Werner is a good chap. Yeah? Well, up to a certain point. He bandaged my burn, but what if he were to burn himself? – Fiedler? – He quickly looked in his direction – Yes, Fiedler is different, he thought, as if, in that one look, he'd suddenly discovered something new about Fiedler, this man who worked alongside him all year long.

Later on he thought: There's still a good hour to go. If George doesn't have any better ideas, he'll have to stay at my place for another night. Strange... George had sworn this Sauer could be depended on. It's a good thing he has me.

'Look, George, if you can't do anything else, you could at least stir the dough with one hand,' Liesel said. 'Hold the bowl clamped between your knees!'

'What is it going to be? I always have to know what I'm making.'

'It's for steamed yeast dumplings. Yeast dumplings with vanilla sauce.'

George said, 'In that case, I'll stir till the day after tomorrow.'

But he had barely begun stirring when he broke out in a sweat. He was still so very weak. And even though it had been a quiet night, he had passed it in a sick half sleep. By now, George thought, Paul must have found one of them, either Schenk or Sauer. He stirred... Schenk or Sauer... he kept stirring... Schenk or Sauer.

From the street there came the sound of barrels being rolled out and an ancient counting ditty sung by the dewy voices of little children.

> 'Fly away ladybird, fly away
> Father's at war
> And Mother's in Pomerania
> And Pomerania's burned to the ground.'

When was it that he had longed bitterly to be a welcome guest behind an ordinary window in an ordinary home? It was when he was standing in a dark driveway in Oppenheim by the Rhine, waiting for the driver who later threw him off his truck.

In the next room, Liesel was making the beds, scolding one of her boys, teaching the other one to count, sewing a seam on her sewing machine, singing, filling a watering can, comforting a sobbing child. Ten times in ten minutes she almost lost her patience, but retrieved it again ten times from some inexhaustible reservoir. —A person who has faith has patience. But what did Liesel believe in? Well, she believed in what or whoever it is that gives meaning to what she does.

'Come on, Liesel, sit down for a while next to me and darn a sock.'

'Now? Darn socks? This pigsty has to be cleaned or we'll choke in the dirt.'

'Is the dough ready yet?'

'It's ready when you can see bubbles in it.'

Would she throw me out if she knew the truth about me? Maybe she would, but then, maybe she wouldn't. Most of the time Liesels like her, harassed as they are and used to all sorts of trouble, have courage.

Liesel moved the tub from the stove over to the laundry stool, set up the scrubbing board, and rubbed so hard that the tendons stood out on her round arms.

'Why are you in such a rush, Liesel?'

'You call this rushing? Do you want me to twirl on my heel between every two nappies?'

Well, at least I've seen all this from the inside again, he mused. I wonder if it goes on like this for ever? Will it always keep going like this?

Liesel was already starting to hang up a few items on the line strung diagonally across the kitchen. 'So, now hand me the bowl. You see these? Those are bubbles.' There was an expression of childlike joy on her innocent, plain features. She put the bowl with the dough on the stove and covered it with a towel.

'Why are you doing that?'

'No air is supposed to get to it, didn't you know that?'

'I've forgotten all those things, Liesel. Haven't watched anybody doing this in a long time.'

*

'Put that beast on a leash,' Ernst the shepherd yelled. Then he called to his dog, 'Nelly, Nelly!'

Nelly trembled with fury whenever she smelled Messer's dog. Messer had a red hunting dog. The dog had stopped at the edge of the forest, wagging his tail and looking up at his master with his long, floppy-eared head.

Messer didn't have a leash, and it wasn't really necessary, for Nelly, quivering with excitement, was of no interest to the hound. He'd been running around to his heart's content, and now he was looking forward to going home. Old potbellied Messer carefully climbed over the wire fence that separated his own section of forest from the Schmiedtheim forest. The Schmiedtheim forest was a beech forest with a band of evergreens along its edge. The piece of forest that belonged to Messer consisted solely of evergreens. They grew in loose groupings up to the back of his house, their tops projecting above the roof.

My dear little wife, Messer mumbled. He was carrying his hunting rifle over his shoulder, and was just coming back from a visit to his brother-in-law, his late wife's brother, a forester in Botzenbach.

Little wife ... hmm, that must be Eugenia, Ernst thinks. Funny little wife. Nelly continued to tremble with fury as long as the smell of Messer's hound hung in the air.

'Ernst,' Eugenia called to him. 'I'm putting your food on the windowsill.'

Ernst sat down in such a way that he could keep an eye on the sheep. Two boiled sausages, potato salad, cucumbers, and a glass of Hochheimer from last night.

'Do you want some mustard on the cucumber salad?'

'It can never be too spicy for me.'

Eugenia mixed the salad on the windowsill. Soft, white hands, but bare of ornament!

'Is Messer going to put a little ring on your finger?'

Eugenia replied calmly, 'Dear Ernst, it's about time you yourself got married. Then other people's stuff wouldn't keep going round and round in your head any more.'

'Oh, Eugenia, dear, whom should I marry? She'd have to have

Marie's little heart and Elsa's little dancing feet, and Selma's little nose, and Sophie's little behind, and Augusta's piggy bank.'

Eugenia started laughing softly.

What a laugh she had! Ernst listened enraptured. She went on laughing, softly and gently, without any false notes. He'd love to think of something to keep her laughing. But now he suddenly turned serious. 'Yes, but the main thing she'd have to have would come from you.'

'I'm really beyond the age for that,' Eugenia said. 'What main thing do you mean?'

'The quality of being so relaxed, so, so . . . something so free that if you get cheeky with her, there's suddenly nothing there at all that you can get at. And you can't even describe it because you can't get at it; that's the important thing, the essential, the main thing.'

'Oh, that's rubbish,' Eugenia said. But she took another bottle of Hochheimer and, holding it between her knees, pulled out the cork and poured Ernst a glassful.

'It's like the wedding at Galilee here at your place. First the sour things, then the sweet. Doesn't Messer scold you?'

'Messer doesn't scold me for such things,' Eugenie said, 'and I like him a lot for that.'

Hermann was sitting at a table in the Griesheim Railway Workshops canteen. He unwrapped the sandwiches Elsa had made for him to eat with his beer – mortadella and liverwurst, always the same thing. His late first wife had been more inventive about sandwiches. A quiet woman, not beautiful except for her eyes, but intelligent and determined, ready to stand up at a meeting and express her opinion from time to time. If she were still alive, how would she have coped with these times? Hermann ate the sandwich with the four precisely cut slices of sausage that always prompted such thoughts, while at the same time he listened to the talk on either side of him.

'Now there are only two, yesterday they were still saying there were three of them.'

'One of them knocked down a woman.'

'Why?'

'He was stealing the laundry right off the line. And she came out and caught him at it.'

'Who was stealing laundry off the line?' Hermann asked, even though he'd understood everything.

'One of the escaped prisoners.'

'Which escaped prisoners?' Hermann asked.

'The ones from Westhofen, where else?'

'He kicked her in the stomach.'

'Where did it happen?' Hermann asked.

'They didn't say.'

'How can they be sure that it was an escaped prisoner?' another man said. 'Maybe it was some laundry thief.'

Hermann looked at the man; he was an older man, a welder, one of those who had turned so silent last year that you forgot about them, even if you saw them every day.

'Well, so what if it was one of the escapees,' a young man said. 'He can't very well buy his shirts at Pfueller's shop. And if a woman like that gets in his way, he can't very well say, "Please be so kind as to iron this for me."'

Hermann looked at this man; he had been hired recently, and yesterday he'd said, 'All that matters to me is having a soldering iron in my hands again. Once I do, everything else will turn out all right.'

'The guy must be like a wild animal by now, knowing what's going to happen to him when they catch him,' a third one said, making a slicing gesture with the flat of his hand.

Hermann looked at this third fellow. They all looked at him briefly. Then there was silence, after which the most important thing would come, or maybe nothing more at all.

But the young fellow, who'd just been hired, shook it all off. He said, 'The excursion's going to be a big event on Sunday.'

'They say our Mainz colleagues are going to do it in style.'

'We'll sail at least as far as the Binger Loch.'

'And there'll even be a kindergarten teacher for the kids on the ship. All the things they're providing!'

Hermann decided to ask a question just the way you hammer a nail into something slippery that keeps sliding away: 'Which two are still left?'

'Left from what?'

'Of the escapees.'

'An old man and a young one.'

'And the young one, he's supposed to be someone from around this area.'

'That's all in people's imaginings,' said the welder, who'd come back as if he were returning to his own people after a long journey. 'Why would he go back to his own home town where there are hundreds of people who'd know him?'

'Well, there are also some advantages in that for the man. People will be much less likely to denounce someone they know than a total stranger. Just imagine, for instance, your denouncing me!'

The man who said that was a guy built like a horse. In the past Hermann had seen him working sometimes as a hall security guard, sometimes at a demonstration, always with his chest pushed out. 'What price the world?' A few times in the last three years he had tried to sound him out, which the fellow never seemed to understand. But then suddenly Hermann got the impression that he understood more than he let on.

'I'd denounce you without the slightest twinge of conscience, and why not? If for some reason you were to stop being my comrade, you'd stop being my comrade long before I'd stop being yours because I'd denounced you.' The man who said this was Lersch, the Nazi shop steward. He said it in that peculiarly distinct tone that people use when they state a principle, a point of view. Little Otto, his boyish face tense, had his eyes fixed on the fellow's lips. Lersch had been teaching the boy how to handle a welding gun and also how to play the spy. Hermann looked at the boy briefly – he was the first squad leader in the Hitler Youth, but the boy wasn't insolent, more the silent type, only rarely smiling, excessively tense in all his gestures. Hermann thought often about this boy, who was, as they say, blindly devoted to Lersch.

The old man answered quite calmly, 'Right. Before anyone denounces me, he'll have to think carefully whether I've even done anything that would make me stop being his comrade.'

On leaving the canteen many of the men gathered in some corner of their workshops. Hermann didn't say anything else. He folded up the wrinkled paper from his sandwiches and put it in his pocket so that Elsa could reuse it tomorrow. He was almost certain that Lersch was watching him, sniffing at something as yet intangible, that would one day in some word, somewhere, become something he could get hold of.

This time, when the bell signalled the end of the lunch break, they all jumped up, relieved that an external signal was ending something that could never be ended from inside.

At midday a group of children trudging home through one of the small streets in Wertheim got into a fight that was more of a game than anything serious. The group split in two and, tossing their school things aside, started beating each other up.

Suddenly one of the fighting cocks came to a stop, bringing the game to a standstill. An old man in rags standing at the edge of the pavement was rummaging around in their school things. He'd found a leftover chunk of bread. 'Hey, you there!' said one of the boys.

The old man plodded off in the opposite direction, away from the city, cackling. The boys let him go. Usually they were eager for any new mischief, but this time they just gathered up their belongings. The old man's cackling and his hairy, wild-looking face repelled them. As if by common consent they never even mentioned him.

Coming to an inn, the old man thought a moment, laughed, and went in. The proprietress was just serving a couple of lorry-drivers, but she stopped to bring the old fellow the schnapps he ordered. Shortly thereafter he got up and went out without paying, still cackling to himself, his head and shoulders twitching. The proprietress shouted,

'Where did that scoundrel go?' And the lorry-drivers made as if to go after him. But the proprietor, who'd just come back from the fishmonger's, it being Friday, didn't want any commotion and kept his wife and customers from going after the fellow, saying, 'Let him go; just charge it to the overhead.'

The old man trotted on his way, unchallenged. He passed through the little town, not taking the main street but by way of a small market. Feeling fairly safe now, walking more erect, his face more at peace, he walked along between the gardens at the edge of the city and up the hill.

Where there were still houses the road was paved, and at the steepest parts there were steps. At the top of the hill it turned into an ordinary dirt road that led away from the Main River and the highway, deeper into the rural interior. Close to the edge of the city a similar road branched off and led to the highway; the main street of the little town, with streetlamps and many shops, was merely that section of the highway that led through the town. But the road with the steps that the old man had just traversed was the shortest route to the small market for those farmers who didn't come from the Main River villages by way of the highway, but from the more remote villages.

The old man was Aldinger, the sixth of the seven escapees, now that Fuellgrabe had voluntarily turned himself in. No one at Westhofen would have seriously believed that Aldinger could have got even as far as Liebach in his flight. If he wasn't caught in the next hour, then he certainly would be an hour after that. In the meantime, it was already Friday, and Aldinger had made it as far as Wertheim. He had slept overnight in the fields, and once the driver of a removal van had given him a lift for four hours. He'd avoided all the patrols, but not through cunning, for his mind was no longer playing a part in this. — While still in the camp, there were already doubts about his sanity. For days he would be silent and then suddenly start giggling at some order. A hundred coincidences could have led to his rearrest at any moment – the smock he'd stolen barely covered his prison clothes. Yet none of them had resulted in his capture.

For Aldinger there was no thinking or working things out in advance. All he knew was the direction in which he wanted to go. This was where the sun stood over his roof in the mornings. This was where it was at noon. If the Gestapo, instead of setting in motion its sophisticated and powerful search apparatus, had just drawn a straight line from Westhofen to Buchenbach, they would in no time have come upon him at some point along that line.

Above the town now, Aldinger halted and looked around him. The twitching in his face stopped; his expression turned harder; his sense for the right direction, that almost superhuman sense, relaxed within him, since it was no longer needed. All this was familiar; here he knew his way. This was the place where once a month he'd stopped his truck. And from here his sons had carried the baskets down to the little market. While they were busy with that he had gazed at the land. Although his village wasn't far away, all these partially wooded, partially built-up little hills, their reflections in the water, the river itself that collected everything only to leave it behind again, even the clouds, the boats in which people drifted off, why, actually? – Before, he used to see all this as something distant and alien. That Earlier Time, that was the life he wanted to return to, that was why he had escaped. Earlier Time, that was the name of the land that started on the other side of the city. Earlier Time, that was the name of his village.

His first days in Westhofen, when the first abusive words and punches rained down on him, he had felt hate and rage and also the desire for revenge. But the punches kept coming more often and harder, and his head was old. By and by his desire to revenge himself for these foul deeds was shattered along with the memories of the foul deeds. Yet whatever was left after the beatings was still powerful and strong.

Aldinger turned away from the Main and plodded along on the dirt road, walking between the ruts created by the trucks. He looked about him, not furtively, but to determine the direction he had to take towards his goal. His face now looked less wild. He trotted down a little hill and up another. He walked through a small spruce forest and through a little forest preserve. The area seemed deserted. Aldinger walked through a bare field, then through a beet field. He still felt pretty warm. Not only the day, but the entire year seemed to be standing still. Aldinger could already feel the Earlier Time in all his joints and limbs.

That day Wurz, the mayor of Buchenbach, had not gone out into his fields as he had planned, as he had, in fact, boasted he would; instead he went to his office, actually his living room, a stuffy, cluttered little room that served him as mayoral and registry office. His sons had urged him to go out to his fields, that it was quite all right to do so. For they wanted to see their father as a heroic figure. But Wurz had given in to his wife, who wouldn't stop her wailing.

Buchenbach was still surrounded by guards, with extra guards assigned to Wurz's farmstead. The people laughed about it. It would never occur to Aldinger simply to stroll into the village. He'd surely find another way to deal with Wurz. How much longer did Wurz want to keep these bodyguards about? Really quite an expensive whim of his. After all, these SA fellows who'd been assigned to guard duty were all farmers' sons who were needed to work on their farms.

Mrs Schultz owned the general store; it sold just about everything the villagers needed. Her niece helped out in the shop. Mrs Schultz had seen Wurz going into his registry office, and she told her niece's fiancé. The fiancé was from Ziegelhausen and had arrived a few hours earlier than expected in the veterinarian's car with a couple of boxes of knickknacks. He intended to ask Wurz that evening to publish the banns. When his aunt said, 'He's in the registry office,' he put on a collar, and Gerda, his bride, went to change her clothes. The young man was ready first and went across the street. The SA guard who was posted outside Wurtz's door knew the young man and greeted him, 'Heil Hitler!'

The fiancé was in the same SA division, not because he couldn't live without a brown shirt, but because he wanted to be able to work, to get married, to inherit his parents' farm, and to live in peace, which he would certainly have been prevented from doing otherwise.

The SA guard guessed that he'd come about the banns and laughed as he tapped on the living room window. But Wurtz didn't answer.

He had been sitting at his desk under the Hitler portrait, and when the guard's shadow flitted across the window, he had ducked down in his chair. Hearing the knocking, he'd slipped off his chair, crawled around his desk, and hidden behind the door.

'Go on in, you two,' the guard said, since by now Gerda had come out dressed in a skirt and blouse. The groom knocked on the door, and when no one called out 'Come in', he tried the door handle, but the door was bolted shut. The guard had followed them, and now he pounded with his fist and shouted, 'A publication of the banns!'

Thereupon Wurz went over to the door and pushed back the bolt. Puffing, he stared at the groom-to-be as he spread out his papers on the desk. Wurz collected himself sufficiently to enable him to recite his little speech about farmers being the root of the nation, about the meaning of the family in the National Socialist state, and about the sanctity of the race.

Gerda was listening gravely to all this; her fiancé just nodded. Once outside, he said to the guard, 'A nice little pile of shit you're guarding there, comrade!' He pinched off a nasturtium blossom and stuck it into his buttonhole. Then he took his bride by the arm and the two walked along the village street, around the village square, and around the little Hitler oak that wasn't yet big enough to provide shade to any children or children's children, and at most might shade a few snails and sparrows. Then they went to the rectory and presented themselves as prospective bride and groom.

By this time Aldinger had put the next-to-last little hill behind him. It was called Buxberg. He was now walking very slowly, like a man who's dead tired but knows there can be no rest for him. He no longer looked around him, for this was all familiar territory to him; he knew every inch of it. There were already some Buchenbach farm fields mixed in among the last of the Ziegelhausen fields. Even though back then already they'd talked a lot about the reallocation and consolidation of agricultural land holdings, from up here the land was still a patchwork that looked like the much-mended aprons of farmers' children. Aldinger climbed up the last little hill with infinite slowness. His gaze was uncertain, but not dull or vague, rather as if it reflected an unexpected, indefinable goal.

Down below in Buchenbach it was time for the changing of the guards. The man posted outside Wurz's house was also relieved. He went over to the inn, where he met two of his comrades just coming off duty. All three were hoping that their comrade, the new bridegroom, would stop by and stand them a round of drinks.

Wurz, tired from the shock he'd had and also because it was midday, laid his head down on his desk, on top of the bridal couple's papers, their family trees, and certificates of good health.

Aldinger's wife had brought her children their lunch into the field, and they had eaten their meal together out there. There'd been occasional disagreements among the Aldingers, just as in all other families. Since the old man had been arrested, however, the family had drawn together. They rarely spoke about their absent family member, neither to outsiders nor among themselves.

One of the guards, in accordance with his orders, had followed Mrs Aldinger, not letting her out of his sight. She walked past the guards at the village gate, a farmer's wife dressed all in black and lean as a stick, looking neither to the right nor to the left, as if none of it had anything to do with her. Nor did she seem to be aware of the guard who had followed her from the house. It could as easily have been the scrawny cherry tree in the neighbour's garden that had been ordered to watch her.

By now Aldinger had arrived on top of the last little hill. This hilltop wouldn't be considered very high by most young people. Still, from there you could see the village laid out below. For a couple of yards hazelnut bushes lined the road. Aldinger sat down among the bushes. He sat there a while, quite calm in the half shade. Bits and pieces of roofs and fields were visible between the branches. He was dozing off when suddenly he came awake again. He tried to stand up. Glanced down into the valley. But the valley no longer lay there in its usual midday splendour basking in the pleasant everyday light. A cool, harsh brightness enveloped it now, both radiance and wind in one, and in the brightness the village seemed clearer than ever and for that reason strange. Then a dark shadow fell over the land.

Later that afternoon two farm children came by to pick hazelnuts. They ran screaming back into the field to their parents. Their father came over to look at the man they had found. He sent one of the children to the neighbouring village to get farmer Wolbert. Wolbert said, 'That's Aldinger!'

Then the first farmer recognised him too. Grownups and children stood there among the bushes, looking at the dead man. Finally the two men made a stretcher out of some pieces of wood.

They carried Aldinger down to the village, past the guards, who asked, 'Who have you got there?'

'Aldinger. We found him.' They carried him, where else, but to his own house. To the guards posted in front of the Aldingers' door they also said, 'We found him.' And the guard was much too flabbergasted to stop them from going in.

When she saw her husband brought back on a stretcher, Mrs Aldinger's knees buckled. But she collected herself, just as she would have if they'd brought him back dead from the fields. A group of neighbours had already gathered outside the door, as well as the two new guards from the village gate, the three SA fellows who'd been sitting in the inn, and the bridal couple on the way back from seeing their priest. Only the guards at the far end of the village street and those posted all around the outskirts of the village to keep Aldinger from entering the village had remained at their posts, since they didn't know about any of this yet. The guard at Wurz's door was also still standing there so as to protect the mayor against possible revenge attacks.

Mrs Aldinger turned back the coverlet on her husband's bed, which had remained freshly made and unused all that time. But then, when they brought in her husband and she saw how ragged, unkempt and dirty he was, she had them put him on her own bed. She put some water on to boil. Then they sent the oldest grandchild to call the rest of the family in from the fields.

The people standing in the doorway moved aside to let the boy through. He already had the downcast eyes and drawn lips of people in a house where a dead man is lying. In no time at all the boy returned with his parents and uncles and aunts. Aldinger's sons' faces bore an expression of contempt for the curious neighbours who had gathered outside the house. Once they were inside their four walls, in a more private setting, their faces took on an expression of grim mourning. And since the dead man was no different from other dead men, their mourning soon turned into the usual more measured mourning felt by good sons for a good father.

After a while it all became more ordered and calm. Those who came to the house no longer raised their arms and shouted 'Heil Hitler!' but instead removed their hats and extended their hands. The SA guards who, but for the grace of God, would have chased the old man and beaten him to death were able to leave with clean hands and unburdened consciences to go back to their own fields. People walking past Wurz's window grimaced, no longer concealing their contempt because of fear that they might be throwing away some advantage for themselves or their families. They probably asked themselves why it was Wurz of all people who had the power. And they no longer saw him surrounded by the lustre of power, but rather as they'd seen him the last four days, quaking in his wetted trousers. And when they thought about it, they now also saw the settlement village with different eyes, insofar as it had been the reason for selecting people. A tax abatement would have been worth more! And for that they should cringe before Wurz?

With the help of her two daughters-in-law, Mrs Aldinger washed her husband, cut his hair, and dressed him in his Sunday best. They stuffed his prison rags into the stove, thus helping the water to boil, as well as a second kettleful with which they finally managed to get the corpse clean and even have some left over to wash themselves before getting dressed in their Sunday best.

The Earlier Time that Aldinger had wanted to return to now opened its gates wide. He was laid out on his own bed. Mourners came by and were served pastries. Gerda's aunt quickly opened the boxes of notions her niece's fiancé had brought in the veterinarian's car; for now the Aldingers would surely need soap, black ribbons, and candles. Now that the dead man had succeeded in outfoxing the cordon of guards around the village, everything was all right.

Fahrenberg received the report: the sixth of the fugitives had been found. He was found dead. What? How? So this then was no longer a concern of Westhofen. It was a matter for the good Lord, the Wertheim authorities, the farm community officials of the man's district, and the mayor of his village.

After hearing the report, Fahrenberg went outside to the place they called the Dance Ground. The SA and SS men who were assigned to this duty were already lined up. Raspy-voiced commands were being issued. In obedience to the orders, a column of prisoners, dead tired and weighed down by dirt and despair, filed by as quickly and sound-lessly as the breath leaving dead souls. To the right of the barracks door the foliage of two undamaged plane trees gleamed an autumnal gold in the last rays of sunlight; for the day was coming to a close and the fog was moving in from the reedy marsh to this cursed place. Bunsen with his cherubic face stood before his SS squad as if he were awaiting the orders of his creator. Of the ten or twelve plane trees that used to grow to the left of the door, all had been cut down except for the seven they still needed. Zillich, standing in front of his SA squad, ordered the four living fugitives to be tied on. Every evening when the order rang out, a trembling passed through the prisoners, internal and weak, like the last frosty shiver before freezing to death. For the watchful SS guards permitted no one to move as much as a finger.

But the four men tied to the trees didn't tremble. Not even Fuell-grabe trembled. He stared straight ahead, open mouthed, as if death itself had yelled at him to finally behave decently. His face too gleamed with a light compared to which Overkamp's police lamp shed only a miserable glimmer. Pelzer had closed his eyes; his face had lost any gentleness it might once have had, all its timidity and weakness; it had turned bold and fierce. He had collected his thoughts, no more mulling things over, no more doubts and evasions; he had grasped the inevitable. And he too felt Wallau was standing by him. On the far side of Wallau stood Beutler, the man they'd caught and beaten up right after the escape. They had patched him up again on Overkamp's orders, although only temporarily. He wasn't trembling either. He too had long ago finished trembling. He had given himself away by trembling eight months ago, at the border, with his jacket lined with foreign currency. Now he hung rather than stood at his unique place of honour to the right of Wallau, which he would never have dreamed of once, and his damp face was flecked with light.

Wallau alone had a focused look in his eyes. Whenever he was led out to the crosses his almost petrified heart gave a fresh leap. Was George among them? What he was now staring at was not death, but the column of prisoners. Yes, among the old familiar faces he had even discovered a new one. This face belonged to a man who had been in the hospital. It was Schenk, the man Roeder had gone to see that morning trying to find a place for George to stay.

Fahrenberg stepped forward. He ordered Zillich to pull the nails out of two of the trees. The two trees stood there now, bare and empty, two genuine crosses for graves. Now there was just one tree with nails still unoccupied, on the far left, next to Fuellgrabe. 'The sixth escaped prisoner has been found!' Fahrenberg announced. 'August Aldinger. Dead, as you see. He himself is responsible for his death. We won't have to wait much longer for the seventh, for he is on his way. The National Socialist state relentlessly prosecutes anyone who commits an offence against the national community; it protects that which is worth protecting; it punishes those who deserve punishment; it destroys that which should be destroyed. There is no asylum in our country any more for fugitive criminals. Our people are healthy; it shakes off the diseased; it kills the insane. It has been less than five days since the escape occurred. Here – open your eyes wide – look and remember this!'

Then Fahrenberg went back inside the barracks. Bunsen had the column of prisoners step two paces forward. Now there was only a very small space between the trees and the foremost row. While Fahrenberg had been speaking and the subsequent commands issued, the sun had sunk beneath the horizon. The column of prisoners were bracketed on the right and the left by the SA and SS squads. The fog hung above and beyond them. This was the hour when all of them felt lost. Those among the prisoners who believed in a God thought He had forsaken them. Those among the prisoners who believed in nothing let the spirit inside them decay even as decay can set in while the body is still alive. Those among the prisoners who believed in nothing but the power inherent in a human being thought that this power existed now only within themselves and that their sacrifice had been futile and their people had forgotten them.

Fahrenberg had gone to sit down behind his table. From there he could look out of the window and see the backs of the crosses, the SA and SS squads from the side, and the column of prisoners from the front. He started to write his report. But he was too agitated for this task. He picked up the telephone receiver, pushed a button, and put it down again.

What day was it? Though the day was already coming to an end, nevertheless there were still three days left before the deadline he had set himself. If they had found six of them in four days, then they would surely find the last one in the three remaining days. Besides, that one was already surrounded; the fellow wouldn't get another minute's sleep. Unfortunately neither would he, Fahrenberg.

By now it was almost dark inside the barracks. He switched on the lamp. The lamplight from Fahrenberg's window cast the shadows of the trees on to the first row of prisoners in the column. How long had they been standing there? Was it already night? Still no command, and the men who were tied on the crosses must be suffering, their tendons burning. Suddenly a prisoner, in the next-to-last row of the column, screamed. The four men on the crosses started violently and were forced back against the nails. The fellow who'd screamed pitched forward against the man in front of him, pulling him down as well, and was rolling around on the ground, howling, by now already being kicked and beaten by the guards. The SA were everywhere.

At that instant Police Commissars Fischer and Overkamp, wearing hats and waterproof coats, came from inside the camp carrying brief-cases. They were accompanied by an orderly with their bags. Overkamp's work at Westhofen was ended. The search for Heisler no longer required his presence there.

Two orders were issued and everything was as before. The man who'd broken down and the man in front of him had already been dragged off. Without looking to the right or left, the two commissars walked over to the commandant's barracks between the crosses on one side and the foremost row of the column of prisoners on the other, seemingly without noticing the strange sights flanking their route. The orderly with the bags remained outside the door, gaping at all of it. In a little while the two came out again and retraced their steps. This time Overkamp glanced towards the trees. His eyes met Wallau's gaze. Overkamp hesitated imperceptibly. On his face, an expression of recognition mixed with 'So sorry, it's your own doing.' Maybe there was also a grain of respect, of admiration.

Overkamp knew these men were lost as soon as he left the camp. At most they might let them live until the seventh man was brought back. Unless someone did something clumsy or lost patience.

Those still on the Dance Ground could hear an engine starting. Their hearts turned over. Of the four men tied to the crosses, only Wallau was in any shape to realise that they were now lost. But what about George, had they found him? Was he already on the way here too?

'That man Wallau will have to be the first one to go,' Fischer said. Overkamp nodded. He'd known Fischer a long time. They were both National Socialists with all the battle medals and awards. They'd previously worked together in the system from time to time. Overkamp was accustomed to employing the police methods customary in his profession. For him harsh interrogations were an assignment like any other. They didn't amuse him, certainly gave him no pleasure. He had always considered those he'd had to hunt down as enemies of law and order as he saw it. Things became vague only when he started thinking about whom he was actually working for.

Overkamp forced himself to stop thinking about Westhofen. – There was still the matter of Heisler. He looked at the clock. They were expected in Frankfurt in an hour and twenty minutes. Because of the fog, their car was doing no more than forty kilometres an hour. Overkamp wiped his window. He saw the road out of the village in the gleam of a streetlamp. 'Hey, stop the car!' he suddenly yelled. 'Come on, Fischer! Have you had any apple cider yet this year?'

Once they were out of the car and standing there in the misty, deserted, fresh-smelling countryside, the tension and anxiety brought on by their work dropped from their shoulders. They ceased thinking about it momentarily. They entered the same village inn where Mettenheimer had sat waiting for his daughter Elli when she had unexpectedly been issued a visitor's pass to Westhofen. A pass she hadn't been at all happy about.

When Paul Roeder came home from work, George didn't have to ask any questions. He could tell from Paul's face how the attempts to find a hiding place had turned out.

Liesel was waiting to hear what the men would say on tasting her sweet yeast dumplings, waiting to hear their *aah*s and *yum*s. But the two men chewed around on them as if they were carrot slices. 'Don't you feel well?' she asked Paul.

'Why shouldn't I be feeling well? Oh well, I ran into some bad luck.' He showed her the burn on his arm.

Liesel was almost glad to discover the reason for the ungrateful, silent chewing. She examined the burn. From the time she was a child she'd been used to seeing all sorts of work injuries in her family. She went to get some salve.

Suddenly George said, 'The bandage on my hand isn't really necessary any more. While you're playing doctor, Liesel, would you get me some adhesive tape.'

Paul watched wordlessly as his wife, without any fuss, unrolled

George's bandage. The older children watched from behind George's chair. Roeder's little shiny blue eyes shot a cold, severe glance at George.

'You were lucky, George, that none of the glass splinters got into your eyes,' Liesel said.

'Lucky, lucky,' George said. He looked at the palm of his hand. Liesel had taped it quite skilfully, rebandaging only the thumb. If he held the hand a certain way, it looked as if nothing was wrong with it.

'Stop! Don't!' Liesel shouted, adding, 'Oh, too bad. We could have washed it out and reused it.'

George had got up and quickly stuffed the old bandages into the stove that was still glowing after baking the yeast dumplings. Roeder had been following all this without moving.

'Yuk,' Liesel said. She opened the window wide and a little stream of smelly smoke wafted out, mixing with the city air: air to air, smoke to smoke. —Now the doctor can sleep in peace. What a risky thing that had been, going up to his surgery! How skilful the man's hands had been! Heart and intelligence in his hands.

'Hey, Paul,' George said quite cheerfully, 'do you still remember Moritz, the old clothes man? And how we used to pester him until he complained to your father and your father gave you a thrashing, and the old guy stood there and shouted, "Not on his head, Mr Roeder, that'll make him stupid, on his arse, his arse!" That was rather decent of the fellow, don't you think?'

'Yes, very decent. *Your* father must have beaten you the wrong way,' Paul said, 'otherwise you'd be smarter.'

For three minutes their mood had lightened; they'd felt a little better. Then the reality of their situation, its unbearable, irrevocable gravity, started weighing them down again.

'Paul,' Liesel said fearfully. Why was he staring straight ahead like that? She wasn't paying any attention to George. Just kept looking over at Paul while she was clearing the table, and then, as she took the children to bed, another quick look back through the doorway.

'Well, George,' Paul said, once the door closed behind her, 'that's how things stand now. We have to think up something better. Till then you'll have to spend another night here.'

George said, 'Are you aware that in the meantime my picture has been distributed to all the police districts? That they're showing it to all the block wardens? And the block wardens are showing it to all the house wardens? After a while everyone will have seen it.'

'Did anyone see you coming up here yesterday?'

'I can't swear to it, but there was no one in the hall.'

'Liesel,' Paul said to his wife, who'd come back into the room, 'you know I have such an odd thirst, please go and get us some more beer.'

Liesel gathered the empty bottles and left meekly to do his bidding. My God, she thought, what's with that man?

'Don't you think we ought to tell Liesel?' Paul asked.

'Liesel? No, do you really think she'd let me stay here if she knew?'

Paul said nothing. Suddenly there was one thing about Liesel that he didn't know, that was impenetrable to him, his Liesel, whom he thought he'd known to the core since they were children. They thought about it. Then Paul said, 'Elli, your first wife . . .'

'What about her?'

'Her family is pretty well off; people like that might know other people – do you think I should go there?'

'No! They're being watched. Besides, you don't really know how she feels about this.'

They thought about it some more. By then the sun had gone down behind the rooftops across the way. The streetlamps were already on. Some evening light still came diagonally in through the window as if seeking out the farthest corners before it was finally extinguished. Both men noticed at the same time that everything their thoughts touched seemed to trickle away like sand. Both were listening for sounds coming from outside on the stairs.

Liesel came back with the beer, this time greatly agitated. 'A funny thing happened,' she said. 'Someone came and asked about us at the inn.'

'What? About us?'

'He asked Mrs Mennich where we lived. But he couldn't possibly have known us if he doesn't know where we live.'

George was on his feet. 'I have to leave now, Liesel. Thanks a lot for everything.'

'Oh, have a beer with us first, George.'

'I'm sorry, Liesel, it's got late. So...'

She turned on the light. 'Next time don't let so much time pass by on our friendship.'

'No, Liesel, I won't.'

'Where are you going?' she asked Paul, who'd got up to go with George. 'First you send me for beer, and now...'

'I'm only taking George to the corner, I'll be back right away.'

'No, no. You stay here,' George said.

Paul said calmly, 'I'll go with you as far as the corner. That much I can do.'

At the door he turned round again, said, 'Liesel, listen, don't tell anyone that George was here with us.'

Liesel turned red with anger. 'So, there is something going on! Why didn't you tell me right away?'

'When I come back, I'll tell you everything. But don't say a word to anyone. It would be terrible if you did, not only for George but also for me and for the children.'

She stood transfixed by the closed door. Terrible for the children? Terrible for Paul? Chills ran down her spine. She went over to the window and watched the two of them, a tall man and a short one, walking between the streetlamps. She was frightened. She sat down at the table and waited for her husband to come home. In the meantime it turned completely dark.

'If you don't leave right now,' George whispered hoarsely, his face distorted with anger, 'you'll ruin everything for me. You're no help to me.'

'Shut up! I know what I'm doing. You just follow me where I'm taking you. I had a sudden inspiration when Liesel came upstairs just now, giving us such a fright. I have an idea. If Liesel keeps her mouth shut, which I'm sure she will because she's afraid for our sake, then you're out of the woods for tonight.'

George said nothing. His head was empty. He followed Paul into the city. Why should he think if thinking didn't lead anywhere anyway? Only his heart kept pounding, as if it wanted to be let out of its inhospitable quarters. Like two evenings ago when he was on the point of going to see Leni. He tried to calm his heart: You can't compare the two; after all this is about Paul. Don't forget that. It has nothing to do with love affairs. This is friendship. You don't trust anyone? But you *do* have to have the courage to trust a friend. Calm down now. You can't keep on pounding like that. You're upsetting me.

'We won't take the tram,' Paul said. 'Ten minutes more or less doesn't matter. I just want to tell you where I'm taking you. I came by there this morning when I was going to see your damned Sauer. My Aunt Catherine, she owns a haulier's garage, a huge business, three or four trucks. A brother of my wife's from Offenbach is going to be employed there. He was in jail, and they took away his driver's licence because they found alcohol in his blood. He wrote a letter in which he says he's coming soon and I should arrange it with her. She doesn't know anything about that yet; doesn't even know him. I'll introduce you there. You say yes to everything, or don't say anything at all.'

'And identification papers? And tomorrow?'

'Just get used to counting one, two, three, instead of one, three. You have to get away. But first you have to find a place to stay for the night. Would you rather be dead tonight and then have good documents tomorrow? I'll come by tomorrow. Your friend Paul will think of something, never fear.'

George touched his arm. Paul looked up at him, made a face, the way children do to keep from crying. His forehead was lighter than the rest of his face because it had fewer freckles. George felt reassured simply by his presence. If only he doesn't suddenly turn round and leave. George said, 'They could nab us any moment.'

'Don't even think about that.'

The city was bright and full of people. From time to time Paul met someone he knew, greeted the person and was greeted in return. Whenever that occurred, George turned his head away. Paul said, 'Don't turn away every time; no one is going to recognise you.'

'But you recognised me immediately, Paul.'

They had come to Metzergasse. There were two car repair workshops on the street, a petrol station, a couple of restaurants. Since Paul came by here frequently, he was greeted often. 'Heil Hitler!' here, 'Heil Hitler!' there. 'Hello, Paul!' here, 'Hello, Paul!' there. They also stopped briefly at the gate of the entryway to the garage located in the courtyard. There were some SA men, two women, the little man from the inn, his nose glowing this evening like a carbuncle. 'We're going over to the Sun Inn to sit for a while,' one of them said. 'Come and join us, Paul.'

'I want to say good night to my Aunt Catherine first.'

'Oh!' said the old man, who felt a chill at the mere mention of her name.

'Come on,' the two women said, taking the old man between them and leading him off.

Just then a truck came out of the courtyard and forced them up against the left wall. When Paul and George finally entered the courtyard, they found Mrs Grab-er, Paul's Aunt Catherine herself, standing by the gate, having just dispatched the truck. The overland truck shipments left at night.

'Here he is!' Paul said.

'That one?' the woman said, glancing at George. She was a strong, large woman, but it was more her bone structure rather than that she was fat. White, shaggy hair above a round forehead, and white eyebrows over angry, keen eyes kept her from looking like an old woman and more like some naturally white-haired creature. She looked again at George. 'Well, come on in!' She waited a moment and then casually brushed the stiff hat off his head. 'Take that off. Don't you have a cap?'

'His stuff is still at our place,' Paul said. 'He was going to sleep at our house tonight, and now our little Paul is coughing and Liesel thinks he's coming down with the measles.'

'Sounds like fun,' the woman said. 'Why are you standing around there in the gateway? Either come in or stay outside.'

'So long, Otto. Have a good time,' Paul said. He'd held on to George's hat when his aunt had brushed it off George's head. 'Goodbye, Aunt Catherine, Heil Hitler!'

In the meantime George had looked at the woman's face more carefully: the terrain he'd have to reconnoitre in the next few hours, and she, for her part, looked at him for the third time, and this time long and intently. He withstood her inspection – neither of them had reason to be kind.

'How old are you?' she asked him.

'Forty-three.'

'Well, then Paul lied to me. I don't run a convalescent home here.'

'Why don't you wait and see what I can do.'

Her nostrils flared. 'I already know what you can do . . . well, hurry up and change your clothes.'

'Mrs Grabber, would you give me some overalls. My stuff is still over at Paul's.'

'Hmm?'

'I didn't know that your business runs through the night.'

Then the woman started cursing at full blast for several minutes. George wouldn't have been surprised if she'd struck him. He listened without saying a word, and with just a hint of a smile that she may have seen, or maybe it escaped her in the lamplight.

When she was done, he said, 'If you don't have any overalls to lend me, I'll work in my underwear. How am I supposed to know the ropes, right from the first minute I get here?'

'Take him back home again,' the woman yelled out to Paul, who'd suddenly come back, with George's hat in his hand. He'd been running down the street when they'd hailed him from the inn, and he'd waved at them. It made him suddenly remember the hat. Now he got a setback on hearing his aunt's angry words. He grimaced.

'Please give him a chance till tomorrow. Then I'll come back and you can tell me how he worked out.' And he ran off as fast as he could.

'Without Paul,' the woman said, somewhat calmer now, 'someone like you would probably go to the dogs. I'll say it again, my business is not a convalescent home. Come along with me.'

He followed her through the courtyard, which seemed much too bright to him and too full of people. People came and went through the courtyard gate, from and to the tavern and the flats. People were already looking at him. A policeman was standing in the garage next to an empty car. Why couldn't the guy have come here earlier? George thought, and he started to sweat. The policeman, though, paid no attention to him, just asked Mrs Grabber for some document.

'Pick out one of these old things to wear,' the woman said to George. The window of a small room that was used as an office faced out into the garage. The policeman watched dully as George tried on one of the greasy overalls lying there. Then he looked up at the lighted window, at the woman's large white head. He mumbled, 'What a broad.'

When the policeman had gone, the woman stuck her head out of the window, supporting her arms in a way that made it clear that this window was her captain's bridge from which she issued commands. She cursed and yelled, 'Get out into the courtyard, you faking slowpoke! The car is going to be picked up in half an hour for Aschaffenburg, get a move on!'

George walked over to stand below the window. He said up to her, 'Would you please tell me calmly and precisely just what I am to do here.'

Her eyes narrowed to slits; the pupils bored into the fellow's face; she'd been told he was a pretty dissolute type who'd ruined his family. But never mind that. She peered at his face, which she at first thought had been disfigured by a fall, but she couldn't find anything. Usually her glare froze anyone it was fixed on, but for the first time she herself now felt a touch of cold. Calmly she began to explain how he was to overhaul the car. She watched him carefully. After a while she came out of her office and stood next to him, urging him on. George's half-healed hand quickly opened up again. When he tied a dirty rag around it using his teeth and the other hand, she said, 'Either you're healed and in good enough shape to work; or you're not; in that case, go on home!'

He didn't answer her, didn't look at her. That's how she is, he thought; so be it. You have to take her the way she is. Eventually it will all be over. And so he did what she asked him to do. He worked fast and doggedly and was soon too exhausted to be afraid or even to think.

Meanwhile, Liesel was waiting in her dark kitchen. When, after ten minutes, Paul still hadn't come back, she knew that he'd gone farther than just to the corner with George. She wondered what had happened. What were the two of them doing? Why didn't Paul tell her anything?

The evening was deathly quiet. The hammering on the fifth floor, all the scolding and cursing on the third, the marches coming from someone's radio, the laughter echoing across the streets from one window to another couldn't drown out the silence, or the soft footfalls on the stairs coming up.

Only once in her life had Liesel ever had anything to do with the police. At the time, she was a child, ten or eleven years old. One of her brothers had got into trouble; maybe it was the one who later died in the war, for there was never any mention of it in the family afterwards. It had been buried with him in Flanders. But the fear they had all struggled with back then was still in Liesel's blood today. A fear that had nothing to do with a bad conscience; it was a poor people's fear, a chicken's fear under a hawk, a fear of being persecuted by the state. An ancient fear that better defines to whom the state belongs than any constitutions or history books. But now Liesel resolved to fight tooth and claw to protect her family, with cunning and deceit.

As the footsteps came to the last landing and were heading towards their flat, she jumped up, turned on the light, and began to sing in a voice short of breath and hoarse with fear. For, she told herself, singing and cheerfulness indicate a clear conscience. The person outside her door did actually hesitate before he rang the bell.

He wasn't wearing a uniform. Liesel's lamp showed an unfamiliar, nondescript, dull face – a secretive face. Liesel thought: He must be a plainclothes man. She knew terms like these, must have picked them up somewhere else, because Paul never talked about such things with her. She was sure the man had his dog tag pinned to the inside of his jacket.

'Are you Mrs Roeder?' the man asked.

'As you can see.'

'Is your husband home?'

'No,' Liesel said, 'he's not here.'

'About what time will he be home?'

'I really don't know.'

'Oh well, but he will come home at some point?'

'No idea.'

'Did he go on a trip?'

'Yes, yes, he went on a trip. His uncle died.'

Half hidden by the door, partly in the shadow, she saw the man's face twitch, obviously in disappointment. He'll leave soon now, she thought.

But the man turned back again. 'Has he been out of town for a long time?'

'Pretty long.'

'Well then, Heil Hitler!' Even his back looked disappointed. He shrugged.

Liesel suddenly had another fright. What if he asks the caretaker?

She tiptoed out into the stairwell in her stocking feet and listened, but he didn't ask anything of the caretaker. When she went back to the kitchen window and looked out, she saw him walking away down the silent street.

The thing that had impelled Franz to go to the Roeders' that night was a half-formed hope, a sort of feel for what might be possible. Walking now through the still streets to his tram stop, he felt disappointed and disheartened. He took a tram to the opposite end of the

city, where he had left his bicycle at an inn. Then he cycled it out to
see Hermann at his house in the development.

Hermann had been so certain Franz would come that he began
to worry when he didn't arrive. Franz rarely stayed away so many
consecutive evenings. This evening he realised that, although Franz
sought advice from him, he himself needed Franz more than he had
been aware of. This advice that Franz calmly asked of him and which
he then followed to the letter – it required Franz in order to formulate
itself in him and then to bring it out of him. When the bicycle bell
finally rang under their window, Elsa wiped off the oilcloth-covered
kitchen table, and Hermann, concealing his joy, got the chess set out
of the drawer.

But Hermann's joy that evening lasted only until Franz had settled
himself at the table. Franz was not his usual self. And he remained
silent longer than usual.

Hermann gave him time. Then, after a while, it came out, with
Hermann listening attentively at first, then amazed, and then worried. Franz told Hermann what had happened to him, how he'd met
Elli three times, in the cinema, in the market hall, and in the attic
with the apples. How they had together rummaged around in George's
life, tried to dig up people from their memories, how he'd followed
various leads, obsessed by the idea that he could actually find George
himself. And how it had all backfired, totally!

'What do you mean, totally?'

But Franz had turned silent again.

Hermann waited. It was wrong and pointless for Franz to tell him
only now about all that he'd done on his own without having first
discussed it with him. Perplexed, Hermann gazed at his friend's somewhat
sleepy-looking face; it was doing a good job hiding his toughness.

Franz began to talk again, but what he said wasn't at all what
Hermann had expected him to say.

'Look, Hermann, I'm really just an ordinary man. The things I
want in life are the most ordinary of things. For example, that I can
stay here where I am because I like living here. This urge to leave that

some people have, for the most part, I don't have that. If it were up to me, I'd like to stay here for ever. The sky isn't too glaringly bright nor is it too bleak and grey. And it's neither too countrified nor too citified. Everything is nearby, smoke and fruit. How happy I would have been if I could have had Elli. Others are on the lookout for all sorts of women, all sorts of adventures. Not me. I don't have that hunger. I would have been loyal and faithful to Elli, even though I know she's not anyone extraordinary. But she's sweet and kind. I'd be content if I could live with her until we were both old and grey. But now I can't even see her any more.'

'Of course not,' Hermann said. 'It was already taking too much of a risk for you even to look her up.'

'It's surely not an extravagant wish to go out with Elli on a Sunday, but I can't. No. Don't act so surprised, Hermann. I cannot have Elli. The big question is whether I can even stay here for any length of time. Maybe I'll have to leave tomorrow already.

'I always wanted the simplest things in life – a meadow or a boat, a book, friends, a girl, peace and quiet. But then this other thing came into my life. It entered my life when I was quite young – the desire for justice. And gradually my life changed, and now it only appears to be quiet.

'Some of our friends when they imagine what another Germany will look like ... my God, what dreams they have for the future.

'But I don't have those. Afterwards I want to still be where I am now, just different. In the same business, only as a different man. To work here for ourselves. And to finish work in the afternoon not too tired to be able to read and learn. While the grass is still warm. But it should be the grass by Marnet's fence, here. It should all be here. Then I want to live in the settlement here or up there at the Marnets' and the Mangolds'...'

'Well, it's good to know that now,' Hermann said. 'But tell me, what does George's friend Roeder look like.'

'He's short,' Franz said. 'From a distance he looks like a boy. Why do you ask?'

'If the Roeders are hiding someone, they would have behaved just the way you described. But they probably haven't hidden anyone.'

'When I got there, the woman was alone with the children,' Franz said. 'I listened before I rang the bell and after I left to make sure.'

Hermann thought, Franz has to stay out of the game entirely from now on. The three words *like a boy* had given him a shock. This was the second time he'd heard those words today. If only I had the time. Backer is going to be in Mainz early next week! Time is the one thing I lack. We'd be able to get the man out, but time…time…

Hermann asked, 'Where does Roeder work?'

'At Pokorny. Why do you ask?'

'I was just wondering.'

But Franz sensed, or thought he sensed, that Hermann was keeping something from him.

That night Paul and Liesel were sitting together on their kitchen sofa. He was awkwardly stroking her hair and round arms the way he used to do when they first fell in love; he even kissed her face, wet from crying. But so far he had told her only a fraction of the truth. That the Gestapo were after George because of things he'd done in the past. That now the new laws assigned terrible penalties for such things. Under the circumstances, could he really have sent George away? he asked.

'Why didn't he tell me the truth? Eating and drinking at my table!'

At first Liesel had been very upset, had railed against him, stamping around the flat, red-faced with anger. Then she'd begun to moan, then to cry. That was over now. It was already past midnight. And Liesel had cried herself out. Every ten minutes she asked, 'Why didn't you tell me the truth?' As if that were the main issue.

Paul's tone of voice had changed, become more serious. He said, 'Because I didn't know if you could cope with the truth.' Liesel pulled her arms away from his hands. She was silent. Paul went on, 'If we'd told you everything, and if we'd asked you right away whether he could stay, would you have said yes or no?'

Liesel answered vehemently, 'I would almost certainly have said no. He's just one man! And we're four – five, actually six with the one we're expecting. We didn't tell George about that because he'd poked fun at us for the ones we already had. And you would have had to say to him, "George, you're one man and we're six..."'

'Liesel, it was his life...'

'Yes, but our lives too.'

Paul was silent. He felt miserable. For the first time he was totally alone. Things could never again be the way they had been. These four walls...what was the use? This tumble of children...to what purpose? He said, 'And then you demand that we tell you everything! That we tell you the truth! If you had shut the door in his face and two days later I handed you the newspaper and you were to come across his name – George Heisler – under the listing "People's Court" and under "Sentence to be carried out immediately", wouldn't you be sorry then? Would you have shut the door in his face if you had known that beforehand?'

He'd moved a little distance away from her. Covering her face, she started to cry again. Then she said, still crying, 'Now you have a bad opinion of me. Bad, bad. You never thought such bad thoughts about me before. And you want to get rid of this bad thing, your Liesel. Yes, that's what you're thinking, and that you're all alone now and that you don't care a damn about us. George is the only one who still matters to you. Yes, sure if I'd known what would happen to him, with the "Sentence executed immediately" – yes, then I would have taken him in. And maybe I would have taken him in anyway. I don't know now. It all hangs by a thread. Yes, I suddenly think I would have taken him in.'

Paul said more calmly now, 'You see, Liesel, and that's why I didn't tell you anything, because at first you might not have taken him in, and then later, after I explained it all to you, you would have regretted it.'

'But some bad things might still happen. And you'll have to answer for that then.'

'Yes,' Paul said. 'I'll answer for that then. I had to make the decision, not you. After all, I'm the man here and the father of our family. For I can say yes to something immediately; whereas you at first might have said, no, and then, maybe, and then in the end, yes. But by that time it would have been too late. In such a case I can decide immediately. We'll talk about it all later. Now, let's first have the kind of coffee you made yesterday when George collapsed.'

'He turned everything upside down! Coffee at night!'

'Tomorrow, if the caretaker asks you who came to see us today, tell him Alfred von Sachsenhausen.'

'Why should he ask me?'

'Because he'll be asked by the police and maybe the police will ask us too.'

At that Liesel got all upset again. 'The police question us! Dear Paul, you know what a bad liar I am. They can tell just by looking at me. I couldn't even lie as a child. Even when the other kids were lying, they could always tell from my face.'

Paul said, 'What do you mean, you can't! Didn't you lie just a moment ago? If you can't lie to the police, then everything here will come toppling down. You'll never see me again. But if you lie exactly as I'm going to tell you, then I promise you that we'll be seeing the Westend–Niederrad match next Sunday with our free tickets.'

'Are there free tickets?'

'Yes, there are free tickets.'

Shortly before midnight George had stretched out in the garage, but only moments later he was called again because the chauffeur who had come to pick up the car had lodged some complaints. Mrs Grabber upbraided George, this time in a low and cutting tone of voice. And then, just as he was about to lie down again, the second Aschaffenburg car came in. This time Mrs Grabber stood over him as he worked and watched closely, criticising his every clumsy move and all his lapses and faults. That fellow Otto for whom he was substituting must have led a pretty shabby, miserable life, he thought. No wonder he was pretending to be ill, trying to avoid this drastic treatment Paul had seen fit to inflict on him, George. He wanted to lie down again, but now he was told to check out the tools and to clean up the garage. Morning was near. For the first time, George had a chance to look up.

The woman was looking at him. Didn't this fellow care about what wheels ran over him? Was it possible that the wheels he'd come under now seemed comparatively gentle to him? She was amazed, and it calmed her down; George calmed down too. She went back to her office and back to leaning out of the window. George had curled up on the bench. Maybe I can get along with him after all, she thought.

George lay there, heavy as lead, under Belloni's coat. Even though sleep was pretty much out of the question now, thoughts raced through his mind, without stops or gaps, following each other with the suppleness of thoughts that come to one in dreams. What if they never come to pick me up? If Paul just leaves me here? In place of that fellow Otto?

He imagined what his life would be like if he had to stay here. Unable to leave this place. Never to get out of this courtyard, forgotten by everybody. Better to get away on his own as quickly as possible. But what if help were coming after all? And he had left only to be captured a couple of hours later!

If they catch me and take me back to Westhofen, he thought, then let it happen while Wallau is still alive. If it's inevitable, then let it happen quickly so that I can die together with Wallau. If he's still alive! At that instant the end seemed inescapable. As the minutes flipped by, all the things that would normally have been spaced out over a lifetime, over years – the straining of all one's powers to the utmost, then the relaxation, the subsiding, and again the painful straining, the exertion – were taking place within his mind in the space of one hour. At last, totally spent, he watched impassively as the new day dawned.

6

FAHRENBERG, fully dressed, was lying on his back with his legs, encased in boots, hanging down over the edge of the bed. His eyes were open; he was listening for sounds in the night.

He covered his head with the blanket. Now at least he could hear a sound, that inner roar that originates from within a person. Just not this straining to hear any more! He yearned for a tone, for any sort of alarm whose origin he didn't know beforehand so that this self-consuming listening would be done with. The sound of a car engine on the highway, the shrilling of a telephone in the administration barracks, in the end even the sound of footsteps going from the administration barracks to the commandant's barracks could have put an end to the waiting. But the camp had been silent, deathly silent ever since the SA had celebrated, in its own way, the departure of the Gestapo commissars. They'd hit the bottle and gone on drinking till 11.30 p.m.; then, between 11.30 and 12.30 a.m., they had 'walked through' the prisoners' barracks because of that afternoon's incident. Towards one o'clock, when the SA men were as exhausted as the prisoners, the dance came to an abrupt end.

Fahrenberg had started up several times during the night. Once it was a car driving by in the direction of Mainz, twice there were cars going towards Worms, there had been footsteps crossing the Dance Ground but they passed his barracks and headed to Bunsen's door. Shortly after two, the phone in the administration barracks had rung and he had expected it to be the report that they had been ordered to pass along to him at any hour of the day or night: namely, that the seventh escapee had been captured. But it wasn't.

Almost suffocating under the blanket, Fahrenberg pulled it off his head. How silent was the night! Instead of being filled with the sound of sirens, of pistol shots and the roar of engines – the sounds of a monstrous search in which everyone was participating – this was the most silent of nights, an ordinary night between two workdays. No searchlight beams crisscrossed the sky. For all the villages round about the autumn stars were lost in the mist; only the soft but penetrating light of a moon that was waning with the passing of the week found those who longed to be found. After a hard day's work everyone and everything was sleeping. It was peaceful, except for a few screams coming from the Westhofen concentration camp. Screams that now and then woke someone who then sat up and listened. The noise made by a warrior horde withdrawing from the region seemed to become louder for a while and then to die away completely. So that now anyone still awake would no longer be kept from sleep by outside sounds.

I'm going to sleep now, Fahrenberg told himself. Overkamp has long ago arrived at his destination. Why did I have to set a deadline? And why make the deadline public? They can't blame me if Heisler isn't recaptured now. No matter what, I have to get some sleep now.

He wrapped the blanket around his head again. But what if he's already left the country? What if that's the reason they can't find him, because he actually cannot be found any more? What if he's walking across the border this very moment? But the borders are being watched as if we were at war.

He sat up with a start. It was five o'clock. A crazy noise was coming from outside. Yes, this is it, he thought. There was the sound of car engines coming from the highway, the staccato commands from the camp entrance that accompany an arrival. Then came a dark, unevenly mounting noise that hadn't yet reached its ultimate pitch, hadn't yet arrived at that bittersweet taste. No blood had yet been shed.

Fahrenberg switched on a few of his lamps. But the bright light seemed to dull his hearing, so he switched them off again. On the verge of going there himself and overcome by his tormenting hope now almost fulfilled, he stopped first to listen to the sounds coming from the camp entrance.

In the last few seconds the noise that accompanied the delivery of prisoners had been getting louder. It no longer seemed to be coming from individual human beings, nor even from a horde subject to an external though questionable authority. It was like a mob breaking out – but each person on his own, by himself, escaping into the limitless wilderness. There's the tone now, but it was already fading; the moment had passed. Blood had been tasted, and like everything else in the world it didn't have quite the taste promised. The bellowing was already getting hoarse.

Fahrenberg's reactions now were quite human. He put his hand on his heart. His lower jaw dropped. His face sagged with disappointment. To his ears all this was a reasonable, clearly identifiable sequence of sounds.

Outside new commands were given. Fahrenberg pulled himself together. He switched a few of the lamps on again. He pushed buttons and plugged things in.

A few minutes later as Bunsen was crossing the Dance Ground, he could hear, through the closed door, Fahrenberg ranting and raving like someone possessed. Zillich had just come in and given his report: Eight new prisoners delivered. All people from Opel-Rüsselsheim who had opposed something or other. Just here for a short cure that would later make their new wage rates more agreeable.

Zillich had expected and endured the new torrent of abuse with a closed, grim face. He was not bowled over by his chief's ranting; it was the man's customary way of letting off steam. But this time there was not a single word, not a single oblique reference to old times, to their solidarity. Zillich waited it out despondently, his large head dropped to his chest. Endowed with a keen intuition for these things, he had in the past always sensed his chief's every mood. In the last week he had felt that Fahrenberg's attitude, his manner towards him had changed. On Monday, they had still shared a feeling of misfortune after the escape of the prisoners. But in the days that followed, Fahrenberg must have begun to shut him out. Would Fahrenberg forget him completely? For ever? If what the others were saying was true, and the commandant was to be reassigned, what would happen to him, Zillich? Once Fahrenberg was reassigned, would he send for him? Or would Zillich have to stay in Westhofen on his own?

Fahrenberg's close-set eyes – in no way eyes that aroused fear or were destined by nature to penetrate to great depths, only meant to peer into clogged pipes and drains – looked at Zillich with coldness, even hatred. Fahrenberg was actually thinking that this blockhead was primarily to blame. The notion had occurred to him sporadically during the past week. Now it was taking hold.

Zillich used the breathing spell to try his luck, a sort of test of confidence. 'Commandant, sir, I would like to have your permission to make the following changes with regard to the guards assigned to the special punishment squad . . .'

Bunsen, standing outside, heard a second episode of ranting. Well, he thought, there won't be many more opportunities for such entertainment. The commission that had investigated the events relating to the escape hadn't yet made any public announcement. But among themselves, the SS officers were agreed that the old man wouldn't last another week.

There was a second breather. Bunsen came in, but only his eyes were smiling. Zillich withdrew, looking like a bull whose horns had been trimmed. Fahrenberg said in the tone of a man whose power to issue orders was incontrovertible in scope as well as duration, 'The new arrivals are subject to the same punitive measures that have been applied to all prisoners since the day of the escape.' He enumerated them in the same tone of voice. With every recitation they became more stringent.

Quite a few of these fellows are already on the verge of collapse and they're going to keel over from this. He's really venting all his anger, Bunsen thought.

Zillich had gone over to the canteen. They were already serving coffee. Distracted, he sat down at his usual place at the narrow end of the table. Ever since Fahrenberg had shouted at him, telling him he was no longer in charge of the special punishment squad, but that Uhlenhaut was, it seemed as if there had been a fog before his eyes. The prevailing atmosphere in the canteen was of strong, hungry young fellows sinking their powerful teeth into solid healthful food: peasant bread with plum jam, for they obtained everything locally. And on top of that the camp management had especially abundant supplies that week because the punishment measures had restricted food allocations to the prisoners. Large metal jugs of milk and coffee were handed back and forth across the table. The guards who had accompanied the latest transport were the guests of the Westhofen SA. The men laughed and chewed their bread.

'There was a weirdo among them,' one of the fellows was saying. 'His mouth wouldn't close. Right off they took him to the slammer and one of them opened it and looked inside and then he said, "The beauty of the workplace."'

Zillich just stared straight ahead, stuffing his mouth with bread.

II

Some of the fog had dissipated, but a few fragments of it still hung here and there between the Marnets' and the Mangolds' apple trees. Franz bounced over two earthen furrows, but today he didn't enjoy the bumps, each jolt shooting straight up into his empty, sleep-deprived head. Then, cycling through a patch of fog, he felt the soft, soothing coolness on his tired face.

As he circled Mangold's farmstead the sun was beginning to come through the fog. But nothing gleamed on the harvested trees any more. On the other side of Mangold's place the land dropped down into an endless solitude. You forgot that the Hoechst factories were down there somewhere in the fog, that some of the country's largest cities were quite close, that cyclists would soon be swarming down the street, bells ringing. Here was the desolation that lay beneath the grain. Here, the ancient stillness just three hundred yards outside the gates of the cities. Once Ernst had passed through with his sheep, the land would be truly bare. This desolation was still unsubdued, and who was there after all who would want to subdue it? Everyone had to pass through it; everyone wanted to go through. It will be good to have a fire at home tonight, Franz thought. He had never really liked Ernst very much. But that morning he really missed him, as if life itself had gone with him to another region.

Once you leave Mangold's place behind, the land, falling away in rolling waves, turns into a nothing of gold-grey mist, as silent as if it were uninhabited. You might think that no men ever came up here. That no legions had ever camped here with their military standards and their gods. That peoples and nations had never collided here. That not even a single man, alone on his little donkey with the armour of his faith about him, had ever ridden up here to tame the wilderness. That powerful rulers had never marched here at the heads of their followers to elections and celebrations, to crusades and to wars. It wasn't possible that this golden-grey nothingness down there had ever been the place where, uncounted times, everything was ventured, where everything was lost, and wagered again and lost again. An eternity must have passed since anything happened here, or perhaps nothing had really started yet.

Franz thought: If only I could go on and on pedalling like this, if only the road didn't lead to Hoechst. But there was already a bell ringing ahead of him, and he saw Anton Greiner standing at the soda shack. I'd like to see the day, Franz thought, when that chap goes by here without buying something. Suddenly a petty expression came to his face which a moment before had reflected only the autumnal silence and solitude. But it went away again, and his face turned sad. Thinking of Anton's fiancée made him think of Elli.

Warm air wafted out of the soda shack window. The young woman had lit her little stove. And she had a new gadget, a hotplate with coffee cups for the workers coming from distant villages.

'How can you drink coffee again when you're just coming from home?' Franz asked Anton.

'Do you want to save my money too?' Anton asked in return. In a glum mood, they pedalled downhill. By now they were in the middle of the pack. Suddenly a horn blew three times and they all swerved to the right as an SS man on a motorcycle came past on their left. It was Anton Greiner's cousin. 'You know, he said some odd things yesterday,' Anton said, 'and he also asked me about you.'

Franz was startled.

'He asked whether you were in a good mood, whether you're laughing up your sleeve.'

'Why should I be in a good mood?'

'I asked him that too. He'd already started drinking. A guy who's had a bit to drink like that is worse than someone who's completely drunk. But the motorcycle is now all his; he's finished with the payments. He said that they were all called in with their motorbikes to search the city. They closed off entire streets.'

'Why?'

'It's still because of the escaped prisoners.'

'With such a widespread control can it really be so hard to find one single man?' Franz said.

'I asked my cousin the same question, but he said a major control action has its problems too.'

'Like what?'

'I asked him. And he said that such a widespread action was very difficult to oversee, to keep control of. And by the way, he's going to get married soon. Guess to whom ...'

'Anton, you're asking too much of me,' Franz said. 'How could I know who your cousin is going to marry.' He was trying to hide his agitation. He wondered whether this SS cousin had really asked about his mood ...

'He's getting married to little Marie from Botzenbach.'

'Isn't she Ernst's fiancée?'

'Ernst, the shepherd!' At that Anton Greiner started laughing. 'Hey, Franz, that guy doesn't count. Nobody's ever jealous of Ernst.'

Here again was something Franz didn't quite understand. But he didn't get a chance to ask for an explanation. They were forced to separate right at the Hoechst town limits. Franz ended up in a small street that was blocked by two large tankers. They all had to get off their bicycles and follow along slowly. The faces of the people were as grey as the air. Only metal surfaces – the handlebars of the bicycles, a bottle sticking out of someone's backpack, the curved surfaces of the tankers – gleamed with a bit of reflected morning light. Close in front of Franz there was a row of girls wearing grey and blue pinafores who had their arms linked, shivering. When Franz pushed his bicycle past them, the girls grumbled. Had he heard one of them say 'Franz'? He turned round. A sharp look from one dark eye was aimed at him. He knew her; it was the girl with the badly twisted mouth, with the bunch of hair covering part of her disfigured face. He'd run into her earlier that week. She nodded to him quizzically.

In the locker room there was a lot of whispering, Woodchip, Wood...

'What's wrong with Woodchip?'

'He's back again.'

'What? Where? Here?'

'No, no, not yet. Maybe he'll come back here on Monday.'

'How do you know?'

'Last night I was at the Anker, and Woodchip's daughter came in, the one who limps. She said he was back again. And so I went upstairs with her. And Woodchip was sitting on the bed, and his wife was putting compresses on him. And he had a bandage around his head. "Jesus, Woodchip," I said. "Heil Hitler!" – "Yes," he said, "Heil Hitler. It's nice of you to come up to see me." "What's nice about it?" I asked. "But tell me about it. What did they do to you? Tell me." – Then he said, "Carl, can you keep a secret?" "Of course," I said. "Me too," he said. That's all. Not another word.'

III

Elli focused her brown eyes on the man who by now, after hours of night-time questioning, was no longer a stranger to her – Overkamp.

'Please try to collect your thoughts, Mrs Heisler. Do you understand what I'm saying? Perhaps your memory would work better if you were confined by yourself, than if you're free to walk around. That can easily be determined.'

Her thoughts were all dried out from the dazzling light. She could think only about what she saw. She thought: Those three teeth of his on top are false for sure.

Overkamp was standing in front of her, very close, and the strong light of the lamp was now shining on his clean-shaven neck so that Elli's face was finally in the shade. 'Did you understand what I said, Mrs Heisler?'

Elli said softly, 'No.'

'If you can't remember anything while you are at liberty – which, by the way, you owe to the fact that you separated on unfriendly terms from George Heisler – then perhaps imprisonment, even imprisonment in a dark cell, might have a more efficacious effect in stimulating your memory. Do you understand what I am saying now, Mrs Heisler?'

She said, 'Yes.' Now that the glaring light was no longer striking her forehead, she could think. What have I got to lose if he puts me in a cell? My work at the office? Two dozen letters a day addressed to stocking manufacturers? Imprisonment in a dark cell? Better than all this light shredding your mind.

Her thought process, which usually was subconscious and dreamy, now for seconds at a time was tackling clearly and vigorously all the things that had to be considered, even the possibility of death. Eternal peace following temporary suffering and beatings, as she had once been taught – back then neither her teacher nor his little pupil with the brown braids would ever have dreamed that these vague teachings would ever be applied in a practical way in everyday life.

Overkamp stepped to one side. Elli quickly closed her eyes as the white light flooded over her, taking her breath away. Overkamp looked at her again with a new and painstaking thoroughness. No lover could have done it better. He had assigned his men to pluck a dozen people out of their deep first sleep today, Elli among them. This young person had answered all his questions with only a soft yes or no. Her small face seemed to melt in the murderous glare of the lamp.

Overkamp began again. 'Well, my dear Mrs Heisler, let's start once more from the beginning. During the early period of your married life – try to remember – when he was still in love with you – not at all surprising by the way – and then when the love diminished a bit – but you always made up again, and things were sweeter than before – that's what it was like, wasn't it Mrs Heisler? And yes, then when the little flame gradually, gradually would no longer flare up properly, when your husband started going out with other women, back then, when you hadn't really got over your love for him, when it still hurt you deeply that your great love should start to go down the drain – do you still remember?'

Softly, Elli said, 'Yes.'

'Yes, so you do remember. You remember when one of your girl-friends made some barbed remarks – then another one. When he didn't come home one evening for the first time, and then not for half a week, without apology and of all people he'd picked that one. You remember?'

Elli said, 'No.'

'What do you mean, no?'

Elli tried to turn her head aside, but the glaring light had the power to transfix a person. She said softly, 'He didn't come home. That was all.'

'And you don't want to recall with whom it was?'

Elli replied, 'No.'

During the interrogation, when the questioning reached this point, swarms of unkind memories would come to Elli's mind – just as Overkamp had expected. They flitted around like moths in the glare of the harsh police lamp: the fat cashier, two or three young girls with a red F embroidered on their blue smocks, a neighbour, a gangly, thin woman from Niederrad, and another one. At first she had been jealous of her, that one, and it had lasted because she had absolutely no reason for it: Liesel Roeder. Back then she hadn't yet been the fat Liesel she was today, only a little plump, with reddish-blonde hair and a cheerful face. Once Elli had come to this point in the interrogation, she also went on to remember the entire Roeder family, as well as Franz, and everything connected with them.

So it seemed Overkamp, as usual, had structured the entire interrogation correctly. His questions had dug out of Elli's memory what they were supposed to dig out. Except that everything had remained inside, inside this woman, so gentle and quiet, sitting before him. Overkamp had the impression that the entire interrogation, as they would say among themselves, had detoured. This was always a devilish point in even the most beautiful of interrogations, a point at which even the best police officer can stumble. Instead of at last loosening up and disintegrating under the insistent, gruelling hammering of thousands of questions, the human self will suddenly, at the last moment, pull itself together and become firm again. And besides, if one really wanted to wear this young woman down, she would first have to have a chance to gather her strength. He turned off the lamp. Soft ceiling light illuminated the bare room. Elli sighed with relief. A golden ribbon of light came in from under the shuttered window; it was morning.

'You may go for the time being. Please be available in case we need you. We'll probably need you again later today or tomorrow. Heil Hitler!'

Elli walked into town. She swayed with weariness. At the first bakery she came to she bought herself a warm cinnamon roll. Since she had no idea where to go, she took the usual route to her office. She was hoping not to run into anyone there at this early hour except for the cleaning woman, and that she'd be able to sit in some corner until nine o'clock. But it was not to be. The office manager, an ebullient early riser, was already there. 'The early bird catches the worm – I've always said as much – and you, Elli, are the juicy worm. If it weren't you, Ms. Elli, I'd swear you'd been out hitting the bars last night. Please don't blush, Ms. Elli. Oh, if you knew how becoming that is – there's something so soft, so weary around the tip of your nose and those little blue rings under your eyes . . .'

If only once in my life I could have a real lover, Elli thought. George – even if he were still alive – wouldn't love me any more. And

I don't even want to think about Heinrich. Franz is totally out of the question. I'll go to see my father this afternoon right after work. He, at least, will be happy to see me. He's always been good to me. He always will be good to me.

IV

They've forgotten all about me here in this courtyard, George thought. How long have I been here already? Hours? Days? That witch isn't ever going to let me out of here. Paul will never come back.

People coming out of the nearby houses walked past on their way to town. 'Well, Marie dear, all the best.' – 'Already up? Heil Hitler!' – 'Don't be in such a rush, Mr Maier, your work isn't going to run away from you.' – 'Good day, my dear.' – 'Well then, Anna, see you tonight.'

Why were they all so happy? George thought. What have they got to be happy about? The fact that another day has dawned. That the sun was shining again. Have they been cheerful all this time?

'Well,' Mrs Grabber said, because he had stopped for a hammer beat. She'd been standing behind him for several minutes.

George thought: What if Paul were to forget me now, and I had to stay here for ever in place of his brother-in-law – passing the nights on a bench in the garage, the days in the courtyard. That was the fate intended for the brother-in-law.

Mrs Grabber said, 'Listen, Otto! I spoke with your brother-in-law, Paul, about your salary; that is, in the event I decide to keep someone like you on here – something I haven't decided yet. I can offer you one hundred and twenty marks...'

'Well,' she said, since he seemed to hesitate. 'Just get on with your work. I'll negotiate with Roeder since he's the one who brought you to me.'

George said nothing. The hammering within him was so loud and hard that he thought the entire city must be hearing it. He wondered: Will Paul come before Sunday? And what if he doesn't come even on Sunday? How long should I wait for him? Maybe I ought to leave here right now, on my own. I don't want to keep thinking in circles; I don't want my thinking to be the end of me. Do I trust Paul? Yes, I do. And so I have to wait for him.

Mrs Grabber was still standing behind him. He had completely forgotten about her. Suddenly she asked him, 'How did it happen that they took your driver's licence away?'

'That's a long story, Mrs Grabber. I'll tell you this evening. Provided the two of us can come to an agreement and I'm still working here tonight.'

V

But Paul, at his job that morning – standing at his usual spot, lips pressed together, legs spread once the breech-block was in place, one-legged like a stork when he turned the lever – was wondering about which man would be the right one to help him.

There were sixteen men in his department in addition to the fore-man, and he was absolutely out of the question. Their naked, sweating chests, firm or flabby, old or young, displayed all the scars that men can get. Some in a brawl, some in Flanders or the Carpathians, some in Westhofen or Dachau, others at the workplace. Paul had seen the scar Heidrich had below his shoulder blade a thousand times. It was a miracle that he had survived after the shot passed through him from back to front, and then afterwards had gone on with his life, the life of a welder at Pokorny.

Paul could still remember when Heidrich had turned up in Eschers-heim in November 1918, straight from the field hospital, hollow eyed, walking with two sticks, in the mood to bring about changes in the country. He, Paul, had just finished his training. What had most captivated him about Heidrich was the large entry-wound scar. Heidrich had soon been able to put aside his two sticks. He had wanted first to move to the Ruhrland, then to central Germany. Any place where things weren't going well. He'd already been shot to pieces anyway. But Noske, Watter, and Lettow-Vorbeck had quickly shot down all his revolts when he arrived there from Eschersheim. Still, no bullets could have made Heidrich bleed like the years of peace ahead: unemployment, hunger, family, the gradual loss of all rights, the split among the classes, the waste of precious time arguing about who was right instead of immediately doing what was right, and then, in January 1933, came the most terrible blow of all. The sacred flame of faith destroyed, his belief in himself. Paul wondered why he hadn't noticed the change in the man before. The man Paul saw that morning didn't want to lose a single hair on his head; all he wanted was to keep working, now and for ever, no matter for whom.

Maybe Emmerich is the man, Paul thought. He was the oldest worker in the department. Thick white eyebrows above stern eyes and a little twirl of white hair on his head. He had once been a staunch member of the organisation; for the First of May he'd always already hung a red flag out of his window on the thirtieth of April, so that it would be fluttering in the breeze at the break of dawn. Paul suddenly remembered this. He hadn't cared a whit about things like that before, odd stories, people's peculiarities. Emmerich probably hadn't been sent to a concentration camp, because he was one of those indispensable, specialised workers and because he was fairly old. His teeth had got pretty dull and he wouldn't nibble at the bait. But then it occurred to Paul that he'd twice seen Emmerich sitting at the inn in Erbenbeck with young Knauer and his friends, although they never spoke to one another here at work. And he'd seen Knauer coming out of Emmerich's house several times in the evening. Suddenly Paul understood the whispering of the people the same way the man in the fairy tale, having eaten a certain food, could understand the songs of the birds. Indeed, these three belonged together, and Berger was one of them too, and maybe Abst as well. Emmerich might have rolled up his banner, but his old, stern eyes were alert and watchful. He and his comrades would at least know of a hiding place for my George, Paul thought. But still, dare I ask them? They stick together and don't let anyone come near them; they don't know me, don't trust me. After all, what am I to them? – Merely little Paul.

Whenever anyone asked him something, Paul had always said, 'Don't include me in that. My main concern is whether Liesel has cooked my soup, even if it's not thick enough for my spoon to stand up in it.'

And now? And tomorrow? He heard it again, George's hurried, hoarse voice, more real, more durable than the man himself lying around on the kitchen sofa, grey in the face with his bandaged hand: 'And why do you think that they let you have this soup, bread and nappies, and the eight hours instead of twelve, and the holidays and free boat trips? – Do you think it's out of the goodness of their hearts? Out of human kindness? They let you have it because they're afraid. You wouldn't have even that if we hadn't got it for you. *We*, not they. In the course of many years, with blood and prison, people like you and me.'

And he, Paul, had said, 'Do you have to start with that again?'

George had looked at him intently, almost the way he'd looked at him yesterday evening as he was leaving Mrs Grabber's courtyard. George's hair had turned grey over the ears; his lower lip was bitten through.

He's lost if I don't find somebody today. I can't be thinking about anything else. But how am I going to find somebody? The bad guys are going to betray me; the good ones are hiding. They're much too good at hiding.

There was Fritz Woltermann, standing on his two powerful legs as if he were a statue. A blue snake with a girl's head encircled his large round chest. Similar smaller snakes were tattooed on his arms. He had once been a welder on a battleship. He was a venturesome fellow. He didn't much care whether he might get hurt; he'd be tempted by the risk.

Paul thought, Yes, Woltermann is the right guy! Now he felt cheered.

But only for a few minutes. Then he started to worry again. It suddenly seemed dangerous to entrust everything that was most precious to him to those reckless blue-snake-encircled arms. Maybe Woltermann wouldn't care if he were killed. But to Paul it mattered. No, Woltermann wasn't the right man.

It would soon be midday. He always heaved a sigh of relief as soon as the sun was above the wooden roof. That was his clock: when the brass caps of his indicator gleamed, then the noonday break wasn't far off. He thought: I ought to be speaking with him during the lunch break, with that man who doesn't even exist.

Maybe Werner. Of them all, he was the easiest to get along with. If two men were arguing, he'd go up to them and smooth things over. If someone was in trouble, he'd help him out. And yesterday he'd bandaged Paul's burned arm like a mother might have.

Maybe he was the right one! A near saint! And always quiet. Yes, I'll talk to him right afterwards. The metal caps flashed in the midday light. Fiedler called out softly, 'Hey, Paul!' Paul hadn't pulled the lever down at the right moment.

No, Paul thought. Some voice in his head warned him, although usually he wasn't very intuitive or shrewd about such things. He'll feel too self-important, that Werner. If I ask him he'd drop some big words. Make some saintly excuse. He wants to keep applying hundreds of little adhesive bandages, settling quarrels, and consoling people for their minor troubles.

For the second time Fiedler softly warned him, 'Paul!'

And Fiedler, he wasn't the right one either. Once when Brand had said, 'Hey Fiedler, in the past you never failed to turn up for any strike or any of the demonstrations,' Fiedler had said quite openly, 'Times change, and we change with them.'

Without turning his head, Paul glanced at Fiedler out of the corner of his eye.

Fiedler saw and mused: Paul gave me that same odd look yesterday too. Is something bothering him? Fiedler was about forty years old. He looked physically fit. He went rowing and swimming regularly. His face was broad and calm, and his eyes were calm too.

Paul thought: There's really nothing in that answer he gave to Brand that would speak against him. An answer that was no more than air. Take a handful of it and what have you got ... All the last few years Fiedler had been evenly calm, almost polite in response to everything that was said. He had been kind and decent to everyone,

Paul thought. As if Fiedler had just reached the boundary of his life up to now and were standing on the threshold waiting to be received, and Paul was the doorman. Yes, he had always been decent. There was the business with the lift at the construction site. It had been brought before the labour board, an unpleasant affair. Back then they'd called in two people from their own department to go over there. The lift had just been installed, and they were among the first to use it. A cable had jumped the track, and all four people inside had suffered serious fractures. Fiedler had broken his collarbone. They could have asked for large damages in court, they could have turned in Schwertfeger, who was, after all, to blame for the disaster. But Fiedler had persuaded the three others to present it as a minor matter, even his own collarbone injury, and not make trouble for Schwertfeger. Which was quite a difficult thing, if you remembered that behind every one of the injured men there were a wife and children bemoaning the loss of working pay and the damages they might have received.

Was that enough to make one trust Fiedler? Paul wondered. Perhaps Brand would have done the same from a feeling of community spirit, or whatever the Nazis now called it. Maybe Brand would have said that someone had to accept the responsibility; that negligence was what was wrong with this community spirit thing; and that Schwertfeger should be punished.

Fiedler had always asked short, calm questions at all the factory meetings. He had always made sure that they would get everything they were entitled to. In that too he was in total agreement with Brand.

The little brass capsule on the indicator gleamed. Almost noon. Soon there'll be the signal for the lunch break.

Something came to mind just then, something so fleeting that he'd never thought about it again until now; it had involved no action, no speech. In the spring, when it was announced that they would all listen to the Führer's speech in the large hall after their shift, one man had said, My God, I have to catch the train. Another one had said, Well, go ahead, no one will notice. A third man said, It's not compulsory this time. He, Paul, had said, If it isn't compulsory, I'll go home to Liesel. We all know what he's going to say anyway. —Suddenly a lot of them had left; that is to say, they had intended to leave. It turned out that all three entrances had been locked. Then there was someone who knew that there was one little doorway open, really a doll-size door, and they were a group of more than twelve hundred employees, and they all wanted to go through that little door at once, including him, Paul. You're all crazy, you children! the porter had said. In all that throng one man had said, This is probably the eye of the needle through which a camel would sooner pass than... Paul had turned round and seen Fiedler's eyes sparkle triumphantly in his serious, calm face.

The gleam of sunshine disappeared from the top of the cap. The sun was now on the section of wall between the two windows to the courtyard. The break signal sounded.

'I'd like to speak with you for a moment,' Paul said, having waited for Fiedler in the courtyard.

Fiedler thought: Something's really bothering him. What could affect someone like Paul?

Paul hesitated. Fiedler was surprised to see that, up close, Roeder looked different than he had imagined. His eyes especially were different. They weren't impish and childlike; they were cold and serious. 'I need your advice,' Paul began.

'Well, out with it!' Fiedler said.

Paul again hesitated, but then he said, calm and direct, 'It's about the people from Westhofen, you know – the escaped prisoners. It's about one...' He turned as pale as he had two days ago when George had told him. Fiedler also had turned pale as soon as he heard the first word. He even closed his eyes. How noisy the yard was. What turmoil had they been caught up in!

Fiedler said, 'What gave you the idea of coming to me of all people?'

'I can't quite explain it. Trust.'

Fiedler pulled himself together. His questions came out between his teeth, hard and gruff, and Roeder's answers were just as hard and gruff. One might almost have thought they were arguing. Their frowning, pale faces made it look as if there was mutual hatred and discord. Until Fiedler gently patted Paul's shoulder, saying, 'Forty-five minutes after your shift, go, sit down in the Finkenhof, and wait there. I have to think it all over first. I can't promise you anything yet.'

The second part of his shift turned into the most peculiar time he'd ever experienced in his work there. Now and then he was able to turn and take a look at Fiedler. Was he the right man? He would have to be.

How was it that he came to me? Fiedler wondered. Was there anything in my behaviour? Ah, Fiedler, Fiedler, you've been so careful for so long that no one ought to be able to tell, for so long that anything they could have noticed about you wasn't even there any longer. It was gone. And so there was really no danger that they'd noticed anything about you.

But there must have been some trace, he said to himself. In spite of all his care, something must unintentionally have remained. And Roeder had sensed it.

I could have said: Roeder, I can't help you. You're wrong about me. I don't have any connections any more, no connections to any of the former leaders, to any of my former comrades. I lost touch a long time ago. But maybe I could have found them, re-established contact? But I didn't; I'm out of touch and I can't help you. Should I have said as much to Roeder after he showed all that trust in me?

How has it come to this – that I'm suddenly alone and out of touch? Never found a way to reconnect after all the many arrests, when the connections were severed one after the other. Or didn't I try hard enough to reconnect, the way you would try to find something without which you cannot live or die?

But things couldn't have got that bad with me – not that bad. I didn't become that hardheaded and uncaring, and I'm still part of it; after all, Paul found me. And I'll find my people again. I'll renew my contacts. Even if I have no contacts, I have to help out in this. You can't always stand by and wait; you can't just ask questions.

It was just that back then when everything went wrong, I was so terribly tired. You tell yourself: When things go wrong, it means at best six to eight years of imprisonment and at worst, off with your head. Then it's no wonder that what they give you as an answer is: What you're asking of me, Fiedler, I wouldn't risk my life for that! And suddenly you're giving the same answer. That got me down back then, when the party leadership got busted, and at the same time George Heisler was arrested too.

VI

'This is our last meal together,' Ernst said. 'If your Mr Messer hadn't sold the little piece of land behind the woods to Prokaski in the spring, I wouldn't have to take his sheep to graze on someone else's property.'

'Oh, well, it isn't all that far,' Eugenia said. 'I can wave to you from my bedroom window.'

'Parting is parting,' Ernst said. 'Come sit a while with me while I eat my last potato dumpling.'

'I don't really have the time for that,' Eugenia said. But she sat down on the windowsill, her head outside in the open and her legs inside the kitchen. 'I have to bake and cook ahead. Our three boys are coming tomorrow. Max, who's with the Sixty-Sixth, is getting his first furlough, Hans is coming home from school, and Joseph, that little good-for-nothing, is coming home too for a change. I'm sure it's because he wants some money.'

'Tell me, Eugenia, *your* boy, does he come here too sometimes?'

'What boy?' Eugenia said coolly. 'No, no, my Robert is never off on Sundays. He's studying hotel management in Wiesbaden.'

'That wouldn't be anything for me,' Ernst said.

'He's doing all right,' Eugenia said softly. 'It's in his blood, dealing with guests.'

'Does he come up here sometimes?'

'Robert? Why should he? Messer might not mind. Hans is never here, and Max is a good fellow, but that Joseph ... If he started shooting off his mouth and I were to contradict him, there'd be a row, and I don't want that.'

'Why should he shoot off his mouth?' Ernst asked because he wanted to keep Eugenia there with him a little longer, and she was already stacking his empty plates, glass, and silverware. 'The boy's father wasn't Jewish, was he?'

'No, luckily only French,' Eugenia said. She had got up after all. 'Well then, good-bye, Ernst. Whistle for your Nelly so I can say good-bye to her too. So, good-bye, Nelly. What a dear sweet little dog you are. Good-bye, Ernst!'

She sat down again on the windowsill, leaning her head out to watch the departure of the herd. Ernst had turned his back to the house. He had his kerchief loose around his neck, put one leg forward and one hand on his hip. Like a keen-eyed commander-in-chief regrouping his forces and thereby perhaps also the entire world, he issued low commands that sent the little dog bounding first here then there until the herd formed a tight, elongated little cloud pushing its way into the small spruce forest.

How empty the meadow was now! Eugenia's heart contracted. Even though she didn't care all that much for Ernst, and the three days he grazed his sheep there resulted only in more work for her and stupid talk. How quickly the little forest had swallowed them all up; maybe they were already coming out into the open on the other side. But the meadow would remain empty till next year! That reminded her of all sorts of things that had come and gone, and once they were gone, nothing was as it had been before. Instead there was emptiness and silence, enough to make you weep.

Walking through the yard after the lunch period, Hermann ran into Lersch. He was calling out curt commands with an expression that Hermann vaguely disliked. Looking up, Hermann saw little Otto roped between the wheels of a railway carriage, awkwardly trying to turn the heavy axle. The yard was below street level. The carrriage could be raised by a crane or moved in such a way that it extended out over the yard. The boy was swaying slightly but holding on tight. One moment he would be facing the yard that must seem very far down to him from up there; the next he'd be facing up towards the carriage that seemed to be in danger of turning over on top of him. A youthful worker who was controlling the train-lifting equipment called something out to the boy, not curt and mocking but rather gay and cheerful. Otto had probably had an attack of fear and awkwardness, the sort of thing that often happens to an apprentice.

Lersch himself had the smooth appearance of any skilled older worker you might come across at his place of work. But his tone of voice, the derisive smile, the gleam in his eyes, did not seem appropriate to this simple operation of teaching a boy to do a job. Hermann walked by him thinking that what was happening here should not concern him. Three yards farther on he stopped because he told himself that everything in some way concerned him.

Hermann waited at the iron staircase for the boy to be dismissed. Otto was standing before Lersch, almost at attention, his white face raised unblinking, childish mouth half open. Once he got Otto to go with him, Hermann said to the boy, 'These things always happen to you in the beginning. You should try not to be so stiff. In fact, just the opposite, try to relax, to loosen up. Don't think at all about the fact that you're swaying in midair. The equipment on the railway carriage and the contraption that's holding you, they've been checked hundreds of times. In the ten years I've worked here, there's never been an accident. And remember, whenever you get that feeling, that there isn't a man working here to whom that hasn't happened. It happened to me too.' He placed his hand on the boy's shoulder. But the boy shrank away almost imperceptibly and Hermann's hand slid off. The boy looked at the older man coldly. He was probably thinking: This is between Lersch and me; you don't know anything about it.

As Hermann walked on he heard the young worker laugh and Lersch calling a short command up to him in a tone of voice that would have been more appropriate in a barracks than a factory yard. Hermann turned round quickly; he saw the boy's face had turned pale with the fear of failing at something far too unimportant for commands or for ambition. What will become of the boy? Hermann wondered. The boy now thinks of kindness as mere talkativeness and solidarity as some quaint old nonsense. Maybe he'll turn into another Lersch, an even worse one, judging from his apprenticeship.

Hermann crossed the two courtyards at street level and entered the numbing noise of the workshop, the continual yellow and white flashes from the welding torches. Here and there he was greeted by a smile, smiles resembling grimaces in the blackened faces. Sideways glances, some shouts that were drowned out in the thunderous noise. I'm not alone, Hermann thought. What I thought just now about the boy is nonsense – sheer nonsense. He's just a boy like other boys. I'm appointing myself his godfather, a kind of secret godfather. I'll get that boy out of Lersch's grip. I'll be able to do that. We'll see who's the stronger man. Yes, it will take time. And what if I won't be granted the time? Then, from this long-term task he'd suddenly assigned himself, so suddenly that it seemed to him it actually had been assigned to him, his thoughts returned to the urgent task at hand. A task that might cause everything to collapse, to fail. Yesterday, right after his shift, Sauer the architect had met him at a spot they had previously agreed was to be used only for extreme emergencies. Sauer was tormented by doubts about whether he was justified in having so arbitrarily turned away a man who had come to see him. His description of the visitor as short, blue eyed, freckled, exactly matched Franz Marnet's description of Paul Roeder.

If Roeder was still working at Pokorny, he knew of a good man there who could sound him out. He was an older man, solid and reserved, who had escaped persecution because in the two years before Hitler came to power he'd kept a certain distance from his former comrades, and the Nazis thought he had turned against them. This man could approach Roeder on Monday. Hermann knew the man, having met him yesterday and again today. He could be entrusted with money and identity papers for Heisler, in case Heisler was really still alive. As he himself stepped into the noise and flames of an ordinary morning at work, Hermann wondered whether it was right to risk so much for one individual. The man who was going to sound out Roeder was just about their only mainstay at Pokorny. Was it permissible to risk one man's life for another's? Under what conditions was it permissible? Hermann weighed it all in his mind, back and forth, and came to the conclusion that yes, it was permissible. Not only permissible, but necessary.

VII

At four o'clock in the afternoon Zillich went off duty. Even under normal circumstances he never really knew what to do with his spare time. He didn't care to join his comrades' excursions into the surrounding towns; their amusements didn't interest him. In this respect he was still a peasant.

There was a rattletrap of a car outside the camp entrance filled with SA men who had got together for a trip down the Rhine. They called to Zillich to come and join them. They would certainly have been surprised if he had agreed to do so, maybe even dismayed. You could tell from the looks that followed him, from the interruption in their laughter, that there was a certain distance between them and him.

Zillich stumped along the path through the open fields towards Liebach. The dry, loose soil did no harm to the shine of his shiny, stout boots. He crossed the path that connected the highway with the Rhine. There was a guard posted outside the vinegar factory today – the most advanced outpost of Westhofen. The man saluted Zillich, who returned the salute. Walking a couple of yards farther on behind the factory, he examined the drainage ditch through which Heisler had probably crawled. He saw the place where, according to Gingersnap's testimony, he had vomited. The Gestapo had reconstructed his escape route all the way to the Darré school pretty accurately. Zillich had retraced it a couple of times already. A few dozen people were just coming out of the vinegar factory – a small seasonal workforce of local farm people. They had all been questioned mercilessly. Now they stopped behind Zillich and for the hundredth time looked down into the drainage pipe. For the hundredth time they said, 'Unbelievable!' 'That takes guts!' 'They still haven't caught that one!' and 'Oh yes, they did; caught all of them – they caught all of them!' A youth with a child's face wearing his father's too-big work clothes asked Zillich directly, 'Did you finally catch him?'

Zillich raised his head and looked at them. With that they separated, pale faced and silent. Men who had been gloating a moment earlier withdrew into themselves. Someone said to the boy, 'Do you have any idea who that was you were talking to? That was Zillich!'

Zillich continued on his way along the field path in the sunny but cool afternoon. Since you couldn't see the river from here, the country around him looked exactly like the countryside back home. Zillich had been a close neighbour of Aldinger's. He had grown up in one of the remote villages on the other side of Wertheim.

Here and there he could see the white and blue headscarves of women bent over the earth. What month was it? What crop were they harvesting? Potatoes? Beets? In her last letter to him his wife had asked whether he couldn't come home, for then they could give their tenant farmer notice. And they could invest the money they had saved because, as the family of a former frontline soldier with many children, they were entitled to quite a few benefits. Moreover, they had finally put the farm in order and cleaned it up because the two oldest boys were now as strong as their father. Even so, they were no substitute for him, and once he came home they could plough up half of the piece of land they'd had to lease out, leaving the other half in clover for the cows they planned to buy.

Zillich put one of his tall boots down on the spot where George had found the little girl's hair ribbon. A few minutes later he had reached the fork in the road where the grandmother, Jumblegranny, had turned off. He didn't go on up to the Darré school; instead he walked directly down towards Buchenau. He was thirsty. Zillich didn't drink on a regular basis, only from time to time.

Now and then he saw the glint of a spade. A farmer's wife working near the path straightened up when she heard his footsteps and, wiping the sweat from her eyes with her fist, continued watching his receding figure. Even as he was walking through the quiet countryside

under the grey-blue sky his insides rebelled at the thought of having
to return home for ever. If Fahrenberg dropped him, or if Fahrenberg
himself were dropped so harshly that he'd never be able to hold on
to anyone else, where was he, Zillich, supposed to go? One memory
in particular tormented him: how appalled he had been when in
November 1918 he had come back to his neglected farm after the war.
He had been appalled at the flies, the mould, the many children – one
for each furlough in addition to the two they had from before – and
his wife as dry and hard as an old loaf of bread. And then, with soft
eyes she had shyly asked him to nail some insulation on the windows,
and to do it in the stable first because the wind was blowing in there.
She had brought the rusty tools out to him.

But he realised now that this time it wouldn't be a furlough, where,
for God's sake, you came home and hammered in a couple of nails
and then went back to where there wasn't any insulation to put up
and no little nails to hammer in. This time, he thought, he would be
going home for ever. Inescapably and irrevocably.

Back then he'd gone to the local inn as it got dark. It wasn't much
different actually from the one here that he now saw gleaming on the
other side of the fields at the edge of Buchenau, built of red brick and
covered with ivy. But that ass of a proprietor back then had poured
him a pretty sad wine. At first he'd brooded, then got furious and
started yelling, 'Here I am, back home again in this shitty place! And
they've ruined our war, our clean, decent war. They've wrecked it. So
now I'm supposed to go back and bum around with the cows. Yeah.
They'd like that. Now Zillich is supposed to scrape the mould off
with his fingernails. Here! Take a look at my hands, look at my thumb.
That was a sweet little throat, let me tell you, as soft as a nightingale's.
Lieutenant von Kuttwitz said, "Zillich, if it weren't for you I'd be an
angel now." They wanted to tear the Iron Cross off von Kuttwitz's
chest. That rabble at the Aachen train station. My Lieutenant
Fahrenberg – that time when he was wounded and Lieutenant Kuttwitz
took his place – and then when they took him away on a stretcher,
he held out his hand to me from the stretcher.'

'It's really amazing,' one of the fellows at the inn had said, still wearing his grey uniform but without the shoulder epaulettes, 'that we could have lost the war with you fighting in it, Zillich.'

Zillich had rushed at the man and almost throttled him. If it hadn't been for his wife, they would have called the police. In the years thereafter they continued to put up with him because they felt sorry for his wife. In the early days after his return, seeing how Zillich was working himself to death, they came and offered to lend him things. They allowed him free use of the threshing machine, occasionally lent him some hand tools. But Zillich always said, 'I'd rather go under than accept things from this riffraff.' His wife would say, 'Why riffraff?' and Zillich would answer, 'Oh, come on, they couldn't get home fast enough to dig up their potatoes.'

In spite of her worries and problems there was also a degree of admiration mixed in with her fear. But the farm kept going downhill; the national crisis hit both the guilty and the innocent. Zillich cursed along with those whose tools he hadn't wanted to borrow. He and his family had to leave the farm and move to his parents-in-law's tiny place. —That was the most terrible year of all. All of them squeezed in together. How the children trembled in the evenings when he came home! Once he'd gone to the market in Wertheim when he suddenly heard someone call out, 'Zillich!' It turned out to be a soldier he'd served with in the war. The fellow said, 'Come and join us, Zillich, come along with us. This is the right thing for you. You're one of our comrades, you have a fighting disposition, you're for the nation, you're against the riffraff, against the system, against the Jews.'

'Yes, yes, yes,' Zillich had said. 'I'm against all that.' From that day forth he didn't care about anything any more. He was done with the oily peace. That was finished and done with for Zillich.

Before the dismayed eyes of the villagers Zillich was picked up evening after evening by motorcycle, sometimes even by a Hanomag car. If only the gang from the brick factory hadn't gone into the SA pub that evening! A look had led to a word, and a word to a knifing.

It wasn't much worse in jail than it had been at home in that stuffy mousehole. In fact, it was cleaner and more entertaining. His wife was humiliated and wailed about the disgrace, but then she wiped her eyes and couldn't help but stare when the SA squad came to the village to celebrate his return. Speeches. Heil! Drinking! How the innkeeper and the neighbours gaped.

Two months later, at the big SA parade, he recognised Fahrenberg, his former lieutenant, on the reviewing stand. That evening he went to see him. 'Do you know who I am, Lieutenant?'

'Good Lord, it's Zillich! And we're both wearing the same shirt!'

And now I'm supposed to waste my time with the cows, Zillich thought. Just looking at this village street, which reminded him so much of his own, filled him with a dull anxiety. Even the doorknob at the inn was just as wiggly as the one back home.

'Heil Hitler!' the innkeeper shouted louder than needed. Then in an ordinary innkeeper tone of voice he said, 'There's a sunny spot in the garden, perhaps you would like to sit in the garden.'

Zillich cast a brief look at the open door leading out to the garden. Dappled autumn light fell through the horse chestnuts on to unoccupied tables already set for Sunday with red-checked tablecloths. Zillich turned away. Just the sight of it reminded him of those other Sundays, of his former life, of the most rotten peace ever. He stopped at the bar. Asked for a hard cider. The few people at the bar who, like Zillich, were there to taste this year's cider all stepped back a bit, frowning. Zillich didn't notice the silence that had fallen all around him. He was soon on his third glass. The blood was already roaring in his ears. This time too his hope for relief was an illusion. On the contrary, the dull anxiety that had already filled him to bursting earlier grew inside him. He would have liked to howl. He knew this anxiety, this fear, from when he was young. It had incited him to do some of the most dreadful, seemingly reckless things. No matter how beastly the behaviour it might inspire, it was the most ordinary human fear. From his childhood on, his innate intelligence, his enormous strength had all been kept imprisoned, untamed, unredeemed, and unusable.

In the war he had found the one thing that gave him relief. He didn't turn wild at the sight of blood, as they say murderers do. That would have been like a sort of intoxication, something that could be cured, perhaps through other forms of intoxication. On the contrary, the sight of blood calmed him. He would become as calm as if his own blood were flowing from a fatal wound, like a self-inflicted bloodletting. He would look and become calm, and then he would leave. And that night he would sleep well.

Some Hitler Youths were sitting at one of the tables in the barroom, among them Fritz and his squad leader, Albert, the same Albert whom Fritz only last week would have obeyed blindly in everything. The innkeeper was Albert's uncle. The boys were drinking sweet cider, and they had a plate of nuts on the table that they were cracking against each other. They then tossed them into the cider to soak in the liquids and when the cider was gone, the nuts would have a sweet taste. They were discussing plans for a Sunday excursion. Albert, a deeply tanned, alert boy with clever eyes, knew how to maintain a slight yet imperceptible distance between himself and the other boys by the way he spoke to them.

Once Zillich entered the room, Fritz no longer took part in the discussion or in the nut cracking. His eyes remained fixed on Zillich's back. He too knew Zillich by sight. He too had heard various rumours about the man, although he hadn't thought much about all that.

Fritz had been summoned that morning to Westhofen and had gone there after a sleepless night, his heart pounding wildly. But a surprise awaited him. He was told he could go home again, that the police commissars had left and all outstanding summonses had become null and void. Infinitely relieved, Fritz had gone on to school. The only thing still missing now was his jacket, and he'd gladly forfeit that as the price for his peace of mind. He'd really thrown himself into his work this morning, busied himself with the Youth Service and comradeship. He avoided Gueltscher the gardener. How could he have blabbed so much to that pipe-sucking old man? For that entire day Fritz had been his old self, the Fritz of the previous week. Why had he been so worried anyway? He hadn't done anything! A few stuttered words. A faint no. There hadn't been any consequences. And something that has no consequences, isn't that as good as if it hadn't happened at all? Until five minutes ago he had been the most cheerful of the boys at the table.

'What are you staring at, Fritz?'

He gave a start. Who was this Zillich? What's he got to do with me? What could I possibly have in common with Zillich? What's he got to do with us! Are the things they say about him true? Maybe it really wasn't my jacket. There are people who look so much alike you could mistake them for one another, so why not jackets too? Maybe all the escapees have been caught by now, mine too. Maybe he didn't recognise the jacket as his. Is this Zillich one of us just like Albert? Are all the things they say about him true? What do we need him for? Why did they catch mine too? Why did he escape? Why was he imprisoned in the first place?

He kept staring at the powerful back, wondering. Zillich by now was on his fifth glass.

Suddenly a motorcycle stopped outside the inn. Without taking his left leg off the footrest, an SS man called into the barroom, 'Hey, Zillich!'

Zillich slowly turned round. His expression was that of a man suspended halfway between his usual state and total inebriation and who can't seem to arrive at either. Fritz watched fixedly without knowing what he expected and why he was so curious. His friends had glanced over briefly, and then, since there was nothing more to see, had gone back to discussing their Sunday plans.

'Jump on behind me,' the SS man said. 'They're looking for you everywhere. I made a bet that I'd find you here.'

Zillich walked out of the bar-room with difficulty, but his step was firm and his posture erect. His fear was gone; it was gratifying to know they were looking for him, needed him. He swung himself up behind the SS man, and the two roared off.

The whole affair didn't take more than three minutes. Fritz had swivelled in his seat to watch their departure. Zillich's face and the looks the two men had exchanged had scared him. He began to feel cold. Something in his young heart stirred, a warning or a doubt, something that some say is innate in a person and others say is not, but develops only gradually, and then, of course, there are those who say it doesn't exist at all. But it stirred in the boy and went on quivering as long as he could hear the motorcycle.

'What is it you need me for?'

'It's because of Wallau. Bunsen is interrogating him again.'

They went inside the barracks where Fischer and Overkamp had set themselves up at the beginning of the week. Outside the door a group of SA and SS men were talking excitedly. Bunsen, who had evidently succeeded Overkamp, called up a few people by name after each stage of his interrogation. Every time he opened the door, they were all eager to learn whom he would call in next.

When Wallau had been taken to the barracks, he had a faint hope that Overkamp might not have left yet and that he was only going to be subjected to another useless questioning. But Bunsen had been there in the barracks along with that fellow Uhlenhaut, who was to be Zillich's successor as the head of the special punishment squad. And in Bunsen's face he could read that the end was at hand.

All Wallau's sensations were fused into one: thirst. Such terrible thirst! He'd never be able to quench it. Every last drop of perspiration had been sweated out of him. He was drying up. What a fire! Smoke seemed to be issuing from all his joints; it was all going up in smoke and steam as if not just he, Wallau, but the entire world, were going under.

'You didn't want to tell Overkamp anything. I'm sure the two of us will understand each other better. Heisler was your close friend. He told you everything. Quick, now, what's the name of his fiancée?'

Well, so they still haven't caught him, Wallau thought, and for one last time he was relieved of the exclusiveness of his own death. Bunsen saw the flash in Wallau's eyes. He struck him with his fist. Wallau hit the wall.

Bunsen said in a voice that alternated between soft and loud, 'Uhlenhaut! Attention! —So, what's her name? Her name! You've already forgotten? We'll have it soon!'

While Zillich was riding across the fields towards Westhofen, Wallau was already lying on the barracks floor. Yet to him it seemed that it wasn't his head that was splitting apart but the brittle, fragile world.

'Her name! What was her name? – Quick! Elsa? – Come on! – Erna – Quick! Martha? – Frieda – Quick! – Amalie – Come on! Leni—!'

Leni – Leni – in Niederrad. Why did George have to tell me her name? Why does that come to mind just now? Why don't they go on with their quick-quick? Did I say something? Did it slip out by accident?

'Quick – Catherine – Quick – Alma! – Quick! – Stop for a moment and sit him upright!'

Bunsen took a look out of the door, and his flashing eyes lit similar sparks in all the eyes waiting for him out there. Then he caught sight of Zillich and gestured for him to come inside.

Wallau, covered with blood, was sitting propped against the wall. Zillich looked calmly at him from the doorway. A bit of light above Zillich's shoulder, a tiny blue corner of autumn, told Wallau for the last time that the structure of the world was intact and would remain so through whatever struggles might come. Zillich stood there rigid for one moment. Never before had anyone looked at him with so much composure, so much dignity. This is death, Wallau thought. Slowly Zillich pulled the door closed behind him.

It was six o'clock, late afternoon, early evening. No one else was present. But already on Monday morning a piece of paper was making the rounds in the Opel works near Mannheim where Wallau used to be the employee representative. 'Our former employee representative,' it said, 'Ernst Wallau, was killed at six o'clock on Saturday in Westhofen. This murder will weigh heavily against them on Judgement Day.'

A visible tremor ran through the column of prisoners when they saw that Wallau's tree was empty. The leaden pressure hanging over the camp, Zillich's sudden return, the restrained noise, the assembling of the SA – all this had already prepared them for the truth. The prisoners were no longer able to obey orders, even if it cost them their lives. A few in the column collapsed, one or other couldn't stay in step, tiny irregularities which, taken all together, broke down the rigid order. The nonstop threats, the ever harsher punishments, the ravings of the SA men who now broke into the punishment barracks every night, no longer had the power to intimidate any of the prisoners since they thought they were all lost already anyway.

With Wallau's death something had also snapped in the ranks of the SS and the SA, something that had prevented them for a few days from doing the very utmost. This utmost thing had been the murder of Wallau. But now came the unimaginable, the undreamed of that comes after the utmost thing. Pelzer, Beutler, and Fuellgrabe were not murdered as quickly as Wallau. They worked on them more slowly. Uhlenhaut, who was now in charge of the special punishment squad, wanted to show that he was a second Zillich. Zillich wanted to show that he was still Zillich. Fahrenberg wanted to show that he still had power of command over the camp.

But there were also other voices among the powerful in Westhofen. They thought the current state of affairs there was unbearable. Fahrenberg had to be dismissed as soon as possible, and with him also the clique he had brought with him or had gathered about him. It was not that those who felt this way wanted to see an end of the hell and a beginning of justice at Westhofen. Rather, they wanted there to be order even in hell.

Fahrenberg, of course, no matter how wild and irrational his behaviour, had allowed the murder of Wallau and all that followed, rather than actually ordering it. His thoughts had long ago focused on one man and wouldn't let go of this man until he was no longer alive. Fahrenberg, as if *he* were the prey being pursued, had stopped eating. The only thing he himself had ordered in all its details was what was to happen to Heisler once he was captured alive.

VIII

'Quitting time, Mr Mettenheimer,' the head wallpaper hanger, Fritz Schultz, called out in a cheerful voice. He'd been preparing to make his announcement for the last half hour.

And Mettenheimer gave the expected answer, 'You will leave that to me, Schultz.'

'My dear Mr Mettenheimer,' Schultz said, suppressing a smile, for he really liked the stern-faced old man with his sad moustache sitting there on his ladder. 'SS Standartenführer Brand will be awarding you a medal. But please come down now; everything's really finished.'

Mettenheimer said, 'There is no such thing as "everything's finished". Yes, it's finished to the extent that Brand won't notice what hasn't been done yet . . .'

'Well then.'

'But my work has to be perfect, whether it's for Brand or for Sondheimer.'

Schultz, amused, looked up at Mettenheimer crouched on his ladder like a little squirrel on a branch, full to the brim with an awareness of fulfilling his obligation before the eyes of a severe but invisible client.

As he walked through the empty but already gloriously colourful rooms to the stairwell, he could hear the other workers mumbling, and Stimbert, the Nazi, was muttering something about going beyond one's authority in the matter of working hours, and about calling someone to account. Schultz said calmly, a twinkle in his eyes, while the others smirked, 'Wouldn't you like to contribute half an hour now and then for your troop leader?'

At that Stimbert's expression changed abruptly. The others looked happy and a bit embarrassed.

Elli was standing on the threshold of the first room that opened to the stairwell. She had come up the stairs softly, quietly. The young apprentice, who had been sweeping up, stood behind her, grinning. She said, 'Is my father still here?'

Schultz called out, 'Mr Mettenheimer, your daughter!'

Mettenheimer called down from his ladder, 'Which one?'

Schultz called back, 'Elli!'

How does he know my name? Elli wondered.

Mettenheimer climbed down his ladder like a much younger man. It had been years since Elli had picked him up at work. Now pride and joy took years off his age when he saw his favourite daughter standing in the large, empty room of the ready-to-move-into house, one of many that he'd papered for her in his dreams. He at once saw the sorrow in her eyes, the weariness that made her face even more delicate. He gave her a tour of the house.

The little apprentice was the first to regain his composure and clicked his tongue. Schultz slapped him. His mates said, 'She's great! How did that old grump ever manage to bring her into the world!'

Schultz quickly changed his clothes. He followed the two, father and daughter, at some distance as they walked, arm in arm, down Miquelstrasse.

Elli said, 'And that's how it was last night, and they'll probably pick me up again, maybe even tonight. I flinch whenever I hear footsteps. I'm so tired.'

Mettenheimer said, 'Try to calm yourself, child. You don't know anything, and that's that. Just keep thinking of me. I'll never forsake you. But right now, try not to think about any of it. Come, we'll go in here and sit down for a while. What flavour ice cream would you like? Mixed?'

Elli would have preferred a cup of hot coffee, but she didn't want to spoil her father's joy. He used to take her for ice cream all the time when she was a little girl.

Now he said, 'Have another waffle.'

At that moment Schultz, his head paperhanger, came into the café from the street. He walked over to their table. 'You'll be at the building again tomorrow, Mettenheimer, won't you?'

Mettenheimer, surprised, said, 'Yes, of course.'

'Well then, I'll see you there,' Schultz said, waiting a moment to see if Mettenheimer would ask him to sit down at their table. Then he held out his hand to Elli, looking directly into her eyes. Elli wouldn't

have minded having this energetic, good-looking young man with
the decent, open face sit down with them. Being alone with her father
was beginning to get a little oppressive. But Mettenheimer just gave
Schultz a sour look, and he took his leave.

IX

'Did you have a quarrel at home, Mr Roeder, that you should feel
more at home here?' the Finkenhof proprietor asked him.

'My Liesel and I never quarrel. But she won't let me come home
today unless I come with free football tickets. You know, tomorrow
is the final game between Westend and Niederrad. That's why I'm
giving you my business so early in the day, Mr Fink.' Paul had already
been waiting more than an hour for Fiedler at the Finkenhof, which
had been named for Fink's father, the first innkeeper here. He looked
out of the window into the street. The streetlamps were on already!
Fiedler had said he'd come at six. And he'd told Paul to wait for him
in the event he was delayed.

Two bottles carved of cork and shaped like dwarfs with caps on
their heads stood on the windowsill. These bottles had already been
standing in that same window when he came to the Finkenhof as a
child with his father. The junk people think up, Paul mused, looking
at the bottles, as if he himself were no longer part of this world in
which people thought up such junk. He thought: My father, he made
it. —Paul's father, a man just as short as his son, had died at the age
of forty-six from the aftereffects of a case of malaria he caught during
the war. His father had said, 'The one thing I still want to do in my
life is to go to Amerongen in Holland and deposit a pile of shit in
front of Wilhelm's door.'

The best thing for him to do now would be to order some spareribs
and cabbage. But I can't do that to Liesel, eating up her Sunday money
here, he thought. Instead, he ordered another light beer. Someone
asked as he passed, 'Are you *still* here or are you here again?'

There comes Fiedler, and he hasn't found anybody, flashed through

Paul's mind. For Fiedler's expression was serious and tense. He acted as if he didn't at first see Paul. But standing at the bar, he sensed Paul's steady stare. Then, as he seemed already on his way out again, he slapped Paul on the back, and casually sat down on the edge of the closest chair. 'Eight fifteen outside the Olympia where everybody parks, a small blue Opel. Here's the licence plate number. He is to get in right away; they're expecting him. —Now, listen, I want to know whether it all worked out as planned. If my wife were to come up to see you, what reason could she give your Liesel for coming?'

Paul looked away from him and stared straight ahead. Then he said, 'Liesel's recipe for sweet yeast dumplings.'

'All right. Tell your wife you gave me a cold yeast dumpling to taste. Then when my wife, Edith, comes to your place to get the recipe and if everything has worked out well with Heisler, tell Liesel to say, "I hope you'll enjoy the yeast dumplings." But if there's been a hitch, then tell her to say, "Don't eat too many or you'll get an upset stomach."'

Paul said, 'I'll go see George immediately. Send your wife over in two hours.'

Fiedler got up; he put his hand lightly on Paul's shoulder before he left. Paul sat a while longer in silence without moving. He could still feel the slight pressure of Fiedler's hand, the barest indication of respect and fraternal trust, the sort of touch that penetrates deeper into a person than any affectionate gesture. He understood now for the first time the significance of the information Fiedler had brought him. At the next table a man was rolling himself a cigarette. 'Won't you let me have one of those, comrade?' he said.

During the time he was unemployed he'd smoked whatever he could get his hands on just to ease his hunger; then he'd listened to Liesel and stopped smoking to save money. Now the badly rolled thing crumbled between his fingers.

He jumped up. He had no patience to wait at the stop for the next tram and so he walked into the city. As the streets and people flew past him right and left, he felt he was playing a part in the course of events. He waited in the dark driveway entrance to the courtyard until he had calmed down. Pressed against the wall, he let a group of people coming out of the tavern pass by. Saturday noises came from the alley. He, too, had always tried to get away on Saturdays from his Liesel by going to a bar, since he felt they had enough togetherness on Sundays. The courtyard was fuller than yesterday. He caught sight of George, who was crouched on the ground and hammering by lamplight. It was about the same time he'd brought George here yesterday. The upstairs room in the garage was lit up; so the woman was there.

George bent down lower, as always when he heard steps approaching from behind. He went on hammering on the metal edge, which he had hammered straight once before but was bent again, and now he was once more hammering it straight. He could sense someone had stopped behind him.

'Hey, George.'

He looked up quickly and just as quickly looked down again, pounded his hammer twice lightly against the metal. He'd seen something in Paul's face that might drive him crazy. Two excruciatingly long seconds passed. He couldn't make out Paul's expression, a festive seriousness with a touch of impishness. Paul knelt down beside him and examined the metal. He said, 'It's going to work out, George. At eight fifteen at the side entrance of the Olympia, a small blue Opel. Here's the licence plate number. Get in quickly.'

George hammered the straightened edge crooked again. 'Who is it?'

'I don't know.'

'I'm not sure I should do it.'

'You have to. Stay calm. I know the man who arranged it.'

'What's his name?'

Slowly, Paul said, 'Fiedler.'

George rapidly searched his memory; a jumble of faces and names over the years. But nothing occurred to him.

Paul said again, 'He's a decent man.'

George said, 'I'll do it.'

'I'm going into the office now and will arrange with my aunt for you to come with me to pick up your things right now.'

To Paul's relief, Mrs Grabber did not raise any objections. She went behind the desk that practically filled the entire little room. The lamp that hung far down shone on her full head of hair, a flaming white mane. Her ledger lay on the table. Charts, calendars, a few letters under a malachite paperweight. Another chunk of malachite housed a clock as well as an inkwell and a groove for pens and pencils. As a sixteen-year-old bride she'd got a kick out of the thing. Her desk was quite commonplace, her office the most ordinary of haulage company offices. There wasn't anything remarkable here, except for her. She made what she could of this spot where she'd ended up. All the courtyard had watched when her husband beat her. And the entire courtyard had watched when she realised that she could beat him back. Both her husband and her lover had been killed in the war. And her child had been dead the last twenty years, choked to death by whooping cough, and lay in a part of the cemetery apportioned to the Ursulines in Königstein. Back then, when she'd returned she'd realised, seeing the staring faces of the people in the courtyard, that they already knew all her secrets. Her lorry-drivers thought: She's run out of steam and given up. But she stamped her foot and yelled at them, 'Are you being paid to gawp? Quick, get back to work!'

From that moment on, no one who worked there had had a moment's rest, nor had she.

Perhaps a little now, perhaps tonight. Should she forbid this man to pick his things up from the Roeders'? Why didn't Paul bring the things here? Oh, in God's name, let him go and get his stuff and bring it here. As to his salary, we'll discuss that when he's finally settled in here. She liked the man. She'll get him to open up in good time. He has something about him that reminds me of home, she thought. He comes from the same area where in the beginning the wind is so cold that any little breeze seems warm to you. You might almost think he's one of my countrymen. But first of all, let him finish moving his things. I'll let him sleep in the shed in the garage. He can set up my dead husband's bed – at last, a practical use for it.

Paul went back downstairs to George. He said, 'So then, George.'
George said, 'Yes, Paul?'

Paul was reluctant to leave, but George said, 'Go on, go.'

He left quickly then, without saying good-bye, without first look-ing out into the street. At the same instant they both felt in their hearts a fine unquenchable burning that you feel only when you think you'll never see each other again.

George took up a position from which he could see the clock in the back room of the inn. After a while Mrs Grabber came out and walked over to him. 'Finish your work now,' she said, 'and go and get your belongings.'

George said, 'I'd rather finish everything here, then I can stay the night with the Roeders.'

'But they have a case of measles.'

'I've already had the measles; don't worry about me.'

She stood behind him, but there was really no reason to urge him on. 'Come,' she suddenly said, 'let's drink a glass to your new job.'

He gave a start. Only when he was busy with his work in the part of the yard in front of the garage did he feel relatively safe. He was afraid something might still happen in this last hour. He said, 'Since I had the bad luck to get hurt, I've resolved not to drink any more.'

Mrs Grabber laughed. 'How long do you intend to stick to that?'

For a moment he seemed to seriously consider this; then he said, 'Three more minutes.'

They got a noisy reception at the inn. The place was full. Mrs Grabber came there often. After a brief flood of greetings nobody paid any more attention to them. They stood at the bar.

George noticed two older people, a man and wife. Both were sit-ting peacefully with their beer glasses, squeezed behind some other people. Both were plump, and both looked happy.

My God, George thought, there they are, the Klapprods from the rubbish collection. What a petition that had been, where the wife was for it and the husband against, and they were tearing at each other's hair until both of them suddenly got furious because we couldn't help laughing at them. But dear Klapprods, don't turn round now. I saw you, but you mustn't turn round and see me.

'Cheers!' Mrs Grabber said. They clinked glasses. Now he won't be able to leave, Mrs Grabber thought. Now it's all settled.

'Well, I'll go over to the Roeders' now. Thanks, Mrs Grabber. Heil Hitler! Good-bye.'

He went back to the garage and changed into his clothes, neatly folding up the borrowed overalls. He thought: Soon I'll bring back your coat and all your other things. I'll look for you and I'll find you wherever you are. In the evening I'll go to watch you perform. I'll watch your acrobatic stunts. Your double – ah, no, only your single somersault. Afterwards I'll wait for you and we'll tell each other how we escaped from this life. I want to know everything about you. Nothing should remain unknown between us. Fuellgrabe may say, You're dead. But who's going to listen to Fuellgrabe?

In the driveway he hesitated a moment before going out into the street. It seemed to him as if he'd left something behind in the yard, something important, indispensable. He thought, I didn't leave anything there. And anyway I'm already outside on the street. I've already gone three blocks. I've left the yard. Too late to go back.

He could already see the windowless wall covered with colourful placards and posters at the end of Schaefergasse. Light falling on the pavement, broken letters of the alphabet, red and blue, not making any sense. In a past life there had once before been a night splashed with such red and blue lights. The cathedral had been ice cold, and he had been one of the youngest back then full of childish fear. He walked down Schaefergasse past the parked cars. He saw the blue Opel, compared the licence plate number. It was the right one. If only everything is all right! If only Paul hasn't let them put one over on him. I won't hold it against you, Paul. Far better men than you have been taken for a ride. Only too bad if things were to go wrong now, at the last minute.

The car door was opened from the inside as George approached. The car immediately drove off. How strange it smelled inside, sweet and heavy. They drove through a couple of narrow streets to the Zeil. George looked at the driver. The man had paid so little attention to him you might have thought George had never got into the car. He just sat there silent and stiff, wearing glasses on a long, thin nose. He was grinding his teeth with excitement. Who did it all remind him of? They were heading towards the Ostbahnhof. They were doing sixty kilometres per hour and yet the man at the wheel was as silent as if he weren't aware of his passenger. Maybe I'm really made of air, George thought. Who does he remind me of – God, yes – Pelzer! How about that! We certainly never dreamed we'd be taking this drive. Except that Pelzer's glasses had been shattered in the village of Buchenau, and yours are whole and undamaged. Why don't you say something? George thought. Where are we headed anyway?

But he didn't ask the question; it was as if he were following the man's wish, or as if he'd never got into the car. The man didn't look at him; he sat there awkwardly half turned away as if George's presence would become real only once he touched him.

They left the East Park behind them. George thought: The trap might clamp shut any moment. Then he thought: No, a man who's set a trap behaves differently. He'd be chattering away, he'd lie, he'd try to soft-soap you. Pelzer might have behaved like this in the same situation. Then he thought: If it is a trap, then . . . They drove into the Riederwald development. They stopped on a quiet street in front of a small yellow house. The man got out. He still didn't look at George. He only indicated with his shoulder that he should get out too and then that he should go into the entry hall of the house and from there into the living room.

The first thing George now noticed was the strong smell of carnations. A large bouquet of white carnations stood on the table; it shimmered in the half-dark room. The room had a low ceiling, but it was quite large so that the lamp standing in one corner illuminated only a small section of it. From that corner someone in a blue smock got up, half boy, half girl, half woman. It was the mistress of the house. She came towards the two, not exactly friendly, having been interrupted while reading the book she then dropped on the chair behind her.

'This is a school friend of mine. He's on his way through here and I brought him along. It's all right if he spends the night here with us, isn't it?'

The woman said quite casually, 'Why not.'

George shook her hand. They looked at each other briefly. The man stood by stiffly and watched to see if his guest would start to turn from a dream into something tangible. The woman said, 'Perhaps you'd like to go to your room first?'

George looked at the man; his nod was barely perceptible. Maybe he was looking at him for the first time from behind his glasses. The woman led the way.

As soon as a small feeling of safety streamed into him, not a certainty, only a hope of safety, he started to find pleasure in the colourful mats on the stairs, the white painted walls, the woman's long legs, her short, smooth hair.

What a miracle to be able to be in this room by himself, to be able to think. Once she was outside, he locked the door behind her. He turned on the tap in the sink, smelled the soap, drank a little water. He looked at himself in the mirror, found his image so strange that he avoided taking a second look.

At just about this time Fiedler arrived at his parents-in-law's flat, where he and his wife lived in one room. Had he been living by himself, he would probably have asked Heisler to stay with him. But Dr Kress had occurred to him instead. Kress used to work at Pokorny and after that at Cassella. Fiedler also knew him from the night school for workers he'd attended, at which Kress had taught chemistry. They met frequently after class, and then it would be Kress who learned from his student. Kress was by nature quite timid, although in 1933 he had stood up bravely for what he considered right. But at one point, Kress had given him the fateful answer. 'My dear Fiedler, please don't come to see me any more with your collection lists, and don't bring me any more banned newspapers. I don't want to risk my life for some pamphlet. But come to me when you've got something that's worthwhile.' Three hours earlier Fiedler had taken him at his word.

At last, Mrs Fiedler thought, when she heard her husband's footsteps on the stairs. Even though there was nothing she liked doing less than waiting, she was too proud to join the others in the kitchen. In earlier years they had all eaten supper together. But after several disagreements it had been agreed to let the two young people be by themselves in the evening. Mr and Mrs Fiedler weren't really young any more. They had been married more than six years. But things were going for them much as they were for many others in the Third Reich. Not only were their outward circumstances and relationships obscure and only semivalid, even their feeling for time had dissolved. They felt at a loose end and were amazed whenever another year had passed.

At first the Fiedlers hadn't wanted any children because they were out of work. Besides, they felt they were intended for other things than the raising of children. Back then they thought that they had to be free without any ties so that they could go out into the streets as soon as they were called on to fight for freedom. They were still young, they believed back then, in fact so young that they would still be young later on; because back then *now* seemed to them like morning, and *later* like evening – morning and evening of the same promising day. They didn't want to have any children in the Third Reich because eventually those children would be put into brown shirts and drilled to become soldiers.

Gradually Mrs Fiedler began to devote all her attention to her husband. She watched over and cared for him, almost the way you do with children whom you have to raise at any cost, while everything that was outgrown might and should eventually be destroyed. The two of them had come closer to each other during the past year in a way that was both good and bad. For the two Fiedlers had lived together during the first Hitler year just like two young people exposed equally to the same danger and the same cool wind. Their love hadn't been weakened by mutual indulgence. Later, as their old friends were gradually arrested or withdrew for some other reason, Mrs Fiedler often wondered whether her husband was speculating about new possibilities or simply waiting. Whenever she asked him, he would usually give her the same inconclusive partial answers he gave himself. When Fiedler hadn't come home that evening, she interpreted all these partial answers as whole ones, and the longer she waited for him, this man who had been punctuality personified, the more certain she was that whatever was keeping him was something connected with their former life together. But this former life together was such that just a breath, just the memory of it, was enough to make one feel young again.

She could see that her husband's face was animated, his eyes shining, while he was still in the entrance hall. 'Now listen carefully, Greta,' he said. 'Go to the Roeders' flat. You know his wife, you've seen her, the fat one, very bosomy. And ask her for her recipe for steamed yeast dumplings. She'll write it down for you and then she'll say something else, a sentence you have to pay special attention to and remember. She'll either say: "I hope you'll enjoy the yeast dumplings," or: "Don't eat too many or you'll get an upset stomach." You have to be able to repeat what she said. In any case use a roundabout way to go there and on the way back too. Go there right now.'

His wife nodded and left. So they weren't up in the air any more. The old ties had been re-established, or maybe they'd never been broken. She'd barely started on her roundabout way to the Roeders' flat when she realised that there were others who had come back to life again after the long hiatus and were unafraid now.

Liesel Roeder didn't immediately recognise Mrs Fiedler, for her eyes were swollen from crying. Disappointed and perplexed, Liesel stared at her unknown visitor, wondering if she might turn into her Paul.

Mrs Fiedler realised that something was wrong. But she didn't want to return home without a message. She said, 'Heil Hitler! Excuse me, Mrs Roeder, for coming so late. It seems I didn't pick the best time for my visit. I just wanted to get the recipe for your sweet yeast dumplings. Your husband gave my husband one to taste. You know they're friends. I'm Mrs Fiedler. Don't you remember me? Didn't your husband tell you about the recipe and that I'd be coming over for it?

'Please calm yourself now, Mrs Roeder, and sit down. Since I'm up here and our husbands are friends, maybe I can be of help to you. Don't feel embarrassed; there's no need for that between us. Especially not in times like these. Please don't cry. Sit down. What's the matter?' In the meantime they'd ended up in the kitchen sitting on the sofa. But Liesel went on crying, tears streaming afresh instead of stopping.

'Please, Mrs Roeder, please,' Mrs Fiedler said, 'things are really not half as bad as they look. Didn't your husband tell you anything? Didn't he come home?'

Liesel said through her tears, 'For a very short time only.'

Mrs Fiedler said, 'Was he picked up?'

'He had to go there by himself.'

'By himself?'

'Yes, he had to,' Liesel said wearily. She wiped her face with her bare arm. 'The summons was here when he came home, and he was so late coming home.'

'So then he can't have come back yet,' Mrs Fiedler said. 'Please calm down.'

Liesel shrugged. Worn out, she said dully, 'Yes, he could have. He'll either come back or they'll keep him there. I'm sure they'll keep him there.'

'You can't possibly be sure of that, Mrs Roeder; almost certainly he'll have to wait. There are always people there who've been summoned, day and night, continuously; it's like an assembly line.'

Liesel sat there brooding. At least she'd stopped crying for the time being. Suddenly she turned to her visitor. 'What kind of recipe, the one for Dampfnudeln, for sweet yeast dumplings? No, Paul didn't tell me anything. He was so scared by the summons. He had to go there right away.' She stood up and rummaged clumsily around in the kitchen table drawer. Mrs Fiedler would have liked to ask her more questions, she was sure she could get all the answers from her. But she was hesitant about asking about things her husband hadn't wanted her to know.

In the meantime, Liesel had found a pencil stub and torn a page out of her accounts book. 'I'm shaking all over,' she said. 'Would you write it down, please.'

'Write what down?' Mrs Fiedler asked.

'Five pfennig's worth of yeast,' Liesel said, crying anew. 'Two pounds of flour, enough milk to make a stiff dough, a little salt. Knead it well...'

On the way home through the night-time streets Mrs Fiedler could have told herself that now all the innumerable, vague coincidences, all the half-real, half-imagined threats were becoming tangible and taking shape. But she had no time for such thoughts. She focused all her attention on taking the right detours and making sure that no one was following her. She took a deep breath. Here was the familiar old air again that touched your temples as if it were stiffened by frost. The old darkness too, under cover of which they'd put up posters, painted slogans on wooden fences, slipped flyers under doors. If earlier that day, someone had asked her how the labour front was coming along or about the prospects for the struggle, she would have shrugged just like her husband. She hadn't experienced anything more unusual than a futile walk to see a weeping woman, but she was back now in her old life; suddenly everything was possible, and possible quickly, because it was suddenly up to her to speed things up. Everything was possible in this new day. A reversal of all circumstances and relationships; their own too. And more rapid than had been hoped for, while they were still young enough to benefit together from this happiness after so many bitter experiences. Of course, it was possible that Fiedler might die more quickly and more terribly than they had feared in the struggles he'd got involved in. Only in times when nothing at all is possible any more does life pass by like a shadow. But those times when everything becomes possible again contain all of life as well as death and destruction.

'Are you sure no one was following you?'

'I can swear to it.'

'Now listen, Greta. I'm going to pack just the most necessary things. If someone asks where I am, tell them in the Taunus. And you do this: Go to the Riederwald development, to number eighteen Goetheblick; that's where Dr Kress lives. It's a beautiful yellow house.'

'Is that the same Kress from the night school course? The man with the glasses? The one who always argued with Balzer about Christianity and the class struggle?'

'Yes, but if someone asks you, say you've never seen him before. Tell Kress that I said Paul is at the Gestapo. Give him time enough to let it sink in. Then he's supposed to tell you where he can be reached in the future. My dear Greta, please be careful. You've never been involved in such a dicey affair. Don't ask me anything else, please.

'So, I'll be on my way now. But I'm not going to the Taunus yet. Early tomorrow morning, Greta, go out to the arbour. If the Gestapo came to our house during the night, wear your windcheater. If they didn't, wear your new two-piece dress. If you don't come at all, I'll know that they picked you up. But if you're wearing your new two-piece dress, then I can join you in the arbour. It will mean the cup has passed me by. Do you have any housekeeping money left?'

Greta gave him the few marks she had left. Without a word she packed up his things. They didn't kiss good-bye; instead, they tightly gripped each other's hands. Once her husband had left, she put on her wind-cheater, for she was a practical woman, and she figured she'd hardly have time to change when the crunch came. If the night went by peacefully, she could take her time tomorrow putting on her good outfit.

Kress was still standing in the same spot in the dark part of the room. His wife went to sit down in her usual place without looking at him and opened her book at the place where she had been when the arrival of the two men had interrupted her. Her smooth, stiff hair, which was rather dull in daylight, was shining brighter now than the light that made it shine. She looked like a slender boy who'd put on some sort of helmet for the fun of it. She said, looking down at her book, 'If you keep staring at me, I can't read.'

'You had the whole day for that. Please talk to me now.'

The woman said, still without looking up from her book, 'Why?'

'Because your voice calms me.'

'Why do you need to be calmed? It's really quite calm here in our house. '

Her husband continued looking at her steadily. She flipped over two, three pages. Suddenly he said in a changed tone of voice, 'Gerda!'

She frowned, but pulled herself together, apparently from force of habit and because she felt that her husband was tired from work and that their evening together had begun. She put the open book face down on one knee and lit a cigarette. Then she said, 'Whom did you pick up there? What a strange fellow.'

Her husband said nothing. Involuntarily she frowned and looked at him more intently. In the dusk she couldn't make out his expression. What made his face so shiny? Was he really so pale? At last he said, 'Frieda won't come back till tomorrow, right?'

'Until the day after tomorrow, in the morning.'

'Listen, Gerda, you mustn't tell anyone that we have a visitor. If someone should ask, say he's a friend of mine from school.'

She said, matter-of-factly, 'All right.'

Her husband came closer. She could almost make out his face now.

'Did you listen to the radio? Did you hear about the escape from Westhofen?'

'Me? Radio? No.'

'A few men escaped,' Kress said.

'Really.'

'They caught all of them.'

'What a shame.'

'Except for one.'

A gleam came into her eyes. She raised her face. It had been this bright only once, at the beginning of their life together. Back then as now the brightness passed quickly. She looked him up and down; she said, 'How about that.'

He waited.

'I really didn't expect that of you. How about that!'

He took a step back. He said, 'What? Didn't expect what?'

'This! All this! Well, really – forgive me.'

Kress said, 'What are you talking about?'

'About the two of us.'

In his room George thought, I want to go downstairs. What was I hoping for up here? Why be by myself? Why should I torment myself in this blue and yellow bunker locked from the inside, covered with handwoven mats, with running water flowing out of nickel-plated taps, and a mirror that shows me mercilessly the same thing the darkness did: myself.

The cool smell of freshly bleached linens streamed from the low, white bed. But even though dead tired, he kept walking back and forth from the door to the window as if he were being punished by being deprived of his bed. —Is this going to be my last lodging? My last, yes, but before what? I *have* to go downstairs; I have to be with other people. He unlocked the door.

He could already hear the voices of the husband and wife from the stairs, not loud, but urgent. He was surprised. The two had seemed almost mute to him, or at most taciturn. He hesitated outside the door. Kress was saying, 'Why are you tormenting me?'

George could hear the rather deep voice of his wife, 'Is it a torment for you?'

Kress, somewhat calmer now, replied, 'Let me tell you something, Gerda. It doesn't matter to you why the man is in danger. Doesn't matter to you who he is. It's all the same to you. Danger is the main thing for you. Whether it's an escape or a car chase – it's the danger that excites you. That's how you used to be, and it's the way you still are.'

'You're partly right, partly wrong. Maybe I was once like that, maybe I've become that again now. Do you want to know what made me that way?' She waited a moment. But whether of not her husband wanted to know the whole story, she went on resolutely. 'All this time you've been saying, there's nothing you can do to combat it, that you're powerless to prevail against it, that you just have to wait it out. Wait, I thought to myself, he wants to wait until they've trampled on everything that was precious to him. Please understand me. I wasn't even twenty when I left my parents to marry you, and I left my home back then because I was repelled by everything there, my father, my brothers, the silence in our living room every evening. But it's been just as silent here in our place recently as it used to be back home.'

Kress listened to her, maybe even more astonished than George on the other side of the door. A thousand evenings it had been like pulling teeth to get her to talk.

'And then, another thing,' she went on. 'Back home nothing was ever allowed to change. It was their pride and joy that everything should stay the way it was. —And then you! You, who suddenly told me that nothing ever remains the same for a second, that not even stones stay petrified, and certainly not human beings – except for me, of course! Isn't that so? Because about me you say, "That's how you used to be, and that's how you are now."'

Kress waited an instant to see whether she had finished. He put his hand on her head. She looked unperturbed, even a bit obstinate. He took hold of her hair rather than stroking it. She was tender and tough, lovable, teachable, maybe – God only knew – she could be changed. He started shaking her gently.

Just then George walked into the room. The two quickly stepped away from each other. Why the devil did Kress have to tell his wife everything? Her expression was no longer one of equanimity, but of cool curiosity. George said, 'I can't sleep. Could I stay down here with you for a while?'

Kress, leaning against the wall, stared at him. No doubt about it. Their guest was here; their invitation, accepted irrevocably. Assuming the role of the master of the house, he said, 'What would you like to drink, tea? Schnapps? Some juice? Or beer?'

His wife said, 'He's hungry.'

George said, 'Tea and schnapps. And as to food, whatever you have.'

This was enough to set husband and wife in motion for the next few minutes. The table was set before him. Bowls and plates were put down. Bottles uncorked. Ah, to eat off seven little plates, to drink from seven little glasses. No one felt quite at ease; the Kresses were only pretending to eat. George stuffed the little white napkin into his pocket; it would make a good bandage for his cut-up hand. He pulled it out again and smoothed it. He was full now and so tired he could drop. But he didn't want to be by himself. He pushed the silverware and plates aside and put his head down on the table.

It was much later in the evening when he raised his head again. The dishes had all been removed from the table long ago; the room was full of smoke. George knew at once where he was. He felt cold.

Kress was again leaning against the wall. George tried for whatever reason to smile at him. His smile was reflected, equally forced and lopsided, on his host's face. Kress said, 'Let's have a drink.' He brought the bottles out again. When he poured his hand shook a little and a few drops spilled. This very act of pouring the liquor wholly reassured George. This was a decent man who was making all sorts of sacrifices to take me in. But take me in he did.

Just then the wife came back. She sat down at the table and smoked her cigarette in silence since the two men were silent too.

You could hear the gravel out in the street crunching under quick, light footsteps. The steps stopped at the door to the house. They heard scraping on the tiles as if someone were looking for the doorbell. George and Kress gave a start when the bell rang even though they'd expected it. George said softly, firmly, 'You met me by accident outside the cinema. You know me from a chemistry course.'

Kress nodded. Like many fearful people, he turned calm as soon as the danger became real. His wife got up and went over to the window. Her face had the expression of arrogance and something like mockery that it always wore in any risky situations. She raised the blind, peered outside, and said, 'A woman.'

'Open the door,' George said, 'but don't let her come inside.'

'She said she wants to talk to you, to my husband. She looks decent enough.'

'How does she know that I'm home?'

'She knows. You spoke to her husband at six o'clock.'

Kress went out to the landing. His wife sat down at the table with George. She kept on smoking, glancing at him now and then as if they were both caught on a dangerous turn in the road or on an icy, exceedingly difficult precipice.

Kress came back. George could tell that the worst possible thing had happened. 'I'm to tell you, George, that your friend Paul is at the Gestapo. The woman's own husband has already left home as a precaution. We are to tell her where we're going – or where you, George, are going so that they can reach you.' He poured himself another glassful.

This time he didn't spill a drop, George thought. His head felt completely emptied, as if, instead of stuffing new things into it, it had been swept clean.

'We can take you somewhere by car, or should we all leave? The three of us in the car? Drive somewhere or other? To the Ostbahnhof to catch a train? Or just deep into the country? To Kassel? Or would it be better to separate immediately?'

'Please, stop talking for a moment...' All the thoughts that had been swept out flooded back into his empty head. So Paul had been nabbed. But why had he been nabbed? Did they pick him up? Or had he just been called in for questioning? They hadn't said anything about that. In any case, he was in their hands. But Paul himself? If they could prove that Paul had sheltered him, if they could really prove that— No, Paul would never give away his new hiding place. Did Paul even know? Well, no, he didn't know where he was hiding. If the middleman was serious, if he was really one of our people, then he wouldn't have given him a name. But Paul had seen the licence plate, and that was enough. George recalled others who'd been stronger than Paul. People with the strength of giants, canny and experienced, who had experience in all sorts of battles from the time of their youth. And they'd been worn down and scared to death until information was streaming out of them from all the cracks. But Paul wouldn't betray him. Daring thoughts formed in George's head that required boldness and a quick decision. He had faith in Paul. He'll lie there where others have lain before him gritting their teeth and where their stubborn silence gradually became effortless and final.

Or maybe they'll only question him. He'll stand there looking small and awkward, carefully, shrewdly giving them innocuous answers. George said, 'We'll stay here.'

'Wouldn't it be better though to leave?'

'No. It would just cause difficulties. They'll be sending information here. Money and identity papers. If I leave now, I'll be lost all over again.'

Kress was silent.

George could tell what he was thinking. 'If you want to get rid of me because you're afraid...'

Kress said, 'Even if I were afraid, I would not send you away. You're the only one who knows this man Paul. It all rests on you now.'

'Yes. All right,' George said. 'Please tell the woman outside that we're staying put.'

Kress at once went out. George was getting to like him more and more – his readiness to subordinate the weaker part of his nature to the stronger after a short visible struggle, even his honesty about his fear without any posturing and talk. He liked the man better than his wife, who by now had smoked all her cigarettes and was blowing away the smoke. She'd probably never owned anything she would be afraid to lose.

Kress returned and leaned against the wall. They listened to the footsteps as they receded towards the development. When it was quiet again, the wife said, 'Let's go upstairs for a change.'

'Yes,' Kress said. 'We won't be able to sleep anyway.'

Kress had created a den for himself with a few hundred books in the attic. From the window there you could see that the house was at the end of the new street, a little removed from the Riederwald development. The sky was clear. It had been a long time since George had seen the open, starry sky. It had always been foggy down near the Rhine. He looked up at it, like all who feel in extreme danger, as if it were arched over him and others like him. The woman pulled down the blinds and turned up the heat, which Kress usually did when he came home early in the afternoon. She removed the books from a few chairs and a corner of the table.

George was thinking: Now they're torturing Paul, and Liesel's sitting at home waiting. His heart contracted with fear and doubt. Had it been right to tie his life to Paul? Was Paul strong enough? By now of course it was too late. He couldn't get out of it now. The Kresses were silent; they thought he was falling asleep. But actually, his hands were up covering his face, and he was getting advice from Wallau: Try to calm down; and remember that what's at stake here has only coincidentally been baptised 'George' for a week.

Suddenly cheerful, George turned to his host. He asked him how old he was and what his field was.

Kress said he was thirty-four. His field was physical chemistry.

George asked what that was, and Kress, much relieved, tried to explain. George listened attentively, but then his thoughts returned to Paul, all bloodied, and to Liesel, who was waiting.

Kress, interpreting George's silence in his own way, said softly, 'There'd still be time.'

'Time for what?'

'To get away from here.'

'Didn't we decide to stay? Don't think about it any more.'

But he himself couldn't think of anything else. He stood up and rummaged through the books. Two or three of them were familiar to him from the time he'd spent with Franz. That time was the happiest in his life. But those simpler days were now hidden under the persistent memories of more turbulent years. Why does one forget the most important thing? George wondered. Because it doesn't stand out, isn't disassociated from you, but instead silently enters into you. George turned to the woman and abruptly asked her about where she came from and her childhood.

She flinched slightly, something Kress had never seen her do, and began to talk. 'My father was very young when he joined the army. He had no special talents, so he left the army at the age of forty-four as a young major. At home there were my four brothers and me, so he had us to torment until we were grown up.'

'And your mother?' George had no chance to learn about her mother because a car stopped so close to their house that they all held their breath. But the car drove off, and by then any desire to talk was gone. George thought again of Paul; he asked him to forgive him for being so frightened just now, as if, like Kress, he was now prepared for all eventualities. Nevertheless, he briefly flinched again when another car came by. They had stopped talking. The night dragged on endlessly and the room gradually filled with cigarette smoke.

7

I

THE NIGHT was just about over. You could see now why, even without moonlight, the fields and roofs were still light: they were covered with hoarfrost. A tiny woman coming from the direction of Kronberg with a sack on her back was tramping towards the highway. There was something witchlike about her sudden appearance in the fields before dawn with the sack on her back and a knobbly stick in her hand, babbling to herself and peering about her in all directions. But as she came nearer she looked less and less like a witch. The sack turned out to be an ordinary backpack, and she was wearing a loden coat with a rabbit fur collar and a little hat that she'd pushed down over her customary headscarf.

Just before reaching the Mangold farm, she jumped over a ditch and bent down to the ground as if to sniff at something there. Babbling angrily, she hopped back across the ditch and went up the road to Messer's house. A light was already on in the ground-floor kitchen. The first light anywhere in the area.

Warm streusel cake just out of the oven to go with the Sunday coffee for the good sons of the family. And what about the not-so-good ones? For them especially, Eugenia thought; the sweet, buttery crumbs would put them in a better mood.

The old woman jumped over the ditch, but didn't head towards the kitchen window. Rather she went farther on into Messer's field. Again she briefly bent down; then, without a moment's hesitation, she went into the little forest, following the same path the sheep had taken yesterday. For she was Ernst the shepherd's mother. On holidays she would take his place for several hours herding the sheep, and the sheep droppings in Messer's meadow told her where they had been grazing yesterday. She knew their routes. Today they must already be at Prokaski's in Mamolsberg.

When she came out of the little forest and on to the land that Messer had signed over to Prokaski so that his farm would remain within the limit for hereditary farms, she saw the flat-roofed, yellow hotel down below to the right on Kronbergerstrasse, next to a single group of hoarfrost-covered evergreens. The fields sloped gently downward, only to rise just as gently upward again on the other side of the road. And the view from there stretched on and on, stopping only at the edge of the beech forest on the highest mountain range less than two hours away. Once the sun rose, the large, round valley would be aglow with autumn colours. But now just before daybreak it was a pale, frosted-over world, the moon so wan you had to search for it.

Ernst's mother cast no shadow as she tramped down the greyish-white slope. Suddenly she stopped in her tracks. Two hundred paces ahead of her she saw a girl walking across the open area between several clusters of fir trees and the strip of forest. For a moment the old woman forgot she was on her way to visit her son this Sunday and not his father. A girl hurrying along like this one had long been a better indicator of Ernst's whereabouts than sheep droppings. Into the pale dawn light she crowed shrilly, 'Hey, miss!'

The girl stopped, scared out of her wits. She looked all around her, but far and wide everything was still and grey. Ernst's mother walked down the hill behind her. She said again, 'Hey, miss.' And again the girl started in fright.

'Miss, you left something behind.'

'Where? What?'

'A strand of blonde hair.'

But by now the girl had pulled herself together. She was a plump, sturdy girl and not very easily frightened. 'Well then, why don't you put it into your prayer book,' she replied.

The old woman laughed, coughed.

The girl stuck out her big, round tongue and walked off.

Overhead the moon seemed to swell and become more distinct as the sky turned blue. Gradually it dawned on the girl who the old woman was. It made her feel sick with anger. The church bells began to ring in the villages. How could she ever have got involved with a chap like Ernst! She'd managed to exercise some self-control whenever the shepherd was grazing his sheep behind her house. But now that he had gone to the Mamolsberg side, she was suddenly running after him! Oh, my God! That old woman, his mother, she'll start a round of gossip about me, she thought. The old witch spreads gossip about all the decent girls. Didn't she even start some rumours about little Marie from Botzenbach? Little Marie, a mere child of fifteen, promised to that Schmiedtheimer SS Messer, who would certainly not accept a girl with a spot on her reputation. By the time she had come through the little forest and arrived outside Eugenia's kitchen window, she was already feeling as proud and melancholy as any innocent girl who gets herself talked about. She knocked. 'Heil Hitler, Eugenia! Since you're already busy baking, would you let me have a little tip of your vanilla bean if possible?'

'I'll let you have the whole bean, Sophie, not just the little tip.' Eugenia kept her supply of ingredients in clean glass jars. 'You're my first visitor this morning, Sophie,' she said, presenting the girl with the vanilla bean and a slice of her hot streusel cake on a cake server.

With sugary lips and streusel cake as her unimpeachable alibi, Sophie crossed the road to her own kitchen, where her mother was already grinding the coffee.

The night was behind them. The two men, George and Dr Kress, started every time a car came by from the Riederwald development or when they heard the footsteps of a night-time patrol, and it got worse each time it happened. It was as if, in the course of the night, their bodies had got lighter.

Mrs Kress drew back the blinds and opened the window. Turning back to the bright room, it seemed to her that the two men had aged and lost weight, both her husband and the stranger. She shivered. Glancing at her reflection in the metal base of the lamp, her own face seemed unchanged, although a little pale around the lips. 'The night's over,' she said. 'For my part, I'm going to take a bath and put on my best Sunday dress.'

'And I'll brew some coffee,' Kress said, 'and what about you, George?'

There was no answer. With the fresh air streaming in from outside, George had been overcome, partly from lack of sleep, partly from exhaustion. Kress went over to the chair in which George had collapsed with his head hitting the edge of the table. Kress lifted George's head and turned it slightly. In a corner of his mind he wondered how much longer he would have to shelter this guest; but he managed to muzzle this part of himself that dared even to ask such a question. You're wrong, he said to himself, I'd even keep his corpse in the house.

Only a short while later, George started up; maybe in response to a door being slammed. Still half asleep, but under the old compulsion, he tried to find an explanation for all the noises he could hear in the house: that sound was the coffee mill; that was the bathroom. He tried to get up, to go downstairs to join Kress in the kitchen. He wanted to fight this overpowering need to sleep – not a good, healthy sleep. But it had already overpowered him again, and he barely had time to tell himself that the new dangers threatening him were going to be nothing but a dream, and that he didn't want to let himself be drawn in. But it was stronger than he was.

So, they'd caught him after all. They'd dumped him into Barracks VIII. He was bleeding from many wounds, but because of his fear of what was still to come, he felt no pain. He told himself, Courage, George. But he knew that the most dreadful torment faced him in this barracks. And here it was already.

On the other side of a table covered with electric wires and telephone equipment but in all other respects an ordinary bar-room table – there were even a few cardboard coasters for beer glasses – sat Fahrenberg himself, staring at him with narrowed eyes and a frozen laugh on his lips. To his right and left sat Bunsen and Zillich, who now turned their heads to look at him. Bunsen laughed aloud. But

Zillich remained gloomy as ever. He was counting out cards from a deck. It was dark in the room but somewhat lighter over the table, though George could see no lamp. One of the wires was wound around Zillich's massive chest; the sight made George feel ice cold with horror. And yet he thought quite lucidly: They're actually playing cards with Zillich. So, there are some tables at which class differences don't count.

'Come closer,' Fahrenberg said. But George stayed where he was out of spite and because his knees were shaking. He expected Fahrenberg to yell at him, but Fahrenberg only winked in incomprehensible acquiescence. At that point George realised that the three of them had thought up something new, something especially nasty and malicious. Something tricky, something that would within the next second strike him in body and soul. But the second passed; the three of them continued to look at him. —Be on guard, George told himself, gather every last bit of your strength. Then he heard a small noise like the crunching of bones or very dry wood. George was puzzled; he looked from one man to the other. Then he noticed there was a dent in the cheek Zillich had turned towards him, as if his flesh were rotting away, and one of the ears on Bunsen's handsome long skull was in the process of crumbling away, as well as a chunk of his forehead. At that point George realised that all three men sitting there were dead, and that he, George, whom they were receiving into their eternal unity, he, too, was dead.

He screamed at the top of his voice, 'Mother!' With one hand he grabbed at the lamp; the lamp struck his leg and fell to the floor. Both Kresses came running up the stairs. George wiped his face and looked around the bright, disordered room. Deeply embarrassed, he offered them his apologies.

Mrs Kress with her naked, thin arms and wet, scraggly hair looked comfortingly young and clean. They took him downstairs into the kitchen and sat him down between them at the table. They poured coffee and set food in front of him. 'What are you thinking about, George?'

'Why it is that it can have so much power over us – If I were a free man now, I might be lying in some dangerous place in Spain. Waiting for someone to relieve me, and he might be shot too. I might get a bullet in my stomach. That wouldn't be any more pleasant than the kicks and blows from those thugs at Westhofen. Why is that? Is it the whole process? Is it those in power? Or is it just me? – How long do you think I could stay here, if worse comes to worst?'

'You can stay until your relief comes,' Kress said so firmly that you wouldn't think he'd been silently asking himself all this time how long he could stand this waiting.

II

Around that time Fiedler was again sitting in the garden house outside the city that he leased jointly with his brother-in-law. Before he'd come here, he'd made certain that his wife was wearing the outfit they had agreed on to indicate that the night had passed uneventfully.

Well, it would seem Roeder hadn't given the Gestapo any information so far. He hadn't betrayed the go-between. Otherwise the hounds would already be after them. So far... so far... that indicated only a certain degree of steadfastness, not what the final outcome would be.

Mrs Fiedler started a fire in the little stove that served for both heating and cooking. The wooden shack had been freshly painted outside and in. It was in such good shape that it seemed as if the Fiedlers had no plans for any moves in the future. Fiedler had taken great care with this garden house, especially in this last, more peaceful year. His wife now prepared to serve him coffee on the folding table that he'd designed himself, a collapsible piece of furniture with many hinges, for many purposes, made of simple fir wood with a beautiful natural grain that Fiedler had brought out with diligent planing and polishing.

He looked out through the small glass pane he had puttied into the window frame, past a hedge on which hung many rose hips, past brown and golden bushes and other hedges, towards the distant church spires of the city. Even if Roeder hadn't given them any information during the night, it was possible he might do so now, in the morning. He recalled what had happened with Melzer, whom they'd always considered a decent young fellow. He had been able to remain silent for three days, but on the fourth his tormentors had led him through the large printing plant where he had worked, and he had pointed out all those he thought were or might be suspect. What had they done to Melzer? What poison, what tongs had they used to pull the soul out of his living body?

What if Roeder came to the factory tomorrow, followed by two shadows, and were to point Fiedler out to them? 'No,' Fiedler said out loud. Even the Roeder he had dreamed up just now would refuse to be drawn into this dreamed-up betrayal.

'What do you mean, "No"?' his wife asked.

Fiedler just shook his head and smiled at her strangely. There was no way Heisler could stay where he was for long. They needed some advice, some help. Hadn't he, Fiedler, been mumbling to himself all year long about being completely isolated and no longer knowing where to turn? Perhaps there *was* a man, one single man – but was he for real? Even though the man worked in the same factory, Fiedler had been avoiding him for a long time. Why? For a whole series of reasons in which, as always happens when one lists a lot of reasons, the principal reason was missing. For instance, Fiedler had thought he was avoiding this man because he didn't want to burden him, because this man had important responsibilities at Pokorny. Another time Fiedler had avoided the man because he knew him from earlier days and might say careless things about him. Thus it seems he had avoided him for two contradictory reasons: on the one hand, because of mistrust, and on the other, because he trusted him implicitly. But now, with Heisler's life at stake, there was no time to lose. There wasn't a minute more for brooding about the pros and cons. Now Fiedler suddenly knew that he had avoided this particular man only because, once he went to him for help, there would be no escape any more. So it finally had come to this, whether he, Fiedler, wanted to stay out of things for ever, to withdraw from everything and everyone, or whether he wanted to continue to be a part of it, to belong. This man, too, had the power to wrest from another his innermost soul.

The man in whom Fiedler placed so much trust – his name was Reinhardt – was lying on his bed in his half-darkened bedroom enjoying his Sunday rest. Sleepily he listened to the sounds in his flat.

His wife was feeding their grandchild in the kitchen; for their daughter was off to some wine festival with Kraft durch Freude. He had married very young. His hair was a mottled grey as if it were just beginning to turn grey or had been grey for a long time and was stained by metal dust.

There was nothing extraordinary to be seen in his lean, ageless face, unless you looked into his eyes. And then only if these eyes were interested in something about you. Then they would sparkle in a combination of benevolence, mistrust, and mockery, and also the hope of finding a new friend.

Now, even though he was awake, he had his eyes closed. Just one more minute and then he would have to get up. He had to try to find the man he had been thinking about for the last hour. If only he wasn't away on some workmen's excursion! Although Reinhardt knew Roeder, the man Hermann had told him about, by sight, it was impossible for him to approach Roeder directly; in this twilight atmosphere of rumours and suppositions, he would be risking too much. The man he'd been thinking about was the right man to sound out Roeder.

Maybe all of it was just imagined. Oh yes, they had mentioned names and places. They had also combed through a couple of streets and searched a few flats. Perhaps they were only using this rumour of the escaped prisoners to make a few arrests, for a few random questionings. The radio had been silent on the subject since yesterday. Maybe they'd already caught Heisler. And only in the rumours and gossip of the people was he still chasing through the city, hiding in imaginary hiding places, escaping again and again by means of countless clever tricks – a dream dreamed by many. Such an explanation seemed highly probable to Reinhardt. Then there was the yellow envelope Hermann had handed him intended for this spectral George. A borrowed passport for a shadow. In such times when people's lives were tightly constrained within stifling limits, anything was possible in the realm of wishes and dreams.

The last minute of his Sunday morning calm was up. With a sigh he put his feet on the floor. He had to go at once to see this man who worked in Roeder's department; he could find out what was real about this story. He, Reinhardt, had to be prepared to learn that the story about the escape was composed of thin air, yet at the same time he had to take it seriously and not lose a moment. His dearest friend Hermann, in spite of all his doubts, had acted immediately the same way, as if there could not be any doubt. From the first moment he had worked to get money and documents. Reinhardt's eyes sparkled when he thought of Hermann – a man who gave one the strength not only to do a lot of very difficult things, but also the strength to do a lot of difficult things to no purpose. The grey of his eyes dulled when he thought of the man whom he had to see now, the man in Roeder's department. He frowned.

Still, the man could give him information about Roeder. He'd been working with him at Pokorny for years already. And he wouldn't talk about who had asked him. But beyond that, the man would probably hesitate to do or say anything, just the way he'd been hesitating for years. And Reinhardt had been observing him closely. Would he succeed today in getting the man to come out of himself, this man who was so fearful, so intimidated?

He sat down on the edge of the bed to put on his socks. Just then the front doorbell rang. Oh, please don't let anything interfere now; he just had to go there today – right now, in fact. A moment later, his wife stuck her head into the room to tell him that a visitor had come.

'It's me,' Fiedler said as he entered the room.

Reinhardt pulled up the blind so that he could get a look at his visitor. Fiedler could now feel those same eyes focused on him, those eyes he'd been so afraid of all year long. But it was Reinhardt who first lowered his gaze and said in embarrassment and dismay, 'It's you, Fiedler! I was just about to go to see you.'

'And I,' Fiedler said, calm by now, 'I decided to come to you. I simply have to confide in someone. But I don't know whether you can understand why I stayed away for such a long time.'

Reinhardt reassured him quickly that he did understand. And then, as if he were the one who should excuse himself, he told a strange story about something that happened in 1923. He said he had been stationed in the vicinity of Bielefeld when General Watter had marched in. Back then he was so terrified that he'd gone into hiding and stayed there for weeks even towards the end, when his terror had already faded . . . because he was so ashamed and angry at himself for having been so frightened.

So having been spared a full explanation of his own actions, Fiedler recounted in detail what had brought him there. Reinhardt listened calmly. The uncharacteristically brusque tone in which he interrupted with questions a couple of times did not match the look on his face. It was that of a man who at last sees again before him that which is most important to him and for which he has gambled everything, something he feels will always exist, even though it may often be far away or hidden to the point of vanishing, of being questionable. Yet now here it was in front of him; in fact, it had come to him.

After he had listened to everything Fiedler had to tell him, Reinhardt got up, leaving Fiedler alone for two minutes so that the man would have time to realise fully the seriousness of the step he had taken, a step that had been at once easy and hard. When Reinhardt returned, he put an envelope down before Fiedler. The heavy yellow envelope contained papers made out in the name of a Dutch tugboat captain's nephew who usually made the voyage from and to Mainz with his uncle. They had been able to contact the fellow in time in Bingen, and he willingly gave them his papers and passport since he also had a regular permit to cross the border in his pocket. The passport photo had been skilfully altered to match the picture on the Wanted posters.

Inside the passport there were a few bills. Reinhardt smoothed the envelope with the side of his hand to flatten it, a gesture both utilitarian and tender. The contents of that envelope represented dangerous, painstaking, detailed work, countless errands, fact-finding missions, lists, work done in previous years, old friendships and connections, as well as the help of the Association of Seamen and Dock Workers – a network that reached across oceans and rivers. But the life of the man who now had his fingers in this network was restricted and hard, and these few bills represented a great deal of money, the district leader's emergency fund designated for special cases.

Fiedler pocketed the envelope.

'Will you be taking it there yourself?'

'No, my wife will.'

'Is she up to it?'

'She's probably better at it than I am.'

After a wakeful night, Liesel Roeder, almost blinded by tears, had fed and dressed the children. 'But it's Sunday,' the oldest boy said when she gave them bread instead of rolls. On Sundays Paul usually went to get warm rolls from the baker across the street. At the memory Liesel started crying all over again, and the children, suddenly intimidated and hurt, dutifully chewed and dunked their bread.

Well, Paul hadn't come home and their life together was over. Judging from the sobs shaking Liesel, life with the now lost Paul must have been incomparably happy. Liesel had invested all her energy, not in the future, not even in the future of their children, but rather in their present life together. Now as she looked with swollen eyes down into the street without seeing anything, she hated everybody who had ever dared to rattle that life, whether with persecutions, threats, or even promises of something better for the future.

The children were still sitting at the table; they had finished breakfast, but remained there, remarkably silent.

Were they beating him? Liesel wondered. She saw her future life destroyed, saw it in detail with all the consequences. But the ruined life of the other was more difficult to visualise, even if the other was Paul. What if they keep beating him until he tells them about George's whereabouts? If he tells them, will they let him go home? Can he just come home right away then? Can everything be the way it was before?

Liesel stopped thinking. And her tears stopped too. In her heart she suddenly sensed that just thinking any further about what might be was forbidden. Nothing could ever be as it had been before. Normally Liesel didn't understand things outside the realm of her own busy life. She understood nothing of the shadows that lie behind the boundary posts of reality, and nothing of the strange events that take place between the boundary posts: when reality glides into nothingness and can never return, or when the shadows feel the urge to come crowding back so as to be accepted as real one last time.

But at that moment even Liesel understood the nature of an illusory world, a mistakenly returned Paul who wasn't Paul any more, a family that cannot then be a family any more; a life together through the years that had stopped being a life long ago on an October night in the cellars of the Gestapo because of a few words of confession.

Liesel shook her head, turned away from the window. She went over to the kitchen sofa and sat down with her children. She told her oldest boy to change his dirty socks for the clean ones that had been drying on a rail above the stove. She took the girl on her lap and sewed on a button.

III

Although Mettenheimer thought he was still being followed, he no longer felt the old fear. Let them watch me, he thought with a kind of pride; they'll finally get a chance to know an honest man.

Nevertheless he kept praying that George might vanish from his life without any harm coming to Elli, and without his having to do anything terrible.

Maybe the shabby little man who'd just sat down on the bench next to him was a replacement for the one in the stiff felt hat who'd almost driven him to despair last week. In spite of that, Mettenheimer waited calmly for the porter's family to come out of the church and unlock the door for him. It was a splendid house, Mettenheimer thought. The people who originally had it built had no deep-seated anger in their hearts.

When viewed from the bottom of the autumnal garden sloping up towards it, the two-storey white house, with its low, slightly curving roof and beautiful entrance repeating the same curve, seemed larger than it was. It had stood outside the city until the city grew to catch up with it. The street had actually been laid out to curve around the house because it was too fine a building to be torn down. A house for a loving couple with faith in the stability of their feelings for each other and of their external circumstances. A couple already looking forward to grandchildren at their wedding.

'A nice little house,' said the shabby little man. Mettenheimer looked at him. 'It's a good thing that it gets swept out now and then whenever new people move in,' the little man said.

'Are you the new tenant?' Mettenheimer asked him.

'Me! Good Lord, no!' The little man started laughing uncontrollably.

'I'm the paperhanger here,' Mettenheimer said.

The little man gazed at him with respect. And since Mettenheimer said nothing further, he got up, raised his arm with a Heil Hitler! and traipsed off.

That certainly was no spy, Mettenheimer thought.

He was just about to get up and check whether he had missed the porter's family when he saw his chief assistant, Schultz, coming from the tram stop. Mettenheimer was surprised that Schultz should be showing so much zeal for work on a sacred Sunday.

But Schultz was in no hurry to get to the construction site. He sat down in the sunshine on the bench next to Mettenheimer. 'Hasn't this been a beautiful autumn, Mr Mettenheimer?'

'Yes, it has.'

'Won't last much longer. Last night there was quite a red sunset.'

'Really.'

'Mr Mettenheimer,' Schultz said, 'your daughter Elli, the one who came to pick you up yesterday...'

Mettenheimer quickly turned to face him. Schultz became embarrassed.

'What's the matter with her?' Mettenheimer asked. For some reason he was annoyed.

'Nothing. Nothing at all,' Schultz said in confusion. 'She is very pretty. It's surprising that she hasn't married again.'

Mettenheimer eyed him angrily. He said, 'That's really her business.'

'Partly,' Schultz said. 'Is she divorced from Heisler?'

Now Mettenheimer lost his temper. 'You can ask Elli herself all that.'

The man really doesn't understand, Schultz thought. Calmly, he said, 'Yes, of course I can. I just thought you would like it if we could discuss it first.'

'Good heavens, discuss what?' Mettenheimer said, taken aback.

Schultz sighed. Then in a different tone of voice he said, 'Mr Mettenheimer, I've known your family for almost ten years. That's how long you and I have been working for the same firm. Before, your Elli often came to our work sites, and when I saw her again yesterday, it went right through me.'

Mettenheimer drew in his moustache and began to chew on it.

Finally! thought Schultz. He went on, 'I don't hold any prejudices. There's this story about George Heisler; there are rumours going around. I don't know the man personally. Confidentially, Mr Mettenheimer, I...I hope from the bottom of my heart that he'll succeed in getting away. I'm just repeating what the others are thinking and saying. And then your Elli could enter a plea of desertion. And there's also the child she had with Heisler. Yes, I know. If he's a good child, then, well, then there's already a child.'

Mettenheimer said softly, 'He is a good child.'

'Yes. And if I were in Heisler's place, I'd say it would be better if

Schultz takes care of my child – after all, he's a man like me – than if the boy falls into the hands of those thugs and is turned into one of them. By the time Heisler's child is old enough to go to work with us, the reign of those thugs will be over.'

Mettenheimer was startled. He looked around. But as far as he could tell, they were by themselves sitting there in the autumn sunshine.

'But if Heisler is recaptured,' Schultz said, lowering his voice, 'or maybe he's already been caught, for yesterday and today there wasn't anything about him on the radio, then there's no getting away any more for the poor man. His life will be over, then Elli won't even have to file a complaint about desertion any more.'

The two men looked straight ahead. Dried leaves from the gardens lay scattered all over the sunny street. Mettenheimer thought: This Schultz is a dependable worker; he's got a good heart and a good mind, he's decent looking. I've always wished for a man like that for Elli. Why didn't he become a member of my family years ago? Then we could have been spared all this.

Schultz said, 'Years ago, Mr Mettenheimer, you were kind enough to invite me to spend some time with your family. Back then I didn't accept. Will you permit me to take up your invitation now? —There's just one thing you must promise me, Mr Mettenheimer: Please don't tell Elli anything about what we've agreed on. If I come, Mr Mettenheimer, and your Elli happens to be there in your living room, it will be pure coincidence. Girls like her can't stand it if something like this has been discussed or planned beforehand. They want to have a suitor who's like that devil at the Römerberg open-air theatre.'

If you're condemned to wait, when the waiting is a genuine question of life or death, and you don't know beforehand what the outcome will be and how long it will take – hours or days – then you take the strangest measures to annihilate time. You try to catch the minutes, to destroy them. You set up a kind of dyke against time, and you keep trying to build up your dyke even if time is already flowing over the top of it.

George, still sitting at the table with the two Kresses, had at first gone along with these attempts. But then, imperceptibly, he had withdrawn. He was determined not to wait any longer. Kress was recounting how he had first met Fiedler. Initially, George had to force himself to listen, but after a while he really became interested. Kress was describing Fiedler as a steadfast man who was not susceptible to any doubts or fears. But then a babble of voices outside the window made Kress stop – it turned out to be merely an ordinary Sunday excursion group. Kress tried another tactic; he got up and turned the knobs on the radio, and part of a morning concert filled a few minutes of time. George asked him for a map and sat back down again; there were still a number of things he wanted to know. Less than two weeks ago, a newly delivered prisoner in Westhofen, using a few wooden splinters, had laid out a map of Spain and drawn the Spanish theatres of war in the damp earth with his index finger. George remembered how the man had rubbed it all out again with his wooden shoe when a guard approached. The man was a printer from Hanau.

George was silent, and time came rushing in.

Suddenly Mrs Kress said, as if some response had been demanded of her, that one of her brothers had gone to Spain to join Franco, and a friend from her youth, Benno, also wanted to go there. He was a friend of her brother's and as children they had played together. She went on talking to keep time at bay, the way you grabbed the next best thing to stuff into a breach. 'And for a long time I didn't know whether I should choose you or Benno.'

'Me or Benno?'

'That's right. I knew Benno better, felt more comfortable with him. But I wanted to go somewhere else.'

Her confession was in vain. The few words she'd said consumed practically no time at all.

'Please do your work, Dr Kress, or whatever you were planning to do,' George said. 'Or take your wife for a Sunday stroll; for a few hours try to forget that I'm here. I'll go back upstairs.'

He stood up, surprising both husband and wife.

'He's right,' Kress said. 'If only one could actually forget, he'd be right.'

'Oh, one can,' his wife said, 'and I'm going to go out to the garden right now and transplant some tulip bulbs.'

Roeder's not going to betray me, George said to himself once he was alone. But he might make some awkward mistake. He doesn't know how to answer questions, doesn't know how to behave. It's not his fault. Your wits desert you when you're worn down by beatings and sick from lack of sleep. Then even the shrewdest head turns dull and stupid, and Paul was surely seen with Fiedler every day. That won't be hard for the Gestapo to work out. But you can't reproach Paul for anything. Again George wondered whether it wouldn't be better if he left this house. Even in the best of circumstances, even if Paul doesn't say anything – would Fiedler also remain silent? What George had been afraid of in Mrs Grabber's workshop in the courtyard was more likely to happen here. He would be stuck in this place. They wouldn't be able to find him. Kress was certainly not the man to help him get away. Wouldn't it be better to leave now than to wait here for days?

He had gone over to the window because he couldn't stand enclosed spaces. He looked down at the white street that cut through the development. On the other side of the development, which resembled an all-too-clean village, you could see parks and forests. George was overcome by a feeling of utter homelessness, followed at once by a feeling of pride. Was there another man besides himself who could look with the same eyes and see this wide, steel-blue autumn sky and this street, which led, only for him, into a total wilderness? He looked at the people walking by down below, people in their Sunday best with children and old mothers and strange packages, a motorcyclist with his fiancée on the pillion behind him, two Hitler Youths with a folding canoe in a rucksack, an SA man holding a child by the hand, a young woman with a bouquet of asters.

Just then the front doorbell rang. Let it ring, George thought; it probably rings quite often here. The house and street remained quiet. Kress came up the stairs. 'Come out to the stair landing for a moment.'

George looked, frowning, at the young woman with the bouquet of asters who was suddenly standing here in Kress's house, three steps below him.

'I was asked to bring you something,' she said, 'and I'm also supposed to tell you to be at the dock in Mainz by the Kastel Bridge tomorrow morning at five thirty. The name of the ship is *Wilhelmine*. They'll be expecting you.'

'Yes,' George said. He didn't move from the spot where he was standing. The woman unbuttoned her jacket pocket without letting go of the asters. She took out a fat envelope and handed it to him, saying as she did so, 'So now I've given you the envelope.' Her manner implied that she considered George a comrade who had to hide although she did not know who he was.

George said, 'Yes. All right.'

Liesel had just been grinding some malt coffee for the children and she didn't hear the hall door being unlocked. Paul was holding a bag of rolls he had bought on the way home. He said, 'Liesel, wash your face with vinegar water and get dressed. We still have time to get to the stadium. Hey, Liesel, what's there to bawl about now?'

He touched her hair, since she had put her head down on the table. 'Oh, Liesel, please stop; that's enough now. Didn't I promise you I'd come back?'

'Dear God in Heaven!' Liesel said.

'God had nothing to do with it, or only as much as He has something to do with everything. It was all just as I imagined it would be. A huge lot of hocus-pocus. For hours they put me to the acid test. Except I never imagined that they would sit there and write down all the rubbish I was spouting, and that after that I had to write my name under it, saying that I myself had really spouted all that. When I knew George, where, for how long, why, who his friends were, who my friends were. And they also asked me who came to visit me the day before yesterday.

'And all the time they threatened me with everything they could possibly threaten me with. All that was lacking was hellfire. They really wanted to make me think they were the Last Judgement. But they are not the slightest bit all-knowing. All they know is what you tell them.'

Later, after Liesel felt somewhat comforted, had dressed her children and herself in their Sunday best, and had washed her face with vinegar water, Paul started up again, 'There's just one thing I can't understand – that people would tell them so much. And why? Because they think the Gestapo already know everything.

'But I told myself: Nobody can really prove that George was actually at my house. And even if someone had seen him, I can deny it. Nobody has proof that it was George, only George himself. And so, if they've got him, then everything is finished anyway. But if they actually had him, they wouldn't have asked me so many questions.'

Twenty minutes later Paul and Liesel went into town. They took a detour to drop the children off for the afternoon with Paul's family. The youngest was taken by the caretaker's wife; they'd arranged all that a few days ago already. Paul had a strong suspicion that the woman had reported him, but otherwise she was helpful and fond of children.

Suddenly Paul asked Liesel and the children to wait. Something had occurred to him; there was something he had to do. He went through a gate and into the courtyard. The little window in the garage was lit as always, even though it was bright as day in the yard. Paul walked rapidly over to the window to tackle the unpleasant task. He didn't want to keep his family waiting long. He called out, 'Aunt Catherine!'

When Mrs Grabber stuck out her head, Paul said, 'My brother-in-law sends his apologies. They forwarded a notification from the police in Offenbach to him. So he had to go back home again, and it's doubtful whether he'll come back. I'm really sorry, Aunt Catherine; it isn't my fault.'

For one moment Mrs Grabber said nothing, then she yelled, 'I don't care if he never comes back! I would have sent him packing anyway! Don't you ever dare send me a bastard like that again!'

'Oh well,' Paul said, 'you didn't lose anything. He repaired your truck for nothing, after all. Heil Hitler!'

Mrs Grabber sat down at her desk. The red number on her calendar made her realise that it was Sunday. On Sundays the removal vans usually stayed at their destinations. She had no family any more and even if she did, she wouldn't have gone home. The disappointment she was feeling was entirely out of proportion to the insignificance of this affair, the fact that Paul's brother-in-law had not accepted the job here. The police notification was probably only an excuse; he just hadn't liked it here. But then he shouldn't have had a drink with me last night. He shouldn't have done that, she thought angrily. That was a mean thing to do.

She looked around at the immense Sunday dreariness, a regular flood of bleakness with a few objects floating on it: a little chunk of malachite, a lamp, a ledger, a calendar.

She rushed over to the window and called down into the courtyard, 'Paul!'

But Paul was already on his way with his Liesel to Niederrad Stadium.

Hermann felt both glad and guilty as he watched and listened to his wife singing as she made herself ready for their Sunday visit to the Marnets. With her damp-brushed hair, stiffly ironed dress, little necklace, and clear eyes she resembled a sturdy child about to be confirmed. Even though it was only ten minutes' walk up the hill, she put a hat on her round head. 'Just to show the Marnets.' Augusta Marnet, her cousin, still couldn't get over the fact that Elsa, dumb little Elsa, had landed this older, well-salaried railway man as a husband.

As they approached the Marnets' house, Hermann gazed with amusement at his Elsa's face. He knew all her emotions, the way you quickly become familiar with the emotions of a little bird. How proud she was of her marriage, which she considered indestructible.

'Why are you looking at me in such a funny way today?'

Was it good or was it bad that she was starting to ask questions? he mused.

A person climbing up the Schmiedtheim heights might wonder about the strong blue light gleaming behind the Marnets' garden fence. It wasn't until you got closer that you realised it was coming from the large glass globe in the bed of asters.

The Marnets' kitchen was hot and steamy. The entire family and their guests were seated around the table. Once a year, after the apple harvest, they baked cakes in pans that were almost as large as the table. Everyone's lips were shiny with juice and sugar, the children's lips as well as those of the soldiers, and even Augusta's parsimonious thin lips gleamed. The hefty coffeepot and the smaller milk jug along with the blue-and-white onion-pattern cups, even they looked like a family. The whole tribe was gathered around the table: Mrs Marnet and her tiny farmer husband; their grandchildren, little Ernst and Gustav; their daughter Augusta; their son-in-law and their oldest son, the two of them in their SA uniforms; their son, the soldier, looking new and fresh in his uniform; Messer's second son, the recruit; and Messer's youngest son in his SS uniform – after all, apple cake is apple cake! – Eugenia, proud and beautiful; Sophie Mangold, a little dulled; Ernst the shepherd, wearing a tie instead of his usual kerchief – his mother was taking care of the sheep; Franz, who jumped up as Hermann and Elsa entered; and, at the head of the table, in the place of honour, sat Sister Anastasia of the Königstein Ursulines, the white ends of her headdress shimmering over the coffee table.

Elsa proudly sat down with the women of her family. Her firm child's hand with the wedding ring reached cheerfully for a piece of apple cake. Hermann sat down next to Franz.

'Last week Dora Katzenstein came to say good-bye to me,' Sister Anastasia said. 'I used to buy the dress material for my orphans at her shop. "Please don't tell anyone, Sister," Dora said, "but we're all leaving soon." And she cried. Yesterday all the shutters were closed at the Katzensteins', and the key was lying under the doormat. When they opened it up, the little shop was bare and everything sold off! Only the yardstick was still lying on the table.'

'They wouldn't have left until the last remnant of cotton had been sold,' Augusta said.

Her mother said, 'If we had to leave, we'd also wait until we had harvested our last potatoes.'

'But you can't compare our potatoes with the Katzensteins' cotton.'

'You can compare everything.'

Messer's SS son said, 'One Sarah less.' And he spat on the floor.

Mrs Marnet would have preferred it if he hadn't spat on her clean kitchen floor. On the whole, though, it was rather hard to make people shudder in the Marnets' kitchen. Even if the Four Riders of the Apocalypse had come riding past on this apple-cake Sunday, they'd probably have tethered their four horses at the garden fence and conducted themselves like decent guests inside the house.

'You got a furlough pretty quickly, Fritz,' Hermann said to his Marnet cousin-in-law.

'Didn't you read it in the newspaper? Every mother is to have the joy of seeing a brand-new recruit in her house on Sundays.'

Eugenia said, 'Your son's a joy to you no matter what he's wearing.' They all looked at her somewhat embarrassed, but she said calmly, 'A new jacket like that is of course nicer than one with holes in it, especially if the holes go deep.'

The others were glad when Sister Anastasia bridged the cool pause that ensued by returning the conversation to her previous subject. 'Dora was very nice.'

'She couldn't carry a tune,' Augusta said. 'We were in the same class at school.'

'Very nice and decent,' Mrs Marnet said. 'What a lot of bolts of cotton she must have dragged around on her back all those years.' But Dora Katzenstein was already well ensconced on a ship full of emigrants by the time this one last little delicate flag was raised in the Marnets' kitchen in a valedictory tribute.

'I imagine you two will soon be getting engaged?' Sister Anastasia asked.

'You mean us?' Sophie and Ernst cried out in unison, moving resolutely away from each other. But from her seat of honour Sister Anastasia could see not only what was going on above the table but also below it.

'When are you enlisting in the army, Ernst?' Mrs Marnet asked. 'It would be good for you. You wouldn't be able to duck out of everything there.'

'He hasn't attended drill sessions for months,' the SA Marnet son said.

'I have a dispensation from all the drill and practice sessions,' Ernst said. 'I'm with the civil air defence.'

They all laughed at that except for the SS Messer son, who glared at Ernst with distaste. 'No doubt you'll have to fit your sheep with gas masks?'

Ernst abruptly turned to Mr Messer, for he sensed the man's eyes were on him. 'Well, and what about you, Messer? You'll probably have a hard time exchanging your beautiful black dress coat for an ordinary soldier's jacket.'

'Won't have to do that,' Messer said.

But before a cold silence or something worse could settle over the company, Sister Anastasia said, 'You learned that from us, Augusta, putting ground nuts on top of the apple cake.'

'I'm going out for a breath of fresh air now,' Hermann said. Franz went out with him into the garden. The sky over the flat land was turning colours and the birds were flying lower. 'Tomorrow the nice weather will be over,' Franz said. 'Oh, Hermann . . .'

'What's the matter?'

'There was nothing on the radio about the escape, either yesterday or today, no more Wanted posters, nothing about George.'

'Franz, stop brooding about this thing. It would be better for you, better for everyone. You're spending too much time on it; it's occupying all your thoughts. Everything that could be done for your George has already been done.'

For a moment Franz's face became animated so that you realised that this man wasn't at all slow and sleepy, but was capable of doing and feeling all sorts of things and emotions. He said, 'Is he safe?'

'No, not yet . . .'

IV

Hermann had to leave shortly after that, for he was on the night shift. He left Elsa with the Marnets and what was left of the apple cake. Franz walked with him part of the way. Since he had no appointment for Sunday, he intended to go back home. But now he didn't feel like listening to any more of the talk in the kitchen, nor did he feel like sitting by himself in his little room. He suddenly felt alone, as alone and abandoned as you can only feel on a Sunday. He was unhappy, depressed, and grumpy.

Should he go for a tramp in the woods? Flushing out lovers in the clearings among the warm dry autumn leaves? But no, if he was going to be alone on a Sunday, then he'd rather be alone in the city. He walked on towards Hoechst.

In spite of having had lots of sleep the night before, he was tired. He could feel the week of hard work in his bones. He couldn't just suddenly turn off his worries, in spite of Hermann's insistence that he keep his fingers out of things, now that everything that could be done to help George had been done.

Franz went and sat down in the garden of the first inn he came to. It was still pretty empty. The innkeeper's wife, who was brushing wilted leaves off the tablecloths, asked him if he'd like some cider. To his annoyance, when it arrived, the cider wasn't sweet any more and had already started to ferment. He might just as well have ordered some genuine hard cider. A little girl came running out from the inn into the garden and started rustling around in the leaves that had been swept up next to the fence. She ran over to Franz and tugged at his tablecloth. The little girl's face was framed by a little bonnet; her eyes were almost black.

Then the mother came out and tugged at the child, scolding her.

Franz thought he recognised the woman's rough, coarse voice; her face was young and lean but pinched a bit by a crooked little hat and a large bunch of hair combed over half of her face. He said, 'She wasn't being bad.'

The woman looked at him with the uncovered eye, almost staring at him.

Franz said, 'We've met before. Haven't we?'

She had turned her head so abruptly that a corner of the left eye had been revealed. It had probably been injured in a traffic accident. She replied sarcastically, 'Oh, yes. We've seen each other somewhere before. You can say that again.'

Seen each other, yes, several times, thought Franz. But where have I heard that voice of hers? 'I bumped into you on my bike the other day.'

'That too,' she replied drily. The child she was holding on to with an iron grip almost twisted her arm. 'But we know each other from somewhere else, from long ago.' She was still looking at his face. Then it suddenly burst from her, 'Franz.'

He raised his eyebrows; his heart pounded twice, a soft warning he was used to.

She allowed him a few moments. 'That time we went rowing, when we went to the little islands in the Nidda River where there was the camp among the fir trees, where you ...'

'A nut!' the child cried, fumbling around the table legs.

'Well, crack it under your heel,' the woman said without taking her gaze from Franz.

But he was gripped by a chill, a sort of anxiety that he couldn't explain. He looked at her, speculatively.

She suddenly bent down and said to his face, sounding quite desperate, 'I'm Lotte!'

He was going to say, Impossible! but swallowed the word in time.

But she must have guessed what he was thinking. She looked at him directly as if she were waiting for a sign of recognition, for a vague reflection of all that she had once been for him – a girl, sparkling with happiness, with slender, smooth, sun-tanned limbs. With shiny, strong hair like the mane of a healthy animal.

When the woman saw that he was at last beginning to remember, a trace of a smile came to her face, and it was only then that he really recognised her, by this trace of a smile. He remembered that in the holiday camp she had served them their food from a board balanced on two tree stumps. Remembered how she had come from the rowing boat wearing a little blue smock. How she'd sat on the ground with her knees drawn up. How she'd carried the flag, tired but smiling, a bit of snow on her thick hair. A girl so beautiful and spirited that she seemed like an emblem, like the figurehead on the prow of their own swift boat. He even remembered that she had married soon thereafter, a big, blond man, a railway worker who'd come down from northern Germany. His name was Herbert. He'd never thought of him after that, just the way you stop thinking of something when all traces of it have vanished. 'Where's Herbert?' he asked.

'There!' She pointed with her index finger down at the brown soil of the inn garden, under the soil on which the leaves of a chestnut tree were scattered along with a few spiny burrs. She pointed so precisely, so calmly that it seemed to Franz that Herbert, whom he had completely lost track of and never even looked up, must be lying below him, beneath this garden, having by chance taken residence under the dried leaves and the tall SS and SA boots and the little boots of their women, for by now the garden had filled with people. Lots of uniformed men and their pretty, young girlfriends. But Franz found them all disgusting. He said, 'Sit down, Lotte.' He ordered some cider for her and lemonade for the child.

'Actually, I was lucky,' Lotte said in a changed, matter-of-fact voice. 'Herbert had already left us and gone to Cologne, and that was where someone informed on him. They wanted to arrest me too. But just around that time something had happened in our department at the factory; a pipe had burst, and I was lying in some hospital, close to kicking the bucket. One of my relatives was taking care of the child and had taken her to the country; she was very little still. Then by the time I got better, my child had already learned how to walk, and

Herbert, well, Herbert, he was dead ... After that nothing else happened to me. I slipped through their net.'

'Don't blow through the straw, you have to suck on it,' she told the child, and to Franz she said, apologetically, 'It's the first time she's ever had the stuff.'

She straightened out the little girl's bonnet and said, 'Sometimes I think dying might not have been so bad, but there was the child. I couldn't leave my child to them! You don't need to reproach me, Franz, or to console me. Sometimes you feel so very alone. Then you think: The others, they've forgotten everything.'

'Who is "they"?'

'You all! All of you! You, too, Franz. Didn't you forget Herbert? Do you think I couldn't see it in your face? If you were able to forget Herbert, how many others have you also forgotten? And your forgetting ... that's what they're counting on ...' and with her shoulder she indicated the adjacent table that was occupied by SA men and their followers. 'Don't deny it, you've forgotten a lot of things. It's pretty awful if you become hardened to it and forget some of the bad things they've done to us. But forgetting the best things, in the midst of all the terrible things, that's even worse. Do you remember when we were still all together? I, for one, I haven't forgotten anything.'

Franz stretched out his hand before he really knew what he was doing. With a gentle gesture he brushed away the absurd lock of hair. He gently stroked the damaged eye, her entire face. At the touch of his fingers her face became even paler, and slightly cooler. She lowered her eyes. That made her look more as she once had. Yes, Franz mused, he just had to stroke it with his hand a few more times, and then the wound would heal, and the old radiance, the lost beauty would return to her face.

But he pulled his hand back abruptly. She stared at him with her dry, healthy eye, which was now so black that the pupil blended into the iris, making it seem much too large. She pulled out a little mirror, propped it against her glass, and arranged her hair.

'Come, Lotte,' Franz said. 'It's still early in the day, come and walk a bit with me out to my people's place.'

'Are you married, Franz? Do your parents live there?'

'No on both counts, only relatives. I'm as good as alone.'

They walked in silence for almost an hour. The child didn't bother them. She walked on ahead, eagerly climbing higher and higher, for she rarely got to go anywhere outside Hoechst. After some minutes, the child stopped for a moment to see how much of the countryside had unfolded below them, and along with the land also the sky. If you could only get high enough, the child thought, then instead of new villages and farm fields, you'd see something quite different – the end of everything, the place where the clouds and the wind came from, the wind that was not separate from the yellow afternoon light and would not unfold to reveal anything more.

Franz could already see the Mangolds' house. He hadn't said anything to Lotte, but then, there was no need to talk. Talk would only be disruptive. He bought a waffle for the child at the little soda shack and a bar of chocolate for Lotte. When they arrived at the Marnets' kitchen, Augusta stared at them open mouthed. They all stared at Franz, at Lotte, at the child. Lotte said hello to them; she was relaxed. She helped with washing the dishes. Unfortunately, only a crusty edge piece was left over from the table-size apple cake. Augusta gave the child that piece along with permission to go outside and look at the blue glass globe in the bed of asters. The others were still sitting around the bare, clean-scrubbed table. Ernst kept looking at Lotte, even though he didn't think much of her looks. It annoyed him that Franz, sleepy-headed Franz, had secretly got himself a woman. Later Mrs Marnet brought out her bottle of plum liqueur. All the men drank a little glassful, but of the women, only Lotte and Eugenia did.

In the meantime, the child had opened the garden gate and walked out into the meadow. She stopped under the first apple tree. The child of Lotte and of Herbert, who had been killed.

At first the child saw only the trunk of the tree. She traced the ridges in the bark with a finger. Then she looked up. The branches turned and twisted and reached up into the air, and yet the whole network of branches remained still. The child was standing still too. The leaves, which looked black from below, were all moving very slightly, and the evening sky shone through the spaces in between. One single slanting ray of sunshine shot through the branches and struck something golden, something round.

'There's still one hanging there,' the child yelled.

The people in the kitchen all jumped to their feet because they thought that a miracle had occurred. They ran outside and looked up into the tree. Someone brought the apple picker. And because the child was not yet strong enough, they guided her hand holding the heavy pole like a giant pencil. The basket at the end of the pole hooked around the apple; it dangled there a moment longer: Good evening, apple.

'You may take it with you,' Mrs Marnet said, probably feeling most generous.

V

Fahrenberg took up a position in front of the column of prisoners, lined up at six o'clock this Sunday as on every other evening of the week. Today, for the first time, it wasn't Zillich at the head of the SA, but his successor, Uhlenhaut. Nor was Bunsen at the head of the SS, for he was on furlough; rather, it was a fellow named Hattendorf, a man with a long, horse-shaped skull. But the prisoners, who before would have been aware of the slightest change, were, after the torments of the past week, in a strange state of dull, stubborn apathy.

None of them would have been able to say whether the three remaining escapees who were now being dragged to the trees were dead or still alive. In fact, the entire Dance Ground in front of the barracks had something about it that made it seem like an intermediate landing station; for this place couldn't be anywhere on this earth, or anywhere in the beyond either. Fahrenberg, as he stood there before them, seemed shrunken and emaciated, and just as tormented as they all were.

His voice bored its way into the numbed heads of the prisoners, single words, phrases, something about justice, about the long arm of justice, about the people and about a tumour on the people, about the escape and about the day of the escape, which would be one week ago tomorrow. But the prisoners were listening to the singing of some drunken peasants from the villages far away.

Then suddenly a jolt went through every single man and through the column of prisoners. What had Fahrenberg said just now? Once they'd caught Heisler, it would all be over.

'Over,' one of them said on the way back; that was the only word that was spoken.

But an hour later in the barracks, one prisoner said to another, without moving his lips, because talking was forbidden, 'Do you think they've really got him?'

And the other replied, 'No, I don't think so.'

And the first one was Schenk, the man whom Roeder had gone to find without anything coming of it, and the other was a new arrival, a worker from Rüsselsheim whom they'd put directly into the bunker. And Schenk said to the other, 'Did you see their sheepish faces? Did you see the way they were winking at each other? And the old man couldn't raise his voice. No, that wasn't for real today. They haven't got him.'

Only the ones right next to them could hear what the two were saying. But the import of their words spread through the barracks as the evening wore on.

Bunsen had taken along two younger friends when he went on furlough. They were good-looking, clever fellows, not quite as brilliant as he was and therefore suitable to be his followers.

While Fahrenberg was speaking, they were driving up in front of the Rheinischer Hof in Wiesbaden. Bunsen, after a quick survey of the scene, entered the dance hall followed by his two companions. It wasn't crowded yet. They were playing a slow, drawn-out waltz as a change from the usual jazz. There were fewer than a dozen couples on the bright dance floor, and so there was enough room for the long white and coloured dresses of the women to swing out in soft undulating swirls. Since most of the men were in uniform, it all had a tinge of a victory celebration, or a feast held to mark a peace accord.

Bunsen had discovered his fiancée's father at one of the tables near the dance floor and nodded to him. His father-in-law to be was a salesman for Henkell and called himself a 'champagne consul', and, he would add, a colleague of Ambassador Ribbentrop, who had emerged from the same business. Bunsen caught sight of his fiancée among the dancing couples. Thinking she was dancing with a stranger, he had an attack of jealousy, until he recognised the lean, newly minted lieutenant as her cousin. When the dance was over, his fiancée came over to their table. She was nineteen, lightly tanned and soft, with sparkling eyes, and the two of them sensed the admiration of those around them and basked in it.

Bunsen introduced his two companions; tables were moved together; the waiter hastily cracked some ice with his little hammer. Hanni, Bunsen's fiancée, explained that this was her farewell party because tomorrow she was starting a six-week course at the SS school for brides. Nothing was of greater importance, Bunsen said. He asked her if she intended to give her fellow brides some private tutoring. Hanni's father gave him a sharp look; then almost as sharply he looked at Bunsen's two companions. He was a witty, clever widower, and he wasn't all that delighted by the handsome young fellow his daughter had fallen in love with. In addition, Bunsen's position in Westhofen seemed a rather odd one for a son-in-law of his. But he had made some enquiries about Bunsen's parents, and it turned out they were ordinary parents, minor officials in the Palatinate, decent people. Sitting in their musty living room during the boring courtesy call he had paid them, he had thought the fact that they had given birth to this rather odd son was attributable to the genius of the race.

The room had in the meantime filled up. Waltzes alternated with Rhinelanders and even polkas. Bunsen's prospective father-in-law, in fact all the older men in the room, smiled whenever the orchestra played a familiar melody from days gone by, reminding them of the good times they'd had before the war. There hadn't been this much genuine festiveness, such untroubled, relaxed merriment in a long time here. You find this kind of relaxation of tensions in villages, in cities all over the world whenever people who have escaped some enormous danger, or think they have, are celebrating. That evening there were no troublemakers present, no spoilsports. That had been taken care of. An entire flotilla of little Kraft durch Freude ships were afloat on the Rhine; Hanni's father's firm had donated a supply of Henkell Trocken to each one of them. There were no disgruntled spectators standing near the dance hall doors, just the little waiter with his little hammer and his expressionless face, cracking ice.

In the same city, the Kresses had parked their Opel among the other cars in front of the Kurhaus. They had dropped George off in Kostheim. For he had to find a bed for the night in a rooming house that catered for rivermen, since with his new papers he didn't quite fit in with the little blue car. For the last half hour Dr Kress had been as silent as during their first drive to the Riederwald development, as if his guest, who had gradually taken on form, was going to vanish again, so that it was futile to start a conversation with him now. There had been no farewells at parting. The two Kresses had maintained their silence afterwards too. They drove here without any prior discussion, both of them feeling the need for some light and for the company of other people. They sat down in a corner of the small room because they felt a bit conspicuous in their dusty traveling clothes. They gazed at what there was to see. At last Mrs Kress broke the almost hour-long silence. 'Did he say anything at the end?'

'No, only, "Thanks."'

'Strange,' his wife said, 'I feel as if I should be thanking him – no matter what might happen to us as a result of this affair – for having stayed with us, for having come to see us.'

'Yes, I feel the same way,' her husband said. They looked at each other in surprise, with a new mutual understanding that neither of them had known before.

VI

After the Kresses had dropped him off in front of an inn, George had briefly considered going in, but decided instead to go down towards the Main River. He strolled across the embankment meadow surrounded by many other people enjoying their Sunday and the autumn sunshine that, they all agreed, was on the verge of turning, like the apple cider, and wouldn't last much longer. George passed a bridge with one guard posted. The embankment widened; he had reached the mouth of the Main much sooner than expected. The Rhine lay before him, and on its far side, the city through which he'd walked a few days ago. Its streets and squares in which he'd sweated blood blended into a grey fortress that was reflected in the water. A flock of birds, in a sharp black triangle formation, was etched into the reddish afternoon sky between the highest towers and steeples, much as on heraldic city seals. When George had walked a few more steps he saw, between two of these spires, Saint Martin on the cathedral roof bending down from his horse to share his cloak with the beggar who will appear to him in his dream: *I am He whom you are pursuing.*

George could have walked right on across the next bridge and taken a room in one of the places that catered for rivermen. Even if there were to be a raid, he had a valid passport. But he was afraid of getting involved in any further questioning, and he preferred spending the night on the right bank and boarding the ship first thing in the morning.

He decided to think it all through one more time. It was still daytime. He turned round and strolled about on the meadows along the banks of the Main. A small village, Kostheim, with walnut and chestnut trees, was within sight of the river. The first inn he came to had a sign reading ZUM ENGEL, with a wreath of brown leaves over it, indicating that it was serving fresh cider.

He went in and sat down in the tiny garden – the best place for simply sitting and looking out at the water, letting things take their course. He had to come to a decision.

He sat close to the wall with his back facing the garden. A waitress put a glass of cider in front of him. He said, 'But I haven't ordered anything yet.'

She picked his glass up again and said, 'My God, what else would you be ordering?'

He thought it over and then he said, 'Cider.' They both laughed. She handed him the glass directly without putting it down on the table first. He took a swallow, which made him so greedy that he emptied the entire glass. 'Another glass, please.'

'Well, you'll just have to wait a minute.' She went over to the guests at the next table.

Half an hour passed. A couple of times she cast a brief glance at him. In contrast to the wild lack of restraint he had shown in drinking the cider before, he was now calmly gazing out at the meadow. The last guests left the garden and went inside to the bar-room. The sky had turned red; a light but penetrating wind stirred even the leaves of the grapevine growing on the inside of the wall.

I hope he left the money on the table for me, the waitress thought. She went out into the garden to check. But he was still sitting there as before. She asked, 'Wouldn't you like to have your cider in the bar-room?'

He looked at her for the first time. A young woman wearing a dark dress. Her face, momentarily animated, was tired from working all Sunday long. She had a generous bosom. Her neck was soft. He thought he had seen her before; she seemed almost familiar. Which of the women from the years gone by did she remind him of? Or was it only a desire she reminded him of? It could hardly have been a very special, unfulfillable desire. He answered her, 'It's quite all right if you bring me my cider out here.'

Now that the garden was empty, he set his chair at an angle and waited for her to come back with his glass. He hadn't been wrong, he liked her, as much as he could like anyone at this time. 'Couldn't you take a break for a while?'

'Oh, hardly. I have a roomful of customers.' But she put a knee up on one of the chairs and an arm on its back. A little garnet cross held her collar closed. She asked, 'Do you work here?'

'I work on a boat.'

She looked at him quickly but intently. 'Are you from around here?'

'No, but I have some relatives here.'

'You speak almost the way we do here.'

'The men in my family always get their wives from this area.'

She smiled without losing the trace of sadness in her face. He looked at her, and she let him.

A car stopped on the street; a whole swarm of SS men walked through the garden and into the bar-room. She scarcely looked up at them. Her lowered glance fixed on George's hand holding on to the chair back.

'What's the matter with your hand?'

'An accident – not healing well.'

She picked up his hand so quickly that he couldn't pull it back in time; she looked at it carefully. 'It looks as if you got into some broken glass – the wound could break open again.' She gave him his hand back. 'I've got to go back inside to serve the new arrivals.'

'Can't very well keep such fine guests waiting.'

She shrugged. 'It's not all that bad. In this area we're pretty hardened.'

'Hardened against what?'

'Against uniforms.'

She went inside, and he called after her, 'Another glass, please!'

It had already turned cool and grey by now. I hope she comes back, George thought.

As she was taking orders in the bar-room, she thought: What sort of chap is that out there? I wonder what kind of trouble he's in. I'm sure he's got problems. Even as she waited on her guests with a proud, skilful cheerfulness, she kept thinking. He certainly hasn't been working on a boat for long. He's not a liar, but he is lying. He's afraid, but he's not the fearful type. Where did he hurt his hand? He was startled when I took his hand, but he looked at me. He clenched his fists when that bunch of SS came through the garden. Does it have something to do with that?

Finally she filled a glass to take to him. Nothing was quite right about him, except for his eyes. She went out to the garden, to let him gaze at her.

He was sitting in the cold evening air and hadn't yet touched his second glass. 'Why did you ask for a third glass?'

'Don't worry about that,' he said. He pushed the glasses aside and took her hand. She was wearing only one thin ring with a lucky lady-bird, the kind of thing you win at a fair. He said, 'No husband? No fiancé? No sweetheart?'

Three times she shook her head.

'Had no luck? Ended up badly?'

She looked at him in surprise. 'Why do you ask?'

'Well, because you're alone.'

She gently struck her heart with her hand. 'That's the source of it all.' Then she suddenly ran off.

Before she could reach the door he called her back to his table. He handed her a bill to change.

She thought: So, that's not his problem. And when she came out for the fourth time into the now-dark garden with the money on a plate and the pebbles crunching, he plucked up his courage.

'Do they have a room for guests here in the house? Then I wouldn't have to go across to Mainz again.'

'Here in this house? What are you thinking! Only the innkeepers live here.'

'And where do you live?'

She quickly pulled back her hand and looked at him almost glowering; he prepared himself for a brusque reply. But after a short pause, she just said, 'Yes. All right,' adding, 'Wait here for me. I have some more work to finish up inside. Then just follow me.'

He waited. The hope that his escape might finally succeed was mixed with joyful anxiety. Then at last she came out, wearing a coat and not turning to look at him. He followed her down a long street. It had started to rain. He thought, half-dazed: Her hair will get wet.

A couple of hours later he started up. Didn't know where he was. 'I woke you up,' she said. 'I had to. I just couldn't listen to it any more. And I was afraid you'd wake my aunt.'

'Was I shouting?'

'You were moaning and shouting. Go back to sleep now and be quiet.'

'How late is it?'

She could answer him, for she hadn't slept a wink. Since midnight she had heard every hour strike. She said, 'Almost four. —Go back to sleep now. It's all right. I'll wake you.' She didn't know whether he went back to sleep or just lay there quietly. She waited to see if the trembling that had attacked him during his first sleep would return. But no, he was now breathing quietly.

Camp Commandant Fahrenberg had left orders before he went to sleep that night for them to wake him up as soon as any report came in about the last escapee. There had actually been no need for these orders because Fahrenberg didn't sleep a wink that night either. He listened to every sound that might in any way be related to the news he was waiting for. And although during the past few nights he had been tormented by the utter night-time stillness, this night from Sunday to Monday he was tormented by horns blowing at frequent short intervals, dogs barking, and the shouts of drunken farmers.

But gradually the noises receded. The countryside sank into the deep sleep between midnight and dawn. Still listening for noises, he tried to visualise all the villages and the roads and paths that connected them to each other and to the three large cities. A triangular net in which the fellow should have got caught by now, unless he was the devil incarnate. He couldn't just have dissolved into thin air. His shoes must have left tracks somewhere in the damp autumn soil; someone must have got him those shoes. Some hand must have cut him a piece of bread, must have filled his glass. Some house somewhere must have sheltered him. For the first time Fahrenberg lucidly considered the possibility that Heisler might have got away. But this possibility was impossible. Hadn't they said that his friends had renounced him, that his own wife had long had a lover, and that his own brother was participating in the search? Fahrenberg drew a deep breath. The most likely solution was that he was no longer alive. Probably jumped into the Rhine or the Main. Tomorrow they'll fish him out. Suddenly he saw Heisler before him, the way he had looked after the last questioning, with the torn lips, the impudent eyes. And right then Fahrenberg knew for certain that his hopes, his expectations had come to nothing. Neither the Rhine, nor the Main, nor any other river would ever yield his corpse, for this man lived, and he would continue to live. For the first time since the escape Fahrenberg realised that he wasn't pursuing one single man whose features he knew, whose strength was exhaustible, but rather a faceless, inexhaustible, inestimable power. But he couldn't bear to think such a thought for longer than a few minutes.

'You have to go now.' She helped George get dressed, handing him each piece of clothing, the way the wives of soldiers do at the end of the last night of their furloughs.

I could have shared everything with her, George thought, my whole life, but I have no life to share.

'Have something to drink before you go.'

In the early-morning light he saw what he was about to leave. She was shivering with cold. Rain beat against the windowpane. The weather had changed overnight. A soft whiff of camphor came from the wardrobe as she took something out, some ugly, dark woollen thing. All the beautiful things I would have bought for you, red and blue and white.

Still standing, she watched him drink his coffee. He was quite calm. She went ahead of him, unlocked the front door to let him out, and went back upstairs again. In the kitchen and then on the stairs she had wondered whether she shouldn't tell him that she had an idea what his trouble was. But why? It would only disquiet him.

She rinsed his cup. The kitchen door opened; an old woman wrapped in a quilt with a short grey braid stood on the threshold. She instantly started reproaching her, 'Stupid Marie, I swear, you'll never see him again. You picked up something nice there, didn't you? Are you crazy? You didn't even know him when you left this afternoon, or did you? Well? Say something! Have you swallowed your tongue?'

The younger woman slowly turned away from the sink; her shining eyes fastened on the old woman cowering there, grumbling. Marie, lost in thought, looked down at her with a calm, proud smile. Her moment had come. But she had no witnesses except for the old woman who, shivering with cold and anger, quickly withdrew again to her warm bed.

What would I do without Belloni's coat! George mused as, head down, he followed the rails. Rain pelted his face. Finally he was leaving the houses behind. The rain hung in strands before the city on the other side of the river. The city seemed totally unreal against the endless dull sky. Like one of those cities you invent in your sleep for the length of a dream that doesn't even last that long. And yet it had already endured for two thousand years.

George had come to the Kastel bridgehead. The guard hailed him, and George showed him his passport. He was already on the bridge when he realised that his heart had not even speeded up. He could have calmly passed ten more bridgeheads. Well, so it seems you can even get used to that. He felt that his heart was now immune to fear and danger, but maybe also to happiness. He slowed down a little to be sure he wouldn't arrive even a minute early. When he looked down at the water, he saw the tugboat *Wilhelmine* with its green loading line reflected in the water. It was quite near him at the bridgehead, but unfortunately not alongside the shore but next to another boat. George was less concerned about the guard at the Mainz bridgehead than about how he could get across the strange boat. But there was no need for concern. He was less than twenty paces from the dock when he saw a man's round head emerge on the deck of the *Wilhelmine*. The man had practically no neck, a round, pudgy face with round nostrils, deep-set little eyes, a face that boded no good to anyone, just the right sort of face in these times for an upright man who was willing to take all sorts of risks. He was obviously expecting George.

On Monday evening the seven trees in Westhofen were cut down. It all went very quickly. The new commandant had been installed before they had even been informed of the change. He was no doubt the right man to restore order to a camp in which such things had happened. He didn't bellow, but spoke in an ordinary tone of voice. Still he left no doubt in our minds that we would all be shot at the slightest incident. He had the crosses cut down at once, for they were not his style. It was said that Fahrenberg had gone to Mainz that Monday, and that he'd taken up quarters in the Fürstenberger Hof. Then, they said, he put a bullet through his head. But it was just a rumour. Maybe that night in the Fürstenberger Hof another man put a bullet through his head because of his debts or an unrequited love. Perhaps Fahrenberg was shoved up the ladder and given even greater power.

But we didn't know about all that yet. And later on so much happened that you couldn't get any accurate information any more. On the other hand, we thought it wasn't possible to experience any more than we had already experienced. But once outside, we found out how much there was one could still experience.

Yet on that evening when, for the first time, they provided the prisoners' barracks with some heat and we assumed the kindling they used came from the seven trees, that evening we felt closer to life, in fact much closer to life than later on, and also much closer to life than any of those other people who think they are alive.

The SA guard had by then already stopped being amazed at the rain. He now turned round suddenly hoping to catch us doing something forbidden. He roared at us and right away handed out a few penalties. Ten minutes later we were lying on our cots. The last spark died out in our little stove. We had an inkling of the nights that were before us. The damp autumn cold penetrated our blankets, our shirts, our skins. We all felt how profoundly and how terribly outside forces can reach into a human being, to his innermost self. But we also sensed that in that innermost core there was something that was unassailable and inviolable.

Anna Seghers (1900-1983) was born Netty Reiling in Mainz, Germany, into a Jewish family. In 1924 she received a doctorate in Art History from the University of Heidelberg, and in the same year her first story was published. During this time, she came into contact with many left-wing intellectuals, including her husband, a Hungarian economist, and began writing in earnest. By the end of 1928, Anna Seghers had joined the Communist Party, given birth to two children and was awarded the Kleist Prize for her first novel, *The Revolt of the Fishermen of St Barbara*. She left Nazi Germany for France in 1933, where she wrote *The Seventh Cross*. After the Nazi invasion in 1940, she was forced to flee again and, with the aid of Varian Fry, she and her family sailed from Marseilles to Mexico on a ship that included Victor Serge, André Breton and Claude Lévi Strauss among its passengers. According to Seghers, she had four copies of her manuscript: one was lost by a friend who was also fleeing the Nazis; one was destroyed in an air raid; one was found by the Gestapo; the last she sent to her publisher in America just as she was leaving France. Seghers gained international recognition with *The Seventh Cross* (1942), which became an international bestseller. It was the basis for the 1944 MGM film starring Spencer Tracy and has been translated into more than thirty languages. After the war Seghers moved to East Berlin, where she became a prominent figure of East German letters, actively championing the work of younger writers from her position as president of the Writers' Union and publishing at a steady pace. Among Seghers's acclaimed works are *The Seventh Cross*; *Transit* (1944); *Excursion of the Dead*

Girls (1945); *The Dead Stay Young* (1949), and the story collection *Benito's Blue* (1973).

Margot Bettauer Dembo has translated works by Judith Hermann, Robert Gernhardt, Joachim Fest, Ödön von Horváth, and Feridun Zaimoglu, among others. She was awarded the Goethe-Institut/Berlin Translator's Prize in 1994 and the Helen and Kurt Wolff Translator's Prize in 2003. Dembo has also worked as a translator for two feature documentary films: *The Restless Conscience*, which was nominated for an Academy Award, and *The Burning Wall*.